# TEWTZ E VONN

# MAIA

TALLYWHOA PUBLISHING

iii

Tallywhoa Publishing
An imprint of Tallywhoa Enterprises, LLC
Columbia, Missouri, USA

This is a work of historical fiction. Some names, characters,
places, and dates are historically accurate, and others are
entirely fiction created by the author. The views expressed in
this work are solely those of the author.

All images and illustrations are either the original work of
the author or are historical images from known archives and
are identified as to their respective source.

Cover art: *MAIA* @ Mary Ratchford Douglass
(Inspired by *Medicine Woman* by Lisa Iris)

ISBN: 978-1-7340057-0-7 (e)

ISBN: 978-1-7340057-1-4 (sc)

ISBN: 978-1-7340057-2-1 (hc)

ISBN: 978-1-7340057-3-8 (sccolor)

Library of Congress Control Number: 2019913185

# MAIA
## Kill Devill Series: Book 1

The Kill Devill series is the story of my ancestors who emigrated from England, Ireland, Scotland, France, Africa and Brazil bringing their histories and heritage with them to build a new world from Barbados to Missouri. For you to hear my story, you must first hear the stories of the Emigrants. The people who came to the new world left their homes, families, and countries first. To go somewhere new, we must inherently leave someplace old. To function somewhere new, we build on what we bring with us from the past.

Maia begins in 1667 with the arrival of my ancestors, Captain Thomas Dewe and his brother Richard, in Bridgetown, Barbados in 1667 to join their brother John and make the family sugar plantation prosper. They could not have imagined I would connect myself to them and their Mayan mistresses, via DNA analysis 350 years later. Truly mind boggling and occasionally hilarious to consider what we can know about them hundreds of years later.

The majority of historical dates, characters, places and artifacts I include in my story are factual references. I have used much artistic license, created some fictional characters and places, a series of murders and criminals, and have embellished with absolute abandon to create a story both historical and fanciful. In short, I created a story for you to read that could have happened, much of which did happen, and I leave it to the reader to ponder. Much of this story is true. I am living proof. Let the story begin...

*With all my love to my sons Joseph, Jonathan, and William, and my grandson Colton.*

# PART 1
# BARBADOS, WEST INDIES, 1667
13°08" N-59°62" W

The earliest known map exclusively of Barbados, it appeared in Richard Ligon's *True and Exact History*, published in 1657. The map identifies 285 plantations by owner, and shows the early development of the leeward coastal region, while the interior remains overgrown and inaccessible. Vignettes depict planters hunting wild hogs and chasing runaway slaves. Curiously, a pair of camels is shown; Ligon wrote that 'several planters imported these beasts and found them useful in Barbados, but did not know how to diet them.'

## THE ANGELINE

# 1

The *Angeline* sailed into Carlisle Bay, Bridgetown, Barbados in the fall of 1667. Captain William Douglass nodded to his First Mate, Charles Michaelson, to drop anchor. The anchor fell from the bow of the ship, plunged through the surface of the sea and grabbed into the seabed with bubbles gurgling to the surface. The *Angeline* rose and fell with the swells of the sea as all hands prepared the passengers and freight to go ashore. The ship strained against her anchorage with each wave and settled with each trough. Charles ran the crew through the routines of dropping and securing the last sails, clearing the decks and passageways as the Captain saw to the security of the ship.

Captain Douglass used his spyglass to inspect the docks and immediate area prior to granting permission for the starboard side gate to be opened and the access ladder let down. He could see the lighters, the shallow draft row boats, were already rowing out to the ship to ferry passengers and freight to shore. What he didn't see concerned him more. She wasn't there. The *Angeline* had arrived early, but she should have been there in the first lighter headed out to the ship. William's native intuition never lied to him. Something had gone wrong.

William collapsed his spyglass and quickly went to his cabin to gather his things for shore. He would personally make sure every box of freight was accounted for as it came ashore and was claimed by the proper owner. Clothes in his duffle, manifests and company logs in his officer's case, and he was headed for the shore boat. As William came out on deck, he and Charles exchanged a glance, Charles was now in charge on ship. The First Mate could raise anchor and run for the open sea with or without her Captain.

Charles moved from the stern toward the gateway as William tossed his duffle to the oarsman in the *Angeline's* shore boat waiting to take him to shore. Turning to Charles as he prepared to descend the ladder William said

"Charles, send the passengers and their freight and luggage to the docks as we normally do. Wait for my signal before you send…the rest. We are being observed from the garrison. She isn't here. Something isn't right. Keep the critical crew on board to run to open waters if you must."

"Aye Captain. I understand. The *Angeline* and all she carries will be kept safe."

Not everything would go to shore. Charles knew in what order to send freight to shore and with whom. William relied on him with good reason. Barbados was Charles' home and he knew the people well. William handed Charles his spyglass and the key to the magazine, grim as he made his way down the ladder to the lighter below.

Charles, William, and the oarsman watched a large reef shark surface, dorsal and tail fin ominous as it circled the lighter and disappeared under the ship. The shark was significantly larger than normally seen in the bay, and far from its normal range it had followed them in from deep waters. Something was brewing with the weather; the fish always knew first. William was well aware ships in harbor attract scavengers that swim as well as row. The Captain kept an eye out and a pistol drawn for the big shark as he waited for the first passengers, Captain Thomas and Richard

Dewe, to board the shore boat. Looking up he called to Charles

"Charles, keep aware of the sharks before you allow anyone off the ship. Arm the main officers if you must." Charles nodded and held up his rifle for William and all others to see he was armed. William added "Gentlemen, we must load quickly and get pushed away from the ship. Watch your step, the last one is a bit tricky."

Richard led the way off the ship and down to the shore boat just ahead of his brother Thomas, grateful for a safe arrival to Barbados and thirsty for fresh water, food, and a real bed. The descent from the ship's deck to the small boats was unnerving knowing a large predator lurked under the ship. Richard wondered if there were equally dangerous predators waiting for them on shore. Thomas knew they were waiting. The glint off a spyglass announced them.

Giles Freeman watched closely from the garrison balcony with his spyglass as the owners of the Tallywhoa plantation and their luggage and freight were shifted from the deck of the *Angeline* down into the shore boat and lighters. Giles took notes of the arrival of prominent landowners on every ship as part of his regular duties assigned to garrison Commander Colonel Duncan McKenzie. Giles studied the unmistakable brothers of John Dewe closely. Somehow these three sons of Colonel Thomas Dewe were part of the Watchers' agenda, the group slowly spreading tentacles across the island. The *Angeline's* crew and dock workers rowed the ship's shore boat and the lighters with steady skilled strokes and delivered Captain Douglass and the Dewe brothers safely to the Careenage docks.

Richard stepped out of the shore boat and stumbled briefly as his sea legs found land, wavered momentarily with the first few steps toward Bridgetown. His steps grew stronger as he gained his land legs and walked confidently toward the market. The aroma of fresh baked bread wafted in between the smell of the sea and fish, beckoning from the market. The gulls called raucously around them, darting and diving for scraps tossed into the sea by fisherman cleaning their day's catch. Richard breathed deeply and called to his brother

"Thomas! They've fresh bread and Kill Devill rum my brother. I'm pretty sure it's this way. I'll save some for you."

Richard followed his nose up the dock knowing the local rum would be easy to come by along with the dense breads made from corn flour, cassava or potatoes, fish, cheeses, and fresh fruits unique to the island. The local foods intrigued his palate, awakened his appetite for both food and pleasure. The voyage hardships quickly set behind him.

Thomas replied "right behind you brother. I'll catch up directly. Try not to get lost in your indulgences before your luggage makes dry land..."

Shaking his head, rolling his eyes, and mumbling 'bastard child, surely mother lied, he had to be a bastard child' as his little brother waltzed toward the market. Thomas conferred a moment with William as they prepared to disembark from the shore boat "Yes, William, please keep me informed of the *Angeline's* schedules, rates, and freight space. And by all means share our details with prospective buyers you come across as well. I feel we can help each other with minimal effort. Thank you for a safe voyage and arrival to Bridgetown. Good to know you, William."

A confident handshake, a smile, backs patted, good will and a few extra coins exchanged, Thomas looked up to see Richard nearing the shore end of the dock. A quick direction to Aaron and Ruben, the personal porters he hired to carry their baggage, and he stepped out of the shore boat and onto the portion of the dock declared public in 1657. Thomas' booted steps sounded the hollow beneath the boards as he continued to mumble under his breath 'when I get my hands on the family bastard child...'

Giles watched as Thomas easily found his land legs as a seasoned traveler and officer can do. Pausing to make arrangements with the crew unloading their trunks and freight from a lighter, Thomas was quick to remember the faces and names of those who took care in their duties and those who did not. He knew they would need reputable resources and cultivated connections with a bit more coin and kind words. Thomas also considered they might disappear a family bastard child for a fee.

Thomas caught up just as Richard was purchasing two bottles of 'Kill Devill' rum along with a round loaf of freshly baked corn and cassava bread and a wheel of cheese. Standing at the sea wall they sliced pieces of cheese out of the wheel with the knife Thomas kept in his boot cuff, tore off chunks of the bread with their hands, and drank the rum straight from the bottles. The rum warmed their insides as the sun warmed their faces, the sea breezes fresh and cleansing. The voyage from England was over and the 'family bastard child' had once again bought his way out of eminent demise with good rum. The cloaked figure in the shadows between the buildings across from the market listened and watched unnoticed as the brothers relaxed and began to take in their new surroundings.

Richard was eager to explore Bridgetown with her welcoming familiar British influence seen in the architecture, garrison, and the horse racing new to the island. But first he and Thomas must find their brother John. Richard had confidence in their abilities and combined assets; they would succeed as they were born to aristocracy and thus the Tallywhoa would prosper. Their brother, John, was waiting for them.

"We need to hire a rider to take word to John we are arrived." Richard stated the obvious to Thomas, crumbs falling to the Scaly-Naped pigeons feasting at his feet. "John will not know we are here as the ship made excellent sail; we are early by a full two days. Do you think he will be keen to see us home to the Tallywhoa? The plantation should be heavy into cane cutting and crushing. We may need to hire a horse and cart or several assinigoes, the little donkeys common across the island, and a guide."

## SCALY NAPED PIGEON

Thomas, ever watchful about liaisons and keeping relationships, washed down a bite of bread with rum and thought a moment before he replied "First, I want to check in with Governor Vagado's commanding officer Colonel Duncan McKenzie. He may have a man we can send to find John and inform him we have arrived. We need to know who we can rely upon and where to find them. Father has long held contacts here in Bridgetown and we must be respectful to them, inform the friendly to our arrival. We must be ever vigilant as gentlemen to present ourselves as such to others. We will need the support of father's established colleagues and business partners. They will be critical to the future success of the Tallywhoa."

"Well then, our first stop shall be the garrison." Richard commented as he nodded in agreement, gazing about at the ladies in the market. He took note of several including a set of twins, all of whom took note of Richard, appreciative of the Dewe brothers' attractiveness and gentlemen's manners. "But surely we can take the time to enjoy our first meal, the view, and familiarize ourselves with our new surroundings."

Thomas knew what that meant coming from Richard, realizing they needed to make haste and be on their way to the plantation quickly or risk losing Richard to his delights. "Indeed, Richard." Gathering up the rum, bread, and cheese into a small cloth sack, Thomas turned on his heel and headed down the sea wall past Richard, gently taking his brother by the elbow in tow away from the market and the ladies. "Let's see the view this direction, and by all means, brother, familiarize yourself with the shops and people along the promenade to the garrison. We may well need to know in the near future where to find the smithy, harness maker, sailmaker, and tailor."

Richard glaring at his brother with disappointment knew not to resist the guiding hand at his elbow. Thomas had kept him out of harm's way far too often to refuse preemptive care. A quick glance back toward the market and he fell in beside Thomas willingly, Thomas' hand gently falling away in response. As they walked, he noted the shops on the way as Thomas had suggested. He knew Thomas was right in taking him along thus, and also about paying attention to surroundings. Barbados was indeed a new world to them, their father's talk of his business and holdings was a tremendous advantage but not the same as being there in person. Richard pondered out loud as they walked the sea wall "Where is father's office here in Bridgetown? Surely he has some sort of representative we should liaison within the city. Any idea where to look?"

Thomas considered how much to share with Richard before he spoke. "Father no longer keeps an office here in Bridgetown. He chose not to rebuild after the fire of 1659. I understand we are to liaison through John and a French solicitor, Henri Izzard. We will meet with John and assess the situation with the Tallywhoa. If we deem it necessary, we can then arrange to consult with Izzard. A social meeting to introduce ourselves will of course be arranged regardless of need. Father sent a bottle of Izzard's favorite *Armagnac De Gasogne* just for the occasion."

Thomas smiled smugly knowing the solicitor would get one bottle, not the entire crate. Oh yes, he would keep a private stock of the finest French cognac all for himself. Why yes, yes, he would. Richard raised a brow, tilted his head oh so slightly and began mentally constructing ways to entice his brother to share the stash he knew would be kept well hidden. This could take some planning. Thomas was quite the clever strategist, difficult to outmaneuver in a wine cellar or on the battlefield. Richard knew the plot would emerge over time, the goal a bottle of fine French brandy. He smiled smugly to himself. Thomas noticed and raised a brow "…give it your best shot, brother. You'll not win…"

Ever since they were boys, they had some challenge happening between them. Headmasters never caught on, exasperated they would give up. The brothers always won, sharing their exploits and loot between them was a given. The Brandy a new challenge, the garrison looming in front of them redirected their attention to the reason for their travels.

## THE GARRISON

They arrived at the Commanding Officer's door at the garrison just as it opened before them. A young officer stepped back to allow Thomas and Richard to enter. He asked "Good morning gentlemen, who should I say is calling? I will gladly let Colonel McKenzie know you are here." The brothers wondered how he knew they were at the door before they knocked. Eyes were everywhere, ears were closer. So noted. Stepping inside the vestibule Thomas and Richard removed their hats and tucked them respectfully under their arms. Thomas handed the sack of cheese and bread to Richard and reached inside his morning coat to retrieve his commission papers as identification.

"Good morning to you, sir. I am Captain Thomas Dewe, and this is my brother Richard. We are just arrived on the *Angeline* from London. Colonel McKenzie and our father Colonel Thomas Dewe are well acquainted with each other, having served together prior. We are here today to let Colonel McKenzie know we have arrived safely and express our gratitude for his services toward our brother John and the Tallywhoa Plantation. Would it be possible for us to meet with the Colonel briefly?"

"The Colonel is in today and will be most delighted to meet with you I am sure. Let me alert him to your presentation. Please wait here for just a moment" The officer immediately turned to take Thomas' papers as an introduction to the Colonel. The Colonel's office door was just to the left and behind the officer's vestibule desk. As his eyes adjusted to the dim lighting Thomas noted the rifle by the inner office door and the sword on the desk just above the ink well and blotter. No doubt there was a loaded pistol in a drawer and another in the officer's pocket. While the décor was casual, the security was sharply defined.

The officer knocked gently on the Colonel's door, went in when asked and quietly explained the visitors waiting at the front desk. Thomas was certain he heard papers being hastily gathered, a drawer sliding home and a key turning in a lock. As he and Richard glanced at one another in recognition they had both heard the key turn, Richard shifted the sack to his left hand and let it hang close to his side. Colonel McKenzie appeared in the doorway ahead of the officer, smiling broadly with hand extended to meet the sons of Colonel Thomas Dewe.

Colonel Duncan McKenzie was a patriarch of the McKenzie clan, a true highland Scotsman. The Colonel was dressed in a finely woven merino wool McKenzie tartan kilt with an ornate sporran and broach pinning the plaid at his shoulder atop the fine white linen shirt ruffled at the chest and cuffs. The Colonel was indeed a warrior and gentleman. Thomas was at once acutely aware he had been wise to find the Colonel first. Like his own father, Colonel McKenzie was not an ordinary man. These were the men who would carve countries out of the new world and establish dynasties to govern them.

Thomas shook the Colonel's hand with a firm grip, noting the clan patriarch's ring with the stag's head carved into the surface. Documents sealed with that ring were mandates accepted without question that no one would dare challenge. The same stag's head was depicted on the broach and sporran latch. McKenzie was indeed a powerful man both in the highlands of Scotland and Barbados.

"Welcome to Barbados lads! What an honor it is to meet the sons of Colonel Thomas Dewe. I hope ye had a fair crossing. Evans bring the dock glasses and my best single malt. This calls for a celebration!" The Colonel waved them into his office, waited for the officer to leave the tray with tulip shaped hand-blown dock glasses and scotch, and with a glance about the hallways closed the door and turned to pour the golden liquor for his guests.

Something about Colonel McKenzie made him a natural leader of men. Perhaps his upbringing and heritage from the Highlands of Scotland had successfully groomed him to be a patriarch. Kind, forgiving, and tolerant toward his subordinates, McKenzie had the constitution to make hard decisions and enforce them as needed. This leader of men was truly a patriarch and protector, a listener and an enforcer. Thomas instinctively knew his command was not something to challenge or ignore. Counting the Colonel as a friend and supporter was a significant achievement that was earned through competence and loyalty. Sharing his best 20-year-old single malt as his guest was a mark of acceptance, and a sign of expectations yet to be revealed.

The Colonel poured two fingers into the dock glasses for Thomas and Richard and at least three fingers for himself. Handing each man a glass he sat back in his chair covered in cordovan leather with dog heads carved into the arms, swirled the scotch to release the aromas as he tipped the glass to his lips. The golden liquor glowed with warmth and allure. The smoky aroma tantalized and begged to be savored slowly, sipped and savored, never rushed. Oh yes, this was fine Scotch as only the Scots can create. Richard contemplated how much it would cost to attain a steady supply; Thomas contemplated learning how to make his own. Perhaps they should build a distillery along with the cane production at the Tallywhoa. Quiet fell gently across the room as the men savored their drinks, no one spoke, eyes closed they reveled in the wonder of what an oak barrel charred on the inside kept safe for the future.

"Tis a fine thing, old scotch." The Colonel returned the men to the present. "Sets a man into a proper frame of mind when respected and appreciated." Thomas sat quietly listening while Richard appeared to be calculating a second pour, though he, too, was taking in every word and gesture the Colonel made. "You must be exhausted after your voyage from London. I expect you have news from England. What's on your mind this fine morning?"

The Colonel's left hand lifted his glass again as he waited for a reply, his right hand resting softly on the highly polished teak wood desk, intricately carved along the edges, a single middle drawer with a key in the keyhole, partly turned. The drawer would not open quickly or quietly. The contents protected from the casual intruder, but the simple

17

mechanism would not withstand an assault by determined hands. Thomas conjectured in his mind the day's itinerary and immediate duties the Colonel must face lay inside the locked drawer with the key half turned. Likely there were small sums of cash, not quite confidential communications of the day, and an assorted array of loose ends representing a cornucopia of triviality. The thought-tired Thomas just to consider. Perhaps the key was still in the keyhole in hopes someone else might take the drivel away, looking for something of value. Thomas mentally gave the Colonel full ownership of whatever might wait in the dark of the drawer.

Thomas swallowed slowly, sat up a bit and began to explain their uninvited meeting. "First Richard and I thank you for taking the time to meet with us. We apologize for the unannounced visit and are most appreciative for your hospitality. We are unexpectedly arrived early to Barbados. Our brother, John, is not expecting us for two more days. We need to organize transportation for our luggage and freight. I understand the journey to the Tallywhoa isn't terribly far, but the roads are mostly paths that can be difficult to navigate in a time conscience manner. Might you have a man who could get word to the Tallywhoa we are in Bridgetown? Perhaps a regular patrol or a local constable might be available?"

"Aye, Thomas. I can send a rider to the plantation to alert your brother of your arrival. Stay a day or two before you and Richard head there yourselves. Enjoy Bridgetown's beauty and specialties and I'll arrange a few introductions while you are here. The rider may return with requests from John, and you may find use of the services of the tradesmen locally. I can offer accommodations here in the garrison for you and storage for your freight until you hear back from John and make arrangements for transport."

The Colonel rose to his feet and opened the door slightly. The Officer who had shown them in immediately appearing at the door, waiting patiently for the Colonel to finish writing the orders he would dispatch as per the Colonel's instructions. "Lieutenant Evans find Giles Freeman. I need him to take a letter to John Dewe at the Tallywhoa Plantation as soon as possible. He is to wait and bring a reply if so requested. Go now, the orders...the letter...will be ready for Giles when he gets here." The Colonel lingered an extra moment looking at Evans, a silent message went between them, almost unnoticed by Thomas, completely ignored by Richard. Lieutenant Evans nodded and quickly was gone to fetch the courier, closing the door silently behind him.

Thomas realized as he watched the colonel write the message, dipping his quill in the ink well gently as he wrote with chimney black ink on fine paper, the Colonel was writing with his right hand. The Colonel was ambidextrous. Thomas wondered if the skill was inherent, or if the Colonel had been forced to learn writing with his right hand in school. Being lefthanded was considered to be a sign of the devil in uneducated circles. The Colonel was an intriguing individual. Thomas knew he would learn more about the Colonel in time, and that he could learn much from him. Fine scotch and fine paper does not a leader or gentleman make. There was much, much more to discover. Thomas felt a chill run up his spine at the thought of how those lessons might be learned.

The Colonel rocked the blotter over the letter to dry the writing quickly and removed the gold sealing ring from his left hand. Folding the letter sides in and top over bottom, he melted sealing wax over the flame of the candle alight by the blotter. Firmly pressing the ring into the warm wax, the impression read clearly as it cooled. The unmistakable McKenzie clan motto, *Lucceo Non Uro* surrounded a Stags head. Richard assumed this was simply how military leaders do business. Thomas knew the seal was in itself a message. *I Shine, Not Burn* was far more than just clan identification. Thomas wondered, to whom, and what was the message?

Colonel McKenzie placed the sealed letter before him on his desk, slipped the ring back on his finger, sat back in his chair and continued to sip the velvety smooth 20-year-old scotch from his dock glass. The message here was straight forward. Good scotch was never rushed, deserved full attention and was meant to be savored, enjoyed in breath and taste. Thomas and Richard happily followed the Colonel's example, sat back and fully enjoyed the best scotch either had ever tasted as they waited for the courier to arrive.

§

Lieutenant Evans knocked on the Bully Tree plank door at the end of the corridor as briskly as he had walked across the garrison courtyard and into the officers' quarters. Sensing the urgency at his door, Giles Freeman responded immediately. Evans was always unsettled at Freeman's appearance. A scar from a sharp sword ran down the right side of his face and left across his chin. A full head taller than Evans, Freeman was an imposing figure and deliciously handsome, his scar gave him a rugged character and a genuineness of expertise. Few dared challenge him; most that did were not still living to say so.

Looking up at Giles, Evans explained his directive "The Colonel needs you at once. He requests you follow me to his office where he will give you his specific instructions and the correspondence to be couriered. The Colonel asks that you wear this with your civilian riding costume."

Evans placed a green silk ribbon in Freeman's extended hand, noting the irony of a silk ribbon across a palm hewn rough by a hard life in service on ships and battlefields. Freeman was well known as the Colonel's most valued officer. On the island only the Colonel's wife, Elizabeth, knew he was the Colonel's son.

Freeman's mother, Elizabeth McKenzie's sister, married into a rival clan. Giles had been raised quietly far from town and prying eyes with support provided by both of his grandmothers. His stepfather knew of the deception before he married Giles' mother, agreed to claim Giles as his own from birth and gave him his name. The clan matriarchs were a force to be reckoned with, and few dared interfere with a child, a male child, guarded by their united interests. An unspoken truce was held about the boy. His mother too young to challenge the matriarchs, his father knew not of his birth, and his stepfather held the secret tightly so the world would never know. When Freeman came of age, he pledged his allegiance to his stepfather who was a revered provider and warrior within his clan. Yet fate put Giles on the course to be the protector of his father.

Giles nodded and softly closed the door. Hurriedly he shed his military regalia, carefully hanging his jacket and kilt on his valet stand. Satisfied his prized tartan was safely and properly stowed, he put on a leather vest, breeches, and tall riding boots. He tied his mid-back length auburn hair with a leather lace and the green silk ribbon over the leather. Wearing his clan tartan or local breeches, Giles was obviously fit and young, virile and strong. A quick glance in his mirror revealed piercing green eyes and a look indicating he was satisfied he had not forgotten anything the Colonel would expect.

The Colonel's communications methods were clever and calculated, while they were observed and noted, they were unquestioned. Giles took his saddle bags hanging on the peg by the door and slung them over his shoulder as he opened the door to follow Evans to the Colonel's office. He would don the spurs and side arm he kept in the saddle bags as the groom saddled his horse, Devlin. Their boots sounding the tell-tale echo as he followed Evans across the cobble stone breezeway to the Colonel's office, Giles avoided the gaze of the enlisted. Suspicious of his frequent assignments outside the capital, their prying eyes could not be avoided. He quickened his pace, the less he was seen the better. Arriving at the Colonel's door, Evans knocked gently and held the door open at the Colonel's response.

Stepping into the Colonel's office McKenzie stood from his chair and motioned to Thomas and Richard as he introduced them. Freeman immediately recognized the Dewe family resemblance in their dark hair, rich brown eyes, and powerful physical build. With minds as fit as their bodies, he already knew his cousins came from a formidable family. The men shook hands as the Colonel explained his orders.

"Freeman I need you to take this letter to John Dewe out at the Tallywhoa plantation. The letter explains the early arrival of his bothers and asks if John will send transportation or if Thomas and Richard should hire someone here in Bridgetown to transport their trunks and freight. They are my guests at the Garrison until we receive word from John."

Colonel McKenzie had stated the obvious as he handed the sealed letter to Freeman. Thomas had an inkling something was just a bit off but could not quite place the reasoning. Richard was rather oblivious eyeing the bottle of scotch on the table, his empty dock glass still in his hand, hoping the Colonel would be in a chatty mood.

Freeman nodded with the standard "Yes, Sir, Colonel. I leave at once and should return by tomorrow in time for afternoon tea." Turning to Thomas and Richard Giles acknowledged them as he slid the letter into the inner pocket of his vest.

"Gentlemen, welcome to Barbados. I'll make haste to the Tallywhoa and return as soon as possible. A pleasure to meet you both."

He nodded to the Colonel, turned on his heel and left the office briskly, almost running Evans over on his way out. Evans stepped back abruptly to avoid being bowled over by the Scot who outweighed him by 50 stone. Evans wondered what the highland people feed their children to grow such men. Perhaps he noticed too much, or not enough. Evans lost in his thought almost closed the door in the Colonel's face as McKenzie, Thomas, and Richard were headed out of the office. McKenzie was instructing Evans to escort the brothers to the guest quarters for temporary accommodations.

"Make sure they have everything they need to be comfortable here as my guests. Assign an attendant to each room to keep it tidy, water pitchers filled, linens changed and such. Prepare their private baths promptly. They likely will want a good hot soak after their sea voyage. Any expenses are to be charged to my personal usury account."

Thomas and Richard were contemplating who would get to their hot bath quickest, the Colonel was dead on, oh for a hot soak. Thomas responded for both

"Colonel you are more than generous. We won't impose on you more than a night or two, but we will accept your offer for accommodations. Thank you for your hospitality and generosity."

Turning to Evans he and Richard nodded to the Colonel and turned to leave the room. As they were leaving the Colonel added to Evans to "Make sure you show them my personal dining quarters. Tell chef to prepare his best, I intend to dine at 8:00 this evening. Get word to the group to join us, my most sincere invitation of course." Evans nodded in acknowledgement, turned and left the office.

Walking past the brothers, he led them down the same corridor he had just come from with Freeman. Making a left through a nondescript arched entry they climbed the stairs to the top floor. Entering the door at the top of the stairs he motioned for the brothers to follow him to the left, heading toward a set of large double doors at the end of the corridor. Speaking softly, he explained "These are the Colonel's private guest quarters. Your rooms are just inside across the hall from each other."

Evans pulled open the right-hand door as he spoke, revealing a hallway with four single doors, two on each side of the hall. The hallway ended at another set of double doors. "The Colonel's private dining room is just through those doors. He expects you at 8:00 this evening for dinner. Try to be prompt, he detests inattention to time. You will find a full bath ensuite off your rooms. The bath attendants have access to bring your hot water and tend your rooms through the door at the rear of the bath. You have complete privacy at your discretion if you slide the interior bathroom bolts.

23

Please leave the access doors unbolted when you leave the rooms for the day. Only your attendant has access if you key lock the primary guest room door"

Handing each man a key as he spoke, Thomas and Richard realized this was no ordinary barracks, the baths' access door were exits unseen by prying eyes. "If there is anything you need, pull the bell chain to alert your attendant and they will respond immediately. Your attendants are directly below your rooms and have access to the garrison kitchen, wardrobe, and physician. They can assist you with directions and information about Bridgetown as well. Enjoy your stay Captain Thomas, Richard. I am also available at any time to meet your needs." Evans waited just a moment before turning to leave.

Thomas thanked Evans, turned to Richard and they both raised one brow in quizzical thought. They turned in unison to slide their keys in the locks and explore their accommodations. Neither had expected to be housed in the Colonel's private barracks or to be provided meals amid good company. Richard knew there would be expectations later while Thomas worried what the full price would be.

## THE CANE MILL

# 2

Giles Freeman knew the way to the Tallywhoa well having been to the plantation many times on errands for the Colonel. His horse Devlin could get there and back without any directions from his rider. More than once the trusty dun had taken him safely home when he was unable to navigate his surroundings on his own. He owed his life to the horse on more than one occasion. Still, vigilance was required along the way. Highwaymen were ever present and might not recognize his trusted mount or him as the Colonel's representative at a distance.

The green ribbon was his passport safely through if the highwaymen could see it as he rode swiftly through the sea oats and through the cane fields along the road. The tall cane hid secrets Freeman did not want to know. McKenzie hadn't just sent him to alert John of his brothers' arrival, he was holding the brothers as his guests. Thomas and Richard were leverage of some sort. Already pawns in the politics of Barbados plantation aristocracy. Freeman didn't like the cloak and dagger behaviors the Colonel sometimes employed, especially when he was stuck in the middle. His apprehension and anxiety were coming through his body subconsciously.

## DEVLIN

Sensing the unease and tension in his rider's legs and hands Devlin set his ears half back and tensed down his topline. As athletic as his rider, Devlin collected himself and focused on Freeman's every weight shift and accommodated the balance instinctively. The horse and rider were true partners, an elegant ballet of athleticism even on their off days. The tension grew as they were nearing one of the stone cane presses. Devlin and Giles could smell the aroma of molasses and fermenting cane residue. Giles shifted his weight slightly and Devlin seamlessly shifted with him to the far side of the road, passing the cane press with as much room as possible. The press was powered by a windmill with arms that swooped tirelessly; the sails stretched taught catching the island breezes. The scattered cane debris attracted wild pigs and wayward people; the Watchers were always watching. Giving both a bit of space was always a good idea.

Once they had safely passed the cane press Giles relaxed a bit knowing the Watchers had seen the green ribbon and had let him pass unchallenged. He let Devlin come down to a walk to catch his breath and extended his frame just enough to cover a bit more ground with less effort. The Tallywhoa was roughly five miles northwest of Bridgetown, and they were almost halfway to the plantation.

The uncultivated areas were alive with lavender blooming between the bearded fig trees and Flower Fence shrubs with purple and white Passionflower vines twining amongst them all. The orange and black Silver Spotted Flambeau butterflies fluttered about with abandon. The aroma was worth a wander through at a full amble even when you were otherwise in a hurry. Green lizards skittered up the tree trunks and under the shrubs while Caribbean Land crabs darted out of their way. Antillean Crested Hummingbirds hovered, dived and darted among the yellow Sweet Pea Shak Shak flowers while the Rain birds darted above after flying insects. With an average temperature of 75 degrees the countryside was a beacon of respite as well as an adventure in staying alive. Ever vigilante Giles came back to focus on the journey as Devlin stopped in his tracks.

Head up and ears forward, Devlin tensed. Freeman followed the gaze of his mount knowing Devlin could see, smell, or hear something he himself could not. Devlin breathed deep and seemed to sample the scents with his nose forward. The breeze was coming from their back and they were upwind. Giles knew they must be close to the source of the smell. Devlin tilted his head, snorting shortly, he inched forward a few steps as he looked for what he could smell. Hesitant, the horse backed up the same few steps and stomped a front hoof as if to call "who's there" to what he could not see.

## SHAK SHAK TREE

Placing his hand on Devlin's withers Giles tried to settle the horse. The shrubs ahead on the left moved ever so slightly and Giles could just make out the shape of a full grown curly red-haired Mangalitsa pig as it stood up to look back at them through the shrubs.

The tusks curling alongside the hog's face were a giveaway this was a smart and very dangerous old boar. Fat and heavy the boar easily weighed over 1000 pounds and could still move with surprising agility and speed if necessary. The wise man would give that hog wide berth and live to hunt him another day. They sat starring at each other for a few minutes. The old boar just stood and watched them as they slowly approached, unmoving from his spot. Something was off. Normally once they are discovered even the old boars will move away from horses or carts. Giles had a sinking feeling he was about to discover one of those secrets he didn't want to find.

Giles gripped with his legs and with Devlin snorting they inched forward along the far side of the road. The boar stood unmoving, starring at them unafraid yet unchallenging. As Giles neared the boar's shrub, he could see another shape on the ground. The boar was protecting something, probably a dead animal left by the road for the pigs to clean up. Looking closer as they began to pass by the boar Giles could just make out a pair of boots partially exposed on the far side of the shrubs. Giles was looking at what was left of a person the old boar was guarding. The stench was intense as they moved down wind of the body. Giles took note of the boots and what clothing he could see from horseback, wondering who was missing and where he was missing from on this beautiful day in Barbados.

The boar turned to face them as they moved past him. The boar's beady dark eyes looking toward Giles and Devlin, he lifted his snout to catch the scent of horse and rider, half wheezed a breath. Giles knew pigs have terrible eyesight and the boar would remember them by smell. Devlin felt the pressure on his sides as Freeman gave him leg and broke softly into an easy lope to move quickly away from the ghastly scene. The sooner they arrived at the Tallywhoa the better.

A party would be sent out to determine who the person was and kill the boar if possible. The bigger question was if the boar killed the person or if the body was left there for the pigs. Bile rose in his throat, knowing there would be little left of the body when they returned. Killer unknown, a chill ran up Giles' spine. Dread filled his being as he contemplated what he must do on the trip back to the Garrison. What had started out as a lovely day out on a simple errand had quickly demised into a ghastly job, complete with the rot and ruin untimely death brings.

Topping the crest of the hill Devlin's head and ears came up a bit as the Tallywhoa came into sight. They crossed the last stretch of distance to the plantation house in haste, both horse and rider anxious to be received and refreshed. Slowing to a jog as they entered the front gates, Devlin came to a stop at the front steps. Giles quickly stepped down, pulled the reins over Devlin's head and handed them to

31

Weezie, the groom at the Tallywhoa who cared for Devlin as if he were her own.

**The Tallywhoa**

Weezie was ever gentle with her hands and soft voice, and always had the large trough filled with cool fresh stream water. Weezie turned to lead Devlin to the stable just behind and east of the main house as Devlin rubbed his head on her shoulder almost knocking the petite woman down. Giles chuckled softly to himself at the comedy between the tiny groom and his beloved mount. Knowing they were completely in love and safe with each other as horses and their women are Giles climbed the front staircase two steps at a time, pulling his gloves off as he approached the door.

The massive front doors opened without a knock. The butler had been alerted by the upstairs maid of Freeman's approach when she saw him crest the hill as she cleaned the windows in the second-floor bath. Giles was reminded a plantation never sleeps, the walls have ears, and there are eyes everywhere. Someone here would know something about the grizzly scene he had passed on the road. Likely no one would say lest he/she be associated with the event. Slaves and servants could be beaten, tortured, or killed at an owner's whim. Although all the slaves and servants respected John Dewe and thought him kind, none dared test the extent of his whims.

The butler ushered Freeman into the two-story library and went to fetch Mister John. The two-story room had windows all along the southern wall. The view from the hill-top mansion overlooked extensive vegetable and botanical gardens and acres of cane fields. The blue sea was visible just beyond the coconut palms and mangroves far in the distance. The stunning vista and island breeze wafting through the windows belied the harsh world of hurricanes, plagues, and politics the people endured to coax their fortunes out of the soil and sea. Giles soaked up the moment of tranquility, sighed at the beauty and irony. He turned away from the window at the sound of boots entering the room.

John Dewe was as impressive as his brothers. Intelligent, handsome, and fit John carried the stamp of man his father Colonel Thomas Dewe put on all his sons. John extended his hand to Giles as he approached from the doorway and welcomed Giles to the Tallywhoa once again.

"Giles Freeman. Good to see you again. What brings you the Tallywhoa on such a gloriously beautiful day?"

John was always exuberant toward guests. They were few and far between in the islands that were weeks away by ship from civilization. Gesturing, he directed John to a seat looking out over the plantation toward the sea. John poured rum into the all familiar dock glasses for himself and Giles. Taking a seat in the chair juxtaposed to Giles, he sipped his rum waiting as Giles retrieved the Colonel's letter from inside his vest.

"The Colonel asked me to bring this letter to you along with news that your brothers Captain Thomas and Richard Dewe have arrived in Bridgetown. They are apparently a full two days earlier than expected and are staying temporarily in the Colonel's private guest quarters at the Garrison. They have trunks and freight that must be transported by cart or the assinigoes. I am to wait your reply if you will be sending transportation or if they are to hire someone in Bridgetown on their own." Giles was direct and succinct, if not a bit brusque. Dreading the conversation about the remains he had discovered by the road Freeman let that information wait until after completing his primary assignment.

John immediately set his glass of rum on the side table and reached over taking the letter from Giles as he stood. "You bring excellent news indeed! My brothers have arrived safely from England. Splendid. Positively splendid!" John walked across to the library table under the window. Picking up the letter knife he quickly slid the blade under the sealed flap and broke open the letter from Colonel McKenzie. With his back turned to Freeman, John opened the letter discreetly reading the cryptic message with apprehension.

*John,*
As you read this you will have been informed your brothers have arrived safely in Barbados and are my guests at the Garrison. Their trunks and freight are currently stored in the Garrison cellars. I have suggested they stay a few days in Bridgetown until transportation to the Tallywhoa is confirmed. Please provide Giles Freeman with instructions if a rig needs to be hired or if you are sending transportation. Thank you for your hospitality and accommodations for Giles until he can return.

*Colonel Duncan McKenzie*

John stood silently at the window for a few moments composing his thoughts in response to the Colonel's letter. McKenzie wanted a delivery directly to the Garrison. The freight for the Tallywhoa was a perfect and legitimate reason for Tallywhoa transport to be seen going into the garrison.

John didn't like it but knew there was no choice. Turning on his heel, he returned to the desk. Dipping the quill in the ink well John penned a response to the Colonel at the bottom of the letter he had received.

*Duncan,*
Thank you for sending word my brothers have arrived safely in Bridgetown. I will send transportation to pick up the trunks and freight along with horses for Thomas and Richard. Please accept the crate of rum as my thanks for graciously hosting my brothers. Look forward to seeing you soon.

*John Dewe*

John refolded the letter as he had received it. Using the blunt end of the letter knife he crushed the Colonel's sealing wax into bits, pouring them into his wax melting ladle that rested in a cradle over a candle. Watching the bits melt back into a usable liquid, John was struck by the irony of repurposing the Colonel's paper and wax. McKenzie would get what he wanted, at a price and at John's convenience. Once the wax was melted John gently took the ladle out of its cradle, tipped the small ladle and poured the liquid back onto the flap of the letter. Pressing the Dewe seal into the soft warm wax, the excess oozed out around the die and quickly set as is cooled. John always felt a certain satisfaction as he sealed correspondence or containers with the family seal. A finality or ownership, he wasn't sure. Either way, he left his mark and handed the letter back to Giles to deliver to the Colonel at the garrison. Giles returned the letter to the inside of his coat, but before he could mention the deceased out on the road John was thinking out loud as was his habit.

"Thank you, Giles, for bringing the letter yourself. Let's go chat with Weezie and let her know you are staying over the night and will be leaving in the morning with the cart and horses for Thomas and Richard. She will stable Devlin for you with care. If she doesn't get to pamper him for at least one night, I'll never hear the end of it." John had started toward the library door when Giles called him back.

"John, wait. Excuse my directness but I must to talk to you for a moment."

John stopped. Turning back to face Giles he was quite surprised. Giles Freeman rarely spoke, but when he did people listened. "Giles, what is it? What has happened? Is something wrong with Thomas or Richard?"

"No, Thomas and Richard are fine. At least they were when I left them in Colonel McKenzie's office. I need to discuss an incident along the road here this afternoon."

John's brow furrowed quizzically. "What are you on about, Giles? What incident?"

"About halfway between the cane mill and the Tallywhoa I came across a dead body. A large Mangalitsa boar has had a go at it for a day or two it appears. I saw boots and the pant legs protruding from under the shrub with the boar. Are you missing anyone from the Tallywhoa?" Giles asked without giving too much information, he really didn't enjoy recanting what he had seen, or smelled.

"Not to my knowledge. I must check with the overseers to determine if everyone is accounted for. I think I would have heard if someone was missing. Regardless, whoever you have discovered belongs somewhere and has a name. What sort of boots did you say? Were they military high tops or something a civilian would wear? Slaves do not have riding boots, save the horsemen and coachmen of course. Oh dear, this is alarming news." John was clearly distressed at the thought of discovering who the victim might be. Mostly because losing a slave would be a significant financial loss to the plantation.

"George!" John summoned his butler who appeared as if out of thin air. "George, I need you to send the boy Tom to find overseer Ian and tell him to meet me at the stable. It's important. Quickly, he must go as fast as he can run to the fields." George turned and went immediately to the kitchen and found Jane, Tom's sister. She ran to the stable to find Tom.

Within minutes Tom was running out the back lot and off around the tobacco barn toward the cane fields. He knew overseer Ian would be organizing to head the workers back toward the slave quarters this late in the day and should be easy to find. Crossing the low water crossing at the creek was always a refreshing few steps in the cool water, then on up the rough coral sand soil toward the main cane stand. Tom could see overseer Ian's head above the cane on the far side of the field. He turned to his left as the way was shorter and flatter than the path to the right which snaked its way through mounds of cane leaves cut from the cane as it was harvested. It was better to avoid the wild pigs and bats that came out in the late afternoon lured in by the fermenting foliage.

Tom came around the far corner of the field and almost full body slammed Moses. Excusing himself as the exhausted slave caught him gently before they collided Tom asked "Moses, you seen overseer Ian? Master John want him right now." Moses set Tom on his feet and turned toward the overseer "Tom, overseer Ian is right back yonder. Slow down so as not to run over him, too. Go on now, it's all right."

"Thank you, Moses, thank you. I sorry I ran into you. Thank you, Moses…" Side-stepping as he spoke, Tom then turned and ran the 200 yards further down the road to the overseer Ian. "Mister Ian! Mister Ian! Master John wants to speak with you at the stable. He sent me to get you right now. He awful upset, don't know why, but he want you at the stable right now. Please, he did say please right now Mister Ian."

Ian knew not to keep John waiting. Ian turned to Patrick, a mulatto small group manager who was not quite an overseer and not quite a slave either. "Patrick, see to it the men get to their quarters. We are in a bit early this afternoon so let them spend a little time in the creek to cool off and clean up. The soap is in the box in the cart as usual. I'll check in to be sure everyone is where they should be by dark."

Patrick nodded and responded "Yessir Mr. Ian. Will do. No worries Mr. Ian. The men will get washed and be in on time." Patrick enjoyed being responsible on occasion. He worked hard to get himself out of servitude and swore he would one day finish out his indenture and have his own place with a family. Both loyal and determined, Patrick was an asset to the Tallywhoa. Unbeknownst to Patrick, he was John Dewe's bastard son issued by a slave owned by Colonel Duncan McKenzie. Ian did what he could to secure a better future for Patrick, meager though that was likely to be.

Ian put his heels in his horse's sides and was off to the stable. His horse, Tiger, was anything but a Tiger. More lazy than smart, the old horse did only what he must. Mister Ian muttered constantly at the old horse the entire way home, but he couldn't bear to part with the nag. Tiger and Ian had been a team for almost 20 years. Classic lazy ass pair. Arriving back at the stable in record time, even Ian was amazed. Ian dismounted to find John and Giles chatting with Weezie.

Weezie glared at Ian as he dismounted and walked toward Giles, John, and her without even a glance or care to Tiger. Breathing heavily the old horse wandered quietly over to the trough for a drink of water, reins looped over his neck, he drank shallowly, raised his head from the trough, cocked one fetlock shifting all his weight to the other hind hoof, let out a long slow sigh, let his ears droop sideways, closed his eyes and went into complete parked-for-the-day mode. Weezie walked over to Tiger and gently released the pressure on the girth to give the old boy some room to breathe and fully relax. Tiger rubber his head on her shoulder in gratitude as John greeted Ian and began explaining the issue at hand.

"Ian, I need to know if all the workers are accounted for. Freeman has found a body by the road between here and the cane mill. Are we missing anyone?" John was mildly alarmed, but not panicked.

"No sir. I know everyone is accounted for at the Tallywhoa. At least they were in the fields headed back to the barracks when Tom came to fetch me. I counted heads and called names this morning and again at noon. I can't say about any workers who are on loan or lease to other owners without sending a runner to check on them." Ian was getting a bad feeling about this line of questions. Something was definitely amiss with someone somewhere, and he did not want to be the person responsible for the loss of a worker. "Do you want me to send runners to the other owners, Mr. John? We will know by morning or tomorrow afternoon at the latest."

Giles wanted to expedite the return to see about the remains before every plantation on the island knew about the incident. "John, I think we might be able to make this simpler if you, Ian, and I go back to the remains. One of you may be able to identify the person or at least which plantation he was from. I'd prefer to not raise an alarm unnecessarily if we don't need to do so. I cannot speak for him of course, but I expect Colonel McKenzie would prefer less publication and more resolution."

"Agreed, Giles. Weezie, saddle up Devlin for Giles, Beulah for Me, and hitch up Wiley to the cart. Ian, would you gather up a shovel and a tarp and whatever else you think we might need to retrieve the body?" John hesitated, thinking about what they might find. He looked at Giles and at Ian before speaking again. "Well, let's get on with it then. We won't know anything until we get there. Ian we will need guns and several of the dogs. Giles saw a big Mangalitsa boar at the site. If he's still there we will have to kill him or run him off at least. Bring the older dogs. I don't want to lose any of my young pups who don't know how to take on a feral boar."

Giles was grateful for the thought of the dogs coming along. Pigs can take on any dog or pack if full grown like this big old boar but prefer to run if given the chance. "Good idea, the dogs. And torches, it could be dark by the time we're done. I don't want any surprises out there in the dark. Let's get on with it, shall we?"

John and Ian nodded in unison. John headed to the house for his guns and some water and rum while Ian went to the shed for a shovel and a tarp. Weezie headed into the barn to saddle the horses and harness Wiley. Giles beat her to Devlin, preferring to saddle his horse himself. Wiley set his massive ears forward in unison as Weezie opened the gate to the lot. He walked into the barn aisle as he did every day in preparation for harnessing. Weezie could have him harnessed and hitched in a matter of minutes and did so. The mule loved her as did the horses, nuzzling her as she pulled the shafts alongside his flanks.

Beulah was a nicely made cross between an Irish Cobb and a thoroughbred. The bay mare with a star on her forehead and two white socks behind had the frame to cover distance easily, heavy bones to stay sound, and the sense to keep herself and her rider safe. Weezie had her saddled and ready to go as John returned from the house. Ian was loading the shovel and tarp in the cart as Giles sat quietly on Devlin. The three men wore grim expressions as they headed out the gate with John and Giles ahead of the cart. John tipped his flask to his lips and silently held it out to Giles. Graciously accepting the flask Giles was more than happy to soften his nerves just a tad. He knew what they were headed for and wanted this over with as quickly as possible.

The dogs were tied in the back of the cart to keep them from jumping out before they were needed. Bred from English foxhounds and mastiffs, the dogs weighed over 50 stone each, could take down a running stag, and were well trained to protect their master. Ian had chosen three he knew to be seasoned hunters and careful to mind. He could manage these and the risks the old boar might present. No boar was worth losing a good dog. They needed dogs to distract and herd the boar off, not challenge him. Old Blue, Duke, and Mammy were the best of the Tallywhoa pack for this job. "Duke be quiet. We'll be there soon enough. Lay down with Mammy. Go on, lay down." Ian directed the dogs who were antsy to get out of the cart and go to track. Dejected, Duke responded and lay down next to Mammy, clearly disappointed. Mammy shifted over to the other hip and sighed with a moan as she leaned on the sideboard of the cart. "Mammy you know I depend on you. You're my best girl, you know."

Ian continued to talk to the dogs as he drove the mule behind John and Giles. John smiled slightly at the overseer who could manage a dozen men with no expression but would cry like a baby if one of his dogs had so much as a thorn in a paw. John giggled. Giles looked at John quizzically, turned to see Ian cuddling Mammy on his lap as he drove. Looking ahead again, Giles giggled, too, and then raised the flask to his lips before passing it back to John.

Wiley plodded along steady and sure as mules do, ears flopping back and forth with every step. The road was bumpy going for an empty cart, so the going was slow. John and Giles had easily left them behind at a slow jog. A few miles down the road Ian watched them in the distance as they came to a stop. Giles was pointing off to his right and ahead of them. The horses were stopped and snorting while nervously stepping back and forth. Ian guessed the old boar was still there and untied the dogs to be ready if the boar charged out from the shrubs. A few hundred feet behind the horses he pulled Wiley up to a stop. The last thing they needed was that boar running up under the cart.

Giles pointed out the shrub where the boar had been earlier. He was sure the old hog was still there. He inched up with Devlin just enough to spook the boar into standing. Devlin backed up as the boar stood.

"Good Lord have mercy!" John exclaimed. "That's the old boar Will Pierce has been trying to find for months. He's clever and fast. Bastard has killed two of Will's dogs already. Ian!" John called out to alert Ian to the quarry. "This is the boar that killed Will Pierce's dogs! Bring your gun and the dogs. Giles and I will flank you. Let's see if we can't get this mean old devil to run out to the east where we can shoot him cleanly. I want this bastard dead today." Giles nodded at the plan.

Ian stepped down from the cart with his rifle in his hand. John had a pistol and Giles had both. Ian unbolted the tailgate on the cart and let it drop. The hounds jumped down at Ian's feet already on alert and ready to hunt. A deep slow growl came from Old Blue. He had scented the hog and knew what the quarry was. Duke and Mammy immediately dropped their noses to scent Old Blues track. The hounds gave voice and moved to take chase. Ian had not let them off lead just yet. He was hoping the boar would run without the dogs getting close enough to get hurt. Walking toward the shrub and the boar the dogs were in full voice and straining against their leads. The old boar turned to face the dogs, put his head down and shook the shrubs.

Giles went clammy, Ian stopped short. John was silent. They all knew the boar was not afraid of the dogs on leads. Ian would have to set them loose to flush him out. John waited until Ian was almost to him. "Ian, Giles and I are going to move a bit more offsides. When the Boar has to look both ways to decide which way to run, let the dogs off their leads. He should turn and run east. Giles draw a bead on that bastard and shoot him when you have a clean shot. I do not want my dogs hurt." Giles nodded as he and John moved offsides the boar, Ian standing where he was with the hounds. John was just about to signal Ian to let the dogs loose when he saw another movement between Giles and the cart.

"Ian! Giles! There's two!" Devlin caught the movement behind him and instinctively turned on his haunches to face the new threat. The sow was camouflaged covered in black mud, had her head down charging at Devlin, squealing in fury as she bulldozed her way through the scrub. Devlin took two strides and jumped clear over her, landing and turning to watch her run past the boar and out across the lower hillside. Her litter of piglets squealed and ran behind as if shot from a canon after their mother. The old boar barked a warning at the men but didn't move. The dogs were wild with adrenaline to take on the quarry.

"Giles, are you good? Do you have a sight on the boar?" John wanted a calculated kill on the boar. One shot. No misses. No errors.

"Yes! Set the dogs loose now!" Giles was ready to be done with the boar. Nothing wakes you up like a sow charging you full throttle with piglets scurrying around your horse's hooves like lemmings running to the sea. Nothing compares. Giles had his rifle up aiming at what he thought was the boar's head. He would wait until the boar cleared the shrub to be sure he got him with one bullet.

Ian held his breath as he slipped the leads off the dogs. Old Blue, Duke, and Mammy set after the boar instantly. The dogs were in full voice and snarling at the same time, the boar saw them coming. Ian raised his rifle to kill the boar, or the sow, to protect them all. Pigs are smart and will work in teams. He had every reason to believe these pigs had been tag teaming their quarry for some time.

The old boar put his head down and came out charging the dogs. Not afraid, he was furious. Ian panicked when he saw the old boar head straight for Mammy. Old Blue set his jaws in the boar's flank and turned him. Duke went for the boar's rear hock, Mammy went for his testicles. The boar roared in fury, spinning and throwing the dogs off just long enough to run straight at Ian. Ian drew down his rifle and fired straight at the boar's head. The bullet hit home, and the boar came crashing down head over heels on top of Ian, the rifle tossed into the ditch as they fell in a heap, the boar's dead eyes just above the tusks dripping with blood onto Ian's chest. While it wasn't the plan the old boar was dead with one shot. The sow was still about and dangerous. Unlikely she would return soon; she would take her babies to safer surrounds. She could smell the boar's blood. She backed into the shadows and hid with her week-old piglets huddled behind her for safety.

The dogs were confused as to what to do. Ian was trapped under the weight of the boar. John and Giles were working to roll the boar off of Ian. Giles went and got Wiley to pull the dead boar off of Ian. The boar was far too heavy for even two men to move. Wiley snorted at the old boar, walked gingerly around and waited for John to hook up the chains around the boar's hocks. Giles noticed Mammy had effectively emasculated the old boar. The testicles were ripped completely out of their bag dragging useless on the ground. Giles smiled at the old bitch and went to Wiley's head, clucked gently, and gave a gentle pull to get the mule started. John drove him from behind and in short order the boar was dragged off of Ian. Giles took Wiley up the side of the road a short distance to get the boar fully off the roadway, unhooked the chains from the boar's hocks and took Wiley back to the cart. As they passed Ian sitting in the road drinking from John's flask, Giles could see Ian was shaking and covered in pig blood.

Mammy was licking Ian's face and whining loudly. The old bitch was clearly afraid her master was hurt. Duke and Old Blue were circling the dead boar growling, touching him with their noses and quickly jerking back. John stood up to evaluate the scene.

"Blue! Duke! Come here. Mammy, he's OK, really. Calm down old girl. Come on, get off of him, give him room to breathe! MAMMY, SIT!" John finally got her calmed down as Duke and Old Blue returned to their master. Slipping their leads back over their heads, John stood up and helped Ian stand. Wobbly and covered in pig blood, Ian was still somewhat stunned by the experience. He bent down slightly to pet his dogs gently on the head, talking quietly as he did.

"Well done, Blue, Duke. Mammy you're a good girl. The best girl I know right now. Good dogs, good, good dogs." Ian was regaining his composure and comprehending they had killed the boar. "Mr. John, If you will hold the dogs, I'll help Mr. Giles see to the body, or what's left of it anyway…"

44

Ian's voice trailed off at the prospect of what they might find.

"Let me have a look first, Ian. I want to see if I can identify him or the plantation he is from before you and Giles move anything. Stay here with the dogs. Let them go if the sow comes back, she'll run I'm sure." John looked to Giles and they turned to see about the body, the reason they were there in the first place. Neither wanted any part of this, but obviously had no choice.

Giles led John around to the side where the boots were protruding. Bending over they peered under the shrub to find the grizzly remains with the face eaten off, entrails strewn about, flesh torn from the back and arms. The right hand was missing entirely, and the left hand was badly mangled but still had a gold ring on the ring finger. A petite finger, slender and feminine held the golden band, emeralds circling a glistening oval diamond. Giles stepped back, turned to John in horror. "John this is a woman. A lady, not just a woman. Only a lady of wealth wears a ring of emeralds and gold. Who do you know that wears such a ring?"

John's mouth dropped open, stunned. He bent down to see the ring on the lady's hand. Standing abruptly and turning away, John was suddenly ill. "Dear God. This is Esmerelda Conn. She is the daughter of Andrew Conn, owner of Emerald Oaks Plantation. I'm sure it is her. She was presented at last spring's Rosebud cotillion. Andrew will be devastated. I must go at once to inform him."

Giles stepped closer to John and intercepted his stride. "No. I need you to ride to the Garrison and report the incident to the Colonel. He will send the appropriate personnel after taking down what you've seen here today. When you return, we will decide who should go to Emerald Oaks. I do not think Andrew, or her , should have to see her in this state. We may have to rely on the ring and clothing to identify her. Perhaps there are personal items, a hair clip or a length of her hair to identify her. Ian and the dogs should remain here as well to keep the sow away from her body."

John nodded and paused a moment. "Yes. Yes of course you're right. I'll go to the Garrison and find the Colonel. This isn't a random accident. She's wearing men's trousers and riding boots. Something's wrong here. I'll be back with a detail as quickly as possible" Turning on his heel, he mounted Beulah. Side stepping past the dead boar, Beulah snorted and blew nervously. Once passed John headed her toward Bridgetown, put his legs on her sides and set her to a fast canter. The Garrison was only a few miles away, but it seemed like thousands. He brought Beulah to a walk to let her catch her breath as they entered the bustling city. No need to draw unnecessary attention. John went directly to the Colonel's office. Dismounting he handed the reins to a soldier guarding the door. Knocking with more energy and anxiety than he had wanted, John came face to face with Lieutenant Evans.

"John Dewe to see Colonel McKenzie at once." John was still flustered and not exactly thinking about etiquette at that precise moment. Covered in dust and blood all over his clothes and smeared along his neck and chin John looked as if he was returning from a war zone. Evan's was startled by John's appearance, a man who he had always seen impeccably dressed and never dirty.

"Yes, indeed, sir. Please come in and I'll get the Colonel for you immediately." Evan's stepped aside to let John into the vestibule. Hastily he went to the Colonel's door and knocked rapidly. "Colonel McKenzie, John Dewe is here with urgent business." Evans was looking John up and down for clues to the state of his distress and checking for obvious injuries. The door opened and McKenzie stepped out with a gruff look on his face. What could John Dewe be thinking coming to his office this way? McKenzie started to admonish Dewe until he took a good look at John. "John. What on earth is the matter, man? You've blood all over ye. Are you hurt?"

McKenzie immediately stepped forward to help John slowly sink into Evans' chair. "Evans get a glass of scotch, and one of water, too. Quick man!" Turning back to John he waited for John to compose himself to tell him what had happened that brought him bloodied and filthy to the garrison.

"Duncan, I have dreadful news. Giles and I have found Esmerelda Conn's body just past the cane mill on the way to the Tallywhoa. At least we think it is Esmerelda. You must come quickly with a detail. Andrew will be devastated. We must get word to him as well. Dear Lord, Duncan. The hogs have had at her for at least a couple of days. There isn't much left…it's horrible…" John's voice trailed off as he cringed at what he had seen.

"John, how do you know it is Esmerelda?"

"The emerald and diamond ring on her left hand. It is the same ring Andrew gave to Esmerelda at the Rosebud cotillion last spring. There may be other items as well, but the ring was obvious, and we didn't want to move the body…what is left of it…before you could see the scene. Duncan, the hogs…there isn't much left to identify. It's horrific. Andrew and Isabella simply cannot see their daughter this way." Standing as Evans returned with the glasses of scotch and water, John took the water and drank it down quickly. He took the scotch and sipped it slowly, washing it down with more water as Evan's poured more into his glass. Finally replenished he turned to McKenzie. "Thomas and Richard. Where are they?"

"Your brothers are down to the market scouting about the trades shops this afternoon. I don't think they'll be back soon, and I truly do not know where to find them quickly. You are welcome to go to their rooms and refresh yourself while I take a detail out to the site. Meet up with them when they return?"

"Thank you for the offer, but no. If that is indeed Esmerelda Conn, I must go with you to inform her parents. I'll return tomorrow with a cart and assinigoes as I said in my letter. Oh, yes, right. You haven't received that letter back from Giles yet. Of course not. No matter, we can discuss details on the way back to where Giles and Ian wait for us." John's thinking was slowly returning to a more conscious level.

"Evans, I need Henry Watts and Joseph Douglass, Brice Ratchford and Jenny Harris. I need a female along to be with Isabella if needed. Find them and have them report to me immediately. But first, take John to my private toilet and arrange for a hot bath and a set of fresh clothes." John started to protest but McKenzie cut him short. "John you cannot show up to Andrew and Isabella's home with their daughter's blood all over you. I don't think you realize what you look like just now."

"What? Oh, no, of course you are correct. I cannot show up with blood all over me. No that is just unthinking of me. But just so you know, this isn't Esmerelda's blood. This is pig blood. Rather a story to be told over fine scotch later, but for now rest assured the pig didn't fare so well. He is quite dead. I'm not injured physically, just shaken up knowing Andrew's daughter is dead under highly suspicious circumstances." John reached for the bottle of scotch and turned to Evans. "Lead the way my boy. The hot water sounds like a gift from God right now. The Scotch a gift from his son, and clean clothes a gift from the Holy Ghost."

Evans stepped to his left, turned and led John down the corridor to the Colonel's private toilet. Pausing at the door to the attendant's quarters, he gave brief instructions before continuing up the hidden staircase behind the portico garden wall. John had never been to this part of the garrison before. He wondered what other secrets might hide along the way. Glancing warily about, he followed Evans up the stairs and through a door into a spacious yet completely private bath. The attendant was already filling the enormous wooden tub lined with muslin with steaming hot water from a tap just above the foot of the tub.

John had never seen anything quite like this before. Running water in taps yes, but not hot water like this. He made a mental note to question McKenzie about this novel idea sometime in the future. At the moment he simply wanted to get in that mysterious steaming vat with the aroma of lavender filling the air as the attendant dripped lavender oil in the bath. Oh, heaven can wait he thought, this works for now.

The attendant shut off the valve and explained how it worked if he wanted to add more, pointed out the bar of soap, a brush, and a flannel to wash his face with. Towels were neatly hung over some tubing apparatus behind the tub. He realized as he touched the tubes, they were hot, thus warming the towels as he bathed. Oh, he liked this arrangement well. The tubing ran back up the wall just a bit and then down to the tap in the tub. Clever. Very clever. Hot water, warm towels, lavender oil, and good scotch. This was going to cost him down the road. McKenzie always found a way.

John stripped off his dirty clothes and stepped into the hot bath. Slowly he slid down into the aromatic water and immediately found wonderful relief from the day's stress. How easy it would be to just stay here for a long, long while. As he drifted into euphoria the attendant interrupted his bliss to remind him his clean attire was laid out for him in the dressing room next to the bath. The Colonel wanted to leave in about an hour, please. John so wanted to just dissolve into the bath but knew he could not. He picked up the soap and brush and made good use of the amenities at hand.

Once scrubbed clean and odor free he arose from the tub, took a towel off the heating tubes and wrapped the warm towel around his waist. He took the second towel off the tubes and used it to roughly dry his soaking wet hair and then worked his way down his body to the waist towel. Stepping out of the tub onto the towel on the floor the water trickled down his legs and ankles, pooling on the mat around his feet. John bent over and dried his ankles. Dropping the towel on the floor he dried the bottom of his feet and removed the waist towel to dry his legs.

Genuinely regretful he must leave the luxury behind he stepped into the dressing room adjoining the bath to find clean clothes laid out exactly as the attendant had described. Quickly he dressed in breeches, linen shirt, and jacket. John discovered his riding boots had been cleaned and polished while he bathed. He could get used to this. Ian? No. Jane maybe. A plan was forming as he prepared to return to the site where Giles and Ian waited.

Back to reality as he followed the attendant out of the dressing room, down the stairs and headed across the breezeway back to the Colonel's office. Turning the corner he came face to face with Thomas muttering on at Richard about the voracity of producing a portion of the Tallywhoa cane crop into rum as well as raw sugar for export to the colonies and England. Coming to an abrupt halt as John came around the corner, Thomas started to excuse himself for being careless when he realized the man was his brother John.

"John! What on earth are you doing here? We weren't expecting to hear from you until tomorrow afternoon. It is wonderful to see you. There's a lovely pub just across the way. Let's celebrate our reunion with a pint or two, shall we?" John, Thomas, and Richard shook hands and hugged as brothers do with genuine pleasure at seeing each other again.

"Thomas I'd like nothing better today of all days. However, I cannot. There has been an incident on the road to the Tallywhoa. I've come to notify the Colonel and arrange for a detail to be sent to investigate. I'm afraid I can't stay and celebrate just now. I will be sending a cart and mule, assinigoes, and horses for you tomorrow if that suits you both." John was anxious to be on his way. "I apologize for being curt, but the Colonel is waiting for me. I promise I will explain everything when you get to the Tallywhoa."

Another brief hug as John stepped past them and hastened to the public door of the Colonel's office. A cart and driver waited with three riders in crisp military uniforms. Beulah was ready to go as she lifted her head and put her ears forward toward her master. The front guard gave John a leg up. Settling into his saddle John was surprised to see the colonel come out of the stable door riding a Clydesdale mare that could easily pull a caisson. Witcher was a war horse, well trained and valuable. Standing almost 18 hands tall, McKenzie's legs came about two thirds of the way down her sides. John wondered why short men ride the tallest horse they can find.

**Witcher & Assinigoe**

McKenzie in command motioned to John to ride beside him with two riders ahead of them, the cart behind them, and the last rider behind the cart. The small entourage moved casually out of the garrison grounds and into the street heading toward the Tallywhoa. No one spoke until they were outside Bridgetown. They picked up a slow jog for a bit before the lead riders kicked into a lope moving ahead to scout for issues. The Colonel was contemplating the course of action to follow.

"Nasty business recovering deceased persons. Notifying the families is the worst part in my opinion. Lives forever changed with one word. I have had to deliver agonizing grief far too many times in my career and it never gets easier." The haggard look on the Colonel's face defined a rare moment of absolute and genuine despair. Rarely was he seen emotionally vulnerable.

John looked ahead out of politeness to the Colonel and replied "Agreed. On the battlefield one expects hardship and loss. But this loss of a young life that should be home with her parents, this is truly hard to accept as God's will. A man had a hand in this untimely demise. I'm sure of it. The question is who and why." John replaced his grief with anger, an emotional state he could work with and accomplish the grim tasks at hand. The group fell silent as they approached the cane mill. The two lead scouts had stopped to wait for the Colonel and the cart to catch up before moving on. Well aware the Watchers were there; they took no risks. They all felt eyes upon them. The silence was deafening.

Colonel McKenzie motioned for the riders to move ahead as he approached. Purposefully not looking about he chose to appear unconcerned. The stillness and quiet was in truth extremely disconcerting. Something was definitely not right. Freeman finding Esmerelda close to the road without being discovered for at least a day or two prior was nagging at the Colonel's mind. Anxious to evaluate the scene the Colonel put his heels against the Clydesdale's side and picked up a slow jog. She covered a lot of ground with few steps, each step making the earth shake as her feet hit the ground. John nudged Beulah to keep up and she did. The driver of the cart slapped the reins gently on the back of the mule, clucked to move him on into a trot as well. The tail rider held back a few lengths to give the team a bit of room, scanned the fields and shrubs for movement and when satisfied the way was clear moved into a trot to catch up. They were nearing the site.

Dread sat heavily upon them knowing there was no happy ending for the family of Esmerelda Conn.

§

Giles and Ian sat in the shade of the cart as they waited for John to return with a detail. The dogs had settled with them out of the direct sun. Aside from a few birds and butterflies there was no movement in the cane fields or the shrubs. The feral sow watched from the shadows where she hid with her piglets. She wouldn't venture out again until after dark and the men and dogs were gone. The dogs knew she was still nearby. Ian knew they could smell her and watched the hillside where she disappeared casually. They would alert if even a blade of grass moved. Mammy's ears went up first, Duke stood and growled low. Old Blue set to barking to alert Ian and Giles of approaching riders. The detail had arrived.

The lead riders were men Giles recognized from the Garrison. The Colonel and John came behind them with the cart following with a petite tail rider on a small grey gelding behind the cart. Giles wasn't quite sure he was seeing clearly at first. But yes, that last rider was indeed Jennie Harris. Not actually a soldier as women were not allowed, Jennie accompanied details when the Colonel felt a woman might be needed. People definitely responded differently to her than the uniformed officers, especially other women. Giles realized her presence was calculated and that the Colonel believed the victim was Esmerelda Conn. A woman would be an asset to notify the lady's parents.

The first rider, Brice, called out "Freeman, where is the victim?" while the second rider, Joseph, was eyeing the carcass of the old boar lying just next to where his horse stopped. Astonished with the size of the animal even in death, Brice had to address him twice to get his attention again.

"Joseph. Joseph this way man. The victim is this way." Dismounting in a single fluid motion Brice was on the ground and headed toward the shrub where Giles was now standing. Joseph followed suit letting Ian hold the reins of both horses. The dogs were milling about half whining half barking under the cart, still tied by their leads to the frame. John and the Colonel pulled up, dismounted and walked over to join the men hunched overlooking under the shrub. Giles and John were both content to stand back and let the others examine the scene. The cart and tail rider pulled up just as the Colonel got a good look at the remains.

Standing up visibly shaken by what he saw the Colonel wiped his brow and covered his nose with his forearm. "Dear Lord, may she rest in peace. Let's cut the brush back away from her. We can't drag her out." The Colonel and John stepped up wind from the body as the men tied rags over their mouths and noses. Henry Watts, the driver, unloaded the machetes and axes from the garrison cart and handed them to Brice, Joseph, and Giles. John pulled on Ian's work gloves to drag the cut limbs away from the body. Ian had already done his duty up close today. John had him hold the horses and keep the dogs quiet. Still shaken, a bit inebriated with rum, and covered in dried pig blood Ian obliged.

The Colonel knew they were being watched. Concerned there was no interference and no evidence the body had been interfered with prior to their arrival, he was becoming more aware something was very amiss. Scanning the area with his peripheral vision he could not say anything was out of place, there was no message for him to discover. The atmosphere was all wrong here. A chill went up his spine at the thought the Watchers knew what had happened and were staying clear in hopes he would figure out what had happened to Esmerelda on his own. The Watchers knew. The realization hit home. Who or what were they actually dealing with? Looking all around them quite deliberately, he saw a shadow move in the trees behind them toward the cane mill. The unspoken message was clear. "You will know who did this, Colonel. We had no part in this. We're watching."

Giles noticed the Colonel wobble a step. Reaching out to steady him was a reaction. "Colonel, are you all right?

You've gone pale, sir. Perhaps you should sit in the shade a bit..." The Colonel turned angrily toward Giles. "I'm fine. Thank you for your concern but I am fine. It's just a bit unnerving to see a lady end up this way. Let's get this shrubbery cleared away quickly." Gesturing toward the tangled foliage, Giles went back to hacking out the bracken while John pulled the limbs back and out of the way. Within 30 minutes they had the area cleared and the remains were clearly visible.

Giles instinctively made mental notes of the details while Jennie drew sketches from the side. Noting exactly where each shrubbery limb had been, damages to the body, the clothing, boots, hair, and the ring still on the finger. Giles stopped cold when he saw the green ribbon that had been in her hair and trampled into the dirt behind her head. The Colonel was staring at the ribbon. As his eyes narrowed, his posture straightened, and his nostrils flared for just an instant in anger. A realization came across the Colonel's face. While the Watchers knew the culprit, they had no part in the killing. Likely they had an idea and would leave clues to tell what they knew. Patience would reveal much. The difficulty would be in keeping her father and John away from the men who had no part in this. Playing with fire was an accurate description although they had no idea at the time.

Giles knew the Colonel well enough to know his silence held more meaning than when he spoke. His look of recognition confused Giles, made him stop and think about the situation with new eyes. The Colonel knew more than he was saying, and Giles went cold with the realization this event was something new, rather someone new. There was a new evil in the Parish. Their job was to catch him.

Jennie tenderly slid the ring off of the mangled hand. Wiping the blood away she handed it to the Colonel along with the ribbon to return to her family. Jennie measured the soles of the boots, recorded the color and fabrics in the clothes. Gently she managed to pull the belt out of the trousers which she passed to the Colonel as well. Turning the belt over the Colonel found the letters E.C. inscribed on the back of the buckle. The tail end of the belt had been chewed by the hogs. As the Colonel contemplated what to say to her parents, Jennie interrupted his thoughts.

"Colonel, sir, I think you need to see this."

The Colonel refocused on Jennie's hand pointing at the entrails laid cleanly out on the ground. There in the muck was clearly a fetus. Esmerelda had been pregnant. The Colonel stepped back as if he had been struck, Jennie stood up slowly not taking her eyes off the tiny baby. "looks to be about 5 or 6 months in the womb, sir. I'm not a doctor but I've helped the midwife birth many and bury far too many stillborn. Esmerelda would have just begun to swell her belly noticeably."

Giles and John looked at each other with the same thought. Who was the father? Could he have done this to rid himself of an unwanted child? In unison they looked at the Colonel who was turning red with fury. Gritting his teeth, he managed to swear under his breath, livid at the stupidity of 'man'. Without looking up he said to the group

"No one is to speak a word about the child. We may catch the bastard who did this by keeping his secret until he gives himself away." Looking up and looking each person directly in the eye for recognition and agreement, they all understood and nodded one by one. The Colonel would find the person responsible for this atrocity and would not be kind when he did. "John, Jennie, we must inform her parents. Giles please assist the men with getting her remains in the tarp and into the cart. We will take her back to the Emerald Oaks immediately. There is nothing more to be gained here. She was probably killed someplace else and dumped here to be found."

The Colonel noticed Ian was still holding the horses next to the cart with the dogs tied underneath. "Ian, once they have the body loaded in the Garrison cart, take your dogs and go home to the Tallywhoa." Noticing Ian was covered in blood for the first time he said "Dear Lord Ian, are you injured? You've blood all over you."

Ian was still shaken but explained how the boar charged him and he shot him square between the eyes, the velocity of over 1000 pounds of charging hog going head over heels knocking him down and landing squarely on top of him, blood soaking into his clothes as the hog bled out from the hole in his skull. Somehow retelling the event made Ian realize how close he came to being killed. He no doubt would have been if had missed with his one and only shot. He couldn't help it but he was crying silently realizing he could have lost his beloved Mammy, too. Looking up the road where the dead boar lay, he decided he earned those tusks. The meat could rot but he would cut out those well-worn tusks as his trophy.

The colonel just sort of stood there looking at Ian then John then Giles who just sort of looked back. John said "Colonel that is exactly what happened. If not for Ian's steady hand on the trigger in a crisis, and his dogs, that old boar would probably have killed us all." Speechless, the Colonel took Witcher's reins from Ian and with a leg up from Giles waited for John and Jennie to get mounted for the ride to the Emerald Oaks.

Giles turned back to the worst part of the job with Henry, Brice and Joseph. Gently they lay the tarp next to the body and rolled the remains slowly into the center. Joseph used a shovel to include the pieces and parts that he could, placing the baby softly into Esmerelda's arms, held by her mangled left hand and the stump of her right forearm. The child would be buried with his mother. Joseph told it was a boy and Giles commented how evil must a man be to kill his unborn son. Carefully they folded the tarp around the remains and lifted the bundle into the garrison cart.

The Colonel and John waited for the men to rinse their hands and faces with the dipper from the water barrel and mount up to lead the way. Jennie fell in the tail rider position again with a full view of the group and the shifting shadows as they moved on. The Watchers were there, angry at the discovery of the child. The perpetrator would not walk free for long and he should pray the colonel finds him first. The women in the shadows had ways that could make the devil sleep with the lanterns lit.

# 3

Thomas and Richard watched John ride off with Colonel McKenzie and a detail of soldiers wondering what had happened to prompt such measures. Something significant had transpired for the Colonel to attend personally. They would have to wait until the soldiers returned to hear the details.

Richard raised his brow and said "Thomas, I've no idea what that was about. We may find out later from John if he returns with the Colonel. Meanwhile, let's get changed and head back to town to the *Running Boar* for a pint and something to eat. No reason we can't relax and enjoy some local fare while we wait".

Thomas rolled his eyes and replied "Richard, you are predictable if nothing else. But you are also correct. We cannot do anything until someone returns with news…and transportation. So, yes. Let's enjoy the local fare this evening since it is obvious the Colonel's dinner plans are scuttled. The *Running Boar* it is." Richard smiled to himself having won over the plan for the evening, pulled the key to his room out of his pocket and headed across the breezeway to his room with Thomas close behind.

The brothers took the time to freshen up and put on clean clothes. Casual yet crisp Thomas was always turned out properly. Richard was a bit less fashion-conscious preferring attire that complimented his masculinity and enterprising nature. Both were highly desirable bachelors. The men had an agenda with clearly defined goals and objectives. They differed in the means to achieving their agenda in ways that complimented the bigger picture. Most of the time. The *Running Boar* was the first engagement in Barbados, the first step in returning the Tallywhoa to full prosperity. They met in the hallway between their rooms, locked the rooms and left the garrison in anticipation of good food and new company.

Walking down the street toward the pub the men passed a variety of carriages, carts loaded with freight, people doing business of all sorts. Activity is enterprise and they were pleased to see Bridgetown was as active as their father had described to them. Lots of money was changing hands in the market and behind closed doors. Bridgetown was a world of contradictions. The ladies were dressed in embroidered silks and fine linens and wore kid leather shoes and gloves. Fine European made carriages pulled by matched teams of horses shuttled them into town and home again. As they shopped the ladies were followed closely by plainly shod servants and slaves wearing their cleanest rough canvas trousers or plain cotton shifts to carry their ladies' purchases and protect them from pickpockets and thieves. The men conducted business in the pubs and gentlemen's club over pints and cards.

Richard looked up to see the sign for the *Running Boar* at the corner of the next block. Thomas followed his gaze and shifted his direction to cross the street toward the pub. Looking briefly over his shoulder, he stopped to let a carriage pass and noticed the twin ladies they had seen earlier at the market. They were headed away from the market, headed home Thomas assumed. The ladies were whispering to each other and giggling about some confidence they shared. Thomas and Richard were unaware the ladies had been observing the brothers from the back as they walked toward the pub. Richard in his vanity assumed it was about him, Thomas was more interested in who they were as they were clearly form a family of means and influence. Someone would know who they were, and it would be easy to find out.

Crossing the street to the pub, Thomas held the door open for Richard who had stopped to watch the ladies' carriage move away. Thomas sighed and called to his brother "Richard. The pint you're buying me is in here, brother" as he motioned with the other hand to enter the pub. Richard glared briefly at Thomas and gruffed retorting "the pint I'm buying you? Oh, hardly bother, you'll be buying mine. After all you're the oldest and I'm the little brother in need of protection from all things evil containing alcohol." Passing by Thomas on his way through the door, Thomas gently shoved him into the pub as bothers will do. Thomas gave Richard that slanty-eyed 'oh please do grow up in this lifetime' look. Richard just smiled and eyed the available tables.

Thomas took control and chose a table well inside the pub toward the rear with seating that allowed him to have his back to the wall and face the door. He wanted to see who came and went form the pub, and with whom. As they claimed their seats at the table, a bar maid came over to wait on them.

"Gentlemen, welcome to the *Running Boar*. What can I get for you this evening?"

Richard casually enjoyed the presence of the girl, a welcome respite from Thomas and his seriousness. And ale. He must have ale. "Pint of ale for both my brother and I, please lass. We are thirsty and hungry. What might you have on the menu this evening?" Thomas sat attentively while Richard flirted shamelessly. A finely researched and deeply practiced art Richard had mastered by age 5. Such the lady's man Richard was a royal pain to take to dinner. The women all wanted Richard; the men wanted to be Richard. Thomas just wanted a pint of ale at the moment.

Thomas interrupted their blushing and fussing "Miss, if you could just bring the ale, and surprise us with some meats and cheeses. Maybe some local fruits and breads. Whatever is good and fresh." Smiling at her as a gentleman should she did a slight curtsy and headed for the bar. Richard simply shifted his attention to her backside as she walked away, tilted his head slightly and smiled lost in his thoughts. Thomas had noticed her finer qualities, just a little less overture and a lot more discretion than his brother. Watching the reaction of the other men in the room to Richard's overtures was always enlightening. He learned a lot about men's constitution from their attitude toward Richard. And he always had lovely women to chat with as well. Richard was good to have along.

The bar maid returned with two pints of ale and a loaf of fresh corn bread. The barkeep was immediately behind her with a platter of smoked fish, sausages, cheeses and fruits. A sharp knife lay across the platter for serving. The barkeep watched Richard expressionless. Thomas assumed he was either family or held her indenture. Either he would put that knife in a man for touching the girl, or he would hold it to a man's throat for the money she earned. Either way, even Richard realized there were consequences to any man who went too far and mistreated the bar maid.

Thomas thanked the bar maid and said "Please keep our pints full for several rounds. My brother and I are indeed thirsty and appreciate your excellent fare and service. How much do we owe you so far? I prefer to pay up front." The bar keep looked at Thomas and knew this man was not about to be indebted. He and his brother were good clients to have about. Watching Richard eyeing the bar maid, he replied to Thomas "Pints and food are a shilling per man, sir". A substantial yet fair price for good food and service was expensive on the island. Thomas laid the coins requested, plus two more to keep the mugs full, on the table and the bar keep quickly picked them up. Nodding to Thomas he went back to his work behind the bar.

Richard had sliced the bread and was cutting into the meats and cheeses, layering the slices on the bread with the point of the knife. Thomas sipped his ale and watched a group of men enter the pub and sit at a table in the shadows across the pub. Richard laid the knife back on the platter and began to eat with fervor. Looking up at Thomas, he followed his gaze to the men sitting in the shadows. Trusting Thomas's instincts, he took note of the clothes the men were wearing, and the weapons tucked into their belts and boots. Most likely these were dock workers finally come to drink and eat after unloading the freight off the *Angeline.*

Thomas picked up a slice of bread and added some smoked fish, bits of a crumbling white cheese, and bit into the layers discovering a delightful aroma and truly fine flavors. Richard was already downing his third slice with a sausage of lamb and sprigs of mint folded in the bread. Garlic and herbs, Rosemary he thought, permeated the lamb with flavor. The ale was cold and a perfect complement to the tray of meats and cheeses. Thomas was more deliberate, but Richard was taking mental notes as well. Other patrons came in for a pint and left. Some were playing cards, smoking pipes or cigars over finer liquors such as rum or scotch. A hum of contentment permeated the atmosphere. A short spat over a card played and dropped ended with the bar keep taking the cards away and leaving a loaf of bread. The evening was edging into night. It was time to go back to the garrison.

Thomas laid two more shillings on the table, stood and waited for Richard to finish up his last bite of smoked fish. Licking his fingers, Richard stood up and tipped his last bit of ale from the mug. The *Running Boar* had been an excellent choice for food, drink, and people watching. The bar maid was easy on the eyes and the bar keep kept the mugs filled. Richard was sure her top was laced higher when they walked in but couldn't be sure after 4 pints. At some point she just sort of disappeared. No matter as Thomas was walking to the door ready to get to the garrison and a warm bed already considering what they had to do tomorrow and wondering if the Colonel and soldiers had returned. Pushing the door open he and Richard stepped out into the street emptied of merchants and buyers.

They crossed over to the sea wall and ambled back toward the garrison. The mosquitos were vicious and prompted them to walk faster. Thomas knew the mosquito nets would be a welcome addition this evening. Richard was wondering how John managed to withstand the swarms of biting insects for so long. Mental note to ask about things that bite on the island. Swatting at the blood suckers the brothers arrived at the garrison noting the Colonel's office was dark and went on up to their rooms.

The brothers unlocked their doors in unison and quickly closed them to avoid letting the insects in with them. Thomas sat and removed his tall boots, standing them next to his bed in military fashion. Stripping down to his nakedness he went into the bath to rinse off and put on his casual evening shirt and loose-fitting drawstring sleeping pants. Soft and cozy from many washings these were his favorite clothes. Returning to the bedroom he noticed the netting had been let down around the bed while they were gone. He put out the candle that had been left to light the room for him, slipped under the net and melted into the soft bed with fresh linens and goose down pillows. He lay awake a short time thinking about the day, the people they had met, the curious interactions between his brother John and the Colonel and fell asleep listening, always on guard.

§

Richard shed his boots and left them where they fell by the chair. He grabbed his shirt behind his head and pulled it off, tossing it onto the table next to him. He unfastened his belt and let his trousers drop to the floor. He picked them up and put them on top of his shirt. He realized at that moment the candle in the lantern was lit when he came in the door,

64

cautiously he scanned his room. His naked body sculpted by candlelight he reached back to remove the leather lace from his hair. Richard shook his head gently sending his thick dark locks down below his shoulder in undulating waves. He looked up to realize there was light in the bath. The sound of water moving about in the tub, a gentle humming eased into the room, luring him to find the source beckoning him closer.

As he walked softly past the table with the candle in the bed chamber, the light fell across his back illuminating the rippling muscles under his skin as well as the scars left by more than one jealous partner of one lover or another. His buttocks muscular, his legs strong, his shoulders carried an air of self-awareness of his beauty as a man. The door to the bath was slightly ajar, the light growing stronger as he approached, the humming clearly a woman's voice. The humming stopped.

Richard pushed the door open slowly, hinges creaking, to reveal the bar maid in the tub, hair tied up with a ribbon, sponge in her hands washing her leg propped up on the edge of the tub. Soapy water ran down her arms and over her chest, dripping off her nipple back into the tub. Smiling slightly, she leaned forward and held out the sponge to Richard. Saying not a word, he took the sponge and began washing her back. Looking over her shoulders he could just see the shape of her breasts above the water. Her hair smelled of lavender. Intoxicated by her aromas he closed his eyes for a moment to fully explore the scents. She murmured something gentle bringing him back to the present. He looked down and found her looking into his eyes, a sly smile on her face.

Richard stood and meant to step into the tub with her, but before he could she stepped out of the tub. She placed one of her hands on the back of the tub, and then the other, bending over to brace herself. Gently he massaged her dark and secret places still damp from the bath. She moaned with the pleasure of his gestures. Richard was a master of making a lady wait. He then carried her breathing heavily to the bed and laid her gently on her back. Richard physically loved a woman the way a woman should be loved, leaving her breathlessly satisfied. When she had caught her breath, she stood and gingerly walked to the bath to fully clean herself. She stepped into the tub and winced as she slowly sat in the hot water. She was bruised and bled slightly from the tiny tears that sometimes happen with unusually well-endowed men.

Once satisfied she was clean, she stepped out of the tub as Richard held the warm towel for her off the heating tubes. He tenderly dried her with a touch gentle and kind. Already dressed in his sleeping pants, he helped her pull her smock over her head and pulled her outer dress snug around her breasts. He laced her bodice up to show her breasts to their best advantage and kissed them both, just above the ruffle line. She felt faint for just a moment as he stepped back and finally spoke.

"My dear, you are a wonder to come home to and a delicious lover. I thank you for spending your evening with me. Perhaps we might again someday". His hand caressing her bottom as he spoke, she felt it difficult to leave but realized she would be missed at the pub. The bar keep was indeed a greedy man who coveted her indenture and the money her services brought into to his pockets. "I've left you a gift in your dress pocket. I hope it is sufficient". She felt in her pocket and found 5 shillings. She would give the three the keep expected to him and hide the other two for herself. Richard continued to speak "I'll be sure to visit the pub when we are in Bridgetown again. The service is spectacular". He walked her to the door of his room and quietly let her out. Watching her leave through the big double doors he noticed she winced as she walked away. He apparently did his job well. Again. He smiled to himself, closed and bolted the doors, and fell into bed pulling the netting down around him as he dropped fully spent and was asleep before his head hit the pillow.

Thomas heard the double doors close softly and half woke thinking 'Richard, already brother?' He was aware of Richard's effect on a woman and closed his eyes with a sigh thinking the poor girl would most likely have difficulty walking the next morning and went back to sleep. The Dewe's men were well known for their prowess, they never disappointed.

# 4

The soldiers led the detail taking Esmerelda Conn's body home to Emerald Oaks. John and Colonel McKenzie rode behind the scouts and in front of the cart driven by Henry Watts. Jennie Harris riding next to Giles Freeman brought up the rear. The trip from the site where Esmerelda was found seemed much further than actual distance of 4 miles away. The contingent was silent, each person considering what might have happened to bring Esmerelda to such an end. Jennie observed the Watchers moving along through the edges of the fields and woods as they went. The men didn't seem to notice.

Turning into the drive up to the big house at the Emerald Oaks the Colonel sat up straighter, determined to be stoic on behalf of the family. John felt his heart break for her parents whose world was about to change forever. The soldiers did their jobs as they should with grace and care for all. Jennie realized the Watchers had disappeared from her notice, but she knew they were there. A chill went up her spine hoping whoever they were, they would be kind to the Conn family in their loss.

### Emerald Oaks

Pulling up to the front steps, the house man greeted the Colonel and immediately sent a servant boy to fetch the stable manager and hands to help with the horses. Inviting the Colonel into the house he turned to hold the door open for the detail. The Colonel declined, asking the man to please ask Mr. Conn to come out to talk with him. The man then realized there was something...someone...wrapped in a tarp in the back of the cart. Visibly terrified and shaking, wondering who it might be the Colonel was bringing for Mr. Conn to see, the house man abruptly went it to find his master without saying another word. He found Andrew Conn in his study working on the financial books for Emerald Oaks.

"Master Andrew? Master Andrew the Colonel McKenzie is here and asking could you please come out front right away."

Andrew did not respond immediately being completely consumed with his figures calculating balances and creating long range planning decisions.

"Master Andrew? Colonel McKenzie is here and wants to talk with you out front. He has a cart with a body in it. I think he means for you to identify the body, sir."

Andrew stopped writing and looked up at the house man with a quizzical look. "Are we missing any workers I am unaware of? What is this about?" The house man was clearly upset and replied "I don't know anything for certain Master Andrew. I just seen what looks like a body wrapped in a tarp in the back of his cart. He asked that you come out to speak. I invited him into the house to meet with you but he said no, for you to come out there."

John frowned as he put his pen back in the pen holder and capped the ink well. Standing he stood and started toward the door to the hallway, walking past the houseman holding the door open. Annoyed to be taken away from his figures he was curious what the Colonel could possibly need him for. The front door was standing open as the house man had left it for the Colonel. Walking straight through he found the Colonel waiting for him on the top step.

"Colonel McKenzie, what a pleasure to see you. What brings you all the way out to Emerald Oaks this evening? Is there something I can help you with? Do you need accommodations or fresh horses perhaps?" Andrew gestured to his home and stable as a gracious host does. Looking at the Colonel and then the faces of the others he knew something was dreadfully wrong, and it involved him. Somberly and with trepidation Andrew asked "Colonel what's wrong. This isn't a social visit is it? Tell me what has happened".

The Colonel's heart sank to the pit of his stomach. This was the absolute worst part of his job. "Andrew, where are Isabella and Esmerelda?"

Andrew replied "Isabella is upstairs in her sewing room. She went up just after tea to work on a dress for Esmerelda.

I'm not sure where Esmerelda is, she may be with her mother or out tending her kitchen garden. Why do you ask?" Andrew was becoming afraid of the answer.

"Andrew, we believe we have found Esmerelda's body. The ring and garments have been identified as hers, at least we believe they are hers. Could she have given those things to someone else, sold them...? We need you to look at the body and tell us if it is Esmerelda or not."

Andrew went ashen and starred at the bundle in the cart.

"Andrew? Do you understand what I said? I need you to tell me if the girl in the cart is Esmerelda or not. We can't be sure due to the damage to the body, specifically her face."

Andrew stood silently starring at the cart. Giles standing behind the Colonel was full of rage at the heinous crime and couldn't look at Andrew without tears himself. Turning away Jennie caught his eye and they connected for a moment, then simultaneously looked away to avoid seeing Andrew's horror looking upon what was left of his daughter.

"Andrew?" The Colonel repeated.

Nodding he understood what the colonel wanted he slowly descended the steps toward the back of the cart. The Colonel motioned to Joseph to pull back the tarp so Andrew could see the corpse. The stench hit him before he could see her. Reflexively he stepped back and covered his nose and mouth with his forearm. He looked first at the boots near him and recognized them as the set he had custom made for his daughter, the Tomboy who preferred to ride as men do and not in a carriage. He looked at the clothes, knowing they were the riding costume her mother had made for her. Last he forced himself to look at her head. Andrew gasped at the horrific scene. There was no face to identify, but he did recognize her hair in an instant. Sobbing uncontrollably, he broke down as a father does discovering their child is dead, brutalized, and rotting. "Oh, dear God. What has happened to my Esmerelda? Who did this? Colonel I must know who did this!"

72

The Colonel let Andrew a few minutes to compose him. "Andrew, here is her belt and her emerald ring. John recognized the ring as hers from the Rosebud cotillion last spring. You have identified her body and so he was correct this is Esmerelda."

"Yes. Yes, this is Esmerelda."

"Andrew. There is something you must know. Ms. Harris is the person we often use to catalog a scene when a body is found. She discovered evidence that Esmerelda was about 5 or 6 months with child.

Andrew, stunned, questioned the Colonel asking "What? Oh heavens no, this is not Esmerelda if you think she was with child. That's simply…" Andrew followed the Colonel's gaze to Jennie Harris who had her hand just above the child cradled in Esmerelda's arms. Andrew had to look closer to convince himself of what he was seeing. There was indeed a wee baby. "How? How can this be?"

The Colonel asked again. "Look very carefully and closely Andrew. You are positive this is Esmerelda? The truth is this girl was with child. The hogs that destroyed her face and took her right hand ripped the womb from her body. Horribly gruesome but it is what happened. Are you sure, Andrew?"

Stunned, Andrew could only nod. Then realized Isabella must be told. "Isabella. I must get Isabella." Sobbing he turned to fetch his wife and found Isabella standing on the top stair crying silently, starring at her daughter's remains.

Isabella held her composure better than her husband. "Yes, Colonel McKenzie. That is our daughter Isabella. Andrew was not aware of her pregnancy. I was letting out her clothes for her because of her condition. I have a good idea who has done this. Joshua the stable manager will help you move her to the cellar. Thank you for bringing her and our grandchild home. Come inside to the parlor before you leave. I have much to share to help you find her killer."

Speechless Andrew nodded to Joshua to do as Isabella asked. Henry Watts drove the mule behind Joshua as he led them to the cellar door. Joshua spoke quickly with a servant girl who scurried off to fetch help. The slaves not only worked the fields, they helped raise the children and prepared bodies for burial. Joshua pulled the cellar door up and let it fall open to the side. He turned to find the servant girl holding a torch for him to light the stairs as Brice and Joseph carried the tarp wrapped body down into the darkness. Joshua set several crates together for them to place Esmerelda's body on until the slave women could tend to her. The body would be buried as soon as a coffin could be brought from Bridgetown.

The Colonel, John, Jennie and Andrew left the soldiers and slaves and went back to the house to hear what Isabella had to share. They found her sitting in the parlor on a love seat beneath a portrait of Esmerelda hanging on the wall above a fireplace mantle. Rarely used in Barbados, the English couldn't design a house without a fireplace. Andrew went to stand behind his wife and placed his hands on her shoulders. The Colonel sat in a chair across from Isabella. Jennie sat next to Isabella on the love seat with a pencil and paper for notes. Jennie noticed a movement at the tree line out the window. The Watchers were there.

Isabella looked directly at the Colonel with no expression to give away her thoughts. The Colonel's eyes narrowed a bit, his features hardened as if he were about to be interrogated. Jennie realized Isabella was not afraid of the Colonel. Isabella obviously saw the Colonel as someone who would answer to her. Colonel McKenzie was ill at ease by Isabella's behavior. This was not at all what he expected from a bereaved mother. The Colonel began the conversation by offering his condolences to the family.

"Isabella, I am so sorry for the loss of your daughter. I will do everything in my power to find her killer or killers. Please accept my condolences to your family."

Isabella replied "thank you Colonel. I am confident you will find the person or persons responsible for my daughter's death. We are of course distraught at the loss of our daughter and grandchild. Andrew was unaware of Esmerelda's pregnancy at her request. The father of the child has not been forthcoming in meeting his responsibilities. Esmerelda chose to not rush into any decisions in the best interest of her child. She did not tell me the name of the father, but I have her diary which mentions a man who is most probably the father. She did not write his name for fear of being found out. I am quite sure I know who he is, Colonel. My hunch is he killed her or had her killed."

The Colonel was stone still and staring blankly at Isabella as she spoke. Andrew was looking down at his wife in disbelief. The house man by the door stood silently listening to every word. McKenzie paused to let Isabella say more. When she did not continue, he spoke with deliberation. "We will need her diary as evidence. Where is it now?" Jennie noticed the slightest smirk on Isabella's face.

Isabella continued "I'm sorry Colonel, but no. You may not have my daughter's diary. I will allow your scribe, Ms. Harris, to copy the pertinent information for your use. She is welcome to stay as our guest and copy the text at her leisure. The transcription shouldn't take her more than a morning. Andrew will see to it she returns safely to the garrison with her documentation."

Jennie looked up at the Colonel and back at Isabella. Andrew looked at the Colonel and Jennie. Everyone in the room was confused as to what just happened. John Dewe stopped breathing as he looked at the Colonel and Isabella. Something didn't add up here. Isabella just starred at the Colonel expressionless. Jennie looked out the window as a movement at the tree line caught her eye. The house man was no longer at the door. When did he slip away? How much did he hear she wondered? How much did the Watchers know? Isabella paid no attention to the Watchers. Jennie realized she was one of them. Isabella was part of the Watchers.

The Colonel started to protest about copying the diary. Protocol demanded the diary in total. He decided to let it go for now. He was sure he could get Andrew to bring it to him later. "Very well Isabella. Jennie may stay and copy the diary information that matters. Thank you for allowing her to stay as your guest to do so." The Colonel paused before asking the question hanging in the room. "Isabella, who was the father of Esmerelda's child, your grandson?"

The color drained from Isabella's face. The child was a boy. They hadn't told her the gender of the baby. She and Andrew had lost their daughter and a grandson. The fury ignited in her belly. Isabella's eyes could have pierced stone as she looked at the Colonel. "I am not certain and choose not to say lest I am incorrect. I will not point a finger at an innocent man, Colonel. I believe the excerpts will lead you the correct conclusion. You must decide for yourself." One eyebrow rose slightly in challenge to the Colonel. The Colonel did not move, did not blink. John, Andrew, and Jennie were all looking at the Colonel oddly. Realization of what they were all thinking finally found his tongue.

"Dear Lord, it isn't me! But apparently Isabella believes it is someone I know and must handle this with care and prudence. Am I correct Isabella?"

Isabella hesitated and replied "Yes. I am quite sure the killer is someone we all know. Someone that is willing to kill to keep secrets. I will add he has no secrets. So you must understand, killing her did not keep his secret and thus his life has little value anymore. Regardless of if you can prove his guilt or not, life as he knew it is still over." A chill spread through the room, the Colonel white as a sheet, the house man was back standing by the door listening.

Jennie glanced out the window but could no longer see the tree line as evening had fallen into night. The Watchers were still there, she could feel them. Jennie wondered if the Colonel knew who he was really speaking with. Isabella was a powerful woman the wise man did not trifle with. Looking down at her notes Jennie wrote 'the come to Jesus moment has arrived; the hunt for Esmerelda's killer begins and will not end well for someone'. Silence hung in the room for a painful few minutes. Isabella never took her eyes off the Colonel. The silence was interrupted when the house man gestured to Andrew.

Andrew walked over to the house man and listened as the man whispered in his ear "Master Andrew, Joshua has sent word the women are preparing Miss Esmerelda's body. They ask if you have a dress you want her to wear for her burial and what to build for a coffin? The women want to do right by Miss Esmerelda, Sir, they loved her very much. We all did." Andrew looked up with tears in his eyes and spoke to Isabella without looking at her.

"Isabella, the women need a dress for Esmerelda. Please find something suitable for our daughter and grandson. We will put both names on the headstone. The boy's father will be known and take responsibility for him. John, would you please stop by the rectory on your way home and ask Father Michael to come to Emerald Oaks at his earliest convenience? I must go to Bridgetown and have the carpenters prepare a coffin for my daughter". The house man left to ask Joshua to prepare a horse for Master Andrew to ride to Bridgetown.

The Colonel stood and assisted Isabella in standing from the love seat. "Isabella, my condolences again. I am so sorry for your loss. Thank you for providing accommodations for Miss Harris to copy the diary information in the morning. I will keep you informed of our progress. Please feel free to ask any questions you may have and share anything you feel is important."

Isabella nodded and dropped her hand back by her side, glancing out the window. Her look was sorrowful beyond consolation. Mothers are not supposed to outlive their children. Isabella had lost her only child and grandchild. There is no greater burden a woman can bear. Jennie was truly heartbroken for Isabella. Tucking the pencil inside the journal cover, she tied the string around the leather binding to protect the contents from prying eyes. She would go over the diary very carefully with Isabella tomorrow. Tonight,

Jennie would stay with Isabella until she was able to sleep. The longest night is always the first night after the loss is discovered. Isabella would never get over the loss, but she would learn how to live with it.

The Colonel, John, and Andrew left the room, walked silently down the front steps and mounted their horses to leave. Henry Watts was seated on the cart waiting for them to leave as a group to return to the garrison. Watts had his flask under the seat that the men shared as they waited. A gruesome day, the men deserved a bit of rum for the trip back to Bridgetown. Brice and Joseph mounted their horses as Joshua gave the Colonel and Andrew a leg up onto their horses. Sorrow filled his face as he stepped back out of the way. Brice led the way with the Colonel, John, and Andrew behind them, the cart behind the men, and Joseph was the tail rider. Jennie watched from the window as they moved down the drive and out onto the road back to Bridgetown. Knowing it would be a long night, Jennie asked the house man to bring wine and two glasses. Isabella stood by the fireplace starring into it as if there was a fire burning.

Retuning with a decanter of wine and two glasses, the house man asked Isabella about the dress for Esmerelda again. Isabella nodded and slowly went up the staircase to find an appropriate garment in which to bury her daughter. There were some baby clothes in her cedar chest for her grandson. He would have a proper burial with his mother. She would hold him once before he was buried. Tears welled in her eyes as she entered Esmerelda's room. Opening the wardrobe with both hands she looked over a dozen dresses Esmerelda loved on fine occasions. She chose one made from chocolate silk embroidered with gold threads and pearls. The matching shoes were carefully put away in a drawer below the dresses. A handkerchief embroidered with Esmerelda's initials would cover her disfigured face and another would cover her missing hand.

The upstairs maid had silently entered the room and was taking the garments from Isabella as she picked them out.

She, too, was in tears. Esmerelda had been almost a sister to her, and her death was devastating. Isabella looked over the clothes and shoes one last time. Satisfied she went into the room across the hall. Opening the trunk at the foot of the bed she rummaged about until she found the tiny christening gown Esmerelda had worn so many years ago. Holding the gown tightly to her chest she wept. Jennie waited as Isabella sat on the floor and then reached to help her stand when she was ready. The maid took the tiny gown and left to take the clothes to the women preparing the bodies.

Jennie helped Isabella back down to the parlor. Wine had been poured into the glasses waiting for them by the fireplace without a fire. As they sat once again, this time across from each other, Isabella looked behind Jennie as if she saw someone there. Jennie turned to follow her gaze and realized there was indeed someone standing in the dark behind the door, not wanting to be seen. Jennie quickly stood and moved to draw her knife from her hip. Isabella stopped her short. "Jennie, she isn't a threat. Please sit down. Facing me, do not look at her, she cannot be seen." Jennie looked at Isabella with a slow understanding and sat as Isabella had asked.

The person stepped out of the shadows and handed a letter over Jennie's shoulder to Isabella. As Isabella reached for the letter Jennie looked up at the window and saw the reflection. It took a moment for the reality to set in it was Elizabeth McKenzie, the Colonel's wife standing behind her. Stunned, her eyes met Elizabeth's eyes in the reflection. Jennie spoke quietly "Elizabeth what on earth are you doing here dressed like a man and cloaked to hide? I think you and Isabella need to explain yourselves to me. The Colonel is expecting details. What exactly am I to tell him?

Elizabeth let her hood fall down her back and replied "Nothing. I was not here. You did not see me. Do you understand, Jennie? I was never here." Jennie looked from Elizabeth to Isabella and understood. Elizabeth was never there. Jennie replied "of course you weren't. But I must know what is going on here. What is all this about. I have a hunch you need me." Elizabeth looked at Isabella who was reading the letter in tears. "Isabella?" Jenny asked "What' is in the letter that makes you weep again?"

Isabella called the house man to bring another glass and fill the decanter again. She was sure it was going to be a very long night indeed.

"The letter is from Captain William Douglass of the *Angeline*. He writes to tell me the ship has arrived safely. My shipment can be put aboard any time." Isabella choked on the last words as she took her glass of wine, tears cascading down her face. Jennie and Elizabeth each took one of Isabella's hands and held her as she cried.

Giles Freeman sat unnoticed out on the porch next to the window. He had heard every word but missed the meaning. Jennie would find him later at the stable when Isabella had finally fallen asleep. The drug he had put in her wine would have her sound asleep soon. The house man was compliant in making sure his mistress slept well that night. Giles made his way to the stables unseen and unheard by anyone in the house. The stable manager had organized a pallet for him in the loft and didn't bother to look when he heard him open the barn door, not realizing he didn't hear it close.

John turned Beulah and headed away from the Colonel and the military detail group when they reached the turn off for the Tallywhoa. Nudging the mare into a lope he could see the lights of the rectory in the distance. Father Michael would still be awake as it was just getting dark. Pulling Beulah down to a walk he turned into the rectory drive and stopped at the private entrance. As he prepared to dismount the door opened and Father Michael stepped out with a lantern and stepped up John and his horse.

"John Dewe? This is a surprise. What can I do for you this evening?"

John settled back into his saddle and explained the situation. "Father Michael, Andrew Conn's daughter Esmerelda has been killed and believed to be murdered.

Colonel McKenzie and I took her body back to Emerald Oaks earlier this evening. Andrew has gone to Bridgetown to organize a coffin with the Colonel and asked that I stop and let you know about Esmerelda's death. I know it would be appreciated if you can go to Isabella as soon as you can safely get to the Oaks. It was horrible Michael. The hogs had been at her for a day or two. There isn't much left to bury."

Father Michael felt weak and stunned by the news. "Dear Lord, No! Esmerelda? How can that be? Of course, I will go to Isabella at once. She should not be alone."

John explained that "Jennie Harris is with her, Father. She is not alone. Jennie can explain more about the incident to you when you get there. But you don't need to put yourself at risk rushing to Isabella. She is fine until you can safely arrive.

"Thank you, John, for bringing me the news. And I am relieved Isabella is not alone. I will get a few things together and head to Emerald Oaks shortly. It isn't far and I'll be safe enough. I will take the parish caretaker with me as well. Be safe getting home, John. You've had a dreadful day."

John nodded and headed back out the drive the same way he came in. Turning toward the Tallywhoa, he nudged Beulah into a simple jog. The rest of the ride home would be uneventful and the quiet was a welcome respite from the truly wretched day. The mare felt him relax a bit and she did, too. A steady pace and they would be home soon.

§

The Colonel, Andrew and the detail arrived back at the garrison just in time to see Thomas and Richard walk past the Colonel's office door returning to their rooms. The Colonel and Andrew stopped at his office door to dismount and handed the reins to the guards at the door. Evans opened the door to let the men in the vestibule. The Colonel quickly briefed Evans that Andrew would be spending the night in the private guest quarters and why. Evans immediately left to prepare his room and alert the attendant. The Colonel ushered Andrew into his inner office and immediately

81

offered Andrew a dock glass of his best scotch. Andrew gratefully accepted as he sank haphazardly into the chair closest to the liquor cabinet. Looking at the floor with his head in his free hand he wept silently. Grief overcame him at last as fatigue took hold of him body and soul.

The Colonel quietly stepped out of his private office and pulled the door almost closed behind him, giving Andrew a bit of privacy. Motioning to the guard inside the door to step outside the vestibule, the guard nodded respectfully and quietly went out with him. The news about Esmerelda was rapidly disseminating across the island. The news would not be a surprise to one man, the question was which man.

Fury filled the Colonel. Based on Isabella's suspicions they were likely looking for a married man who was probably much older than Esmerelda and with heirs not to be displaced by a bastard child. The Colonel was no saint and never claimed to be. He had strayed from his marital bed once and always regretted having done so. He believed he had done right by his wife and children since. McKenzie did not know anything about the child kept from him, that his wife Elizabeth helped hide from the clan patriarchs to protect the child from his own people. God pity those who hid the child should he ever find out.

As he stood outside the private door to the vestibule with the guard, he noticed a local bar maid slip through the shadows at the far end of the garrison corner. She crossed the street and disappeared into the night. Her gait seemed odd, as if she were in pain and considered sending the guard after her. On second thought if she were in trouble she could easily have come to the guard as he was sure she saw both the guard and him. Spent from a wretched day, he went back into his office and found Evans had returned and was explaining to Andrew about his room and bath.

The Colonel motioned with a nod it was time to take Andrew to his room. Dock glass full of scotch in hand Andrew fell in behind Evans and followed blindly up the stairs and to the room next to Thomas. Evans realized

Andrew was not coherent any longer and helped him remove his jacket and boots. Pulling the rope for the attendant, he waited for him and the two soldiers managed to get Andrew into a hot bath. Evans returned to the Colonels office to close it up for the night. The attendant stayed discreetly out of the room until Andrew needed assistance getting safely out of the tub and into the bed. The Colonel's scotch is an excellent way to fall quickly asleep. The bit of powder the Colonel added helped expedite the process.

Evans found the Colonel sitting at his desk with his scotch in his left hand, eyes closed, apparently asleep. Gently he tried to take the glass from the Colonel lest it be dropped and broken on the stone floor. "Leave it, Evans, please. I'm not asleep just yet." The Colonel mumbled as he sipped his scotch. Looking wearily at Evans he realized how long the day had been for the lieutenant as well. McKenzie stood and left the office heading toward his quarters scotch in hand. Evans was grateful for the consideration and locked up the necessaries and the inner door and bolted the vestibule door from the inside.

Evans' quarters were off the vestibule well hidden from the public yet immediately accessible by the Colonel or the guards. Exhausted he stripped down and washed with a flannel and a bowl of cold water, slipped into his night clothes, and crawled under his netting. As he relaxed he remembered the sounds of intimacy coming from Richard's room as he left the attendant setting up the bath for Andrew. Tired as he was, Evans had a mental image of Richard naked. Silently and alone he began stroking himself gently, flannel cloth in the other until he climaxed. Dropping the soiled flannel cloth on the floor he rolled over and was asleep in moments. Like all well trained military he slept with one ear always on alert. This night the garrison was truly quiet. Even the horses slept without stirring.

Except for the Colonel's Clydesdale war horse Witcher. She was the alpha mare, the Watcher who never slept and saw or heard everything in the sleeping stable. She stood in the shadows at the back of her stall facing the doors. One hind foot cocked and resting, her lower lip hung limp beneath her muzzle, eyes not quite closed she listened with ears pointed sideways to hear from all 360° around her. Her right ear perked up at the soft footsteps as her lady slipped unnoticed into the garrison through the hidden panel at the back of the unused stall at the far end of the aisle. Witcher's nostrils twitched in recognition of the lady's scent of lavender cloaked in linen and silk. A low throated nicker as the petite lady stopped to give Witcher a sugar cube with loving hands that could not reach the withers of the war horse. Witcher loved her woman and would protect her, and the Colonel, with her own life. As educated and successful women do, Elizabeth McKenzie had her network of protectors well-constructed.

Easing out of the aisle and into the garrison breezeway, Elizabeth quickly moved through the shadows to the attendant bath entrances. The door left unlocked for her by another Watcher had well-oiled hinges and opened without a creak. Elizabeth entered the chamber full of linens and toiletries, removed her cloak and hung it on a peg by the door. She disrobed her trousers and shirt and redressed in her night gown and robe. The door to the stairway to the Colonel's bath was at the far end of the chamber. Elizabeth let herself in with her key the Watchers had made for her and made her way up to the bath. The tub was full of hot water with lavender soap and a sponge on the stool next to the tub, towels hanging to warm on the pipes. Elizabeth managed to sit down in the tub, grab a square of flannel, and lather the bar of lavender soap as the bed chamber door opened. Duncan McKenzie smiled as he entered to find his wife naked, wet, and warm.

Elizabeth smiled coyly at her husband as he picked up the sponge and sat on the stool. The ritual began as she leaned forward and let him gently wash her back with the sponge, rivulets of soap and water running slowly down her spine, sliding unhindered over her hips and down the crevasse between her buttocks. Edging quickly into inebriation, Duncan shifted and began to caress her left arm with the sponge, followed by tender kisses from her wrist to her neck, nibbling her ear with his lips, the sponge drips making lines down her chest as he held her chin up with the sponge in his left hand. Closing her eyes part way in response to the warmth of the water and partly the heat of her husband, Elizabeth succumbed to the delicious stimulation from the sponge as Duncan washed down her neck, around each breast. Dipping the sponge into the water to rinse the soap off her delicate alabaster skin, Duncan pledged his fidelity to himself once more.

Duncan had never forgiven himself the misguided infidelity in his youth and chose to believe Elizabeth did not know. If she did, she had never let on. Duncan truly loved Elizabeth who had born him twin daughters and raised them to be fine ladies. As all men do, he had also wanted a son and heir to his name and clan but it was never to be. Elizabeth could not bear more children after the twins and their complicated birth that almost took their mother's life. He cherished Elizabeth so much it made his heart ache at the thought of losing her. He began to wash her legs and feet with a loving heart and a grateful soul.

Elizabeth had dainty feet with tiny toes, almost childlike and easily hurt. Little did Duncan know about the depth of the woman whom he washed. She was everything he knew and could imagine and so much more. He stood and offered his hand to help her step from the tub. Elizabeth arose with her hand in his. Wrapping her in a large warm towel she sat on the stool and Duncan began to unpin her hair. Falling in a long thick braid Elizabeth's hair reached the floor. Unbraided is was almost ankle length when standing, waves of auburn tinged with golden strands glistened in the candlelight as Duncan began to brush it out from the end working up to her head.

Elizabeth sipped the scotch in Duncan's glass as he slowly worked the tangles from her hair. Her husband had good hands and better scotch. What more could a woman want? Smiling slyly to herself and thoroughly enjoying the pleasure of Duncan's hand in her hair and on her shoulders, she moaned softly, encouraging him not to stop. He moved her hair off the back of her neck and nuzzled her, taking in the smell of her as he reached around from behind and slid his other had under her towel to caress her. Tilting her head back on one shoulder she exposed her neck. Duncan held her close as he caressed her neck with his lips and breath, one hand slipping lower. As he found her points of sensitivity she moaned, wanting him to go further.

Realizing he had stopped, Elizabeth opened her eyes to find Duncan cradling her with tears running silently down his cheeks. "Duncan whatever is the matter husband? Why do you weep? Have I offended you in some way?" She was suddenly afraid he had discovered her liaison with the Watchers or something more dangerous about a son he didn't know he had. Elizabeth tensed waiting for Duncan to respond.

"No, my love, you have not offended me. You my wife and our daughters are my life for which I am eternally thankful. I cry out of the guilt I hold for having so much beauty and goodness given and kept safe for me while others suffer unimaginable loss."

Elizabeth raised her left hand and placed it on his left cheek as he rested his chin upon her shoulder. Holding him close they sat in silence for a few moments, just breathing each other in. She let go of the towel with her right hand letting it fall away from her slightly. Reaching down she guided his hand. Relaxing into his touch he shifted her back to a sitting position and wrapped the towel back around her. He reached over to the wall and pulled the attendant call rope. Their backs were to the door when the attendant responded in the doorway.

"Colonel what is it you need, sir?"

86

"My lady needs her bed warmed before she retires. Please fetch the bed warmer pan and warm the linens on our bed." Duncan mumbled slightly as he muzzled Elizabeth's hair.

"Yes, Colonel. Immediately, sir." The private disappeared and returned quickly with the bed warmer pan filled with hot coals. Making his way into the bed chamber he discreetly and respectfully looked away from the couple still nuzzling each other by the tub. Passing the pan between the sheets for a few minutes the linens heated, the down comforter held the heat in for the few minutes it took for the attendant to leave and Elizabeth to enter.

Duncan watched Elizabeth walk into their bedroom, glancing over her shoulder and dropping the towel at the door. The woman knew how to entice her husband to bed, with style. Duncan removed his clothes and slipped into the tub to wash away the day's ills. Turning the tap to add more hot water, he picked up his glass of scotch where Elizabeth had set it down. Funny, he was quite sure there had been significantly more than a swallow in the glass when he came into the bath. He smiled and chuckled to himself. His wife was a clever creature indeed. Soaking in the bliss of a hot bath, Duncan let his mind go blank and his body go limp. The lavender scent ensconced the experience with pleasure and good thoughts. He was dragged back to his senses by the sounds of Elizabeth snoring in the next room. Duncan smiled and laughed to himself, wondering what he had missed out on under the warm sheets that night. Ah, well. There was always the morning to follow. He drank the last of the scotch, put the glass on the stool, slid deeper into the tub and fell asleep.

Cold and shivering, Duncan awoke still in the tub. Elizabeth was standing over him with a warm towel waiting to dry and wrap her beloved husband as he stood and stepped out of the tub. "Husband you're sure to catch ill if you chill in the tub for too long." She gently pulled the towel around his shoulders to ward off the night air.

The same towel that wrapped her from nose to toes barely covered Duncan from shoulder to knees. He reached up and cradled her face in his hands, kissing her passionately as the towel fell to the floor behind him. Her hand went around his waist and folded upwards toward his shoulders. She felt his erection mature against her as they kissed and fondled each other. Pulling her tight against him he rubbed himself against her firmly, hot and anxious to know her secrets. She moaned, sweat beading on her body, she was on fire with desire.

"Husband, please…oh please give me more…"

Elizabeth braced herself as Duncan was in complete control, and he used that control to satisfy his wife first and then satisfy his lust as he pleased. Catching his breath a bit, Duncan kissed Elizabeth on her back and fondled her breasts in appreciation, caught his breath, and returned to the bath. He stepped into the tub and washed himself standing up with a soft flannel and the lavender soap. He felt better than he had in a long time. Elizabeth was truly a wondrous lover. Stepping out he toweled dry and took the wet flannel to clean Elizabeth. She was cold and shaking when he returned. He gently cleaned her, making several trips to the bath to rinse the flannel and properly clean his wife. Once he was convinced he had her properly cleaned Duncan fell into bed. Elizabeth slipped in next to her fully spent husband, breathing hard as he fell into a well-earned sleep. She prayed Duncan would return safely each night, she knew she would never find another man to take her as he did. Together they slept unmoving until morning.

# 5

Jennie watched as Isabella sipped her wine, head beginning to nod as the drugs took effect. Somehow Isabella managed to not drop her crystal glass and finished her last drop of wine. Amazed, Jennie was truly in awe of her ability to consume three glasses of rich red wine, one laced with sleeping drugs, and still be awake enough to set her glass down delicately on the side table, stand by herself and walk to the stairs.

As Isabella stepped in front of Jennie she commented softly "you do understand Elizabeth was not here tonight. I'm sure you do. Think about our conversation and the value your participation would have for our group, and our families, too. I watched you looking for the Watchers in the tree line. You already were aware of our presence. Now you understand our purpose and why discretion is valued above all else. We will not discuss this again in my home. Word will be sent to you when the next conclave happens. I do hope you will attend. I look forward to the positive impact you would bring to our work." Wobbling a bit more than she was used to, Isabella turned and made her way up the stairs.

Jennie followed her discreetly; fearful she might fall down the stairs. Isabella continued her conversation with herself and Esmerelda as if she still lived "Esmerelda, your brown silk dress. It is your favorite isn't it? I am sure it is. Would you tell me if it were not so?" Isabella seemed to see her daughter standing next to her walking her to her bed. "And the matching shoes. I picked those as well for you dear." She cocked her head as if listening and responded "why yes, I did find your christening gown for little Michael. He is so precious. We will miss him. Our hearts are broken for you both my daughter." Jennie watched as Isabella held a complete conversation…with no one.

The tone changed when Isabella began pleading "but you must tell me for certain who his father is, my daughter. He must have his name and be blessed for burial in consecrated ground with you. What do you mean you cannot say? Of course, you can tell me. You MUST tell me before the Colonel figures it out, and you know he will. What of his reputation?" Isabella's hands were on her hips as she turned in the hallway to face who ever wasn't there that she was arguing with. "I really do not care about HIS reputation. I care that my grandson has his name and is rightly recognized by the ch…" Stepping back as if she had been accosted "STOP this nonsense now! We will know who his father is eventually. I am quite sure he is named after him already, isn't he? How do I know? I'm not stupid girl. I'm your mother and I know YOU very well, and the men who come sniffing up your skirts even better." Clearly put out Isabella turned sharply, wobbled and almost fell catching herself on the railing of the balcony, stood straight and walked with purpose into her bedroom.

Jennie stood outside the door completely bewildered with what she had witnessed. Was that the rantings of a drunken mother who had just lost her only daughter and grandson, or did she just witness something quite unknown to her rational world. She stepped closer to the doorway to assist Isabella should she need her. Sitting on the side of her bed looking down at her feet Isabella softly said "Please, Esmerelda, let Jennie be here for me this night. Help her help me learn to live without you. I know you will always be with me, but tonight I need Jennie's help".

Jennie was beginning to truly wonder what in the world was happening when she felt a warmth embrace her, holding her briefly before evaporating into the hallway. Isabella spoke to Jennie then "she won't bother you anymore Ms. Harris. Please help me with my shoes and laces. Call for the maid and she will lay out my sleeping gown and help me retire." Completely speechless Jennie did what Isabella asked. When the maid was there and ready to help Isabella change, she paused and glanced at Jennie to give Isabella her privacy. Jennie nodded and softly spoke to the girl "I'm going out for some air, but please come find me if you need anything I can do for Isabella or Andrew". The girl nodded in understanding as Jennie left the room closing the door softly behind her.

Once down the stairs she stepped out the front door for some fresh air. She realized Giles was no longer on the porch and assumed he had gone to the stables already. Jennie had a hunch Giles knew about Elizabeth being at Emerald Oaks if he had stayed on the porch by the window long enough to overhear them. If he had, she knew Giles would be silent unless he was forced to share overheard conversations. She noticed the stable door was ajar. Someone had deliberately left it open. Quietly she made her way across the yard in the shadows; unseen and unheard she slipped inside the stable without moving the door. Giving her eyes time to adjust to the dim light of the inside of the stable she could see moonlight coming down through the door in the loft used to load hay into the barn.

She could see the roughly hewn staircase leading to the loft. As she stepped close and put one hand on the railing, she looked up to find Giles sitting on a bale of hay looking out the doorway into the moonlight. The dim light described every feature in his handsome face kindly. His green eyes looked black in the night, his auburn hair down around his shoulders tousled roughly as if he had just pulled the lacing off for her. His shirt tail hung loosely over his sleeping pants and the lacings at this chest were undone to let the cool night air in, the linen billowing out with the gentle breeze. He had pulled his boots off wearily and washed naked in the lot by the horse tank. Getting the stench of death off of him had been a challenge with cold water and a small bar of soap but he managed. The butler had brought the clean shirt and sleeping pants along with a blanket and pillow. It was the best they could do on short notice for a soldier.

Jennie smiled and blushed as she watched him in the moonlight. Giles really was a fine piece of real estate, a good man anyone woman would cherish and take care of if he chose her to do so. She really didn't want to spoil the moment, but she needed to talk to him before they all slept. "Giles?" She spoke his name softly to not alert the groom or dogs. Looking down the staircase he could not make out who had spoken to him in the darkness at the bottom.

"Giles, it's me, Jennie. May I come up and chat for a few minutes?" Recognizing her voice Giles nodded and swiveled on the end of the bale extending his hand to help her clear the last step at the landing.

"I take it Isabella is asleep?" Giles asked nonchalantly, he knew she had to be as much of the drug as he had put in her glass. Jennie nodded and asked "what did you give her? I saw the Colonel give you something earlier as the butler stood there with the decanter of wine. Please tell she will wake tomorrow."

Giles did a double take and realized Jennie was truly concerned about the drug. "She'll be fine Jennie. It isn't anything dangerous, truly. Just helps a person relax and drift off to sleep peacefully." Giles could see Jennie wasn't convinced. "Why do you ask? Has something happened to Isabella? Did she fall or in some way injure herself?" Giles was beginning to become alarmed by the frightened look on Jennies' face. "Jennie. What happened?"

Jennie wasn't sure how much to tell Giles, he might shrug it off as a woman and her vapors as men are want to do.

Isabella's behavior had spooked Jennie and her anxiety overruled her reticence. "She was talking to Esmerelda. As if the girl was standing right there in the hall with her. If I hadn't seen it with my own eyes…I swear something pushed her backwards. She was demanding to be told the name of the baby's father. She argued with no one there all the way into her bedroom. She even told…Esmerelda…to let me alone, that she needed me with her tonight. Giles something touched me. I SWEAR something wrapped around me as it passed out of her room. And was gone."

Giles looked at her with a stare she had never seen before. Jennie felt completely foolish having told Giles about the incident. Looking back at him, still staring at her he asked "Jennie, did she say the name of the boy's father. Think Jennie, what exactly did she say?"

Stunned at Giles' question Jennie paused and quoted Isabella's words "Isabella said something like 'he's named after his father isn't he Esmerelda? His name is Michael isn't it. He will have his father's name'" Jennie paused to let Giles absorb what Isabella has said. Giles knew immediately what it meant and stood abruptly to lookout at the cane fields and starry sky. Jennie stood slowly and asked "Giles, what did I say? What is it? You're scaring me, Giles. What?"

Giles tilted his head back and closed his eyes silently praying in his mind 'dear Lord, please do not let this be so. Anything, anyone, but him'. Jennie had stepped closer and in front of him to get his attention softly. "Giles what on earth is wrong? You look like you've seen a ghost. Please tell me what this is all about."

Giles opened his eyes and looked down at Jennie, moonlight cast across the side of her face and glistening in her eyes. 'God you do send temptation my way in many forms. Must you put her in arms reach, in the moonlight, in a loft of hay…'?

"Giles?"

"You're sure she said Michael. Think Jennie."

"Yes. I'm positive she said 'Michael'. Who do you think she meant..." Jennie cut off her own question when she realized what Giles was thinking. "Oh, Giles no. Not that Michael. Not FATHER Michael. I won't even think that is possible. No." A shiver ran up her spine because she would think of no one else now that Giles had put the idea into words.

"Yes. I mean that Michael." Giles looked stricken at his own thoughts. "This is a wretched thought but must be considered. I don't think you are aware there have been a number of complaints, comments really, brought to the Colonel's attention about Father Michael's behaviors toward certain parishioners. We've never been able to prove anything against him and have kept very quiet in our observations. So yes, he will be on our list of people to question as we investigate Esmerelda's death." Truly stricken at what he had to say out loud to Jennie he sat heavily on the bale of hay. 'Michael. FATHER Michael. Please God let it not be him'. Giles had a sinking feeling he was going to discover yet another secret he did not want to know.

Jennie sat next to Giles on the bale of hay. She and Giles were good friends. They looked out for each other professionally as they could. She definitely needed someone close to the Colonel to keep the Cretans in the barracks respectful to her. Giles was a man that needed the simple cares a woman can provide. He consulted her on things and relationships he didn't understand to do his job better when families and women were involved. He had been raised in a strong patriarchal community and recognized he was not well prepared to work with women competently as a soldier. Giles put his arm around Jennie, and she leaned against him.

Both considered the ramifications if there was more between them and had managed to avoid building an intimate relationship. They both knew they were losing that battle. Giles could smell the scent of citrus in her hair and he couldn't help but wonder what other aromas he would find upon her. He closed his eyes and let the moonshine rest upon his face as he tried to remember how his mother smelled, her face, her laugh. It was all so long ago he couldn't remember the details. Jennie's scent always brought the fleeting mental images back to him though. Something on the edge of his consciousness was trying to come back to life in his memories. Opening his eyes, he sighed as the pictures dimmed once more.

Jennie felt his focus shift as he placed his chin on top of her head and his arms drew her closer. Lord the man could hold a woman just right. She knew what she wanted. She knew he wasn't ready. She resigned herself and snuggled closer in the dark, brushing her cheek against his chest just to feel the realness of him. She loved him dearly, yet something kept him locked away from her even though she knew he loved her with all his heart. He knew he loved Jennie and wanted her, all of her, but could not or would not build a life with her just yet. Jennie was confident in time that might change.

Giles thought about a life with Jennie much of his waking moments. The life of a soldier was hazardous and unpredictable. He wanted a stable life before he took a wife. Jennie had made him think this way. The thought of leaving her alone with his children to raise without him terrified him. He held her closer and brushed his cheek reflexively in her hair. Oh yes, he loved her. The ache in his loins would not let him turn away from Jennie's touch and scent. Jennie sensed a change in his demeanor. She could feel his body warming next to her. She knew she should leave. She didn't.

Giles' hands were trembling as he traced the shape of her neck and her chest with his fingertips. His breath was warm and shallow, coaxing her to melt into his arms. "Jennie..." His voice whispered so softly she wasn't sure if he said her name or if she wished he had. "Oh, Jennie..." Giles deftly picked her up and carried her to the blanket spread out under the moonlight. Laying her head upon the pillow he looked into her eyes for acknowledgement or rejection of his advances. He found a pure and loving glow radiating from her entire being. Her soul was wrapping around him like a glove.

Giles bent to nuzzle her neck and was sliding his hand up her thigh when a voice called up the stairs.

"Mr. Freeman? Mr. Freeman Father Michael is here and would like to speak to you and Miss Harris. I think Miss Harris has gone for a walk I can't find her. Mr. Freeman could you come to the house and speak with Father Michael?"

Giles looked toward the staircase and replied "Yes, I'll be there shortly. Thank you for letting me know Father Michael has arrived."

"Mr. Freeman, if you see Ms. Harris please ask her to hasten back to the house. I believe she may be able to answer some questions for Lady Isabella. I do not want to waken my Lady if we do not have to do so."

"Not to worry. Miss Harris won't have gone far. She will turn up directly. I'm sure of it. And NO, do not wake Lady Isabella under any circumstances. I'll be there in a few minutes. Make the priest comfortable while he waits."

"Yes Sir, Mr. Freeman. Thank you, sir."

The footsteps grew quiet as the houseman left the barn. Giles was already pulling on his boots and jacket by the time Jennie was down the staircase and headed out the back of the barn to not be seen retuning to the house. Disappointed their moment was interrupted, yet grateful at the same time. Jennie was sure that one day she and Giles would be a couple in every sense of the word. She smiled at the thought as she let herself in the kitchen door at the big house and made her way into the parlor where Father Michael was waiting. Father Michael was standing looking out the front window with a glass of wine in his right hand and his left hand tucked behind the small of his back. The expression on his face made him look like the cat that swallowed a canary. Jennie sensed something was awry. Giles was right to forewarn her.

The Priest most definitely was more than he presented to the world.

Jennie spoke as she began to pour a glass of wine for herself. "Father Michael. How good of you to come. Isabella is finally asleep. I will answer any questions you have as best I can. Anything Isabella must answer will have to wait until morning. How can I help you?" The Priest turned from the window in response to Jennie's question.

"Ah, Miss Harris. I am so glad you were able to be here with Isabella in this most horrible of circumstances. I came as soon as John Dewe shared the news with me earlier this evening. I am stunned and shocked at the loss of Miss Esmerelda. The immediate question I have is what can I do for the family? Obviously, we must prepare a service and burial for Miss Esmerelda as soon as possible. I understand Andrew is in Bridgetown to organize a coffin, and the slave women are preparing Esmerelda's remains for burial. Ghastly job. I do not know how they can do it". The thought of touching the remains of a corpse so desecrated revolted the Priest. He sipped his wine a bit faster.

Jennie confirmed the Priest's comments "Yes, Father Michael the women are preparing the body for burial. Isabella picked out a dress for her daughter to be buried in earlier this evening. She also selected handkerchiefs to cover her mangled face and hand. Andrew went to Bridgetown with Colonel McKenzie and the soldier detail that recovered Esmerelda's remains."

The Priest nodded and sipped more wine. "Thank you again for staying with Isabella. That was very kind of you. Andrew will no doubt be back tomorrow morning so you shouldn't be inconvenienced long. I expect you could leave at dawn if you need to do so."

"Actually, Father, I am stayed behind to collect evidence that might identify Esmerelda's killer. Isabella believes she knows who killed her daughter". Jennie was not divulging knowledge of Esmerelda's diary or her son. If Giles' fears were founded, they needed the Priest to implicate himself.

The Priest was looking out the window again swirling his wine in its glass. Looking down into the swirling red liquid he casually asked "what evidence does Isabella have about her daughter's killer? Does she really have some sort of evidence, or is she a heart broken mother speaking out of despair?" Father Michael starred at his wine swirling in his glass expressionless. His demeanor gave Jennie the creeps.

Jennie was mentally constructing a trap for the Priest. If he was the father of the baby and Esmerelda's killer, she had every intention of catching him. "I honestly do not know. Isabella was…is…completely overcome with grief. She is distraught over the loss of her only child. Hopefully she will clarify her thinking in a day or two and I will be able to sort out what she means. I can say Colonel McKenzie intends to know who did this heinous crime and punish him severely. That's why I am here, Father, to catch who ever killed Esmerelda Conn." Jennie was matter of fact in her speaking words carefully chosen. She intended to tell the priest just enough for him to fear he would be caught and try to cover his tracks. He would make a mistake and she would catch him. The priest's expression had gone cold and hard, still starring into his swirling wine, his lips drawn tight, his grip on the glass forceful, and his left hand balled in a fist behind his back. Giles was correct, oh yes, there was definitely more to know from and about this Priest.

Giles walked into the parlor and startled the Priest into looking up to see who had arrived. The Priest went ashen and held his glass out for the houseman to refill. When no one took the glass from his hand the Priest realized the houseman was not in the room. Giles stepped up and took the glass to refill for the Priest "Father Michael, I am so glad to see you have arrived. Let me get you a bit more wine." Giles took the glass from Michael's hand and stepped to the sideboard to fill it. Father Michael stood frozen in his steps.

"Why, um, thank you Mr. Freeman. I didn't realize the houseman had stepped out. How kind of you to pitch in." The look on Michael's face was anything but Priestly.

Calculating and cold, no warmth and no air of piety. Father Michael was a polished piece of work both Giles and Jennie could easily see. "I wasn't expecting to see you here, Giles. Good to see you and Miss Harris both, of course". His less than genuine sincerity made a mockery of his station as a Priest. "I assume tomorrow you will accompany Miss Harris back to Bridgetown?" Jennie glanced at Giles who simply smiled at the Priest.

"Actually, no. I will be staying on until Miss Harris has completed…" Jennie was staring straight at him "…until Miss Harris has completed any tasks Lady Isabella has for her, and also visiting with the servants and workers who knew Miss Esmerelda. The Colonel intends to catch whoever did this to Esmerelda." Looking the Priest straight in the eye Giles continued "We will find who committed this horrible crime. I believe the Colonel intends to hang him. And for what it's worth, dispose of the remains as fish food at sea. I've never seen Colonel McKenzie quite this angry and determined before. God help the poor soul who did this."

A chill ran up Father Michael's spine. His eyes narrowed and his palms grew sweaty with anxiety. This was not going to end well for anyone, especially the father of Esmerelda's child. Isabella must know the truth, or the Colonel would not have left two of his soldiers here to protect the family. Or use the family to catch the killer. Colonel McKenzie was clever. Giles was correct; the Colonel wouldn't stop until he found the guilty party. The priest looked at the house man who had returned to the doorway.

"Father Michael, the guest room is ready for you, sir, at your convenience. Mister Andrew asked I prepare the room for you and see to your needs. Is there anything you need, Father Michael?" The Priest thought 'hemlock. Tall glass, with a side of arsenic' would do nicely.

"Thank you, but no. I'm fine just now. I will go up when I've finished my wine." The Priest smiled vaguely at the houseman who nodded and went off to the kitchen to arrange with cook for breakfast the next morning. Looking about the room Michael observed "this really is a lovely home. Emerald Oaks has always been a happy place. Andrew is a kind man and good to family and workers alike. The family is always generous with others in time and goods. Miss Esmerelda will be sorely missed by the children at the orphanage. Did you know she taught the homeless children to read? An amazing young lady indeed".

Jennie responded "Really? No, I was not aware of Esmerelda's work there. What a kind memory of her, thank you for sharing that with us Father Michael. People should be remembered for their goodness." Jennie lied to the Priest to draw out more information. She was well aware of Esmerelda's work at the orphanage. Jennie was a patron, giving of her time and money graciously. Jennie had been raised there herself and had met Esmerelda there many times teaching her how to work with the children. The first piece of evidence the Priest knew Esmerelda's life patterns fell into place. Jennie said a mental 'thank you, Father Michael' for giving it to her so easily.

Giles was expressionless as he melted out of focus toward the wine decanter. He turned away as if he wasn't paying close attention, knowing full well Jennie was lying to get more information. Jennie could get information others could not just because she was a woman and men like Michael saw her as weak and unable to think or analyze. Oh, how wrong they were. Jennie had a mind like a steel trap. The wise man didn't try to outsmart her for they would not win.

Father Michael finished his wine and sat the glass down on the sideboard. "It has been a particularly long day. I think I'll retire for the evening. We can talk more tomorrow after Isabella wakes up and has had time to breakfast and compose herself. Good night Giles, Miss. Harris." Giles nodded to the Priest as he headed up the stairs. Jennie and Giles exchanged a glance that noted the Priest knew exactly where the guest room would be.

Jennie longed for a hot bath and bed herself. "I'm ready to retire myself. We can compare notes tomorrow, Giles."

Giles nodded and turned to the house man standing by the door.

"Please see to Miss Harris this evening. I expect she would appreciate a hot bath and a warm bed. We've all had a long day and tomorrow will be stressful as well. Do you need anything more from me tonight? If not, I'll head back to the loft."

"No, Sir, I do not need anything from you Mr. Freeman. I will get cook to heat the water for Miss Harris to have hot bath. Been a right bad day for everyone." The houseman left to help cook prepare Jennie's bath.

Giles knew Jennie would not lack for anything. Andrew had given clear instructions to his staff before he left. Giles just wanted to be near Jennie when he could be. While their relationship wasn't a secret, they did not advertise it either. In time they would make their worlds come together. The waiting was a bitch. Jennie was almost to the top stair when she looked back and smiled at Giles. He nodded and left for the loft, knowing he would think about Jennie as he fell asleep. He would worry about Esmerelda's killer in the morning.

# 6

Thomas stood leaning on the walkway railing overlooking the garrison courtyard and breezeway as he sipped his Earl Grey, savoring the lemon and sugar concoction slowly as he watched the garrison awaken with the dawn. The plate of fruits, breads, and cheeses the Colonel's cook set out for breakfast was a perfect complement to the hot porridge served with cream and honey. Scrambled eggs with grilled sausages and tomatoes were on their way up from the kitchen. The aromas were tantalizing, warm, and rich with herbs. Early morning had always been Thomas' favorite time of the day. Observing the order of things as they awoke helped him set the schedule and tone for his day. He sipped his Earl waiting on his eggs and sausages wondering if Richard would be seen before lunch.

The sound of the cook setting platters on the sideboard signaled the service of the hot foods. Thomas walked back inside the dining area and found a platter with the grilled sausages and tomatoes and a bowl of eggs covered with linens. Setting his mug down at a table near the window where he could still see the doors, he took up a plate and served himself. He turned to find the cook had left a plate with a small round of warm bread with a pot of fresh churned butter on the table next to his mug. Oh yes, he could get used to this kind of living. With a sigh he realized that wasn't going to happen any time soon. Still, the service was lovely, and he enjoyed every moment.

Thomas was just finishing up his last bit of bread with butter and jam when Richard appeared. Richard was up and about at this early hour? Thomas spoke to his brother kindly "Richard, good morning brother. I'm surprised to see you up and after your breakfast this early. Work up an appetite last night did you?" Richard silently filled a plate with man sized portions of everything on the sideboard, smirking as he impaled a sausage on a fork and bit the end off. The cook had brought up a warm round of bread and a pot of butter for Richard and stood waiting to see where Richard would sit.

Richard spoke simply to Thomas "I trust you slept well also, brother? "The cook set the bread board on the table Richard chose next to and facing his brother.

"Sir, what can I get you to drink this morning?"

Richard replied "Hot tea. Honey to sweeten if you have Earl Grey, please."

"Yes of course, sir. I'll get that for you now" The cook scuttled off and down the access stairs to the kitchen below them. Thomas poured more from the small teapot into his mug, added a slice of lemon and two cubes of raw sugar and stirred slowly. Watching Richard attack his food...'really Richard, no one is going to take it from you' ...Thomas opened the conversation about the day's expectations.

"I expect John will be here by mid-day with a cart and horses for the journey to the Tallywhoa. Until he arrives, I would like to go to the market and replenish a few personal supplies. What do you have in mind for the morning?" Thomas sipped his tea gently as it was hot and wonderful.

Richard paused chewing a bite off of the sausage still stuck to his fork. "I could do with a trip to the market as well. I noticed a shop next to the Gentleman's Club that sells tobacco and liquor. I'm curious what they stock and how they price their goods. The Tallywhoa may be wise to expand and diversify products to become significantly more profitable, in my opinion."

Thomas replied "I agree. Buying the competitions product is the best way to analyze the competition and the market. We can meet the producers as John arranges introductions for us, learn what is actually required to create such diversification." Richard nodded in agreement as he continued eating. Watching Richard finish his third plate of food Thomas wondered how they could have the same mother. The brothers were stamped with their fathers features so where, Thomas chuckled as he mentally wondered, did Richard acquire his unique attributes? Their mother would swat him with her fan if she could. Thomas chuckled louder and Richard looked up at him quizzically.

"What are you laughing at Thomas? Did I miss something?" Richard was looking about as if he had truly missed something important. Thomas just looked out the window and sipped his Earl. Brothers. You gotta love em. Smiling to himself, Thomas emptied the little pot of tea into his mug, stood and stepped out to watch the courtyard as Richard finished his breakfast. There was no hurry since the market and shops would not be open for at least another hour or so. The sun warming his face, Thomas simply stood there absorbing the life around him.

Richard pushed his plate away from him, stood up and with mug in hand went to stand by Richard to watch the busyness of the garrison in her daily functions. Richard simply wasn't cut out to be a military man. Far too many restrictions on what a man could do, and he preferred being his own boss at all times. Thomas was the only person to whom he would subordinate. In truth, the brothers loved each other dearly and had on more than one occasion put their lives on the line for the other.

"Thomas it is a glorious morning." Sipping his hot tea, he was feeling more alive after a couple mugs of caffeine laden brew. "Anything of particular interest happening in the garrison? They do seem to be busy as bees and obedient as sheep." Richard was always amazed men could actually live together in barracks and not kill each other at random.

Thomas considered all he had seen that morning. "Lieutenant Evans, the Colonel's main assistant, has taken three letters directly to the Colonel's quarters before you awoke. A courier has been sent out with responses. We don't know to which letter or letters since he was carrying a courier's satchel. The cook sent a kitchen helper to the kitchen herb garden to cut fresh herbs for our grilled sausages and tomatoes. The eggs in the basket carried in his other hand were fresh from the hen house I assume. Six pigeons and eleven sparrows have been vying for the crumbs of crust the cook tossed out. Leftovers from yesterday most likely. The key mystery is who are the twins that are visiting the Colonel as we speak?"

Richard raised one eyebrow and inquired "the same twins that were in the market and carriage yesterday"? Pretty girls always had Richard's immediate attention.

"Why yes, I think they are the same twins we saw yesterday in the market and the carriage. You don't suppose they are the Colonel's daughters, do you? What a marvelous thought indeed!" Thomas knew how to push Richards buttons. Looking away as Richard glared at him the twins appeared from the Colonel's quarters and headed back across the courtyard toward the street entrance. Accompanied by Evans they were escorted and acknowledged by the soldiers as the Colonel's daughters should be.

Thomas looked over and could just see the Colonel in his doorway watching them walk away and noting how every man greeted them or looked at them. Oh yes, it was obvious these were his daughters. Mental note to self, Thomas thought, 'twin daughters and a father who will kill for them'. He commented casually to Richard "I think not Richard. I prefer to live to see tomorrow."

Richard sipped his tea and replied "brother, I intend to see many tomorrows, thank you. I think I'll finish dressing for town. Shall we meet in the courtyard in say half an hour?" Watching the twins leave the garrison he considered how his list of available ladies just shrank by two. Leaving his mug on the table by the door next to Thomas's mug Richard returned to his room with Thomas right behind him. Neither man had seen the Watcher in the shadows observing them watching the twins leave the garrison. The brothers out of sight, the Watcher silently dropped her hood with her signet ring clad right hand and slipped out of the garrison.

§

John Dewe was finishing his breakfast as Weezie hitched Wiley to the cart. Patrick saddled Beulah for Mr. John and two extra saddle horses for Thomas and Richard. Ian had loaded the cart with the load of goods ready to go to the auction house and the special crate for Colonel McKenzie. John and Ian would ride ahead of the cart, Patrick and Moses would drive the cart, and the extra horses would be tied to the back. The cart would be slow going behind the assinigoes loaded with sacs of sugar for the auction. John and Ian would amble along, stop and wait for the cart to catch up, and amble along again. Ian stepped inside the kitchen door to let George know the horses and cart were ready. John overheard, quickly finished his tea and headed for the door pausing momentarily to grab his coat off the hall tree and his hat off the peg.

Patrick and Moses were waiting by the cart with the extra horses tied on behind. Ian gave John a leg up onto Beulah, mounted Tiger in one motion, picked up his reins and the group headed out the gate. Weezie waved as they left, hoping Ian would remember to stop at the apothecary and pick up the salts and Sulphur she needed to make poultices for the livestock and the workers. Small clouds of dust stirred up behind the cartwheels and the hooves on the dirt road, the cart and harness clanked and jingled as the mule walked on steady and sure. John and Ian were quiet, both anxious about passing by the dead boar and the place they found Esmerelda's remains.

As the small convoy approached, they could smell the dead boar before they could see him. Rot comes swiftly on an island in the Caribbean replete with maggots, flies, and stench. The horses, assinigoes, and mule tilted their heads and cocked one ear as they walked past the bloated rotting hog, the men covered their faces with their arms as best they could. The scattered branches were all that remained of the shrub where Esmerelda was found. They all deliberately looked away from the spot. Especially Moses. He couldn't bear to look at where Miss Esmerelda had been dumped. Moses' daughter was the upstairs maid at Emerald Oaks and grew up with Esmerelda doing everything together until they came of age and separated by their place in life. Moses' heart ached for Andrew and Isabella.

They were nearing the cane mill when Moses noticed shadows moving through the tree line. "Mister John..." Moses started to point them out to his master when Ian interrupted. "Moses, I see em. They won't bother us today I don't think." He involuntarily reached up and touched the green ribbon tying back his hair. The movement did not go unnoticed" The Watchers slipped back into the shadows and let them pass unchallenged. Moses looked from Ian to the trees and back again, realizing the green ribbon was a message to someone. He would remember that. John decided to change the subject to a lighter topic.

"Ian, when we get to Bridgetown, we will stop at the garrison first and leave the horses there. From there I want you to take the cart and assinigoes to the auction house. After Patrick and Moses have unloaded the sacks of sugar for the sale, return to the garrison to unload the crate for the Colonel. Once Lieutenant Evans has stored the crate we must load the cart and assinigoes with the freight Thomas and Richard brought from England. And their trunks of course. Once that is done fetch a pint for each man from the garrison stores. Evans knows the Colonel always lets them have a pint. Hot work loading and unloading freight."

Ian responded "Yes sir, Mister John. We will take care of the deliveries and the loading. Do you have a time when you want to return to the Tallywhoa?" Ian was hoping they would have a bit of time to enjoy their pints, but not so long as they would be returning past the cane mill in the dark.

"I can't be sure until I've had a chance to talk to Thomas and Richard. My expectation is they will want to load and leave fairly quickly, but not so much as to make the trip difficult. I have a few stops myself in town so it won't be immediately. Did Weezie or George give you any lists of goods they need for the stable or house? I know they normally do when we bring the cart."

"Just a few things, Mister John. Weezie needs salts and Sulphur for poultices and George mentioned cook is out of flour and vanilla if we can find it easy like. George gave me 2 pounds out of housekeeping to buy what I could find. I think cook wants to bake something special for Miss Esmerelda's wake. I hope that's all acceptable with you? No one really had a chance to ask…" Ian knew John wouldn't care but always cleared expenditures before they were made if at all possible.

"Yes, of course. Those are all necessaries and the special cake for the wake is a must do. Women do those things and I'm lucky to have Cook to think of them for me since I haven't a wife to think of such things. Ask cook when we get back to make extra cakes for the workers, too. They have worked particularly hard this season. We should all celebrate Miss Esmerelda's life. Yes. I like that idea. Buy several bottles of vanilla if you find good quality product." John reached into his vest pocket and pulled out two pounds worth of coin and passed them to Ian. "This should be enough to get what cook and Weezie really need. They both do excellent work and I want them to keep doing so."

"Yes, Mister John. I know where to get the best products. Thank you, Mister John. I'll take care of it personally." Ian was sincere and would indeed see to the task himself. Patrick was listening to how Ian and Mister John spoke to one another respectfully. He liked that in Mister John. He always spoke respectfully even when he was angry with a worker. John could be hard on his workers and Patrick knew he liked certain lady workers better than others.

There was a steady stream of female slaves and Irish servants who found their way to the big house when they came into childbearing age. While it was never spoken it was common knowledge that when the girls became pregnant, they would be worked in a special group to facilitate their childbearing. The mothers of still born children were often sold off or leased out as wet nurses to suckle the children of other gentry. The girls who produced babies that thrived were rewarded with recurring pregnancies sired by the men of Mister John's choice. Breeding slaves was common practice on Barbados. Buying slaves was prohibitively expensive so John raised his own to improve the profit margin of the plantation. Patrick knew he was the product of the slave breeding, but he did not know which of the gentry was his father. The cart hit a pothole in the road and jolted Patrick back to the present.

The group was coming into the fringe of Bridgetown already bustling with activity. The horses put their ears up at the confusion while the mule didn't seem to notice. They passed by the market on the way to the garrison. The vendors hawking their goods for money or barter were chattering the qualities of their wares. Shoppers dickered and haggled over prices, eventually settling on common amount and exchanges were made. Commerce and enterprise make the world go around, even on a tiny island in the Caribbean.

Making their way through the crowded market street to the garrison was slow. Eventually they arrived outside the stable doors. Patrick jumped down from the cart and untied the horses from the back. The guards opened the doors for him to bring the horses for Thomas and Richard inside for

110

fresh water and to rest up for the trip back home. John dismounted from Beulah handing the reins to a guard.

"Ian. When Patrick returns go ahead and take the cart and assinigoes to the auction house and unload the sugar as we discussed. I'll check in with the Colonel and try to locate my brothers. Let Evan's know when everything is loaded and ready for the trip to the Tallywhoa. The storage security detail will know what freight is to be loaded for Thomas and Richard." John started to walk away when a thought occurred to him. "Ian. A thought. If you run across Andrew Conn let him know we are here. He might have interest in traveling back together later. Given the purpose of his trip to Bridgetown..." John's voice trailed off at the obvious thought.

"Yes sir, Mister John. I'll let him know we're here. I expect his driver will be waiting with his cart and horses here at the garrison somewhere." Ian was pleased to work for Mister John for he was truly kind to others in need when he could be. John Dewe knew loss and hardship. John's wife Patience had died in childbirth several years past. John never really recovered from the loss and grief and thus had never allowed himself to love another woman. There were many servant and slave girls to satisfy his needs in other ways, but he had not been able to open his heart and love again. John had arrived at the Colonel's office door. Evans let John into the vestibule, glanced about briefly outside before closing the door behind them.

Ian was leading the way to the auction house as Patrick drove the mule and Moses watched the crowds. Bridgetown had grown tremendously since he was first brought here as a boy. This island was his home now and he knew he would die here. Most of his children were still here on the island. A few had been sold or traded to other owners with plantations on nearby islands. Many slaves came into these islands, but few ever left.

Moses had lost count how many children he had, at least 25 or 26 that he knew of had been born and named. Like the father of the Dewe brothers, Moses left his stamp on his sons. Tall, strong, smart, and attractive they were always in demand and were valuable property. Moses was in his early 50's and was still siring children. He knew of six women that were carrying his child at the time. Two at the Tallywhoa, three at Emerald Oaks, and one at the Pierce farm. Moses wondered how they were doing when Patrick brought the mule to a halt. They had arrived at the auction house.

Patrick applied the brake to the cartwheel and wrapped the reins around the lever. Jumping down he hurried to the back of the cart to help Moses unload the bags of sugar. Each bag weighted about 50 pounds and there were about 20 bags. The men had it unloaded and stacked on pallets ready for the auction later in the week. The bags had the Tallywhoa trademark stamp on the burlap. Tax stamps would be applied when the taxes were paid out of the receipts. Moses and Patrick climbed back into the seat to follow Ian back to the garrison. The trip back was much quicker with the empty cart.

Ian dismounted from Tiger and handed the reins to the guard. "Hold him for just a couple minutes while we get the cart and assinigoes inside, thank you, sir" Ian addressed the soldier respectfully. Once they were through the doors, he took the reins back and followed them inside. A stable groom led tiger to a stall to untack, water, and groom him. Tiger would be rested and ready to return to the Tallywhoa.

The cart rumbled through the stable stopping once on the way to the garrison storages. Evans was there waiting to take the crate for the Colonel as was the custom to the private quarters. Ian and Patrick held opposite ends of the crate following Evans into the bath access chamber full of linens and hot water boilers. Patrick lost his balance and put his hand out to catch himself, grabbing the cloak hanging on the peg by the door. Ian stopped momentarily for Patrick to rehang the cloak and move on. Ian noticed a letter with a red seal had fallen out of the cloak onto the stone floor. Evans quickly picked it up and moved to replace it into the cloak pocket when he realized the seal on the letter was the Colonel's personal crest. Slowly he replaced the letter, clearly confused about what it was doing in the pocket of a cloak in the bath attendant's access chamber.

"Lieutenant, this crate is heavy. Can we move along, please?" Ian was ready to get the freight loaded, find the goods Weezie and Cook needed, and enjoy that pint Mister John had promised them. Evans nodded and continued to lead them through to another smaller chamber between the baths and the colonel's barracks. The lieutenant unlocked the door mostly hidden in the shadows and pushed it open to reveal a large storage closet. There were crates similar to the one they carried already stacked in the room. Ian and Patrick heaved the crate on top of several others on the far wall. As they left Evans locked the door and followed them back to the cart. Moving on they continued down the access way to the stores.

Lieutenant Evans opened the storeroom doors and indicated for Moses to stop the cart past the door to make loading the freight easier. Ian, Moses, and Patrick followed Evans into the warehouse to identify which freight was to be loaded and in what order. The cart and assinigoes would be fully loaded and heavy on the return trip to the Tallywhoa. The mule would walk along steady to provide as smooth a ride as possible. Rolling up their sleeves the men began to move the crates out of the warehouse and load them onto the cart. Some crates required two people and others a single man could manage. Ian noticed the crates were numbered on the outside.

"Evans, do you have a manifest for the crates? I assume there is something that indicates what is in each of the crates by number." Evans hadn't noticed the numbers and called for the storehouse foreman. The foreman quickly appeared with a manifest. There were 6 crates 2' x 4' X 18", 3 wooden 50-gallon hogsheads, two large trunks, and an assortment of other random sized smaller boxes and bags. Ian counted a total of 15 items on the manifest and only 14 loaded on the cart. He had checked the numbers as they were loaded. Item number 7, a wooden barrel containing 'D-Flour', was missing. Ian made a mark by the item on the paper and would tell Thomas later.

Ian and Patrick walked beside the cart as Moses drove the mule back to the main Garrison. They parked the cart and unhitched the mule to let him have water and rest before they headed home.

"Moses, Patrick come with me to the canteen. Mister John was to arrange a pint of ale for us." Ian was always pleased when John extended kindness to the workers. Slaves or not, they worked hard for the plantation and deserved to enjoy a bit of pleasure on occasion. Ian entered the canteen while Moses and Patrick waited outside. The Colonels kindness ended at the door for security reasons. Admitting Ian was stretching the rules far more than the Colonel liked as it was. Stepping up to the bar Ian identified himself to the soldier tending and serving.

"Good morning. I am Ian, Mister John Dewe's overseer. I understand Mister John was to arrange for a pint of ale for myself and the two workers waiting outside. Did he have time to speak with you about this?" Ian always asked and didn't dare order a soldier, even a barkeep. The young soldier looked confused and began to refuse, looking past Ian he saw the Colonel in the doorway waiting to see what the young soldier would do. Clearly the young man was unsure, and the Colonel nodded affirmatively and gave him thumbs up, indicating Ian would get anything he wanted.

"Why yes, Mr. Ian, I can provide you with whatever you need." Hurriedly he filled three pints of ale and handed them to Ian.

"Thank you. We are indeed thirsty, and this is just the ticket." Smiling Ian picked up the pints and took them outside to Moses and Patrick. They stood in the aisle just outside the Canteen, but not in public. The Colonel did not want to advertise his benevolence to the general public. The

114

ale was cool and dry. Pints empty Ian returned them to the barkeep with a smile and another thank you.

"Moses, I think it would be best if you stayed with the horses and mule, and Patrick you come with me to fetch the things for Weezie and Cook. Mister John will want his animals watched and Patrick can help me carry the packages." Moses nodded and headed back to the stables while Ian and Patrick went outside and headed for the market. Ian was hoping to make a quick trip into the market, get what the women wanted, and return to the garrison. Patrick was enchanted to go to the market. The book vendors were particularly intriguing to Patrick. Mister John insisted all his workers have basic reading skills. Patrick could read and write far better than anyone realized and craved books to read. Ian and Moses knew and cautioned Patrick to be very careful about letting people see him do so off of the plantation.

Ian and Patrick found the salts, flour, and vanilla. Ian bought 10 pounds of the salts, 50 pounds of flour, and two 1-litre bottles of vanilla. Patrick tossed the flour over his shoulder and had the bag of salts in the other hand. Ian carried the bottles of vanilla carefully as they looked for the apothecary for the sulfur. The Apothecary shop was across the street from the market itself. Patrick stood outside with the bags of flour and salt. Ian tucked the bottles of Vanilla in Patrick's shirt and went in the shop to find the proprietor.

Seeing Ian enter as she stood on a sliding ladder to reach a jar on a high shelf the shopkeeper's daughter spoke to Ian politely. "Is there something I can help you with today, sir? Just a moment while I climb down, and I'll be glad to assist you." Ian immediately stepped over to take the jar from as she descended the ladder.

"Let me hold that for you, miss. Be careful, these ladders are a bit treacherous in skirts I should think." He held out his hand, took the jar and set it on the counter then reached up again to take her hand as she stepped down the last few rungs.

"Thank you, Mister…?"

"Ian. I'm the overseer for Mister John Dewe at the Tallywhoa. I'm in need of some flowers of sulfur for the horse manager. Do you have any flowers today? I know she likes the finely ground for poultices and medicinals." Ian discovered himself quite enjoying a lady salesclerk for a change. Made the day just a bit softer.

"Yes, we do have the fine ground. How much are you wanting today, Mr. Overseer Ian? We sell it by the pound." The shopkeeper's daughter smiled sweetly at Ian; he was kinda cute in a gruff older man sort of way.

"Weezie asked for 10 pounds if you have it". Ian was honest with the girl and then wished he hadn't been. He liked the idea of coming back for more.

"I think so. Let me check in the back. We normally have 10-pound sacks." The girl disappeared behind the curtain covering the doorway, returning shortly with a 10-pound bag. "Is there anything else you need today Mister Ian?"

"No. That's all that is on my list." Ian hesitated just a moment before asking "Do you have any sweet-smelling oils for soap making, Miss? I think Mister John might let the ladies make up something a bit more civilized if they had some scent oils." Ian had no idea what made him think of buying scent oils.

"Why yes, we have a few. Some lavender, rose, and clove today. Since you're buying 10 pounds of sulfur, I can let you have the little bottles to sample."

"Oh, the women will really like that miss. Thank you!" Ian was pleased with himself. He paid the shopkeeper for the sulfur and tucked the small dark brown bottles wrapped in muslin in his shirt pocket for safe keeping. Outside he motioned to Patrick and they headed back to the garrison and another pint of ale if his luck held. Crossing the street they came across a book vendor at the end of the market area. "Mister Ian, did you want to see about a gift for Mister John? He likes books, don't he?" Patrick had slowed down as they approached the books in the crate at the edge of the market.

Ian slowed for a moment and realized Patrick desperately wanted to look at the books. Looking just past Patrick he saw Thomas and Richard headed their way. Greeting the brothers Patrick turned to see them and stepped behind Ian and turned where his face could be seen. "Mister Thomas, Mister Richard. Patrick and I were just on our way back to the garrison. Do you think Mister John might like one of these books? He is hard to get gifts for and I am always on the lookout. What do you think?"

Thomas and Richard stopped and looked at the titles in the crate. Running his finger along the spines, Thomas considered each book a moment before going to the next. Richard followed as Thomas moved his finger along. "Actually Ian, I think we ought to see what John already has in his library. Furthermore, I have a crate full of books to take to the Tallywhoa. Let's look through those as well. No need to duplicate what we already have. You may have one of the new titles I've brought with me to give as a gift if you like. John would truly like that." Thomas was genuine in his value of books and always encouraged reading and literacy. Even among the slaves he encouraged literacy.

"A crate full of new books? Mister John will be so excited. Yes, I agree. Let's see what there is before we buy one here. We will be back again soon. Thank you, Mister Thomas. Patrick, we need to get back to the garrison and hitch the mule." Nodding Ian and Patrick moved on toward the garrison. Thomas watched them go and wondered what just happened. Richard was still considering the titles in the crate. Thomas began to walk off, Richard caught up in a few steps.

Ian and Patrick disappeared into the stable doors as Thomas and Richard went into the Colonel's office. John and the Colonel were in the inner office chatting. Evans followed the brothers to the door and stood to the side for any instructions the Colonel might have.

"John, it is good to see you safely arrived back in Bridgetown. Richard and I are anxious to get to the

117

Tallywhoa. We can be ready to go with just a few minutes lead time. I believe the cart is loaded and ready?"

"Just waiting for Ian and Patrick to return with the items the women wanted from the market. They should be back any time now. Once they are back, we will meet up with Andrew Conn and head back together. I think he will be waiting for us at the edge of town at the undertakers."

"Ian and Patrick are already returned. They were just ahead of us. Ian had purchased a few things in the market for the women I understand. Patrick seemed to have his hands full. I expect they will be ready to leave within minutes." Thomas was anxious to get to the Tallywhoa.

"I only need a few minutes to gather my things. Shall we all meet at the carts then?" Richard was already headed toward the door, paused and waited for Thomas. "Colonel, thank you for your hospitality. You have been a wonderful host. Anytime we can do the same for you please let us know." Thomas nodded and the brothers headed to their rooms to fetch their things.

"John, thank you as always for the consideration you provide. I look forward to seeing you again soon. Well, no not really. I will be out for Esmerelda's burial tomorrow afternoon. But another time when things are better, we must all sit down and share some scotch and good stories." The Colonel and John stood at the same time.

"Yes of course Colonel. As always, we work well together. Thank you for taking care of my brothers. Anything I can do to help find Esmerelda's killer you need only ask." The men shook hands and John headed out the door to the garrison stables. Stepping outside he found Moses waiting in the cart with the assinigoes ready to go. Patrick was holding the horses. John was checking the load on the cart to be sure it was secure when the McKenzie twins walked up on the way into their father's office.

"Why, John Dewe, what a pleasure to see you again." Mary politely spoke, Minerva nodded in acknowledgement. "I see you are on your way home to the Tallywhoa. Have a safe trip. Pleasure to see you again, as always." The girls did a short curtsy and moved to enter their father's office when Thomas and Richard appeared between them and the door.

"Thomas, Richard let me introduce you to Colonel McKenzie's daughters Mary and Minerva McKenzie." The girls curtsied again toward the brothers "Pleasure to meet you both, Mister Thomas. Mister Richard. You must excuse us we are late for a meeting with father. Perhaps we will see you again soon?" Mary was clearly taken with Thomas, blushing as he kissed her hand. "The pleasure is ours ladies. We look forward to visiting sometime soon." The brothers stepped out of the way as Evans held the door open for the girls with a cold stare directed to the Dewe brothers, all.

Thomas and Richard got a leg up from Patrick. John was already up on Beulah and they were ready to head home to the Tallywhoa. Last stop was to pick up Andrew Conn on the way out of town. Tomorrow would be a hard day for the community. Meanwhile, they had freight to get home and were looking forward to finally arriving at their destination after a very long voyage. It was truly good to be headed home with John once again. It had been far too long.

# 7

Jennie awoke early, dawn barely breaking. She quietly dressed and made her way into the kitchen knowing Cook would have tea made and breakfast well underway. A hot cuppa earl in each hand she ambled out to the large covered porch off the back of the house facing the stables. Giles was there watching the sunrise. She handed him a cup as he pulled her close to warm her in the cool morning.

"Sleep well?" Giles wasn't a morning conversationalist.

"Ummm, yes. And yourself, how was the loft?" Jennie sighed at the memory of the almost moment in the loft last night.

"Full of hay and a rather persistent cat determined to curl up top of me. Purred all night long. Though she was warm…" Jennie snickered at the mental image.

"Well, at least Andrew has Cook well trained. The tea this morning is lovely." She snuggled just a little closer, still enjoying the thought of a purring cat in total domination of Giles. She giggled.

"The little tigress kneaded regularly to make sure I was still breathing. I have cat hair all over me. I think I breathed some in…did you know I don't like cats? "Jennie couldn't help but laugh out loud. The mental image was probably funnier than the reality. Giles couldn't help himself and smirked a giggle as well.

The humor faded with the thoughts of the day. Esmerelda and her infant son would be buried this afternoon and Jennie would be working on the diary all day. Giles would quietly watch the comings and goings of people at Emerald Oaks and at the cemetery later. Both Jennie and Giles expected the killer would be among the mourners. They hoped to get an idea of who that might be.

Cook leaned out the door and called them in to breakfast. "Mr. Giles and Miss Jennie breakfast is ready if you be hungry. Come on to the kitchen table and eat. Going to be a long day. All y'all gonna need a good breakfast to do all that ya needs to do." She hesitated just a moment to see Giles and Jennie begin to make their way inside. Clearly, if Cook called you in to eat, you complied with grace. So, they did.

Cook directed Giles and Jennie to serve their plates from the stove. Sausages, eggs, and porridge were hot, steaming with aroma. On the table were fresh fruits, cheeses, and breads. Plates brimming, they sat and enjoyed their breakfast. Life was hard on Barbados, Cook's breakfast made one day a little easier. Jennie offered to help with their dishes but Cook refused and shushed Jane over to clear the table and refill their mugs with hot Earl. Jane was a precious girl. Jennie had been watching her as they ate. There was something about Jane that piqued Jennie's sixth sense. Something was different about this child, very different. Cook was aware of Jennie's inadvertent awareness of Jane, hoping Jennie would simply not notice Jane's likeness to her mother. Jennie was trying to place what was tickling her brain when Andrew came into the kitchen.

"Giles, Miss Harris, I trust you've been well cared for? I see Cook has created her regular cornucopia of breakfast choices." Andrew turned to Cook "A fine turn out, Cook, well done! I'll sit in here this morning with Mr. Freeman and Miss Harris." Jane quickly pulled out a chair for her master. Graciously Andrew sat and scooted himself in as Jane pushed valiantly. Andrew was indeed a kind man, especially to the children.

"Andrew, I would like to get started reviewing Esmerelda's diary as soon as possible. Until Isabella wakes up I will interview some workers if that is all right with you." Jennie sipped her tea casually leaning back in her chair.

"Yes, I understand. Do you know who specifically you need to speak with? I will have Joshua and Cook arrange a schedule." Andrew was sincere about finding his daughter's killer and was well aware someone at the Emerald Oaks might know who it was, or enough to know where to look. Andrew leaned back as Cook set a plate in front of him. "Cook, some butter and preserves please."

"All the house staff first I think. The plantation managers, too. I also want to go to the worker's quarters. They see everything that goes on. I want to know what they've seen and not shared." Jennie paused to give Andrew time to eat and consider.

"Esmerelda's maid can tell you much about my daughter. They grew up together and were inseparable. Adulthood has been more difficult for them, but they still confided in each other I'm sure. Cook, send Jane up to fetch Esmerelda's maid."

"Thank you, Andrew. I've got my journal. May I commandeer the back porch for interviews?"

"Yes, yes that would fine. Cook make sure there is a pitcher of lemon water and glasses for Miss Harris and Mr. Freeman out on the table. We can make the morning pleasant if we try." Andrew had a grief-stricken look as he considered the day's activities centered on burying his daughter and grandson. Tears welled in his eyes as he sipped his Earl. Little Jane came over and hugged him "Please don't cry Mr. Andrew. Miss Esmerelda is still here in our hearts and always will be. She love you, Mr. Andrew. She do." Andrew hugged her back. So noted by Giles and Jennie.

The curious moment was broken when Toby stepped into the kitchen as Jane scurried off to find the upstairs maid.

"Mr. Andrew, Ms. Isabella is awake and is on her way down for breakfast. Where should we serve her this morning, sir?"

"In the dining room at her usual place at the table, thank you Toby."

"Yes, sir, Mister Andrew." Toby took the china filled with Isabella's standard breakfast items from Cook. No doubt he had already set her place at the table. Toby would be waiting to seat her when she entered the dining room.

"Miss Harris, Giles, I will see to my wife and then send the maid to the porch for your interview. If you need anything do not hesitate to ask. Cook will keep her eye on your needs as well. I want my daughter's killer found." Andrew's eyes had hardened and gone cold. Jennie felt a shiver run up her spine. Andrew was far more than he presented. Jennie was afraid to know; Giles didn't want to know. They both knew they were bound to uncover secrets best left alone. Andrew was a dangerous man when truly angry, and today he was seething lethal fury.

Andrew left the kitchen to see about Isabella. Giles and Jennie headed out to the porch with their mugs of Earl. Jennie had her journal open and was reviewing her prior notes when the maid appeared.

"Good morning Miss. Mr. Andrew says you need to speak to me. About Miss Esmerelda." Nervously the maid sat down in the chair as Giles gestured. "I don't know how I can help you, but I'll try to answer your questions best as I can." Jenny gave Giles a glance to back off a bit, the girl was clearly afraid. Giles turned away to look at the fields as he sipped his tea, listening but not looking.

"Thank you for coming to see us so quickly. Most appreciated." Jenny sat back a bit to be less threatening to the girl. "Just a couple of questions. First, do you know who the father of Esmerelda's baby is?"

The maid squirmed, uncomfortable with such a personal question about her mistress. "Mam, I don't know such things." Looking down to avoid Jennie's eyes the maid was trembling slightly. Jennie waited a moment to let her think.

"Well I'm sure you are aware of gentlemen callers Miss Esmerelda spent time with. Was there anyone…special…to her? Or anyone who was threatening her? Please tell us what you know to help us find her killer."

The maid continued to look down and spoke slowly "Miss Esmerelda had many gentlemen callers. She be pretty, and smart. Mr. Andrew, he make sure she could read, write, do numbers better than he could. I think he plan for her to be Mistress over the Emerald Oaks someday. I knows other owners did not like that. That Miss Esmerelda could do numbers and all. Say she knowed too much. Mr. Andrew, he want her to learn everything. I think her, Miss Esmerelda, was more woman than those men were men. No offence intended Mr. Giles, but she was. They didn't like that none. No not at all."

"WHO didn't like that? I need to know who…anyone in particular? Did someone threaten her? Who?"

"There was a couple of em dat told Mr. Andrew she had offended them by telling they sons' 'no'. Dat Miss Isabella needed to be taught her place. Mr. Andrew didn't like dat none, none at all. Mr. Pierce and Mr. Andrew had words once. But it was Mr. Fuller dat threatened Mr. Andrew. Say he goin ruin Mr. Andrew if Miss Esmerelda didn't apologize for embarrassing he son like dat. Oh, he was right mad, dat one."

Jennie was busy taking notes as Giles casually kept watch of the activities going on around them. Toby was listening just inside the study window behind the Maid. Cook was taking her time putting the scraps out for the chickens. Tom was shushed away by Joshua as he headed to the stables from the slave quarter. There were no secrets here. Nothing could be kept quiet for long.

Jennie addressed the maid "is there anything else you can tell me? Was there anyone Miss Esmerelda was spending time with Mr. Andrew did not know about?"

The maid thought for a minute before responding "I can't say for sure, but I don't think so. Only man she seem interested in was one of the Izzard sons. She was nice to him. At least she never said nothing bad about him. George I think is his name. Seems a real nice man, a gentleman."

"Well, that's a start, thank you. I will follow up with Mr. Izzard and Mr. Fuller. Discreetly of course. If you think of anything else, please let Mr. Andrew know and I'll come back. Is that OK with you?" Jennie was good at getting people to talk to her, especially women. The slave girls were taught to be quiet and not see or hear anything. Their lives depended on their silence more times than not.

Giles watched the maid walk back into the house through the kitchen door. He also noticed the shadow move from beside the window in the study. He and Jennie would compare notes later where they could not be overheard. Emerald Oaks kept dark secrets. The thought made him cringe. He sipped his hot earl and motioned for little Jane to refill his mug while Jennie finished up her notes about her conversation with the maid. Jennie looked again at little Jane as she poured the tea and went back to the kitchen. She had the same eyes as the maid. Unmistakable the girls were related.

"Moses." Giles spoke quietly to Jennie without looking at her.

"Moses...what?" Jennie wasn't sure what Giles was talking about.

"Moses is the father of the maid and little Jane. They have his eyes, and it is commonly known that Moses is one of the top breeding bucks on the island. My apologies if I have offended you. Moses is the common thread between Jane and the maid. It's obvious once you look closely at Moses. Andrew keeps Moses busy all over the island."

Jennie wasn't offended. She was stunned. She knew the owners engaged in barbaric practices to create slave holdings as cheaply as possible. Somehow the concept hadn't been quite so real before. The concept of the plantations' interconnectedness could complicate the investigation into Esmerelda's death. Wow. What and who were they really investigating. Jennie looked at Giles and saw him starring into his tea.

"Plantation culture is very ugly when you pull back the curtain of gentility hiding who and what they really are." Giles had a weary, wary look. Jennie realized he knew far more than he was saying. She also realized the Colonel had left him at Emerald Oaks as her bodyguard. This was no ordinary incident they were investigating. Anyone asking questions was a threat to someone.

Jennie closed her notebook without saying a word. Isabella was walking toward their table. Giles stood up to offer the lady his seat as a gentleman does. Isabella declined the offer and invited them into the parlor. Jennie assumed the leather-bound journal she carried was Esmerelda's diary. Together they went in through the kitchen to the parlor.

Isabella turned to Jennie and handed her the journal. "Here is Esmerelda's diary. I hope you find it useful in identifying the father of her baby, and perhaps her killer. My hunch is they are the same person. I have suspicions but I prefer you come to your own conclusions first. We can chat later. I will answer any questions for you that I can. I ask you keep the diary here in the parlor or return it to me. No one else should have access. These are my daughter's private thoughts and I would like to keep them private if possible. I am sure you understand"

Jennie nodded "Yes, mam. I understand. Thank you for sharing what you can. I will be quite careful with the diary and the information within." Looking up Jennie noticed Father Michael in the doorway starring at the diary. Following Jennie's gaze Isabella turned to see who was there.

"Father Michael, thank you for coming. Let's go to the dining room. George will bring you a breakfast plate and we can discuss Esmerelda's service." Isabella and Michael left the parlor and went to the dining room.

Jennie sat at the desk in the parlor and opened her journal next to Esmerelda's diary. Skimming the pages she found entries for almost every day beginning the first of the year. The first few months were uneventful with comments about the Rosebud Cotillion coming up, what she would wear and who would attend. The tone of the entries changed immediately after the cotillion. Several days after the cotillion there were no entries. When the entries began again, they were written in a very different tone. A distinct sadness wove itself into the fabric of the comments. Jennie frowned at the heaviness in the entries. Something had happened at the cotillion or immediately thereafter. Jennie did the mental math and realized that was probably when Esmerelda became pregnant. Jennie thought 'Esmerelda, tell me what happened to you and who was involved. I need you to help me'.

Jennie deep in thought causally flipped through the rest of the pages. As she did, a card that had been tucked between pages fell out on the desk. It was a dance card from the Rosebud Cotillion. Ten names were listed, five on the front and five on the back. Eight were checked off, the last two were not. The eighth person on the list was John Dewe. The ninth person was Samuel Fuller. The tenth person was George M. Izzard. Jennie sat up abruptly. Something had happened at or after the cotillion. Jennie knew where to look first.

The entries after the cotillion were sporadic and became fearful when Esmerelda realized she was pregnant. She was clearly terrified what would happen to her and her child. George was the man who was helping her, offering her refuge if needed, prepared...wanting... to take her as his wife. Esmerelda was refusing to agree. Why, if he was the father of the child, would she refuse? The entries stopped a few days before Esmerelda was killed. No father of the child was clearly identified, no hint at who would have killed her. Jennie knew the last three men on the dance card were suspects. One of them was likely the killer. She would need Giles to help question them. Jennie was learning that dark secrets hid behind the gentry's façade. She quickly closed the diary and sent George out to find Giles.

# 8

Isabella and Father Michael sat the dining table. Michael was explaining between mouthfuls what to expect at the service. Graveside Catholic mass would be said at the Conn family crypt. The family would receive guests at the house immediately following.

"Isabella, do you or Andrew have any requests or questions?" Father Michael asked between mouthfuls of sausage and eggs.

"No, I think we know what to expect. We just like to believe we will not bury our grown children, don't we?" Isabella was pragmatic yet cold. "I expect the slaves have Esmerelda prepared and placed in her coffin. Her father and I will see her once more before the lid is placed. A prayer I think before?"

"Yes of course Isabella. Anything you want interred with her, you can place with her at that time. Do you have pall bearers chosen?" Licking his fingers, Father Michael could multi-task completely uninhibited.

"We will have to check with Andrew. I expect he has that taken care of." Tears were rolling down her cheeks unchecked at the thought of her daughter being carried up the hill to the crypt in a wooden box. At least she would rest nearby. Father Michael put his hand on Isabella's to comfort her and cried with her. Losing an adult child is cruel beyond words, and he had none to comfort Isabella and Andrew. Father Michael sat at the dining table with Isabella while she cried.

After some time, Isabella composed herself and she sent Toby to find Andrew and then assigned him to clear Father Michael's plate away from the table. Isabella stood as Andrew entered the dining room. Father Michael stood, too.

"Andrew it is time we said our farewells to our daughter and grandson. I have a keepsake I want buried with her. I will get it and meet you and Michael in the hallway. We can go down into the cellar together."

"Yes, I think we should do as you say, Isabella. Michael and I will wait for you in the hall." Andrew was broken hearted losing his daughter, but also for Isabella's loss of her only child. It was common knowledge that Andrew had many children around the island. Some were born to black slaves and some were born to Irish slaves. Only Esmerelda had been his heir.

Waiting in the hall for Isabella Father Michael contemplated about whom had killed Esmerelda. He had known about the pregnancy. Girls got pregnant regularly, even the daughters of the gentry. What had happened to Esmerelda? He was certain the paternity of the child was a critical piece of the puzzle and was determined to discover his identity. Esmerelda had been grief stricken and truly terrified. Her mother, upon discovering her daughter was with child, refused to let her wed a man who truly loved her and wanted to raise another man's child as his own. Something was very, very wrong in this house. As God was his witness, Father Michael would see Esmerelda rest in peace.

Isabella stepped down the last step and took her husband's arm. Father Michael followed, and Toby came close behind with a torch. Toby pulled open the cellar doors and lit the torches on the staircase. In the middle of the cellar was the coffin Andrew had purchased in Bridgetown. Inside the coffin lay Esmerelda. She wore the brown silk dress her mother chose for her, one handkerchief over her mangled face, another over the stub of her right arm. Tucked in her left arm was her wee baby dressed in her christening gown. The boy was so very tiny, but perfect.

Before Andrew could stop her, Isabella stepped closer and picked up her grandson. She would hold him just once. He would be held by his grandmother and be loved. Stepping toward the torch burning in the holder at the foot of the stairs, Isabella took a good look at her grandson and froze where she stood. Her fears were confirmed. This child was sired by a black man. Esmerelda's terrified state had made Isabella suspicious. Slave or not, it was illegal for black men and gentry women to have intimate relations. Andrew would have killed the child or given him to a wet nurse at another plantation to suckle had he lived. Still, this was Esmerelda's son, her grandson, and he would be blessed and buried with his mother. The child had no part in his creation or his demise. God would love him, and so would she. Smiling with love filling her broken heart and rage burning in her gut, Isabella tucked the wee bundle gently back into his mother's arms. Isabella kissed, said a silent prayer and placed Esmerelda's Lapis Rosary on her chest with the crucifix resting on her grandson.

Michael led them in prayer together as a family for the last time. As he blessed Esmerelda with the holy water, he caught a glimpse of the baby, the black baby in his white mother's arms. At that moment he knew what had happened and who had done this to Esmerelda. Only one man could be so callous and cruel. He stepped back seething with rage inside and let Andrew and Isabella cry over their child and grandson while they said their final goodbyes. There would be hell to pay and Father Michael intended to hold the door open for him. Isabella, Andrew, and Father Michael left the cellar as Toby and Joshua nailed the lid of the coffin shut.

Walking out into the sunlight the three were momentarily blinded by the sun until their eyes could adjust. Blinking, the cart and mule came into focus. Moses was standing at the head of the mule patiently waiting for the procession to begin. Toby went into the house and brought everyone outside to take Miss Esmerelda up to the family crypt. Jane brought Miss Isabella her parasol to keep the sun off. The servant women stood out of the way as Andrew, Joshua, Toby, and Giles carried the coffin up from the cellar and put it in the cart. Moses climbed up into the seat and slapped the mule softly with the reins. The family followed the cart slowly up the path toward the crypt. No one spoke. The only sound was the coffin bumping in the cart as the wheels hit holes and rocks in the path.

Father Michael led the group in the graveside mass for Esmerelda. Not quite the full cathedral kind of mass, but a lovely service for a young mother taken too soon from her family. The men carried Esmerelda to the crypt, lowered the coffin into its place and placed the slab over the top. The women placed flowers on the top of the slab. The mason carving the inscription would place the headstone when complete. The group followed the cart back to the house. Esmerelda and her child were buried, but their secrets were not.

The entourage returned to the house somber and tired. Cook had refreshments prepared and arranged on the dining room table, in the parlor, and study. Neighbors and friends were already there with more arriving to pay their respects. The coming and going would continue into the late afternoon. Everyone brought food. Isabella and Andrew went through the motions of greeting everyone and offering refreshments. Toby and Cook made sure everyone was well cared for and listened to the bits of conversation they could overhear discreetly. Giles and Jennie mingled unobtrusively in the study and parlor.

John Dewe and his brothers Thomas and Richard arrived early afternoon. Andrew was delighted to have the distraction of introducing the recently arrived brothers to his guests. John mingled with his brothers and engaged Andrew telling stories about local relationships, shenanigans, and polite politics. The men were sipping whiskey when Colonel McKenzie arrived with his wife Elizabeth and daughters with a security detail. The Colonel left Elizabeth and the twins with Isabella after paying his respects and joined the men in the study with Lieutenant Evans shadowing his movements. The rest of the detail was outside or in the kitchen.

"Duncan, so kind of you to come. I trust you have found refreshments in the dining room? Or would you prefer something a bit more substantial?" Andrew raised his glass to suggest whiskey was an option.

"Andrew, I am so sorry for your loss. Esmerelda was a lovely girl who will be missed by all who knew her. Elizabeth, the twins, and I share our deepest condolences with you and Isabella. That said, yes, I'd love a bit of your whiskey. Thank you." Andrew looked to Toby who was walking toward them with a glass of whiskey for the Colonel.

"Ah, thank you Andrew. The perfect host as always." The Colonel took a long sip and savored the golden aged liquor.

Thomas and Richard sipped their whiskey slowly. Thomas spoke first "I'm sure Richard shares my regret we did not have the honor of meeting Miss Esmerelda. Beautiful like her mother, and kind as well. Did she and your twins know each other well, Colonel?

"Yes, they were good friends since childhood. There aren't many girls their age on Barbados. They did many things together and were a joy to have around. Silly, funny, and smart they were indeed a trio to behold!" The Colonel and Andrew both chuckled reminiscing about their daughters.

"Yet as adults they had gone their separate ways somewhat. The twins really functioned in Bridgetown society and Esmerelda enjoyed the expanse of the countryside. I suppose it is a reflection of their origins." Andrew missed them all.

"Aye, Andrew they grow up much too fast. They do indeed." Smiling the Colonel toasted the girls and looked for Toby to refill his glass. Toby was already at his elbow. Obviously, he had served the Colonel before. Um hmm. Andrew muffled a giggle.

Richard brought the conversation around to future enterprises. "Andrew, Colonel, I'm wondering how bad is the criminal element in the area, really? Things appear to be relatively quiet and routine for the most part. What am I not seeing?"

Andrew replied "Richard, we really have very little crime in terms of theft or assault in a blatant way. Mostly we deal with the unscrupulous buyers and auction workers. Weights, measures…math…doing honest business is foreign to many of the people we must deal with as growers. Would you agree, Colonel?"

Thomas noticed the Colonel stiffened and for an instant gave cold look at Andrew. "Yes, for the most part I agree. We do have the market and pub brawls when sailors come ashore. A whore gets herself a black eye on occasion from a drunken client. The typical reprobate behavior that comes with a port assignment. Rarely do we have serious theft or assaults. Premeditated murders are almost unheard of." The Colonel sipped his whiskey considering what not to say. "We do have an interesting underground information network on the island. I haven't been able to identify exactly who they are. I can say they are clever, everywhere, and seem to know everything before anyone else does. I call them the Watchers."

Richard queried "the Watchers? No idea who they are, how they communicate or where they live? How completely fascinating. Do they have an agenda?"

Andrew shrugged "we have no idea. They just sort of appear and disappear, leave information as needed. Rather creepy actually."

136

Thomas wondered "so you do you believe these are slaves or indentured servants, or, who exactly? They could be quite valuable if approached carefully I'd think."

"Well first we have to figure out who they are, I've several theories as you describe. They truly seem to evaporate before our eyes and reappear when and where we are to be led or blocked. They are manipulators and we suspect some criminal activity but cannot prove anything. Eventually, I will catch them. They have foiled too many plans and advances for the plantation owners of Barbados." The Colonel was clearly antagonized by the Watchers. He knew they were in the room watching but had no idea who they were.

Each man had his own ideas of what plans that were foiled might be. Thomas had a hunch it was more about the Colonel acting on behalf of the Crown appointed Governor than the plantation owners. The sugar industry was rife with corruption. Fortunes were made and lost almost daily. John and Andrew were avoiding looking at the Colonel as Toby refilled their glasses again. Father Michael had been watching out the window taking mental notes of who was arriving and with whom.

"Oh, my lord…" Father Michael said under his breath a wee louder than intended.

"What Father? Is something wrong?" Andrew stepped to the window to see what Michael was looking at. "Ethan Fuller. He actually has the gall to show up here and with Samuel in tow. Unbelievable." Andrew quickly left the room to meet the Fullers at the door. He did not want them in his home, good intentions or not. The Colonel turned to follow as Evans stepped deftly between the Colonel and the doorway blocking him in to guard him. Giles slipped out behind Evans and was at Andrew's side in an instant. The detail was behind Fuller in two steps. Evans stepped aside and let the Colonel lead the way to the doorway.

Surrounded, Ethan and Samuel looked around a bit bewildered, but not surprised. Ethan said "Andrew, Samuel and I came to offer our sincerest condolences. Despite our differences we are truly saddened by your loss. Esmerelda was a lovely girl. I am horrified for you and Isabella. I apologize if we have caused you distress. Samuel and I will leave now if that suits you and the Colonel." Nodding to the Colonel respectfully, Ethan and Samuel turned to leave, their horses still at the bottom of the front steps. The Colonel started to speak but Andrew stopped him with a raised hand.

"Ethan, Samuel, thank you for paying your respects. I will let Isabella know you were here, but now is not the best time to do so. I'm sure you understand. My wife and I have lost our only daughter and she is inconsolable and distraught. Safe journey home."

Samuel nodded respectfully, his father half so and smirked all the way to the gate. Giles watched them closely. Samuel was genuinely heartbroken and grieving openly, Ethan was gloating. Giles went cold and took a mental picture of them as they rode out. He would be able to pick them out in the dark by the sound of their horses' hooves from a distance. Giles casually strolled out to where their horses had stood and noted the shape and size of their hoof prints. They are unique to each horse. Samuel's horse had the larger hoof of a crossbred and was shod only on the front. Ethan's was a more refined print indicative of a thoroughbred, was shod all around, and had heeled shoes on the front but not the back. Giles could recognize the prints again anywhere. He watched as Ethan and Samuel disappeared from sight over the hill, Ethan taking off and leaving Samuel to catch up as they went. Parenting was not Ethan's strongest suit.

Returning to the house the Colonel was watching Giles as he came inside. He knew Giles had seen something important and wanted to know what that was. Andrew went back to chatting with guests and motioned for Thomas and Richard to follow him. They were at the doorway of the parlor when Andrew commented "Colonel, do introduce Thomas and Richard to your lovely daughters. I believe they have met informally outside of your office by chance. A wonderful opportunity for formal introductions, don't you think?"

The Colonel smiled "Why yes of course Andrew. Where are my manners? Thomas, Richard these are my daughters Mary and Minerva." The girls curtsied as they were introduced. "Daughters meet Thomas and Richard Dewe, brothers of John Dewe and owners of the Tallywhoa Plantation." Thomas and Richard made the requisite short bow.

Richard was attracting Minerva's attention unintendedly while Thomas offered his arm to Mary to escort her to the refreshments at the dining room table. Richard followed suit for Minerva. Richard could feel their father's eyes on his back and his officers moving closer. These girls were off limits regardless of introductions. Although Minerva brushing close against him as they made their way through the doorway belied their father's ability to keep them chaste. Richard preferred to live to see the next sunrise and deliberately did not respond to the physical invitation. Jennie noticed the girl's wanton behaviors hadn't changed since, well, ever. Their mother just smirked, shook her head, and went back to conversation with Isabella.

Jennie slipped out of the parlor behind the girls to find Giles in the hallway with the Colonel and Andrew, watching the girls with Thomas and Richard through the doorway. Laughing quietly, the gentlemen were filling the ladies' plates with treats and Toby was serving wine in stemware as asked. Jennie noticed Cook was watching the tables to keep them full as people cycled through all afternoon. Father Michael stayed in the parlor with the ladies almost the entire afternoon, leaving when the Fullers arrived, he had not returned. Curious, Jennie asked Andrew "have you seen Father Michael recently? He seems to have wandered away."

The Colonel and Andrew shrugged. Evans said "I believe he is upstairs Miss Harris. You might try the ladies drawing room, or I could go up and let him know you are asking for him if you prefer?"

"Oh no, I don't think that is necessary. Isabella may miss him in the parlor and now I know where to find him if needed. Thank you, Evans." Jennie returned to the parlor to find the diary on the desk where she had been working earlier. Isabella must have left it out accidentally. Jennie picked up the journal to return it to Isabella and found an envelope underneath with her name on the front. The seal on the back was almost identical to the Colonel's personal seal. Turning her back to the room Jennie broke the seal and opened the letter to find an invitation. The Watchers were calling a conclave at the cane mill that night. She would be there.

Jennie slid the letter into her pocket as she turned around to face the room. No one had noticed. No one was left in the room but her. Isabella and Elizabeth were talking as they walked down the hall to the dining room. Giles stopped at the parlor doorway momentarily and walked out the front door, clearly expecting Jennie to follow.

Jennie found Giles out on the far end of the front porch. She walked up and past him looking away toward the fields. Giles had his back to the fields able to see the doors and windows, or rather who was at the doors and windows. They were out of earshot and could speak casually but were still careful.

"Jennie, there is something going on with Ethan Fuller and his son Samuel. The incident at the doorway was orchestrated by Ethan. Samuel was dragged along by his father. Ethan was gloating as they rode out, Samuel is afraid of him. Father Michael knows something about them as well. Let's see where the Priest goes when he leaves tonight. I want to know his thoughts. My hunch is the Michael that Isabella was referring to was not the Priest after all. Or this is all a coincidence. I wanted you to know where I am off to in case you need me later. I will be back very late or early morning. I'll let the Colonel know we plan on taking another day to gather information before returning to the garrison."

"Oh my. I think you are on to something significant. I found evidence pointing to Samuel as well. Esmerelda's dance card from the Rosebud Cotillion. She danced last that evening with John Dewe and did not with Samuel or George Izzard, the last two names on her card. Something happened to her at the dance or after. One or all of those men knows what happened."

Giles was staring at the back of Jennies' head. The evidence was beginning to look ugly. "So, who is the Michael that Isabella was referring to? We're missing something." Giles was studying the faces through the window. Isabella and Elizabeth were chatting with the other plantation owners' wives. He noticed Elizabeth slip an envelope to each of them discreetly. The letters went into their skirt pockets or into their bodice none of them opened the letters or acknowledged the receipt. Jennie followed Giles' gaze and saw the letters discreetly hidden away in her peripheral vision. Giles focused on the women.

"Jennie…any idea what those letters are about?"

"What letters?"

"The letters Elizabeth McKenzie gave to the other ladies. What is that about?"

Jennie couldn't lie to Giles. "I didn't see exactly so I can't say for sure. I can ask Isabella later. Probably some sort of ladies tea or something." Jenny was looking away so Giles couldn't see her face. She hadn't lied, but she hadn't been fully truthful either. She wanted to find out what the Watchers were really about before she said anything. They might have information about Esmerelda's killer.

"Ask Isabella. I don't want any surprises. I'll see you in the morning." Jennie nodded and returned to the guests inside the house. Giles quietly left for the stable to saddle Devlin. Could be a long night. He sent Tom to Cook to get a sack of food for the road and a jug of water. Blanket rolled and tied behind his saddle, food in his saddle bags, he silently led Devlin out the back and mounted out of sight of the house. He rode to the rectory and waited for the Priest to return.

# 9

Isabella went to the parlor after dinner to read, closing the door and drawing the curtains the light from her lantern could be seen under the door. Jennie slipped out of the house unnoticed shortly afterwards and made her way through the evening shadows to the stable. Hearing rustling coming from the stalls, Jennie grabbed a pitchfork to defend herself and her horse. Peeking into the stall where her horse was stabled, she could see he was already saddled and ready to ride. Confused, she began to turn around when Isabella's said "are you going to ride him or look at him? We haven't much time to get to the mill. Be quick."

Stunned Jennie put the pitchfork against the wall, brought her horse out of the stall, mounted in one motion and followed Isabella who was already headed out the back to the tree line. Slowing to a walk to safely move through the dense Locust, Cedar, and Ironwood trees, the full moon lit their way, the native flowers perfuming the air. Isabella's horse made a stop and seemed to drop into a hole. Jennie realized as she followed, they were slipping down into a gulch to keep hidden from view. Creatures of the night scurried away and around them. Jennie prayed they didn't scurry up a group of wild hogs or Highwaymen.

As abruptly as they entered the gulch, they were suddenly on the road toward the cane mill. Isabella kicked her stallion, Satan, and they were two dark shadows running in the night. If she hadn't seen this with her own eyes, she never would have believed Isabella was a talented horse woman and athlete. The realization the Watchers were women of means and significant talent made Jennie squeeze her gelding's sides a bit more to catch up to Isabella. The plantation wife was a façade fading with the shadows they galloped past.

As they neared the cane mill, they could smell the dead boar and the horses looked with one ear cocked and a snort as they passed the corpse. The mill coming into view Jennie could see at least a dozen horses tied in the trees just beyond. Isabella went straight to the doorway of the mill and stopped. Motioning to Jennie she dismounted and handed the reins to Maria to lead their horses out of the moonlight. Jennie was right behind Isabella as they entered the mill.

Lanterns lit the inside of the mill completely. Jennie looked around to see the matrons from every significant plantation, a number of proprietor's wives, and an assortment of other women from Bridgetown and surrounding areas. There were 18 women in attendance. Isabella was apparently one of the group leaders along with Elizabeth McKenzie, Weezie, and Cook. One woman looked familiar, but Jennie could not remember where she had seen her before. Pondering who she was Isabella began to speak.

"Ladies, thank you all for being here tonight. As you all know, we buried my Esmerelda today. What you do not know is Esmerelda was with child. Without going into detail, I can say we know the father was black and we believe he, or his owner, was the man who killed Esmerelda. I am asking you to help me find her killer. Elizabeth and I have invited Miss Jennie Harris, an official with the Colonel's contingent at the garrison, to join our group. Jennie can be of great help to us in this matter and others in the future. Please share with her anything you would share with

Elizabeth or myself." Pausing, a murmur went through the group and then they began to step forward to welcome Jennie to their group. Pleased with the response Elizabeth spoke next.

"Ladies, thank you for your kind welcome of Jennie. Who has something to share tonight?" Elizabeth looked around the group looking for contributors.

"Ms. Elizabeth, Ms. Isabella I have some news." Weezie stepped forward. "Mister says there is a new ship coming to port soon. A French ship that wants to trade what they plundered from Antigua. Mister's brothers bring news the French are at war with the English. They are talking about taking the ship and all her goods. Refit the ship to run sugar to the colonies. Mister says we beat the Dutch Admiral de Ruyter in 1665, we can beat the French that come to Barbados, too. I think we can get a nice share of the plunder if we are smart about it. Add the funds into our savings and investments."

Stunned, Jennie could only stare at one and then another of the women. This was an investment and banking group. Women with lots of money and the power that comes with lots of money.

"Ms. Isabella, Ms. Elizabeth, I have news, too." Maria stepped forward. "Father Michael says there will be a Bishop from Rome to visit soon. He is hiding everything he can and has a second set of church records just for the Bishop to see. He says the Bishop is here to take everything he finds back to Rome and will leave the island in poverty. Father Michael is working diligently to keep what's ours here in Barbados. I think we might need to keep the Bishop from Rome distracted while he is here."

Elizabeth raised a brow. "My, that is interesting news indeed. A bishop from Rome! When is the Bishop expected to arrive?"

"Father Michael says sometime in the next couple of months he thinks, depending on the weather, sailing and such."

"We will organize a social calendar that compliments Father Michael's church calendar. The Bishop will be kept busy and out of trouble. Perhaps we can convince him to leave a contribution here instead of taking the food from the orphans' mouths." Elizabeth was smiling devilishly and Jennie thought, 'dear God, they are extortionists as well'. A movement by the door caught her eye. The women turned as a group and stepped aside to allow a small cloaked figure to come to the front. Elizabeth and Isabella nodded and stepped back. The figure walked straight to face Jennie and stopped.

Looking up at Jennie she reached up with old wrinkled and arthritic disfigured hands to drop her hood back off her head. Her hair was completely white, and her eyes looked to be completely blind. She reached up and gently felt Jennie's face. She ran her hands down Jennie's arms and across her stomach. Holding her hand against Jennie's womb she began to speak in a language Jennie had never heard before. A younger woman standing behind the old woman a few paces began interpreting and speaking to Jennie.

"Maia, the grandmother says the old ones have brought you here because you carry the blood of our people. You have been chosen to preserve our ancestor's link for future generations. Men will try to take you and make you their weapon against others. The ancestors will not let them. Do not be frightened no matter what happens the old ones are always with you as they have always been with her."

The old woman began singing in a voice none had ever heard before. The younger woman stepped back and was looking behind Jennie. Jennie felt something touch the back of her head and ran down her back, wrapping around her and the old woman, the energy growing until they were glowing white and the sound was deafening. The women were all terrified and standing far away from them.

The old woman stopped singing and the glow died away. The grandmother said to Jennie "Remember, Maia, you carry the blood of our ancestors. The old ones are with you always. You are blessed." She pulled her hood up over her head and turned to leave with the girl the way they came in.

Jennie was speechless, stunned she looked around the room at the others. Weezie stepped forward toward her. Utter astonishment written across her face, she spoke "You! How can it be you? Who are your people, that you carry the blood of our ancestors?"

The old woman was just passing through the door stopped and turned to speak to Weezie. The girl with the grandmother interpreted again "She is Maia, the chosen. The old ones have brought her here. Maia is of our blood. I have seen her in my visions many times. Her father was of the others. Her mother was from the old people, older than the islands. She will carry our future in her womb before this time tomorrow. All of you must care for Maia and prepare to move our blood to Carolina. She carries our blood, and the truth of our ancestors. So it is and shall be." The old woman turned and left, no one dared utter a word.

Elizabeth whispered to Isabella "how could she know of 'Carolina'. The grandmother comes from a tribe of natives in Brazil. There is no possible way she knows of 'Carolina'..., and why on earth would she think Jennie has Caribbean native blood? Who is Maia?"

Everyone in the mill was looking at Jennie who finally said "I have absolutely no idea what that was about. I think she has me confused with someone named Maia. She is obviously blind, you did see her feeling my face, didn't you?" They all just sort of looked at each other and Jennie, bewildered. Regardless, the old woman had never been wrong in her guidance. Jennie would be cared for and protected at all costs.

Isabella brought them back to reality. "Ladies, it is getting late and we must all get home before we are missed. Remember to travel in pairs as far as you can for safety, and care for each other. We shall meet again next full moon for an accounting of funds. Nothing written down, just bring a recent tally so we can judge our full measures. Thank you, all, for being sisters."

The others all nodded and hugged as they left the mill to head home. Jennie stood with Isabella and Elizabeth to leave just ahead of the girls that would lock up the mill. Isabella spoke softly to Jennie "you mustn't let the old woman frighten you. But take everything she said very seriously. Take no unnecessary risks of any kind. And I must ask who the father of your child is?"

"Isabella I am not pregnant. It is not possible that I am and have no intentions of becoming with child anytime soon. The old woman is wrong about that. I'm sorry, but she is just wrong." Jennie was a bit indignant, and a lot perplexed.

Elizabeth stepped closer "Jennie. The grandmother is never wrong. At least she never has been in over 100 years. Yes, she is well over 100 years old. Never question her or her prophecies. Never. You must understand. This is the first time we have seen her in many years. We know of word from her and about her. Most of the women have seen her for the first time tonight as you did. Believe me when I tell you, if she says you are chosen and will carry the blood of our ancestors in your womb by this time tomorrow, you will."

Jennie stepped back a step and looked from Isabella to Elizabeth and back. They were serious. They believed the old woman. Every word she spoke. What in the world was going on here, really? "Well, ladies, time will tell I suppose. Isabella, you are correct we need to get home before we are missed. I'll see you back in Bridgetown soon, Ms. Elizabeth. Travel home safely." Jennie and Isabella mounted their horses and headed back to Emerald Oaks. Elizabeth and the groom that held her horse mounted up and headed back to the garrison.

The old woman and girl watched them leave from the hilltop. Once the women were out of their sight, they removed their cloaks and carried them in a basket as they walked in the moonlight back to their small village in the mountains. As they passed through the outcroppings the women were joined by others, old ones the Europeans could not see. Jennie often saw them but did not realize the people around her could not. The grandmother walked with a strong purpose this night of her 139th birthday. She had lived a long life to ensure the blood of the ancestors continued through the veins of the young. She would live many more years to receive them when they returned. Smiling she raised her face to the moon and sang as she walked home. A glorious night, the last for many full moons to come.

Jennie and Isabella rode swiftly returning to Emerald Oaks. They walked the horses back up the gulch and through the trees for safety and to let them breathe. Unsaddling their horses, they heard the dogs begin to bark. Someone was coming up the lane. Hurriedly Isabella returned her saddle and bridle to the tack room and began to towel off her mare. The stable boy came in and took over. Isabella nodded and put her finger to her lips, indicating to the boy not to say a word. She turned and ran to the back of the last stall and vanished. Curious, Jennie looked over the low wall between the stalls in time to just see the panel close behind Isabella. Shocked, Jennie realized there was a passageway from the stable to the house. To the parlor. Isabella was in the parlor when Jennie left the house. Things were beginning to fall into place how the Watchers went about unseen and unheard. McKenzie was correct. They hid in plain sight.

## MAIA

# 10

"Jennie? Where have you been out in the night?" Giles was walking through the doorway holding Devlin's reins. "It isn't safe for you to be out by yourself at night, Jennie. You know better!" Giles was getting scared-angry and fast.

"Giles, I wasn't alone." Jennie gestured with her head toward the stable boy. "Notice he is rubbing down the mare, too." Hoping Giles would buy her story wasn't her strong suit.

"Jennie, I don't know what you're up to, but I do not like it. We need to talk." Giles looked to the stable boy and handed him Devlin's reins. "Rub him down well, and water him slowly. When he is fully cool let him have some hay and a half serving of grain. I'll not have him colic from ill keeping."

"Yes, Sir, Mister Giles. I take real good care of Devlin. Like he my own. Thank you, Mr. Giles. No worries." The boy took the reins from Giles and led Devlin to his stall. Jennie and Giles headed up the stairs to the loft where they knew they would not be overheard.

Jennie stood in front of the open door looking out at the moon lighting up the cane fields. Giles sat down on the bale of hay behind her and gently pulled her down to sit with him. Wrapping his arms around her he held her tightly.

"Jennie. You must be more careful. I know full well the stable boy was not out riding with you on Isabella's horse. Whatever you and Isabella are up to...you must keep me informed of where you are going and in general, why. There are evil people on this island..." Giles bowed his head and touched the side of his cheek to the back of her head. "I could not bear it if something were to befall you, Jennie. Do not make me suffer thus."

Jennie turned to face Giles in the moonlight. Reaching up with his left hand he cradled her face, longing to kiss her and love her physically as he loved her in his heart...completely. Jennie smiled and said "Giles. I am truly sorry if I made you worry. Yes, I was out with Isabella. I can honestly say you have nothing to fear for my safety when I am with her. Isabella is probably the most capable human being I have ever known in terms of taking care of herself. If I am with her, I am safe. Know this."

Jennie stood in front of the door again and continued "Giles, there are strange things happening among the plantation owners. Things are not what they seem..."

Standing up behind her Giles caressed her shoulders and nuzzled her hair. "I agree. Tonight, I went to the rectory to meet up with the priest when he returned. I had some questions for him. He was evasive as I expected he would be...but he knows much more than he is letting on. I hid out of sight for a while just to see if anyone would show up after I left."

"Really? Did anyone come to see Father Michael? Jennie's curiosity was piqued.

"No. But someone left. I almost gave myself away...almost. Samuel Fuller was apparently there before Father Michael or I arrived there. I don't know if he overheard my conversation with Michael, I don't think so, but it doesn't matter. I heard him shouting, begging Father Michael to help him...I'm not sure what that was about, but he was distraught about something. In the end he rode out toward the Fuller plantation quite upset." Giles felt Jennie tense as he spoke. "What did I say? You've gone cold…"

"Samuel Fuller was the name on Esmerelda's dance card that she did not dance with. Samuel and George Izzard after him. She danced last with John Dewe at the Rosebud Cotillion last spring. Samuel was refused by Esmerelda…Ethan had hot words with Andrew, threatened him as I recall." Turning to face Giles she asked "do you think Samuel could be Isabella's killer? Or he knows who that is? Samuel doesn't strike me as a man with the ability to physically hurt a woman…is he?"

Giles wondered out loud "Samuel seems more of an ethical young man, wanting to demonstrate integrity…his father on the other hand…Ethan could hurt someone. He probably has before. Samuel specifically. So, we still don't know who "Michael" is. Do you think Isabella could be throwing us off track deliberately? We're missing something. Yes, I want to know more about Samuel and George Izzard, too." Giles was quiet, lost in his thoughts for a few minutes, then asked quietly "Jennie, what were you and Isabella doing and where did you go? I am aware of the Watchers. Long before you discovered Elizabeth McKenzie in the parlor. They are not new to me. I know much about them, who many of them are and what they are about. What do they want with you?"

Jennie realized he really did know. No reason to try and pretend he didn't. "I'm not quite sure how to explain what they want. I expect you know they are a very clever group of powerful women. Their husbands are deceived in interesting ways. Some know more than others I expect. They function as an investment group, a social support group to each other…they do shape policy and actions on the island in ways I never could have imagined. But I totally understand how they do, now that I've met them as a group. These are not women to be trifled with, Giles. They could be very dangerous. They have access to confidential dealings, have amassed significant assets, and manipulate the economy of the island. Yes, they do. In short, these are amazing individuals who happen to be women. Their public image is quite a carefully orchestrated façade. Bottom line leave them alone. Forget their association exists. Please trust me on this. We can utilize my inclusion into their group. At least for a little while."

"Yes, they could be most helpful. As long as they are not breaking any serious laws…stealing or extortion or such. I expect there are many things they could share information wise…"

"Giles leave them alone. As in LEAVE THEM ALONE." Jennie had never been so forceful or directly insubordinate to Giles professionally before. He was quiet a moment. Then asked

"Jennie, what do they want with you?" Giles was cold and suspicious about the Watchers motives.

"I'm not entirely sure. Mostly to include me in their 'sisterhood' of sorts. They haven't asked anything from me. At least not yet. Well, if you don't count the old woman's prophecy that I've been 'chosen'…oh this is nuts. They are a bunch of women with time on their hands and money to invest. A girls' club. That's all they are, really."

Giles stepped back and quietly whispered "what old woman? Jennie, who are you talking about?"

Perplexed at his reaction Jennie turned to face Giles. "An old woman showed up just before they adjourned. I'd never seen or heard of her before. She spoke a language I've never heard spoken either. There was a younger woman with her who interpreted for her. They called her 'the grandmother'. Elizabeth McKenzie says she is way over 100 years old and normally only get messages from her. That most of the Watchers had never seen her before tonight, but they all knew of her and her 'prophecy' talents apparently. Prophecies…really…spare me…" Rolling her eyes she crossed her arms and looked up at Giles. He wasn't humored. He was staring at Jennie as if he'd seen a ghost.

"Describe the old woman."

"Well, she was…old. White hair and looked to be blind. She felt my face as if she couldn't see me. Short…maybe 4 feet tall. I guess you'd call her tiny. They all revered her though. The younger woman walked behind her and translated every time the old woman spoke. It was a strange language. A native language I think…you know, Indians of some sort but I honestly don't know. It wasn't European I do know that."

"What did she say. Think carefully, Jennie."

"Nonsense stuff. She's a crazy old woman that they humor. Why does that matter to you so much? You look frightened…Giles?"

Giles looked at Jennie for some time before he stepped closer to her again. "There are some old stories about the island. I have seen them come true in the past. Strange things do happen here I can't explain. Be careful Jennie. Don't assume the old natives are harmless. They stay up in the hills to themselves most of the time. But there are stories…just be careful Jennie." Giles reached down and lifted Jennie's chin up with his hand. "I'd be heartbroken if anything were to happen to you."

Giles bent down and kissed Jennie tenderly before he realized what he was doing. Jennie smiled and leaned in closer to encourage him further. He picked her up and set her on the hay bales stacked two high which put her at face level. Jennie pulled him to her and kissed him, not waiting any longer to be a couple at least in their own private liaisons. Enough of being interested, it was time to decide to build a life together or not. She didn't have an issue with taking some time to do so, but it was time to get on with life. "Giles, I want to be with you. *YOU, Giles.* I'm not sure how or where or when, but I want us to work. I have for a long time…" she smiled and kissed him again.

Giles pulled her close to the edge of the bale, her legs hanging over the edge, he stepped between them and pulled her pelvis close to him. She could feel his erection through their clothes. She wanted him as badly as he wanted her. "Jennie…oh, God, Jennie…" He was nibbling her hair, her ears…nuzzling her neck…God he wanted her.

Jennie reached down and slid her hand in his pants. Her hand, so soft and delicate, made him catch his breath. He pulled away just far enough to give her room to loosen his belt and pull him free of his clothing. He was throbbing with desire. He picked Jennie up and stood her on the first bale. He slowly undid her shirt and let it slip off onto the hay bales behind her. She deftly kicked her boots off and let her trousers slid down around her ankles. Stepping out of them, she kicked her pants behind her with her shirt. Naked in the moonlight, Jennie was a stunningly beautiful woman. Giles pulled the lacing off her hair and watched her hair fall down around her waist. Reaching up he touched her breasts as he kissed her neck. "Jennie, I must bathe first. I've been on the road all day and I am not fit to…be…with you like this." Wrapping his blanket around her he handed her his hairbrush and her journal. "Write about what you want…when I get back…read it to me then…I'll brush your hair as you do…think about…us…together."

Jennie blushed though he couldn't see it. He could feel her warm at the thought. He kissed her once again and disappeared down the ladder headed out to wash up at the pump. Jennie sat with her back to the ladder with the journal in the moonlight and set to write what she wanted Giles to do, to be with her. She could hear him splashing in the water basin as she wrote. And then she didn't.

Shortly she heard steps coming up the ladder to the loft. Smiling to herself she closed her eyes and tilted her head back to greet Giles caress as he returned. The breath was warm, but the hand with the ether-soaked rag over her mouth and nose to keep her from screaming wasn't Giles'. Her world went black as the hood was pulled down over her head. Jennie heard garbled voices saying, 'get the journal, there on the floor' and 'use the blanket…with us…too many questions…a lesson' as she succumbed to the drugs putting her into a sedated state. The last thing she remembered was being carried down the stairs and thrown over a horse in front of a rider.

Jennie began to come around in a strange place she had never been before. It took a few minutes to realize she wasn't dreaming. Groggy she tried to see where she was, but the bag was still over her head. Dim lights filtered through the weave of the fabric. She was being pulled to stand up. Someone was leading her. She bumped into a table and her hands were pulled across the surface and tied to a ring anchored in the wall behind the table. The man's hands were tying her ankles to the table legs. Jennie realized she was completely naked. She couldn't fight back but she could scream, and she did.

Laughing the man pinched and twisted her nipples abusively and she squirmed in pain. She heard another set of footsteps enter the room.

"Is she ready yet?" The voice was clearly anxious to get started.

"Yeah. She's ready…ripe and ready. Bring the breeder."

Jennie had to process what was going on, but she quickly realized what they were intending to do. She was terrified, but they didn't plan to kill her. At least not yet. Footsteps entered the room and she couldn't breathe.

"Well done. She is definitely ready. Michael. Do your job." The man stepped back, and another man stepped up behind Jennie. She gasped as the man thrust himself inside her hard. He put his seed inside her and left.

The boss man stepped behind Jennie and began to sew her shut. He used a gold silk thread and closed her up almost. He deftly sutured her up using the stitch unique to Michael's covers. Jennie cried with agony and shook as he stitched. A practice many owners used to identify which woman had been bred by whom. This man used it to send a message 'I can shut you up any way I choose. I own you'. Rinsing her off with rum, he untied her legs and hands from the wall and table. Pulling her away from the table Jennie could barely walk. Unseen hands dressed her in haste. The linen shirt was rough against her bruised nipples and the rough slave's trousers bit into her crotch like a rasp.

She felt herself being picked up and carried outside and thrown back over a horse and a man's legs. She tried to remove the hood and he grabbed her crotch. The pain was unbearable. "Leave it if you want to live to bear the child bred in you this night." Jennie relaxed and didn't resist again. They moved along quickly for some time and eventually slowed and came to a stop. He grabbed her crotch as he had earlier and warned her "do NOT say a word about this night. To anyone. You were chosen by the grandmother to carry the child within you." He squeezed tighter and Jennie couldn't breathe. "Understand me girl. You do NOT have a choice in this. Remember we own you and you will abide your cover."

Hands reached up and took Jennie down from the horse and carried her back to the loft at Emerald Oaks. He put her down gently on the pallet on the hay. A meek cry of pain as she settled down into the hay and fell in a restless sleep. The drugs were working their magic. She would awaken and find herself sewn down and so bruised and swollen she would be unable to walk normally for days. Giles held her in his arms as she slept, tears rolling down his face into her hair. Why did they have to take Jennie, his Jennie?

When they came for her, he couldn't stop them tho he did try. Overpowered they held him against the barn as Jennie was carried away. He knew who they were and what they would do. Jennie would never be the same and he cried for her, rocking her in his arms as the drugs held her in the darkness of sedation. He was thankful she would sleep for a while and give her damaged body time to heal, and the breeder's seed to take hold. These were the men who impregnated Esmerelda, he was sure of it. But why did they kill her? And why Jennie? What possible reason could they have to do this to Jennie?

Giles sobbed into Jennie's hair, afraid to let go of her, afraid they would come back and take her from him again. There was indeed evil on this island. Driven by the fortunes of men the evil spread through the night preying on anyone the devils could profit from.

There was a rustle at the ladder as Giles heard a woman's skirts climbing up to the loft. Isabella's softest voice gently called to him. "Giles, is Jennie with you? I can't find her."

"Yes, Isabella, Jennie is here. Please come and help me. She has been brutalized in the night. I can only do so much."

Isabella ran to find Giles holding Jennie with tears streaming down his face.

"Dear Lord. What happened to her? Giles...what happened to Jennie?"

Giles said through sobs "I, I tried to protect...her. There were

too...many...Oh...God...Isabella...I...couldn't...protect... her..." Giles held Jennie tighter through his tears. Isabella knelt next to them.

"Giles. Let go of her a little. Let me look at her"

Giles held Jennies tightly and tried to keep Isabella from touching her. "No...no...let her...be..."

Isabella became a bit more insistent.

"GILES! You MUST let me look at her. Release your grip a little. I will not hurt her. She is injured, Giles. She must be tended." Still crying Giles released his grip on Jennie enough that Isabella could look her over.

"She's been drugged. I think I know what this is about...God, what have they done..." Isabella pulled up Jennie's shirt and found her nipples bruised and bleeding from the assault. "Giles I must look...lower...hold her steady..." Looking away, he held Jennies so Isabella could slide her trousers down far enough to look at her genitals quickly. "Bastards! The fucking Bastards!" Giles looked down to see what Isabella was looking at. His face went ashen when he saw the stitching that almost completely closed her. He knew what it meant. He had seen it done to slaves and indentured servants.

"Isabella, why would someone do this to Jennie? Why?" Giles was sobbing again as they pulled the trousers off all the way. She would need skirts for a while. "I will kill the men who did this. I know who they are."

Isabella shot a livid look at Giles. "No, you won't." He did a double take and was aghast at Isabella's suggestion. "You must leave this to me, Giles". If you interfere you will cause untold suffering to others. Help me get Jennie to the house and in a real bed. She will need care for several days. She will be safe in the house with me. You have no choice but to trust me on this. Do you understand, Giles?" Unspeaking he nodded his head. Somehow, he knew Isabella spoke gospel on this incident. He would let it settle for now. He would kill them. He would kill them all.

They wrapped Jennie in the blanket and Giles carried her to the house and up to Esmerelda's bedroom. Gently he put her on the bed and was quickly escorted out by Isabella and the slave women. Clearly in charge, Isabella had Jennie stripped, bathed, and treated superficially in minutes. Jennie was beginning to come back to consciousness and was crying soft cries of agony as they touched her battered body. Giles balled his fist outside the door in rage. Leaning his head against the closed door he could only listen as the women ever so kindly and gently cared for his love.

"Ms. Isabella, you see what been done to her, here?" Giles knew she was looking at the stitches.

"Yes, I saw what they did. I am so angry…she is not a breeder; she is a free woman. How dare they!"

"Yes, Ms. Isabella. But the stitching and the thread…it's the same what was done to Miss Esmerelda. Same buck been at her as well." Isabella took a closer look at Jennies wound. She recognized what the slave was telling her, she just hadn't thought about it in the rush to get Jennie to the house and cleaned up.

"Who? What Buck covered Jennie? Do you know who uses that thread and that stitch? Tell me now girl if you do!"

The girl was afraid and stepped back from Isabella.

"I think it be that new buck Mr. Fuller got from up in the mountains. Hear say he is big as a horse and gets all his covers with child first go. His issue bring top dollar and the Misters pay a big fee to use him on their women." Frozen in place the slave waited for Isabella to reply.

"Really. Now that's interesting news. I had suspicions but nothing to confirm them until now. But why Jennie? She isn't a slave or indentured breeder? We're missing something. Tell me more about this buck Mister Fuller owns."

"Not much else to tell Ms. Isabella. I hear he is one of them native people up in the hills. Speaks some English but mostly that gibberish they talk. The Misters like the mixed get from his people because they can take the heat and climate here without dying like the others. I got no idea what they want to do this to Ms. Jennie for. Mr. Fuller still mad about Esmerelda tellin his boy 'no'? He did see Ms. Jennie here at her funeral and all."

Isabella looked at the slave hard. She realized the woman spoke honestly and was afraid of what was happening to the women on the island. This was cruel, what they were doing. But it served the owners' purposes. Cheap labor to build empires requires a steady supply of women bearing slave babies every year. Jennie had been raised at the orphanage. Her mother was likely an indentured girl who couldn't keep the child due to scandal. Once the child was born she would have been given over to a wet nurse at the orphanage and the mother sold off or sent to whore with the harlots. There was indeed evil on this island. Driven by sugar, the sweet food driving Europe into a frenzy of addiction to the stuff.

"Fuller may be involved. But I don't understand why Jennie would be a target. There's more to this than we know. I will find out. When I do, I think we will know who killed my daughter and grandson." Isabella looked straight at the

163

slave. "Take the best care with Ms. Jennie. Remove those stitches before she wakes. She will most likely be with child and she must heal completely. I will return in a few hours and we will get her back into a hot bath. She needs to fully awaken first. Call me if she needs anything you can't provide on your own." Isabella turned to leave the room.

Giles almost fell on Isabella as she opened the door.

"Giles, I assume you heard everything."

"Isabella...are you serious...this was to deliberately impregnate Jennie? Why? She is a free woman...makes no sense...? And you know Fuller did this to her? The Colonel must be informed, Isabella! This cannot be allowed to continue. They brutalized her...they...they..." Tears ran uncontrolled as he raged.

Isabella calmed him with her soft hand on his arm. "Giles. You MUST let me deal with this for now. When the time is right, they will be punished. Oh, yes. They most certainly will. But right now, Jennie needs to heal and come back to trust you. That may be very hard for her. You are correct. They brutalized her in a way no woman should ever be subjected to. But she was. Let us care for her now until she is better physically anyway. If not by tonight, tomorrow she may be ready to see you. We will talk more before you see her. For now, go take care of yourself and get some breakfast. Please."

Giles looked down at Isabella. Compassion and love in her eyes for both he and Jennie. Something he recognized as only a mother can do. He also realized she lost her daughter, and Isabella was not going to let Jennie's mother lose Jennie. Whoever Jennie's mother might be. Isabella had a new purpose and a solid lead on her daughter's killer. Giles knew to stay out of the way.

"Yes. Yes of course, Isabella. Thank you. I'll be downstairs for breakfast after I clean up." Giles turned and went downstairs and back to the barn. He stayed at the pump and cleaned up slowly. Exhausted from the trauma, he climbed the ladder and fell asleep in the hay, completely unaware of the cloaked figure that watched him. She put Jennie's journal down on the bale of hay by the door, descended the ladder in silence and slipped out the back of the barn and into the trees.

The Watcher was livid at the Mister. She now knew he was being fed information from a mole among them. Somehow, he knew about the grandmother's prophecy and came for Jennie. She couldn't prove anything yet, but she would get evidence and make sure Giles could find it in the journal. She disappeared into the trees, unseen and unheard, determined to avenge the women violated by this evil among them.

# 11

Thomas awoke to the aromas of Earl Grey, frying bacon and fresh baked bread. Hoping to garner a hot cuppa Earl he pulled on casual trousers and a loose-fitting shirt and padded barefoot downstairs and into the kitchen. Sarah was busy cooking for a household of men and didn't notice Thomas enter the kitchen. Thomas took a mug off its hook over the sink and turned to pour himself some Earl.

Sarah had the knife point at his throat. Thomas reflexively leaned backward over the sink, hands in the air. "Da field hands eat out da cabins. Who are you and what you doin in mah kitchen?" Pressing the knife point a little tighter in Thomas's neck, her eyes narrowed with her other hand on her hip.

"Captain Thomas Dewe. At your service. I think." Thomas stood waiting for the knife and the female fireball holding it to stand down. He realized he must look like a field hand…barefoot and unshaven. Her hand was as steady as her stare. Thank God.

"You kin to da Mister John?" Sarah was eyeballing Thomas nose to toes with extremely suspicious golden-brown eyes set in high cheekbones, and jet black hair in a braid that reached her knees.

"Yes, John is my brother. Richard and I have come to help John with the Tallywhoa. And you are?"

"Sarah. Her name is Sarah." John strolled in grabbed a mug and poured himself some Earl. Sarah still had the knife at Thomas's throat. "Sarah, this is indeed my brother Thomas. I have another wayward relative who may emerge today as well. That would be Richard. If you would be so kind, please ask all the questions you want while you have him at knife point, and he is still in need of a hot cuppa Earl." John sat down at the kitchen table. "A woman always gets more from a man when his throat is under siege." John spooned two scoops of sugar into his steaming tea. Thomas was seriously giving John that 'just wait till I can reach you, brother' look. "Sarah, the bacon is burning…"

Sarah immediately turned back to her bacon and pulled the pan off the stove. Muttering about 'men', 'my kitchen', and 'coulda say sumpin' she grabbed a cloth and took the kettle off the stove to pour Thomas a cuppa Earl.

"I sorry Mister Thomas. I thought you be one of them new field hands come in tuh other day. You sprise me, dats all. Breakfast is bout ready. Sit wid Mister John and I git y'all a plate."

Smirking, John sipped his tea as it cooled. Thomas was considering his retributive actions after breakfast. Dunk the man in the stock tank, put salt in the sugar bowl, or have Richard steal his woman. Realizing John seemed completely unattached he was down to the stock tank or salt. Sipping his Earl, he realized Sarah made a fine cuppa Earl. The knife at his throat moment set aside, they were off to a great start.

John couldn't contain himself any longer and burst out laughing. "Welcome to the Tallywhoa, brother. I am brimming with joy you and Richard are safely here. Please, be kind to Sarah. She is the best cook on the island as well as a native healer, and as you witnessed, the best security guard I've ever had. Her mind is as sharp as her knife."

Sarah brought two plates of steaming hot sausages, eggs, and potatoes to the table. Bread with pots of fresh butter and

168

honey were in the center with fresh fruits in a bowl next to the bread board. "Mister Thomas, more Earl?" Thomas nodded and Sarah filled his mug, and then John's.

"It's good to be here, brother. I've missed you and the fun we have when we are all together. It's been too long and far too many miles between us. Breakfast looks positively heavenly this morning, Sarah. Thank you."

Sarah started to respond when Richard stumbled yawning into the kitchen. Fully unkempt, he grabbed a mug, filled it with tea and plopped down at the table. Blinking he looked from John's plate to Thomas', breathed in the aromas and started in on his tea in earnest. "Damn, who's the cook? That looks wonderful. After my Earl, kitchen girl, but looks and smells wonderful, yes." Eyes closed he leaned back in his chair to waken slowly with his Earl. John almost choked as he stood to stop Sarah from whacking Richard with a large diameter cast iron skillet. One does not refer to Sarah as the kitchen girl. No. Richard ducked, spilled his tea and turned his chair over landing flat on the floor on his ass.

"Whut you mean 'kitchen girl'? I be da chef! I ain't yo 'kitchen girl'. Oh hell no." John caught the skillet in mid second-swing and took it from Sarah.

"Richard, meet Sarah. Chef of the Tallywhoa. Please refer to her as such in the future." Thomas was laughing so hard he had tears running down his face. John held his hand out to help Richard up off the floor. Richard swatted him away thinking 'Bastard. I know HE was the family bastard child…'. John went back to his chair while Richard recovered himself from the floor. Setting his chair upright he sat down in a bit more civilized manner. Muttering Sarah brought Richard a plate of hot food. Richard looked from Thomas to John and back again, watching for Sarah with his peripheral vision. 'Killer breakfast' had a whole new meaning at the Tallywhoa.

"Well, y'all gonna stare at it or eat it?" Sarah was still stating her authority and staking out her turf. All three men began to eat in unison. Turning back to the stove Sarah smiled a laughing smile. John knew all about her show of authority. They played this game every morning. They were each other's best company and dearest of friends. Richard and Thomas would eventually figure out they'd been had. Maybe. Sarah wasn't a slave or indentured servant. She was a 4' 10" mixed blood native, a free woman kept safe by John as his 'chef'. A perfect match they were completely in love, but by law could not marry. Everyone knew nobody cared. A meal with John Dewe at the Tallywhoa was always an experience. The Tallywhoa parties were legend. Sarah took their plates as they finished their meal and refilled their mugs with tea as the men planned their day.

Leaning on his elbows John sipped his tea while thinking out loud. "Now that you are finally here, I suppose the first order of business is to unload the freight you brought with you from England. I'll get Ian to get some men to unload the crates. I assume the manifests are accurate enough he will know where things go. The stable, the house…the mill?"

Thomas replied "Yes, everything should be straight forward. I would like to inventory everything myself before distributing around the plantation regardless. There is often shrinkage of goods during a sea voyage. I don't want your men to be accused of theft of something that never made it off the ship."

"Excellent thought. That could be disastrous. Thank you for thinking of the workers in that way. Too many owners don't care enough about their workers or use them to embezzle from dealers. I'll get Ian to organize unpacking enough for us to inventory and then distribute as necessary. Did you bring a money tree by chance?"

"Sadly, no. No money trees. We did however bring some fruit trees and grape vines. Time will tell if they survive. If they do, they will be a welcome addition to the kitchen gardens I'm sure. Rather mundane materials for the most part. Mother sent some fabrics and notions, and a box of books for the library. Children's primers for the orphanage along with some slate boards and chalk. A veritable cornucopia of necessaries from England as defined by mother."

John laughed at the image of their mother preparing the manifests and packing of freight. She would have been totally in her element. "How is mother, Thomas? We hear so little being so far away. And father? What news do you have from him?" John was suddenly homesick for his parents, at least contact via words of others.

"Mother was well when we left England. Sends her love as always with good brandy and a few gifts. I'll bring them down later. The last news I had from father was just before we left England. He is still in the Virginia colony establishing trade routes and providing protection as an officer of the crown to the colonists. There have been some nasty incidents with certain groups of natives further out in the territories. Building his empire, I suppose. He has an interesting plan to take the sugar crops to the colonies and not just Europe and England. The sugar he calls white gold. Claims sugar will create empires among the colonies by establishing the plantation business model there to grow cotton, tobacco, and lumber. I think he's on to something. Time will tell."

John nodded and stood saying "All things to consider over that fine brandy mother sent. How about we get on with the day starting with a tour of the Tallywhoa while Ian breaks open the freight? I'll meet you both at the barn."

Thomas and Richard went upstairs to finish dressing for chore work while John stepped over and wrapped his arms around Sarah. Nuzzling the top of her head he held her close, feeling her belly for the growing child therein. Smiling, the thought of his own child pleased him so much. Sarah was a strong, intelligent woman and would be a fine mother to this child of theirs. God had been kind to give him another good woman to love. The slave and indentured girls were nothing but a way to relieve his lust when needed. John was a good man who also had a dark and wickedly dangerous side. This morning he was happy to hold his woman and child to be and take his brothers out to see their plantation and create a strategic plan. John was euphoric. A last quick nuzzle, he snagged an extra sausage from the pan and was out the kitchen door headed to the barn.

Thomas and Richard met up with John at the barn. The large double doors were open letting the sunlight illuminate the boxes of freight. Ian and a handful of workers were prying the wooden lids off and comparing the contents to the manifest list.

"Ian, when you're done cataloging the inventory Thomas, Richard and I will check it over and countersign the counts. We can then begin distributing the materials to where they belong. Weezie should have the horses ready to go for the tour around the Tallywhoa. I expect to return in about an hour or two at the most. Any questions before we head out?"

"No, Mister John. Patrick is helping me with the manifests, so we have two teams going through the materials. If there are any issues we can discuss when you get back. Lovely day for a ride, gentlemen." Ian nodded to Thomas and Richard respectfully. "Take care at the creek. It drops off deep on both sides of the crossing just so you know. Do you plan to ride through the cane, Mister John? I mean, if you plan to leave the path, I think one of you should have a gun." Ian was still traumatized from having the big boar fall dead on top of him. Patrick had noticed Ian carried his pistol and rifle anytime they went to the fields since they found Esmerelda's body. Ian looked at the brothers to see if anyone had a weapon.

"Ian, excellent suggestion actually. Thomas do…oh I see you have your weapon. I'd say we're set then?" John looked to Thomas and Richard who nodded. "Let's see if Weezie has the horses ready."

The men went round the front of the barn to the stabling area on the side. Weezie had all three horses ready to go.

"Weezie, these are my brothers Thomas and Richard. Gentlemen meet Weezie my stable manager. She takes care of all the livestock at the Tallywhoa and is gifted with the horses in particular. My personal mount is Ms. Beulah. We've been partners for some time now. You're welcome to try out different horses as you like, but I recommend you consult with Weezie just for convenience. She breaks all the riding horses and knows them well. If we don't have anything that really suits you, we can look into something else in the near future. Barbados is a small island with a remarkably high-quality equine population. Weezie, who have you saddled for my brothers today?"

"Mister Thomas I have Tinker for you. He's more thoroughbred than cob. Moves well to a military trained leg and goes well with a light curb. Bold over jumps and settles well when halted. I think you will find him quite nice." Weezie led Tinker out of his stall. Indeed, he was a fine thoroughbred cob cross. Thomas knew any horse that nuzzles their keeper is a good one. So is the keeper, he thought.

"Yes. I think he looks like quite the nice ride. I like his looks. Healthy, strong, and intelligent. Soft eyes. Kind. Thank you, Weezie. Glad to give him a try." Thomas led Tinker out into the lot to mount. John had mounted Beulah using the mounting block by the drive. Tinker was already trained to lead to the block and stop. Thomas already liked this gelding. Nice. Kudos to Weezie!

"Mister Richard. I think you'll enjoy Miss Jezabelle." Thomas burst out laughing. ONLY Richard would get the mare named Jezabelle. Weezie and Richard glared at Thomas. Thomas stifled his laugh and turned his attention to mounting Tinker. Smart man.

"Jezabelle is a good mare Mr. Richard. Soft mouth, kind, and sensitive to your leg and weight. She can run like the wind and jump like a deer. Fast and surefooted. She's smart. She keeps herself safe and thus her rider, too. Beware to not make her angry. She will not tolerate being man-handled or abused in any way. She remembers everything. She will do anything you ask, as long as she knows what you want.

Jezabelle is one of a kind Mr. Richard. If she bonds with you, she will love you always. She is a partner, not just a horse."

Richard's eyebrows rose as Weezie led Jezabelle out of the stall and into a small lot. "Come with me, please, Mr. Richard." Weezie tossed the reins up over Jezabelle's head and led her to the center of the lot. Weezie walked back to the gate and left the horse standing in the middle alone. "Mr. Richard, please walk about halfway to her and stop. If she comes to you without being led, she's willing. If she stands there and looks at you, rests one hind foot, she doesn't care. If she walks around you and comes between you and I, well…let's hope that's not the case."

John and Thomas were sitting on their horses watching outside the gate as Richard walked halfway to Jezabelle. She turned to look at Richard and tossed her nose up and down a few times, just looking at him.

"Turn away from her Mr. Richard. Don't look at her."

Richard turned 90 degrees and looked at Weezie. After a minute or two he felt warm breath in the back of his neck, and a nibbling on his shirt. He smiled and stepped away a few steps and stopped. Jezabelle followed and stopped, nibbling his shirt again. Richard grinned and turned toward the mare. She put her face down for him to rub her ears. Yep, the mare owned him lock, stock, and barrel at that moment. Weezie giggled. John rolled his eyes. Thomas called to his brother.

"Richard. The ladies are always nibbling your neck. Why would your horse be any different? Hmm? No. Of course not. Come on let's go see the grounds." Thomas muttering under his breath to John about not encouraging Richard's predilection for being attractive to all things female.

Weezie held the gate open as Richard led Jezabelle out to the mounting block. He figured out her name was sarcastic. This mare was anything but a Jezabelle. She was loyal, kind, loving, and would dump your ass in a second if you were to mistreat her. Richard was already falling in love with

Barbados. Why yes, yes, he was. Watching Weezie walk back to the stable was a lovely sight as well.

"Richard. This way, brother. Lord…" Thomas shook his head while John was walking ahead on Beulah. Richard just smiled and ignored Thomas humming as he rode past him to catch up to John. Tinker broke to a jog to catch up to Jezabelle and Beulah. John was watching the way Jezabelle had taken to Richard.

"Weezie has told me Jezzie would find her rider on her own one day. And indeed, it seems she has. We will take the time to let you put her through some challenges. Weezie is right, Richard, Jezzie is really a special mare. Everyone loves her, few can get along with her…except Weezie of course. That woman steals the heart of every horse that comes into contact with her. I have reason to believe they nicker to each other about her in the night…seriously. 'No Weezie, no pony rides at the Tallywhoa'. I wouldn't even try."

Thomas was intrigued. "Tell me about Weezie. Is she a free woman, too?"

Richard added "yes, what exactly is with the women on Barbados? Even the European ladies are quite different here, behavior wise. They are quite independent. Downright strong willed. Is it my imagination or are these behaviors encouraged by all the plantation owners?"

"Brothers you are correct. The ladies on Barbados are independent, strong willed, smart, and if riled they are ruthless. They are what women should be. I pity English men who have never known one of these women. My wife, Anne, was such a woman. I wish you both could have met her. I miss her. I think I always will. That said my 'Chef', Sarah, is a blessing to me in so many ways. We would wed if we legally could. She carries my child by the way. I'm ecstatic, of course." John was smiling and giddy as he talked about Sarah. They were good for each other. Thomas and Richard could see that and were truly happy for them.

"Congratulations John. Good on ya, brother. Well done! Did ya hear that Thomas? We're to be uncles!" Richard was the kind of man that loves his ladies and is just silly around children. Other peoples' children. Someday, he thought. I will have a family of my own. When "she" comes along, he knew he wouldn't be able to resist her…the kind of woman John was describing made him smile. A partner for life, not a subordinate and not a servant. A vivacious, smart, capable person to match him wit for wit. Richard was daydreaming when they came to the creek and Jezabelle stopped short, almost tossing Richard over her head.

The stream was crystal clear and ran in bursts of faster water, and then slower stretches. The crossing was often dry or nearly dry. During rains the creek would flash flood in torrents that would cease as fast as they rose. The horses instinctively knew to slow down and walk carefully thru water crossings. Weezie was right. Jezabelle kept herself safe, and thus Richard was safe. Beulah and Jezzie paused and then crossed single file with Tinker coming up last. Safely to the other side the men came out on the path around the perimeter of the cane fields.

The lands of the Tallywhoa were beautiful. The hidden dangers commanded attention and respect. The stunning scenery camouflaged the reality of the harsh living conditions. The brothers all knew bringing the Tallywhoa into renewed prosperity was a daunting task. They rode the perimeter and along the cross sections of the fields. John pointed out the native vegetation and wildlife, and he explained the cycles of the plantation. The production of sugar from cane is arduous and labor intensive. Thomas and Richard both realized they had much to learn from John and the workers. Arriving back at the barn, Weezie and Patrick met them to take the horses in and untack them. Richard chose to take care of Jezabelle himself. He was quite taken with the mare. He was taken with the stable manager as well.

Thomas and John went back around where Ian and the workers had cataloged the materials in the freight crates.

Richard untacked Jezzie and was brushing her down when Weezie came in to take over.

"Mister Richard. How was your ride with Jezzie? Was she a good girl?" Jezzie gave a low soft nicker to Weezie and nuzzled her shoulder. Richard smiled. Yep. This was a good one. Horse wasn't bad either.

"Yes, Weezie. Jezzie is a fine mare. I like her. A lot. We got on splendidly. Your assessment was quite accurate. She will raise fine foals as well I expect. I assume John has a breeding program for the livestock well laid out?"

"Well, yes and no. We do, but I do most of the planning. Mister John seems to like the outcomes and leaves it to me. There isn't that much choice on the island to begin with. So, there isn't much decision making in reality. That said. Barbados has some really fine horse flesh to choose from…compared to what people first think we might have. Very few nags. It is too expensive to ship large animals to ship poor quality. I'm glad you like her. I'll make sure she is well cared for if you need to go assist your brothers with the freight."

Richard hesitated. "All right then. Thank you Weezie. I may bring her some carrots or sugar cubes later…if that's all right?"

"I don't like to give them treats on a regular basis. It teaches them to bite. Once in a while is ok, tho. She will be either in her stall here, or out in the bigger lot out back. Be aware that Beulah thinks she is alpha mare and wants her treat first. I recommend you catch Jezzie and bring her out of the lot by herself before you try to work with her. Funny but horses are jealous creatures sometimes. Not to worry. I'll see to it she is well taken care of. I always have." Smiling a wry smile, she took Jezzie's lead rope form Richard and led the mare outside to the lot.

Richard was watching them walk away. Fine set of legs on that filly. The horse wasn't bad either. Yes, they were going to be friends. He would make sure of that. Turning he went around the stable front and into the warehouse part of the barn to help his brothers with the freight. Thomas rolled his eyes at the expression on Richard's face as he walked in. John looked from Thomas to Richard and back again. Realization finally hit home with John and he flat cracked up laughing. Thomas thought to himself 'I'm living in a circus. MUST I live in a circus, Lord...just shoot me now...' as Richard feigned ignorance of the situation. Again.

The men set to distributing the materials to the appropriate workers and teams. The household goods were being carried in under Sarah's supervision. Thomas looked at her more closely knowing she held his brother's heart and carried his brother's child. John deserved this joy in his life. He had spent many years dedicated to making the Tallywhoa pay dividends for the family. It was time for him to reap the rewards, whatever that might be. Pleased to find good things in the future for his brothers and the Tallywhoa, Thomas set to do his part. Richard was thinking about Weezie. Evening would come and he would have to come see about Jezzie. Why yes, yes, he would.

# 12

"Mr. Giles?" A voice at the bottom the ladder was calling up to the loft to wake Giles up. Groggily he became aware of his surroundings and the voice of Joshua speaking to him. "Mr. Giles, Ms. Isabella is asking for you to come to the house. Miss Jennie is awake."

"Thank you, Joshua. Tell Ms. Isabella I will be there directly." On his feet and dressing as he spoke, Giles looked out the open loft door and realized he had slept all day. Evening was descending. As he reached for his trousers on the hay bale, he found Jennie's journal laying on top of them. He froze realizing he had not put it there. Someone had been in the loft while he was sleeping. He looked around the loft knowing the person was no longer there. He wanted to know how they came up the ladder without him knowing. Stepping into his trousers he scanned the room and realized there were dark corners and sections where the hay was uneven. It would be easy to hide there in the shadows. Had someone been up here when he lay down to rest? The thought made his skin crawl. Someone had indeed been up here, watched him undress and lay down to sleep. The question was, who? Giles picked up the journal to inspect it more closely. It was untied and fell open to a place held by Jennie's pencil. The writing was not Jennie's. The message was to him.

Stunned, he sat down on the bale to read the anonymous note.

'Ethan Fuller is not the head of the snake. When I know who killed Esmerelda and raped Jennie, I will give you the proof. For now, Jennie must comply, or they will kill her. The buck who covered Esmerelda and Jessie was Michael. If she bears a child by him it will be a slave by birth. This is how women are controlled on Barbados. Leave a message in the journal to contact me. Use the crate by the empty stall at the back of the barn. *The Watchers.*'

Giles starred at the page rereading the message repeatedly. This was organized crime. Sophisticated, cruel, and felonious. But why Jennie? What benefit could possibly come from brutalizing Jennie, forcing her to carry a slave baby? Jennie was a free woman but not wealthy, nor a plantation owner's wife or mistress, she was not in any position of power or decision making. Something was missing. He would find it. Tucking the journal inside his shirt he pulled on his boots and headed for the house. Jennie was awake and he must go to her.

Climbing down the ladder he took care to observe there was a crate by the last stall. It wasn't there earlier. He went out the front of the stable to be clearly seen as he headed to the house. He held his hand against the journal to make sure he didn't drop it and to make sure the watcher could see he had it. He didn't dare look around directly. He couldn't see anything out of place or unusual, but he could feel he was being seen. Hurrying, he quickly covered the space to the house. Entering through the kitchen he headed for Esmerelda's old bedroom. At the foot of the staircase Isabella called him into the parlor.

"Giles, could we have a word?" Isabella was standing in the parlor door gesturing for him to enter. He glanced up the stairs and then turned to enter the parlor after Isabella. She closed the door behind him. They were alone in the parlor. He was sure there were ears listening.

"Thank you, Giles. I wanted to let you know about Jennie. She is awake and has had some food, a hot bath, and has slept some off and on. She has been brutally traumatized and physically assaulted. Violently and aggressively raped and battered. The…stitching…was a message as well as a method of cruelty. Which has been removed while she was still drugged. I am quite sure Ethan Fuller is directly responsible and that his breeding buck, Michael, is the buck who raped Jennie at Ethan's direction. I do not understand why Jennie was targeted but clearly, she was. This was not a random attack. I also believe they were the perpetrators behind Esmerelda's pregnancy and murder. I do not understand their motives for any of this, or who is really behind Ethan's actions. I think Jessie was getting too close. But I have no idea how."

"Isabella, I agree. I have no answers and many questions. I will find out who did this and they will be punished. There is someone on Barbados who is extremely dangerous and is using the brutalization of women to get what he wants. We cannot look the other way. I will be most careful and will quietly piece this together. Oh yes, yes, I will. In the meantime, I must see Jennie. I realize she may not respond to me yet. She may blame me for not stopping her abduction. I did try Isabella…" Giles choked up and couldn't speak more, tears welling in his eyes again.

"Giles let's go up and see if she will see you. You may be what she needs. You are what she needs, but it may take her a little while to realize that." Opening the door Isabella led the way up to Jennie. Giles was close on her heels. He hesitated at the door when Isabella indicated he should wait outside for a moment. Isabelle spoke to Jennie, but Jennie was silent. Isabella motioned to Giles to come in and talk to Jennie.

"Jennie? Please speak to me, Jennie…" Tears were rolling down his cheeks in anguish as he knelt by her bed.

Jennie reached up to wipe his tears away. Giles took her hand and kissed it, tenderly and with all the love he could. Jennie was silently crying when he looked up at her. She reached for him with both hands and he took her in his arms as she sobbed silently at first, screaming in terror as he held her secure. The ladies left them alone in the room to heal together. They held each other for a long time without speaking. When they could cry no more, Giles sat on the bed holding her on his lap with his arms around her. Jennie clutched his hands so he could not let go.

"Jennie. We must talk about what happened. When you're ready. I must find who did this to you...and Esmerelda." He felt her tense.

"Esmerelda? What do you mean...?" Jennie was suddenly aware this was sinister and evil and not just about her. Giles considered what to say before he spoke. "Isabella and I believe the men who...assaulted...you were the same men who killed Esmerelda."

Jennie sat up and turned to face Giles. "Giles speak plainly. What are you saying to me?" Giles knew Jennie deserved the truth and he gave it to her. "Isabella is convinced Esmerelda was pregnant with a slave baby sired by Ethan Fuller's breeding buck named Michael. The workers who are caring for you recognized the thread and stitching pattern used on you as the same that was used on Esmerelda. The thread and pattern are used to identify women bred by Michael. Owners pay a lot of money to have him cover their women."

Jennie turned away in shame. Giles held her tightly. "Jennie, this isn't your fault nor was it Esmerelda's fault. There is someone to blame and I will find him." Jennie was crying silently again as she reached down, feeling for the stitches. "Isabella had the stitches removed while you were drugged, Jennie. That you do not have to suffer again. Ever."

"Dear God, Giles...they intend for me to be...bred by a ..." A silent scream came from her as she began to sob into his chest. Giles held her strongly, safe in his arms where she should be. "Jennie, cross that bridge when you get there. If you carry a child sired by Michael, it isn't the child's doing. You will be its mother and the child will be loved by both of us." Giles had a feeling deep in his gut she was already carrying a child exactly as they intended. He wanted Jennie more than ever. This was his woman and would not let anyone hurt her again. He just wasn't sure how. These were evil, organized, and wretched men. He swore to himself he would kill them all. Each and every one of them. Giles was seething with inner fury when Isabella hesitantly stepped into the room.

"May I come in, Jennie?" Isabella was being as respectful as she possibly could. She was far too familiar with the assaults on plantation women. Stepping to the end of the bed she placed her hands on the foot board as she addressed the couple. "Jennie would you like Giles to stay here with you? I mean in this room with you for at least a few nights? I can easily arrange whatever you are comfortable with." Isabella waited patiently for Jennie to think about her situation.

Jennie buried her face in Giles chest and nodded. Yes. Oh yes, she wanted Giles in the room with her. Giles smiled and mouthed a clear 'thank you' to Isabella and held Jennie closer. "Yes, Isabella, I will gladly stay with Miss Jennie as much as I can. I will need to see about Devlin and a few other details. I assume one of the workers or you can sit with her while I go to the stable?" Isabella knew there was more he couldn't say in front of Jennie.

"Of course, Giles. Jennie will not be alone for a moment until she is better. Just pull the bell cord by the bed when you need to go out, or if Jennie needs anything at all." Raising one brow, she sent the message she quite understood she had been put on notice to guard Jennie with her life. Giles had a reputation as a guard for the Colonel. She didn't have to imagine what he was capable of. Jennie had a formidable warrior tending her needs. Isabella fully grasped the ramifications. "I'll be downstairs in the parlor if you need me."

Giles nodded softly as Isabella left. He sat upright in the bed leaning on the headboard and held Jennie closely. She drifted in and out of sleep most of the afternoon. Finally, she slept soundly, and he was able to lay her head on a pillow and tuck the linens tightly around her. He pulled the bell cord and the upstairs maid came silently into the room. She sat in a chair within arm's reach of Jennie. She had a club she hid out of sight beneath the chair cushion. Isabella had made herself quite clear. Jennie would not suffer any aggressions at the Emerald Oaks again. Anyone who allowed it would be whipped and sold, or worse. Giles nodded approval at the maid and quietly made his way out of the room and down the stairs.

Isabella was sitting in the parlor with a glass of wine, starring at the fireplace with no fire burning in it. She motioned to Giles to come in and close the door. Sitting across from her, he waited to hear what she had to say.

"Giles, I am grief stricken with what has happened to Jennie. I truly do not understand why someone would do such horrible things to her. I don't think she was that close to knowing who killed Esmerelda and probably never would have found any concrete evidence. I think there is another motive that has not yet presented itself to us. When Andrew returns from the fields, perhaps he will have an idea. He left shortly after you brought Jennie in from the stables. I know he was angry, but he was absolutely terrified as well."

"I can understand his feelings, Isabella. Especially that all this has gone on under his nose, at his own home. Tell me what you know about Esmerelda. Where and when did they abduct her? I am assuming you mean she was abducted. What other similarities are there you can definitively identify? I agree there is something more to this with Esmerelda and Jennie. I understand slaves and indentured girls are treated as chattel for the law sees them as such. But Esmerelda and Jennie are...were...neither. Tell me everything, Isabella. This is not the time for feigning embarrassment or delicacies." Giles was quite forward with the matron. Isabella was a strong, powerful woman who also knew when to yield.

"Esmerelda was abducted at the Rosebud Cotillion last spring. We were unaware she was missing until we returned home and discovered she was not at home as was expected. Of course, we waited up all night, sick with worry, confident in our daughter's ability to take care of herself. In the very early light there was a knock at the kitchen door. By the time we got there who ever had knocked was gone and Esmerelda was in a heap on the ground. She had been drugged as Jennie was. Andrew carried her up to her bed. The women helped me undress her and discovered she had been assaulted and stitched, exactly as Jennie was. Esmerelda had been horribly beaten, whipped, burnt with a branding iron, too. I didn't tell her father about the stitching and the rape because I didn't want him telling his friends. My hunch was we would catch them if they gave themselves away. Clearly they don't care."

Giles had his head in his hands in dismay, fury in his soul. "Dear Lord, Isabella. What is this all about? This isn't just one mentally deranged man attacking random women." Giles looked up at Isabella. "This is a well-organized group executing planned attacks on targeted individuals." Giles and Isabella starred at each for a moment. "Isabella do you have any idea what this is really about? You must tell me if you do."

"I wish I knew. I have two ideas, neither I can prove. First, you are aware France plundered Antiqua last year. Is it possible this is the French creating havoc on the English plantation owners? We know they want Barbados as well. So, the French are a genuine concern. Second, I have a very different theory I believe you will scoff at, but hear me out, please. I think the natives brought here from Brazil in the 1630's to teach the colonists how to grow local foods are following some old prophecy their elders have taught them for generations. "Giles rolled his eyes and started to chastise

185

Isabella for speaking nonsense when she cut him off. "Here me out, Giles. Please." He sat back and listened.

"The natives were lured here from Brazil with promises of wealth and fortune and land of their own in exchange for helping the colonists facing starvation survive in a strange land. Of course, they were lied to, the land never really happened as it was presented to them. They have been angry ever since."

Giles nodded his head "yes, I am aware of the sensitive relationship with the natives up in the hills. There are things we believe are their doing but can never prove anything."

"Exactly. There is a very old woman they call 'the grandmother', their matriarch and group chief or leader of some sort. She has kept in contact with some of the wives of the plantation owners. I think she believes we are a matriarchal society as they are. Which you are well aware we are not." Giles silently challenged that thinking but knew better than to say so to Isabella. Irony. "The old woman is well over 100 years old according to them. I think she actually is. Her memories are far too clear about historical events to be hearsay. Regardless, she is their matriarch, holy woman, healer and apparently a very powerful shaman…a prophet." Isabella raised her hand as Giles began to protest. "Seriously, Giles, 'the grandmother' is the most powerful woman I have ever met. I think her prophecies have something to do with these assaults. The breeder buck Michael is a half-blood native. The women have interesting stories about him and why the maste's want him to cover their slaves and indentured women."

Giles looked at Isabella stunned. "Are you suggesting this is being organized by an old woman trying to keep her tribe from dying out? Dear Lord…" Giles stood up and went to the window looking out over the fields toward the hills. Yes, they could be watching everything the masters do, and with whom. He felt himself go cold all over.

"I realize how that sounds. I know the old woman to the point I have met her a few times and find what she says other worldly. But Giles, her prophecies spoken to me have always been correct. She warned the Governor about the fire in 1659 but he laughed at her. She warned the French would take over Antigua. No one cared then, but they do now. The prophecies of 'the grandmother' are eerily accurate, Giles. I've learned to pay attention to what she says. I think you need to as well." Sitting quietly, Isabella let Giles digest what she had said.

"What does she have to do with Esmerelda, and Jennie? I don't get that connection."

"I don't think she had anything to do with Esmerelda. I think that was Ethan Fuller exacting his vengeance for Esmerelda refusing her son. He wanted to ruin Esmerelda for any other man. At least in his eyes he achieved that. I don't understand why he killed her...unless Esmerelda threatened to expose him somehow. I suppose that is possible."

"But why Jennie? What has she got to do with anything or anyone? I don't understand, Isabella. Why was Jennie targeted? I don't think she knew enough or ever would to be a threat to Ethan Fuller. So why, Jennie? Something to do with the watchers? Yes, I know about your group."

"Giles I'm not sure. The grandmother came to our meeting the night before Jennie was abducted and prophesied that Jennie had been chosen. She said Jennie would be with child by the same time the next night to carry their heritage into the future as the old ones had ordained long, long ago. Jennie scoffed at the idea, quite sure that was not going to happen."

"So how did the grandmother know in advance? Or did she make it happen? There is more we don't know about this isn't there, Isabella? What do the watchers have to do with her?"

"She has been friendly to us and our causes. She has never asked for anything, just shares some odd predictions occasionally. Eventually they have all come true. In detail. If you are a nonbeliever in the supernatural, she will make a believer out of you. Seriously." Giles looked out the window silently thinking, not seeing anything in particular. "Giles?" Isabella wondered where he mentally went off to.

"Isabella how do you protect yourself from such people? Genuine or not they are very dangerous. I know there are things that happen in this world I cannot explain. The highlands are full of forces unseen and beyond our understanding. You do not have to convince me of that, I already know very well they exist. I also know that unless you provoke them, they are generally not out to be harmful to people though they certainly can be. In the highlands, as on Barbados, the actions of living people are the extension of their belief in such things. The spirits of the old ones have never harmed any living person. Is the motive simply revenge on the colonists for bringing them to Barbados and not living up to their promises?"

"I am amazed. I had no idea you held such beliefs. I don't know…the motive could be revenge, or to ensure their blood is passed forward perhaps? I rather wish you could meet the old girl. She is truly one of a kind. Quite probably the most powerful individual I have ever met. I will say I can't see her doing things to be hurtful. That is totally contrary to the relationship we have had with her. If she is orchestrating impregnating women…I just don't see that. No, I really don't see that. More likely she really was warning Jennie, not encouraging her. She came all the way down from the hills to tell her in person so…"

Giles cut her off "she came down from the hills herself? She was HERE? Well at the mill I gather, but still. How did she get there in the dark without any local person noticing? Think Isabella. Every detail matters."

Isabella was standing, her hands crossed over her abdomen somewhat intimidated by the irate and terrified scot. Giles was a very powerful man who had been overrun by thugs, and then, they handed Jennie back to him directly. These were calculated actions, he was right. "There was a younger woman with her that translated everything the grandmother said. I had never seen her before, but that means nothing to my knowledge. She wore a very old dark cloak. She would have been invisible in the dark, unmoving. And she was happy telling Jennie she was chosen by the old ones. Yes, she was happy, not gloating or mean. Truly happy. She seemed to know Jennie, she called her Maia, and had come to warn her, tell her the good news so to speak." Isabella had a strange look on her face as she contemplated the incident from a different perspective.

"Isabella, do you know who Jennie's parents are? I know she was raised at the orphanage. Do you happen to know? My hunch is there may be an answer there."

"No, I do not know. Father Michael may know. We should talk to him. He should be told about Jennie, too. The other girls from the orphanage may be in danger, too. I'll send Joshua to the rectory and ask the Father to come by as soon as is it convenient for him to do so."

"Actually, I think we should go to him. I understand you ride quite well." Giles was looking at Isabella with one brow raised, daring her to deny it. "I'll have Joshua saddle your horse. Let's go quickly before Jennie awakens. Make haste Isabella." Giles was directive and not taking 'no' for an answer. Isabella was out the parlor door and up the stairs before Giles was through the kitchen. Focusing on the stable and looking for Joshua, Giles didn't bother to look directly at the tree line. He knew the watcher was there. He would leave the journal with the day's findings when he returned from the rectory.

§

Finding Joshua as he entered the stable Giles quickly gave instructions and went to saddle Devlin himself. Joshua sensed urgency in Giles and had Isabella's horse ready in short order. She was walking into the stable as he led the horse out of the stall. Taking the reins from the groom, she turned and mounted and was out the door with Giles close behind. He started down the drive when Isabella headed west toward the cane field and the creek. She put her spurs in the horse's side and was off. Giles didn't have to ask Devlin to go after her, he was already close behind.

Isabella obviously knew where she was going. Giles had no clue and had concerns about the creek and fencing and…holy buckets she ran through the creek without slowing down. Devlin was on her heels and closing rapidly, but the water slowed him down a bit. Giles looked up to see Isabella pulling away toward the trees and thickets. She was mad, running her horse into the brush like that. And then she disappeared completely.

Terrified Giles put Devlin in a dead run to find Isabella. Coming up to the tree line where Isabella had vanished, Devlin put on the brakes as they slid down an embankment and out onto the road. Isabella waited until Devlin was safely on the road and let her dancing horse move out again in a run toward the rectory. Her route had shaved off at least several miles to the rectory. Devlin quickly caught up to Isabella. Isabella pulled her horse down to a slow jog to let him breathe before they arrived. Giles realized at that moment Isabella was riding Satan, Andrew's prized stallion. Quizzical, he thought about it and couldn't remember ever seeing Andrew touch the horse, much less ride him. Jet black all over you would not see him in the night.

"Giles you look surprised. Did you really think Andrew, MY Andrew could manage a fine stud like this on his own? Andrew is a wonderful man, but he isn't a horseman. He simply doesn't speak their language and doesn't care to learn. Satan is mine. Years of breeding the right crosses to get him. He is one of a kind and is siring wonderful foals." Isabella reached down and patted the big black on the neck. He clearly loved the touch and responded kindly to her every touch and whisper.

Arriving at the rectory, the church grounds keeper and stable manager took Devlin and Satan into the stable. Giles and Isabella knocked on the private rectory entrance. Father Michael answered the door.

"Giles, Isabella. This is a surprise. Oh dear, what's wrong Isabella? Do come in. Tea is ready." Giles and Isabella went in past the priest who looked about the yard before closing the door. Turning toward his unexpected guests he led them into his kitchen and poured three mugs of tea. Isabella spooned sugar for them and stirred, handing each man a mug.

"Father Michael, Giles and I are here with disturbing news. Miss Jennie was abducted and brutally assaulted, raped and...stitched...as Esmerelda was." The priest found a chair and sat down in disbelief. Isabella and Giles found chairs across the table from him. "Michael, we need to know about Jennie's parents. We are trying to figure out why someone would do this to her. What can you tell us about Jennie's family? You must tell us what you know."

"Isabella you know I can not divulge confidential dealings with orphans. Seriously, you know better..." Giles cut him off.

"Michael, you will tell us what we need to know. Someone is doing horrible things to the women on this island. I intend to find out why. Today. NOW Michael. What do you know?" Isabella had her hand on Giles' chest to keep him from going across the table and putting his hands around the priest's throat. She fully believed he would. She was right.

Michael's eyes went large. "Really Giles, that tone is not..." Giles was up and across the table in the priest's face.

"NOW, Michael. Or your second set of church records becomes available to the bishop."

Michael was ashen. How did Giles know about the second set of books? This was not good. Not good at all. He looked at Isabella who raised one brow in anticipation of his response.

"Very well, but you must never say how you came by this information. Seriously. If people believed I gave out confidential information at random, no one would trust us to

191

care for the orphaned children. Please. The children would truly be the ones to suffer."

"Point taken Michael, Esmerelda would agree I am sure. She loved working at the orphanage. I will always be grateful you let her work there. What do you know of Jennie's parents and family? We must know everything, Michael. No matter how trivial you believe the information may be."

"Jennie came to us from her father. Or rather, her mother's husband who did not want to raise another man's child. "

Isabella sat back in her chair. "Oh. That doesn't bode well for a marriage. Men can bed and breed a dozen illegitimate children, but God help the woman whose indiscretion is found out by her husband." Fury filled her eyes. "Who were her parents, Michael. You're hedging about their identity."

"Isabella, please, you don't want to know these things. Truly." Michael was trying to keep Jennie's secrets, secret. Giles was beginning to wonder what the real story was. Something was very wrong here.

"Isabella, Jennie's mother is dead. She died shortly after Jennie was born. Her husband said she took her own life out of despair for her wicked adultery. I'm not so sure but can't prove anything. My understanding is her lover wanted the child but could not risk destroying his own marriage with such a scandal. And Jennie ended up here with us permanently.

"Who was her mother, Michael? And who is her father still living, I assume?" Isabella was getting cold and angry. Giles was getting the picture Isabella wasn't seeing.

"Isabella, I think we should leave this alone for right now." Giles saw the relief on Michael's face and the glare of utter fury on Isabella's. Let Michael think about this a day…"

"Oh, hell no! These wicked men have killed my daughter and have raped and probably impregnated Jennie. I will NOT wait. I will know now, Michael." Standing and looking down at Michael, her hands on the back of her chair, gripping so tightly her knuckles went white. Giles tried again to reason with her. "Isabella, please…"

Isabella finally caught on.

"What are you afraid of Giles? Michael? Start talking. What are you trying to keep from me? This is about me somehow…isn't it?" Michael wouldn't look at Isabella. Starring into his tea mug silently. "MICHAEL, TELL ME NOW!"

"Please, sit down Isabella. I always knew this day would come. I'm glad Giles is with you." Michael had regained his composure and resigned himself to the reality that the time had come to tell Isabella everything. "What I said is true. Every word. Jennie's mother was Ann Dewe, John Dewe's wife. Her father is your husband, Andrew. They wanted you never to know, Isabella. What happened isn't what you are thinking right now I am quite sure. Ann Dewe was a native girl from up in the hills. She was quite a beautiful woman with wiles to make a man do what she wanted him to do. She could seduce the devil himself. Jennie is half native by blood. Andrew wanted Jennie so very badly he cried when he had to give her up to us. He carried her to us himself Isabella. He fell from grace, but he loves his family and children very, very much. You must never forget that. It almost killed him to let her go. Esmerelda would've had a sister in his eyes. Try to forgive him his indiscretion, Isabella. I truly believe he has been completely faithful to you before and since Ann seduced him. Andrew truly loves you so much, and yes was afraid he'd lose everything over a bastard native baby."

Michael turned to Giles and continued "John was furious at Ann. I imagine most men would be, but he held a silent, brooding anger that scared even me for Ann's safety. She was what she was, but she was still one of God's children. To be honest, I think John killed her. He has a dark side that we see glimmers of on occasion. But I am not sure of anything. Just a gut feeling. Ann hurt him terribly being pregnant with Andrew's child. I feel certain John still harbors deep pain about the incident. Would he go so far as to instigate what was done to Esmerelda and Jennie? I honestly don't know. But he has had quite a few years to brood over the outcomes."

Isabella sat speechless, ashen and stunned. Giles stood behind her looking at Michael shocked by what he had heard. The pieces fit. Damn but they fit perfectly. "I understand what you are saying Michael, but why would he kill Esmerelda when he had her abducted and covered by a very expensive breeder? That makes no sense. The glory would've been Esmerelda giving birth to a slave baby. Why kill Esmerelda?"

Michael looked at the stricken faces of Giles and Isabella. "I do not know why Esmerelda was killed. I do not know why Jennie was assaulted. We can conjecture or we can try to find evidence to answer these questions." Michael waited a moment for Giles and Isabella to consider options. "Let's not make any assumptions. For starters we should not assume the actions were instigated by the same person. Although it seems clear that Ethan Fuller is assaulting women in the most heinous way possible. Are these actions his idea or is someone paying him? He is brazen and believes he is immune from repercussions for these actions. Why? Is someone protecting him from prosecution? I could go on, but you get the idea."

"Father Michael, I think I need to speak to my husband. Andrew went out to the fields early and had not returned before I came here with Giles. I have questions about his whereabouts and his commitment to his family. I ask you to keep yourself in the wider community and listen. Whoever is behind these attacks will give themselves away. One of us will hear of it. Thank you for being honest with me. I will let you explain to Jennie about her parents as soon as she is well enough to know. She was Esmerelda's half-sister, and thus she will always be loved by me and Andrew. I regret Esmerelda did not know. She would have been thrilled to have Jennie as her sister. We must get back to Emerald Oaks. Jennie may be awake, and Andrew may have returned." Isabella and Giles started toward the door to leave.

"Father Michael, make no mistake I will have justice for all the women these men are assaulting. These heinous crimes must end. I trust you will cooperate with my efforts, and the efforts of all the women I work with. Please do not make me regret putting my faith and trust in you. You are indeed a priest, but you are a man first. Remember that." Isabella turned and left the rectory without looking back. Giles' eyebrows rose as he looked at the Priest.

"Michael do not underestimate Isabella. She is far more powerful than you understand. Her resources go beyond the realms you and I know. She is a woman, a matriarch, and she has support in communities you and I cannot. I trust you will heed her words and collaborate as she has requested. She is correct about one thing without question. It was of God's choice you are a man, and your choice to be a man of God. Thank you for your audience and information. I will be back if needed. You know how to find us if you have news." Giles nodded respectfully and left.

Isabella was already aboard Satan and ready to ride. The rectory stable hand was holding Devlin for Giles. He mounted in one motion and he and Isabella were on their way to Emerald Oaks. Isabella had fury in her eyes and a fire in her belly. A wicked combination in a woman scorned. Giles had hopes Andrew was a penitent man. The trip home was uneventful and direct. Satan could indeed hold his own in any circumstance. Isabella was a talented horse woman. If he hadn't seen her ride the stud himself, he would not have believed what she could do with 1200 pounds of hot-blooded equine in the dark of night through blinding brush and uneven terrain. Neither she nor the stallion faltered. Not once. The big black was smart, strong, and trusted his rider explicitly. Giles wondered if one or both of them could see in the dark as cats do. Clearing the trees and scrub they found the path through the cane field directly back to the stable.

Satan found her heels in his sides and disappeared into the dark before Giles realized what was happening. Devlin's head went up and off he went after them, catching up as Isabella slowed the big black to walk quietly into the stable paddock.

## SATAN

Hearing the big black snorting as he did after a run, wired to run more he was trotting almost in place as Devlin walked along. Collected and ready to go the stud was the most impressive animal Giles had ever seen ridden. Isabella, petite Isabella had him totally at her command with fine soft hands and quiet voice. Devlin just moved over a bit to stay out of biting and kicking range. The big black was a virile stallion after all, and he could have the whole path if he wanted it. Giles realized Isabella was the feminine match to the stallion. The thought of her feminine talents in other situations crossed his mind. He wondered if Andrew had a clue what he had for a wife. Giles looked up as Joshua and the stable hand walked out to meet them and take the horses from them as they dismounted.

"Thank you, Joshua. Make sure he is well cooled and fed properly when he has calmed. We had an excellent ride. Satan is truly a marvel. Don't you agree Giles?" Isabella spoke without looking at Giles. Satan walked away from her with Joshua. Giles had dismounted and handed the reins to the stable hand with similar instructions about Devlin.

"Yes, Isabella I agree. A delightful ride. A joy to watch Satan put through his paces. Truly a magnificent animal. Let's check on Jennie and see if Andrew is about yet. Thank you, Joshua, for taking such good care of Devlin."

"Joshua, have you seen Andrew this evening?" Isabella was ready to confront her husband.

"Yes, Ms. Isabella. Mister Andrew came in about 15 minutes ago. George was all lathered up like he been rode hard a good ways, too. Mister Andrew know better than to treat him that way. Just thought you should know. He listen to you about the horses and all. George is a good horse. No need to abuse him like that. He headed for the house."

"Thank you, Joshua. I most certainly will talk with Mister Andrew about George. He does know better than to abuse one of my horses. Oh yes, he does."

§

Isabella and Giles headed for the house. Isabella was firmly ahead and ready to take on a bear. She and Giles were going to find out everything there was to know about Andrew, John, Esmerelda, and Jennie. Giles was a nice back up but was nothing compared to Isabella in full glory. No man in his right mind would ever challenge this woman and not suffer consequences. Oh, no. Isabella was one hell of a woman. Giles had learned that in short order. She had to be exceptional to live the life of a plantation owner's wife on Barbados. He stayed clear of arm's reach. He suspected there were claws at the end of those lovely slender fingers inside the finely made riding gloves. Sharp claws that could rip out a man's heart while still beating. Smart man, Giles.

Entering through the kitchen they headed toward the stairs. Isabella saw Andrew through the open parlor door. She stepped into the opening and greeted her husband.

"Andrew, darling! How wonderful you're home. Let me go up and check on Jennie and change into more suitable attire and I'll be right down to hear about your day." Andrew smiled, nodded, and raised his glass of scotch in acknowledgement. Giles thought 'run Andrew, run for your life while you still can'. He nodded innocently at Andrew instead and was up the stairs two at a time to see about Jennie. No way was he getting between Andrew and Isabella gone she-cat on the hunt for a rat. Oh, hell no. Nope, Huh uh. Not happening. Smart man, Giles.

Isabella stopped at Jennie's door, knocked and opened the door far enough to speak to Jennie. "Jennie, Giles is back from an errand. Shall I send him in?" Jennie nodded. Isabella stepped aside as Giles went to sit with Jennie for a bit. Giles and Jennie didn't speak with words. He just held her closely and laid his cheek against her hair. Jennie responded with a death grip on his arms, secure in his presence. She fell asleep, unafraid in his embrace. Giles would have to wait to talk with her about what Michael had to say about her parents. Perhaps there would never be the need. Time would tell, and Jennie needed that time to heal. He stayed with her while Isabella changed into her plantation wife attire before returning to talk with Andrew.

A soft single knock on the door signaled Isabella was headed down to the parlor. Giles pulled the rope for the maid and gently laid Jennie on her pillows as the maid came in to take over her watch. Giles kissed her tenderly on her forehead and slipped silently out of the room and down the stairs. Isabella was already seated facing Andrew with a glass of wine being handed to her by Toby. Seeing Giles enter the room he asked "Mr. Giles, would you prefer scotch, rum, or wine this evening?"

"Scotch please Toby. Thank you. Three fingers." Giles stepped over to the sideboard and took the glass from Toby, his back to Isabella and Andrew. He could see Isabella's convincing gentlewoman expression in the mirror over the decanters of liquor. God she was good at presenting what she wanted you to see. He wondered if Andrew had a clue. Sipping the scotch, Giles casually stepped to the windows overlooking the cane fields so he could observe the tree line. He couldn't see anything or anyone obvious, but he knew the watchers were there and somehow would hear every word uttered in this room that evening. Toby didn't seem the character to be part of such a group. He would listen and try to discern who the mole might be at Emerald Oaks assisting Isabella in her works. Isabella was cleverly interrogating her husband, tho Andrew seemed oblivious.

"Andrew, did you have a successful day? How are things coming with the cane fields this year? I assume you have some status to report." Isabella sipped her wine and focused on the glass as if this was her priority. Andrew sipped his scotch and starred at the floor.

"Oh, well, yes I guess you could call it a successful day. The fields are maturing nicely considering their plantings. We should begin harvesting on schedule barring anything unforeseen. So far, the sugar ants are not on Barbados. I fear that eventually they will find their way to our island. A catastrophe if they do. A few hogs ready to butcher soon. I think we will have enough to share at least one or two with the orphanage again. I'll visit with Father Michael soon." He swirled his scotch and watched the swirls spiral from the center to the edge between sips. "How is Jennie this evening?"

"She seems to be much better than she was when we found her. I understand she has slept some and Giles has spent quite a bit of time with her. Jennie has been horribly traumatized, Andrew. She will never be the same. There is a high probability she may be pregnant as a result as well. Like Esmerelda was abducted, assaulted, and returned here to suffer the trauma inflicted upon her by a group of wretched men." Isabella was staring straight at Andrew. "What do you know of these men and these assaults? I am quite sure you know more than you have shared."

Andrew looked up at Isabella and reality hit him. She knew. He looked at Giles who was also staring straight at him. They both knew. Ashamed, he looked in his scotch and began to cry. "You both know what they are doing. Do you know why?" Giles and Isabella were silent. "I take that as a 'no'."

"Enlighten us, Andrew. Tell us why someone would assault with the intent to impregnate your daughters and kill one of them." Isabella's eyes were fire laden daggers. Andrew was ashen.

"I...who...how...God..." Andrew had his head in one hand, scotch in the other. Tears rolled down his cheeks. "You were never to know, Isabella. Truly I have never strayed but once in our marriage and I have regretted it ever since the moment it happened. I loved you then and I still do. I could not bring Jennie in our lives and destroy your...our...trust in each other and our family." Andrew stood and finished his scotch, setting the glass on the sideboard. "What do you want to know, Isabella? I will answer what I can."

"Tell me...us...what is really going on Andrew. We are not stupid. Esmerelda is dead and Jennie horribly damaged. Perhaps forever. It is time for you man up, Andrew. I don't care about an indiscretion with an Indian girl. Lord knows how many illegitimate half breed slaves we have that carry your looks. Yes, I know what goes on, Andrew. But this is different. What in God's name is going on?" Isabela was standing with one hand clenching her wine glass, the other in a fist at her side. Giles stepped within reach of separating them if he must, speaking to refocus Isabella's attention long enough to diffuse her fury. A little.

"Andrew. This isn't a game. This is criminal and deadly. This isn't about birthing an extra slave baby or two. Oh hell no. Even I can see that. What is this really about that someone has assaulted both of your known daughters, and killed one of them?" Giles was speaking to Andrew while watching Isabella. Andrew could easily provoke her into violence, and she could be lethal, he was sure of it. He couldn't blame her. Hell, he might help her. Andrew took a deep breath, looked at the ceiling and turned to face his wife.

"At first I thought this was some form of retribution over Samuel Fuller being spurned by Esmerelda. Ethan using Esmerelda to do so. Until Esmerelda was killed. I honestly do not understand why he would kill her after abducting her and…impregnating her with a native baby. Yes, I know it was Fuller's breeding buck Michael. Esmerelda isn't the first or only woman at Emerald Oaks to carry his issue. I am always present for the cover of Emerald Oaks women and know exactly what Fuller does, the way he marks them with thread and stitching. No different than other breeders, really." Giles blanched at the offhand reference, noting the slave women had no human value to Andrew. Isabella was clearly mortified. Andrew looked at them coldly.

"You want to know the truth; you are going to hear it as I know what the truth is." Andrew refilled his scotch glass and continued. "There are indeed…wretched…men in our world. I am always present at the covers to make sure my women are treated well. I do not allow the assault as Esmerelda and Jennie have suffered. Oh, no, I most certainly do not allow injury or trauma. The women I pay to have covered know why they are there and do not give them cause to rape or beat or whip them. They may or may not want what is happening, but they are not assaulted or abused. They are there for the purpose they serve, and they know what that is. Yes, some women want to be chosen for specific breeding. Most do want the privilege of carrying valuable get. Their lives are better when they do. They are stitched to make sure no other buck gets at them without evidence. I realize this is horrific to you Isabella, but in reality, it prevents the women from future assault by bucks who want to rut a woman without fear of impregnating her without permission. That happens frequently if they are not sewn down. Emerald Oaks has practiced this method for some years now. I'm surprised you didn't know, actually." Andrew sipped his scotch waiting for Isabella to respond.

"Dear Lord, Andrew. What have you become? You are telling me our daughter...daughters, really...have been assaulted, raped, and impregnated by someone wishing to destroy you? Us? Emerald Oaks? Ethan Fuller or John Dewe may be behind this?" Isabella sat down in front of Andrew as he continued.

"Yes, Isabella. That is exactly what I'm saying. The sugar plantations are part of a high stakes financial game between the wealthiest men on earth. The women required to run a plantation be she a matron, such as you and Esmerelda, or a slave such as Jennie or any other slave woman, mean nothing to those people. Absolutely nothing. It's wrong, it's horrible...it's the way it is. I don't agree with their means or desired outcomes and do not condone their control tactics." Andrew was nearing the bottom of his scotch glass again.

"Andrew, I think Isabella and I are well aware of the dark side of planation life. We are personally acquainted with the reality. The questions remain. Why Esmerelda and why Jennie? This has something to do with you and Ann Dewe and Ethan Fuller. We all know he is doing the abductions and using his breeding buck Michael to cover them. We don't understand why. Or maybe the question is WHO is behind Ethan's actions? All this over Samuel being spurned? I hardly think so. John Dewe gone mad over his wife Ann who was an adulteress? I really don't see that given he has a new woman who does carry his child. We are missing something, Andrew. What might that be?"

Andrew thought a bit before responding. "Hear me out before you nay say what I am going to share with you. I could be completely wrong I admit up front. I have a hunch the French taking possession of Antigua has something to do with theses assaults. Jennie and Esmerelda are not the only 'free' women to suffer Fuller's tactics with drugs and Michael. This has been going on a while now. So far none of the owners have been able to figure out who exactly is behind the actions. To date there are 7 women who have been abducted, raped, and impregnated by Michael in the last 18 months. Eight counting Jennie. We honestly do not know what is going on or why. I wish I did. I am hoping Jennie may be able to tell us something useful. We must put a stop to these actions." Andrew was clearly angry, frustrated, and disappointed in himself. "Isabella if I could change things I would. I can't undo what's been done."

Isabella stood again and addressed her husband. "Andrew, we have no need to discuss your infidelity ever again. We must focus on finding Esmerelda's killer. We must also see to it Jennie is well cared for. She could have been my daughter, too. I genuinely wish you had come to me when her mother died. I would have taken her and loved her as my own. I do now. We will explain the situation to her when she is ready to hear the truth. Until then, we will care for her and guard her safety. If she is with child, we will raise it as our grandchild for it is. Do not bring this up to me again, Andrew. I'll not be kind." Isabella left the room and went up the stairs to see about her daughter, Jennie. Giles raised his brows at Andrew, thanked him for the scotch and went out through the kitchen to the stables. He had a message to leave in a crate.

Making his way across the stable yard he noticed the birds were flying low toward the hills in flocks, and the frogs in the creek were loudly calling. Entering the stable Giles made his way back to the stall with the crate. As he stood writing hastily in the journal, the panel at the back of the stall opened slowly. A cloaked figure eased out in the shadows. She paused at the stall door and moved to leave through the back of the barn. Giles stepped between her and the door. Startled, she tripped over the hem of her cloak and fell backwards, her hood falling away from her face. Giles was standing over Elizabeth McKenzie. "Well look what the cat dragged in." Giles uttered to the woman splayed out on the floor. "So, this is how you get in and out of the house. Hidden passages in all the plantation owner houses I expect." Elizabeth scrambled to her feet and stepped back from Giles.

"Giles, you mustn't tell anyone I was here. Do you understand?" Elizabeth was shaken and afraid, hoping she sounded forceful.

"And why should I not reveal you to your husband, Mrs. McKenzie? I should think the Colonel would be most interested in his wife's whereabouts after dark." Giles smirked and stepped toward her, grabbing her arm to deflect her attempt to strike him. "No, Elizabeth, you will not assault me. You have no hope to prevent me from doing whatever I choose. I suggest you start talking and telling me everything quickly." Giles was glaring with fury at the woman. Elizabeth was clearly terrified and put her hand up to shield her face. Giles realized the woman had been abused to demonstrate such defensive reactions.

"Elizabeth. I am not going to hurt you. I am going to let go of you and you are going to tell me what you know about the assaults on the local women. I don't know who is behind them, but I will find out, and why. I am sure Ethan Fuller is the implementer, but as the message in the journal said, he is not the head of the snake." Letting go of her wrist and taking a step back, Elizabeth calmed considerably. "Now Elizabeth, tell me what you know. And tell my why the secretive journal messages?"

Elizabeth looked perplexed. "I know only what you do after hearing Isabella and Andrew speak tonight. But what journal messages? I have no idea what that is about." Giles opened the journal to the message left for him in the loft. "This message. You didn't leave this message as I slept?"

Elizabeth took the journal and studied the message for a couple of minutes. "I know nothing about this. I do not recognize the handwriting and have no idea who wrote this message." Pondering, she looked at Giles and said "Let's find out. Put in something no one else could know. We will find out soon enough who the person is when the information leaks out and gets to one of us. I have a hunch, but I am not positive. I think you know her, Ethan Fuller's daughter, Hannah. She is heavy with child and will drop soon. I expect another of Michael's covers. Ethan is a sick twisted man. As I understand, this is the third time he has used one of his breeding bucks to cover his own daughter. She hates him so much I expect she is the one setting him up to be caught."

Giles was pale with horror. "Dear God, Elizabeth. I knew Ethan was vile, but this...this is indeed sadistically evil. Do you think she would be capable of killing Esmerelda? Is she a threat to Jennie?" Giles turned toward the stall and leaned on the wall, suddenly nauseous at the thought of a father abusing his daughter in such a way.

Elizabeth said "I don't know Giles. Let's set a trap for this wayward watcher and discover who our infiltrator is." Elizabeth handed the journal back to Giles and they began to compose a message. 'No positive news. Will ask questions about hiring a breeding buck tomorrow. Breadcrumbs to lure the goose.'

Giles closed the journal with the pencil placed between the pages, tied the string around it and put the journal in the crate. He and Elizabeth left the barn through the back door. The wind had picked up and her horse was nervous. Giles helped Elizabeth mount up and watched another rider fall in beside her as she reached the tree line. Giles noted they were careful. He went back through the barn and out the front to be seen as he went back to stay with Jennie. Ian's hounds were whining and had their tails between their legs. Giles frowned and looked in the direction the dogs were looking. A storm front was heading for the island. The clouds were exceptionally dark and ominous. His spine tingled and the hair stood up on the back of his neck. Looking up he noticed a movement in the window. The maid was vigilant. No one would get near Jennie. But Giles was concerned. The Rain Birds were flying inland ahead of the impending storm.

**Rain Bird**
*Gray Kingbird*

# PART 2
# THE HURRICANE OF 1667

# 13

Thomas was in the library organizing the new books on the shelves George had cleared for them. He looked forward to reading them in the quiet of the evenings. Sarah's fine supper and John's wine were the perfect setup for an evening with a good book. Thomas smiled at the idea of sharing such evenings with a wife someday. Mary McKenzie came to mind as a consideration. She was smart, reasonably attractive, and well connected socially. And he liked her. He wanted to get to know her better. Meanwhile, he would assist John and Richard with the Tallywhoa and build something worth sharing with a fine woman.

John and Richard walked toward the stables together. John looked up to see the birds in flocks flying low and to the hills. He stopped to watch them for a moment, curious what had sent them flying in the evening. The horses were milling in the lot and pacing in their stalls. The dogs were hiding and whimpering. Something wasn't right. Richard noticed the animals acting odd as well.

"John, what's with the dogs and the horses? Is it the wind that has them nervous?" Richard wasn't sure what to think but knew the weather was changing.

"I'm not sure. But there is a front moving in. Look toward Bridgetown...you can see the dark clouds are hanging low and moving toward the island. A strong storm it would appear. We will shutter the windows directly." They continued to the barn. Richard headed for the stable and John headed to the warehouse area and slave cabins.

Richard found Jezabelle fretting in her stall as were the other horses. Ears twitching back and forth, pacing around and in general unsettled. Weezie came into the aisle from the tack room. "There's a storm coming. They know before we do. Been a long time since I've seen them this nervous. You can help me shutter and secure the doors and windows. I'm sure it will blow over." Richard nodded and began to help Weezie secure the barn. He and Weezie brought the horses in from outside and put them in the empty stalls, tying two smaller horses in stalls together to get every animal inside. John brought the sheep inside the warehouse and was shuttering the chicken coop when the rain began to fall.

The wind kicked up driving the rain sideways and bending the palm trees. Leaves and debris flew through the air crashing into limbs and buildings. The noise was deafening. The men knew they were in the direct path of a deadly hurricane. John sent Ian and two field workers to help George shutter the house. Richard was in the stable with Weezie when the winds picked up fiercely and John was out shuttering the slave buildings. John waved at Richard to stay in the stable until the storm passed, and he would stay at the cabins. Ian and the field hands were in the cellar with Thomas, Sarah, George, and the housemaids.

Richard and Weezie were in the tack room in the center of the stable. The exterior walls were made from coral stone with wood and stone combined for the interior framing and roof. Richard and Weezie soothed the horses as best they could, eventually retreating to the tack room to shelter themselves. They were both soaking wet and decided to remove their drenched top shirts. Richard noticed in the close proximity that Weezie was a truly beautiful woman.

With her hair down around her shoulders dropping to below her waist, her shirt slipping gently off one shoulder, he could see her delicate female figure hidden under her masculine stable manager clothes.

Richard had removed his shirt and wore only his trousers and boots. He had taken the lace out of his hair, letting it fall down below his shoulders. He stepped and reached for a blanket from the stack on the table. Weezie shifted out of the way as she felt the heat from his body almost touching her. She blushed as she turned away to give him privacy. Richard unfolded a blanket and wrapped in around her shoulders. Weezie startled when he touched her and could feel his breath at her neck. Reflexively she leaned into him as he held the blanket around her.

Richard nuzzled the back of her neck and side of her head when she yielded into his touch. He slid one hand inside the blanket to caress her. She closed her eyes and leaned into him closer. Weezie turned to face Richard. Smiling in the light of the lantern, she let the blanket slip off her shoulders and into Richard's hands. Nibbling and kissing his chest, Richard took her face in his hands and kissed her delicately, caressing her breast with one hand and holding her neck with the other. He held the warmth of himself against her and rubbed just enough she could feel the size of him. Slowly he undid her lacing on her shirt and pulled it over her head. He undid her trousers and massaged her with his hands. Richard nibbled her nipples and her neck. He wanted her to enjoy the entire experience. Both of them did.

When their love making calmed, Richard kissed and fondled her as the wind escalated in fury. A limb slammed into the side of the barn and startled the horses. They realized the storm was more intense than they had originally thought. They pulled their clothes back on and sheltered under the table. Richard and Weezie held close together wrapped in a blanket hoping the storm would pass quickly. Richard wondered if John had made it to the cellar with Thomas.

Richard and Weezie shifted the table to the other side of the room and remained underneath. They held each other tightly, terrified of the second storm wave that would finish off what the first wave weakened. The horses screamed as the wind collapsed the barn around them. Richard cried at the thought of what Jezabelle and the other horses were bearing through the storm. He knew much livestock would be lost or so severely injured they would have to be killed. Weezie clung to Richard terrified and afraid the winds would take them all away, never to be seen again.

## SLAVE CABIN

John was in the slave cabin used as a breeding shed. Built of coral stone it was the sturdiest and most wind resistant of the slave buildings. The cabin was built for privacy and ease of maintenance. As the winds kicked up John was well mounted into a slave girl. He had been waiting to break her in for several months now. She was ready to breed, and he always had first go at them.

This girl was particularly pretty, young and fresh. He would lock her in the shed safe from other men and cover her repeatedly until she was pregnant, or another girl caught his eye. This one was satisfying him nicely. He took great pleasure in taking his time. She had screamed with the first thrust. He was a well-endowed Dewe man and left the evidence every time he covered a girl. The pain was excruciating for her the first time. In days to come the pain would be less so.

John held her head down against the breeding stand. He wanted her too sore to walk the next few days and she would be. If all went as he planned, she would be ill with morning sickness about the time she was back to normal between her legs. Once he was sure she was with his child he would have her sewn down to prevent other men from mounting her without his permission. He would cut her back open as the baby was born. Depending on the delivery and health of the baby he would either breed her back himself, hire Fuller to put Michael on her, or turn her over to Moses or Patrick to cover her. This was business. Plantations required slaves and this was an island. The girl he was mounting had a sister he needed to break in soon along with four other young girls he was noticing. The thought made him more aroused.

The wind grew stronger and louder, driving his lust and frenzy. He shot his seed into her and after he withdrew, he pushed a wad of linen in her to keep his seed inside her. John stepped back and wiped himself with a linen rag. He sat on the bench behind the girl still in the breeding rack and watched her shake. Motioning to the other girl in the corner to cover the shaking girl with a blanket, he took out his flask and swilled a long swallow of rum.

After about half an hour he motioned for the girl to come to him. She was heavy with child and waddled over to where John sat. She fondled him into a second erection. John stepped up behind the girl in the breeding chute and pulled off the blanket. Removing the wad of linen, he wiped her off with the wad of linen and tossed it aside. Positioning himself he mounted her again. Aggressively he mounted her over and over. The girl had tears running down her cheeks from the pain and tried not to scream but failed. She didn't try to resist him; this was her duty. John covered her five times that night. When he was spent, he pushed another linen wad inside her to hold in his seed. Exhausted he lay down to sleep leaving her chained in the rack. The other girl pulled the blanket over her to help her stay warm.

Somewhere near midnight amid the driving rain and the roaring winds, John awoke to the sounds of the other girl in agonizing pain. Her time had come to drop her baby. Her water had broken earlier while he slept, her contractions had become incapacitating quickly. The storm was too fierce to fetch the midwife slave, so the girl was on her own. John pulled her shift up to check her progress to discover she was sewn down. He looked closely at the stitching pattern scar and realized this girl carried from one of Moses' covers. He had nothing to cut her open with. He didn't want to lose a good wench or a slave baby, but she was basically on her own unless the storm passed quickly.

The girl's contractions increased rapidly. John stripped her and made her squat with each contraction to help move the baby down. Her water drained out through the small opening left when she was sewn and down her legs as she walked or squatted. After a couple of hours, she began to be unable to walk with the contractions, the baby was moving into the birth canal. The girl was writhing in pain, screaming as the contractions pushed the baby out of her uterus and through her cervix. She began to push between screams and squats. She was straining and pushing trying to deliver the baby out of her body, but she was sewn shut. The baby's head bulged against the labia sewn together. Shrieking in agony, pushing as hard as her body demanded she repeatedly tried to push the baby out. The tiny opening began to tear as she pushed. The baby's head pushing through tore her open slowly and with difficulty, and with a final scream tore her open clear to her anus.

The baby's head was halfway out when it became stuck. The girl pushed and pushed with the head moving out to the chin and then receding back inside her. Even John knew something was wrong. He bent her over and she held the back of a chair as he wrapped his hands in linen cloths to grip the baby's head. As the next contraction racked her with excruciating pain she screamed and shook as she tried to push the baby out again. John grabbed the baby by the chin and the back of the head. He held tight so the baby could not slip back inside the girl. The girl was shaking violently from the pain and pressure. John told her to push harder and longer with each contraction. The baby was firmly stuck. John pulled harder as she pushed and tried to twist the baby around to free it from whatever was holding it fast. He felt something give and the baby lurched out a bit, one shoulder came free. The girl was screaming as he twisted and pulled the baby out of her. Finally, fully out, John turned the baby over his arms face down and spanked the infant to make it cry and take its first breath. The baby didn't move or cry. John rubbed it with a linen and spanked it again. Slowly the infant began to move. John spanked it a third time and the baby wailed. John wrapped the baby in his mother's shift and set him on the table.

The girl was pushing again, a second head was crowning. The second baby slowly began to emerge as she pushed. As the shoulders came into view the baby stopped. It was stuck. John went to pull this baby gently as he did the other but this one wouldn't budge. The girl was screaming as she pushed, John pulling harder he heard something break in the baby, but the baby slid out a bit. The next contraction he pulled hard again as she shrieked. It took three more devastating contractions to get the baby to move. John pulled with force and pulled the second baby out of his mother.

Trembling and bleeding she couldn't move from where she was, the girl watched john towel off the infant and wrap him with his brother. Another contraction racked her body and she expelled the after births from both babies. Torn inside and out, the girl was bleeding profusely. Weakly she slumped to the floor. John picked her up and put her on a blanket and pallet by the back wall. He brought both babies to her and set them to nurse one on each tit. She was not strong enough to hold them securely and John had to put them back on her tit repeatedly, but they nursed. The second baby had a broken collar bone but otherwise they seemed fine. He was concerned the girl might not live but did what he could for her given the circumstances and a blanket.

John released the girl from the breeding stand. She pulled her shift back over head with trembling hands and shaking all over. She gingerly made her way over to her sister and lay down beside her. Tears rolling down her cheeks she lay on her side holding the new babies in position on top of their mother. The wind was roaring more fiercely than John had ever witnessed and suddenly stopped. The eye of the hurricane was passing over them. He ran to the door and managed to pry it open just enough to see devastation outside the shed. The house was gone. The cellar doors still held flat and the stable was fallen in on the windward side. The loft was gone entirely. The winds began to pick up from the opposite direction as the eye of the storm moved past the Island. Praying the cellar was not flooded and the tack room walls strong John secured the door to the shed at the winds hit them full force again.

§

Jennie was sleeping and Giles was sitting in a chair next to her bed reading a book when the winds hit gale force velocity. Giles carried Jennie downstairs and into the cellar with Isabella and the maids. Giles went outside to safeguard the horses and cattle and secure the windows and doors on the buildings as the storm gained strength. Once Toby and Andrew were satisfied they had done all they could they returned to the cellar and the slaves went to the bigger underground stores taking sheep and dogs with them. None of them slept well, the wind howling and rain pounding the roofs and windows.

They could hear the windows breaking and roof being torn off the house above them. They held each other close as Isabella fingered her rosary in silence. Andrew couldn't sit still. Fretful he paced and sat. Stood and paced. He put his hands over his ears and tried not to hear the winds destroying his home. As the eye of the storm passed over the island the silence was deafening. Andrew started up the steps to look at the damages. Giles stopped him.

"Andrew, wait! The hurricane has not passed over us entirely yet. It will be several hours…morning before it will be safe to go out again." Giles was standing with his hand on Andrew's shoulder, imploring him not to risk going out. Andrew hesitated. Frustrated he went back to where he had been seated.

"Yes, of course. Thank You, Giles. The waiting…is so difficult." Andrew had his head in his hands again. Isabella was watching him in the light of the lantern. Her husband, the adulterer. Her husband, the man whose behaviors may have brought about the death of her only daughter.

"Do not fret Andrew. We have survived storms before. We will again. We will rebuild again. We must. We must also be prepared to assist our neighbors and loved ones to help them recover from this disaster, too." Fingering her Rosary harder and faster she was saying what the others needed to hear and she wanted to believe. The beads were getting shiny from the oils on her fingers. The small gold crucifix glittered in the lantern light, a genuine light of hope in the darkness as they felt the foundation of the house tremble.

The roof was torn off and the walls ripped apart. It sounded as if canons were blowing the house to bits. Terrified they huddled praying they would not be sucked out of the cellar as the storm passed over them. The maids were crying silently muttering in a language the others could not understand. Giles held Jennie tightly, his chin on the top of her head, eyes closed as he prayed for deliverance for them all. The storm raged for several more hours as it passed over the island. About dawn the winds began to lie down and the rains let up. The cellar was wet but didn't fill up entirely.

§

Ethan Fuller was on his way home from a Bridgetown breeding when the winds and rain became unbearable. Ethan, Samuel, two henchmen, and his buck Michael were approaching the rectory when the full force of the storm set upon them. They managed to get their horses inside the stable and ran inside the orphanage as the stable manager was ushering the children and aides into the cellar. Among the aides were the McKenzie twins who were there to teach the children reading skills that week. Last in line was Mary McKenzie holding the hand of a young boy and carrying his toddler sister.

The stable manager held a torch to get them all safely into the cellar. He knew the routine to safeguard the children in inclement weather, including a hurricane. As the door flew open and Ethan and his group entered, the stable manager motioned for them to shut the door and quickly join them down in the cellar. Mary McKenzie handed the young boy down to another of the women aides, and then his young sister. She went down the stairs with the stable manager behind her.

Ethan recognized her and called down to the stable manager he was going to make sure the building was secure. Samuel looked at his father suspiciously, knowing something was not right. Ethan grabbed his son by the sleeve and dragged him away from the cellar door.

"Do as I say, boy." Motioning to the men they started away from the cellar. Once out of earshot Ethan found what he was looking for, an empty room he assumed belonged to the stable manager.

"Go back to the cellar and get the girl who went down last. Alone if you can or bring the stable manager with her. He won't be a problem. Quick. This is business Samuel. Time you learned."

"Father, what on earth…"

Ethan cut him off curtly "NOW, BOY! QUICK AS I SAY!"

Samuel knew his father was an awful man and was terrified of him. He made his way back to the cellar and called for the stable manager to bring the girl with him. He said his father had found a girl child that needed her attention immediately. All lies, but he didn't know what else to say or do.

The stable manager made his way up the ladder with the torch and helped Mary up after him. They followed Samuel down the hallway to the manager's quarters. The henchmen quickly overpowered the stable manager and Mary. Ethan was smiling his evil smirk as he looked her over, up and down.

"Yes. She is the perfect choice. The Lord giveth and I taketh away." Ethan's laugh was cold and hard as steel. Samuel was beginning to understand what was about to happen.

"Father, NO! You cannot do this to her. She is a free woman of gentile birth. You cannot do this to her. NO!" Ethan turned on his son snarling.

"Watch and learn, boy. Business is business. When the Lord provides you the means to give you what you want, you'd best take them. You won't get a second chance. Now. Stand over there in the corner. Watch. And. Learn." Ethan took Mary's hands and pulled her over to the table in the center of the room. "I changed my mind, boy. You must learn to manage your investments firsthand. Over here. Hold her hands behind her like this." Ethan pulled Mary's hands over her head and behind her, forcing her to lie back along the 8-foot dining table. Mary's screaming angered Ethan and he put his hand over her mouth, telling her if she continued to scream, he would cut her tits off. Mary ceased screaming even though she was terrified. Samuel pulled her backward until her ass sat at the edge of the tabletop and held her hands down while his father tied them to the legs at the far end of the table. The stable manager struggled to get loose and help her. He was grossly overpowered. The men enjoyed making him watch.

Ethan instructed Samuel with gestures to pull up Mary's skirts and remove her shoes, pantaloons, and stockings. Next, he undid her top lacings to release her breasts and began to fondle them. Terrified, Mary tried to kick Ethan which was a mistake. Ethan merely gestured to the second henchman to hold one of her legs while he held the other. Completely restrained both men used one hand pinching and twisting her delicate places until she screamed. Ethan massaged her gently to arouse her to accept Michael when he was ready to mount her. Once she was ready, he motioned to Michael.

Samuel couldn't help but feel sick at what his father was doing to this girl. He couldn't stop what was happening and much to his anger, he himself developed an erection and lust to take her himself. Ashamed of his own reaction, he looked away and tried not to listen as Michael stepped up to the girl and prepared to mount her.

Michael gently caressed Mary. He didn't like being hurtful if he didn't have to be. He knew his job, but he saw no reason to damage a woman and make her hate men. Ethan and the henchman were stimulating her nipples and restraining her legs for him to have easy access to her. He was throbbing but he still made it a point to be gentle.

Mary was crying yet responding physically to the stimulation. Michael gently positioned himself and slowly began to seat his penetration. Once he was ready, he placed both hands on her hips and thrust. Mary screamed as he penetrated her fully. She would remember her first cover for days to come and would most likely find herself with child as a result. Ethan, Samuel, and the henchmen twisted and pinched as they held her down.

The pain was unbearable at first. Bleeding and bruised Mary couldn't breathe. After a bit she began to lust herself. She didn't understand what was happening to her, but she reveled in the new feelings and couldn't help but want him more, harder, deeper. Covered in sweat and moaning with pure desire, she felt herself short of breath and racing toward a goal.

The winds were picking up and they needed to get back to the cellar. Ethan knew what Michael was preparing for the girl in the end. Michael was unusually lustful and he mounted her viciously. They could all tell Mary was reaching an explosive climax. As her climax waned, the pain from the virgin cover came back with a vengeance. Michael could hold back no longer, he held himself tightly inside her out of breath and feeling he had emptied himself.

Michael stepped back as Ethan began to sew Mary down. He smiled wildly knowing the great Colonel McKenzie would have to bear the thought his daughter had been covered by Michael. The child she would carry would be less than a slave, a disgrace to the entire family. Mary was ruined for marriage to any decent man. Nothing could please Ethan more. Sewing Mary down he took great pleasure in her screams as he did. Ethan took extra stitches to make sure it was perfect. There would be no doubt who took his daughter's virginity and covered her with a half breed native buck.

Samuel untied her arms and Ethan pulled her dress down over her bleeding crotch as he scooted her off the edge of the table. The pain was excruciating. She fell to the floor in agony between her legs. Ethan and Samuel picked her up and made her walk back to the cellar, blood and bits of semen running over the stitches and down her legs. Mary was shaking and in tears as she was pushed down the cellar stairs. Ethan and his men tied the stable manager to a rack of food in the cellar and lay Mary on a stack of food sacks at the back. Ethan sat next to her crotch, grabbing her whenever she tried to move away or speak. She quickly learned to submit and be silent. Exactly what Ethan intended.

Ethan was concerned about the storm's magnitude and duration. This was no ordinary tropical storm. This was a full force hurricane that would decimate the island. Ethan figured if he died tonight, he would die happy having had Michael cover Mary McKenzie. What serendipity. What an opportunity to hold the advantage over the colonel. He smiled and grasped her crotch, squeezing her stitches just enough to send raging pain through her. Repeatedly he antagonized her though the night. As morning came and the storm began to subside, he reached under her skirts and felt her badly swollen, horribly bruised crotch. He pinched her nipple with one hand and grabbed her crotch hard with the other to awaken her and inflame her swelling around her stitches two-fold. Mary gripped her hands into fistfuls of her skirts to avoid screaming, letting Ethan do as he wished knowing she could not stop him.

# 14

After several hours the winds stopped, and the rain lessened. The hurricane had passed. The survivors crept out of their hiding places to survey the damages. Thomas and George could not push open the cellar doors. There was an enormous tree limb down across the door, pinning it down. The cellar had about a foot of water in the bottom but all the inhabitants, human and canine were fine. Thomas knew they would have to wait until someone came by to free them. Surely Richard or John would be out and about soon. The horror of the reality they may all have perished outside of the cellar sank Thomas to his knees. Wait was all they could do for now. They waited.

Richard and Weezie crawled out from under the table to find the tack room held secure due to the debris that fell upon it when the roof and loft were blown away. Crawling out they shoved away timbers and boards. They came into the aisle area to discover the horses still in their stalls. Soaking wet they had superficial cuts from the flying debris. Tiger had a splinter of lumber impaled in his neck. Richard had doubts they could save him, but he knew Weezie would try. Beulah and Wiley were huddled and shaking. Beulah had a non-fatal gash on her head where a falling timber struck her.

The mules were clinging to each other tails to the wind. Tinker was down in his stall shaking. Richard couldn't see any obvious injuries until he lifted his head and tried to roll up on his belly. A gash had opened his gut and exposed his entrails, falling out on the floor. Weezie gasped but knew they would have to put him out of his misery. He would not survive no matter what she did. Sick at heart over the injuries, grateful for the uninjured, Richard made his way outside the barn to find the house was completely demolished, flattened to the ground and mostly blown away.

He slogged his way to the slave cabins and found most of them were gone completely as well. The breeding shed was still relatively intact. Calling for John he heard him reply from the shed. Richard pushed away the limbs and debris from the door and pulled on the door as John pushed out. The door scraped open just enough for John to step outside to survey the carnage.

"Dear God. Oh no. NO, NO! No, dear God NO!" Hands on his head John was frantic to find Sarah and the others. Richard heard the newborns whimper and went in the shed to see who else was there. The girls huddled on the palette. The girl with the new babies stared out though barely living eyes as her sister held her and the babies to keep them warm. Richard could see the sister had bloody semen running out of her and pooling on the floor. 'Good Lord, what had John done to them' Richard calmly told the sister to keep the babies and their mother as warm as she could. He would be back as soon as possible to help them. The sister nodded with tears rolling down her cheeks. Richard turned and, in his haste, ran into the breeding stand. Blood tinged, semen soaked linen rags scattered about told the story. Richard felt nauseous at the realization of what the slave owners did to keep their slave holding growing. John was among them, but by no means the worst of them. He could hear John calling for Sarah and Thomas.

Richard squeezed back out the door of the shed to help John find the others. The slave cabins were gone, almost no trace at all. The dogs were missing as well, but he could hear Mammy and Duke whining at John's calls.

"John be quiet a moment. Listen. The dogs…" John stopped to listen and sure enough that was Mammy and Duke! They were in the Cellar. The doors were pinned shut under an enormous tree limb. Richard and John ran to the cellar calling for Sarah and Thomas. "Thomas, Sarah are you all right? Who is in the cellar with you? Thomas? Sarah?"

Thomas replied "Yes, yes we are all fine! Wet and cold but we are all fine. Sarah, George, and the maids are here with me. Oh yes, Mammy, Duke, and Old Blue. Ian brought them in with him just as the wind hit gale force. Can you get the limb off the doors?"

Richard was already on the way to the barn to get the mule.

John explained the scene. "Richard has gone to get Wiley to pull the limb off the cellar doors. Weezie is tending the horses. We will check on the sheep and other livestock once we have you out of the cellar. Thomas?"

"Yes, John, I understand."

"Thomas, the house is demolished. Almost entirely gone. Debris is everywhere. The breeding shed is still standing. There are two girls in there that need Sarah's help as soon as she can get to them. One has new twins born in the storm. I don't think she will live unless Sarah can help her quickly. The birth was…horrible…"

"I must go see about the other slaves and livestock near the house. As soon as we get you out. I assume the other slaves are drowned or they went into the hills to hide. They know how." John stood up and surveyed the horizon. The visible cane fields were flattened where the cane was ripped out and blown away into heaps along the tree line. He could see the creek had turned into a raging river with mature trees washing down with the torrent. John was ashen as the reality of the devastation hit home. Richard had arrived with Wiley harnessed with chains to pull the tree limb off the doors.

Weezie was at Wiley's head as Richard worked the chains. Wiley slipped in the mud and went to his knees twice before he could break the limb loose from the door and mud holding it in place. The big draft mule took hold with his hooves and leaned into the collar pulling the limb free. Wiley kept going until Weezie told him to whoa. John and Richard were flat in awe of what Weezie could do with equine. They both knew that mule would never have kept trying for them. Weezie hugged the mule and he nuzzled her hip. She backed him up a step to take the tension off the chains and Richard released the chains from the tree. Weezie led Wiley back to the remains of the barn.

Richard and John lifted the cellar doors open. Thomas and George helped the ladies climb out of the cellar followed by Ian and the hounds. They were all speechless at the devastation of the Tallywhoa buildings. Sheep were running loose in the yard and some were still trapped in the ruins of the warehouse. As they stood not knowing what to do first, the slaves began to reappear from the hills. Wet and bedraggled they were all accounted for and relatively unscathed. Moses and Patrick had taken them to the caves when the birds flew out and the dogs began to whine. Moses had been through hurricanes before and knew the signs.

## THE CAVES

Sarah grabbed the midwife slave and ran to the breeding shed to tend the girls there. Sarah came back out calling for Patrick to bring clean linens and more blankets. Start a fire going for hot water and soup. The slaves knew what to do and set to the business of recovery. Moses and the other men began to inventory the livestock for injury or missing. Those that were uninjured or salvageable were gathered up in one area. The animals that could not be saved were humanely killed. The cane fields were gone or so damaged there would be almost no harvest. The kitchen gardens were seriously damaged but not as much as the cane fields. The gardens would return in a few days or weeks.

Once the livestock was relatively settled, temporary structures were put together to keep the worst of the rain out until reconstruction could commence. All said, the Tallywhoa people were unscathed, there was food to be had, and shelter was within reach. The men knew the rest of the island was probably not so lucky. The plantations closer to sea level would be drowned in the storm surge. Tomorrow one of them would ride to Emerald Oaks and the Rectory to check on others.

Moses knew there would be masses of deaths. He had seen the aftermath of a major hurricane once before as a child. This storm was the fiercest he could remember. Coming down the hill from the caves he and the others could see the ruination of the cane fields and other crops. Dead livestock intermingled with wandering strays were scattered across the fields. The creeks were rushing torrents with carcasses washing down to the sea. In a few days the smell would be suffocating, clean water difficult to find in the lower areas of the island. Moses grieved for the loss may families would experience both material and human. He bent down to pick up a shirt that had blown out of the house when the winds took the roof off. Close by the others were gathering what they could carry as they trudged through the mud toward the house. Dread written on their faces as they slowly came into view of the devastation, activity had already begun to cleanup and rebuild. The able bodied joined in without hesitation. They had to work as a cohesive unit to survive.

John, Thomas, and Richard organized groups to collect the debris, sort it for useable materials, and begin constructing temporary structures for people and livestock. Ian and Weezie had tended the horses and sheep. The chickens were scattered about and would come home to roost at dusk if they were able. The hogs would be found and herded back in increments using the dogs and men to group them up. They would use feed to lure them into the catch pens. Some would avoid capture all together and become feral if not shot first. There would be plenty of meat to eat. Vegetables would take some time but could be replanted.

The immediacy was to create sanitary waste sites and water boiled to kill any disease or parasites. The biggest threat in the next few weeks would be toxic water and diseases such as cholera, typhoid, and dysentery. The unprepared and ignorant would die in droves. With luck the Tallywhoa would survive and rebuild to thrive once more. John, Thomas, and Richard were determined they would.

Thomas was concerned about the state of the island. He voiced his concerns to John and Richard. His military officer training was kicking in, to their advantage.

"I'm sure you both realize the entire island is a wasteland just now. Looters and people injured and desperate are likely to show up sooner rather than later. I want to check in with the parish priest and get a feel for what to expect. Father Michael is a long-time resident of Barbados and will have insights on how to prepare and proceed with reconstruction. We need to take care of us and the Tallywhoa. We must also take care of our neighbors, literally and figuratively. John, can you spare Patrick and Weezie for a day or two? I'd like to take them with me to the parish to check on the priest and the orphanage. I have a bad feeling about the children's welfare just now."

John considered for a moment, taking mental inventory of who would be left at the Tallywhoa. "Yes, Thomas, I think you can take them with you for a day or two. Include a couple bucks for strong backs and a couple of the slave girls, too. I think you may find need of them. We will continue as we are. By the time you get back we will have shelters put together for everyone. Extra space will be available for the children if the orphanage is uninhabitable. Take the mule and cart, and chains. Patrick and George managed to set it on its wheels, and it seems ok. I'll get the women to gather up supplies for you. Anything else?"

Richard considered the conversation and added "Take two of the dogs with you. They will respond to Weezie or Patrick if Ian isn't there. You may need them for security if things are as desperate as we believe they may be." Looking from John to Thomas who were both looking at him John said "seriously, brothers. The most dangerous days may yet follow. I am deeply afraid. Entire fortunes have been lost in one day. The wicked will be upon us quickly to victimize the weak."

Neither John nor Thomas had ever heard or sensed Richard as afraid of anyone or anything. Both had missed the highly intelligent thread in his being that could assess and analyze a situation for threats and advantages. Their brother was not the careless free-wheeling ladies' man they had always believed.

"What? Do you both think I'm daft? You've both underestimated me and underrated my value always. You've both been wrong. Remember if you can miscalculate my metal, so do my enemies. These scars on my back are not from foolish endeavors, brothers. Oh no. You've always assumed. You've always assumed wrongly. Take the men you need, Thomas. And the mules and cart. You will need them to transport the children to the Tallywhoa. We will be ready for your return." Richard turned from his brothers and commenced organizing the party to the parish. Thomas and John were speechless as Weezie and George headed for the stables to organize the horses while Ian went to fetch Patrick and some help as John requested.

Ian found Moses first and asked him to take over for Patrick in marshalling the groups at the Tallywhoa after he chose the men and women to travel to the parish with Thomas. Moses immediately set to pull together the team and the groups to set to reclaiming and reconstruction. The young bucks who thought Moses was old and useless quickly learned otherwise. A lifetime of hard work made Moses smart and strong as an ox. His grief at the thought of his children scattered around the island being in harm's way set him to master the uninvited hardships with vigor.

Moses knew there was one way to overcome natural disasters. Get the work done as fast and thoroughly as possible. Take care of everyone, for they are all our relations. *Metakuye Oyasin* the old ones from the north said in prayer. He had heard this from his great great grandmother when he was a boy. Moses prayed for the people as he worked. He prayed to the ancestors, the old ones, and the creator for all the people, as he labored beyond his physical capacity. His spirit was driven with love. The young bucks and girls followed his lead without question. They learned how to love unconditionally that day amid complete devastation. Moses stood tall as the group left to go to the parish. A dark feeling held him in grief as he watched them go.

§

Stiff but unharmed the group began to stir. Giles and Andrew climbed up the steps to open the doors above them. After some struggle they managed to force open the door, the debris on top of the door falling away as it opened. Giles was first to exit the cellar with Andrew close behind him. Both men stopped short and looked around completely stunned. There was nothing left of the house above the stone knee walls. Debris littered the area. The stable roof and second story were gone as well. The horses were still tied in the stalls or wandering about the yard. Giles would have to assess the damages and injuries as he could. The slave cabins were obliterated except for the few stone walls incorporated into the sheds. Sheep were milling about in the yard and the remaining chickens had feathers missing.

Isabella, Jennie, and the others made their way out of the cellar to witness the carnage as the slaves began returning from the caves in the hills. Isabella went into crisis mode and began making assignments.

"Giles, you and Andrew check the horses and livestock. Joshua you and Toby find the carpenters and organize clearing of debris and building temporary shelters." Realizing the fireplace that never held a burning fire still stood, she directed Cook to start a fire in the fireplace and set a cauldron of water to boil. "Andrew, please organize food gathering and brought to cook. We will all be eating from the same pot tonight." Looking about at the carnage and the still living she said to all "we are blessed by the hand of God, for we live still. Houses can be replaced, chickens can be raised, and cane can be replanted. Give thanks to the almighty we are unscathed in what truly matters."

They all nodded, stunned at the scene before them. Everyone began clearing debris and collecting up salvageable materials and foods. Tools were retrieved to a central location. Makeshift barriers were put together to corral the sheep, cattle, and horses. The chickens would come back to roost that night if they put something together for them to come to roost. A detail of two men took shovels to dig an emergency latrine down wind and water from the house and cabins. A curtain of debris and sheets would provide a bit of privacy. Everyone was on task with no arguments and little conversation. Jennie wasn't sure what she could do.

"Isabella, what can I do? I feel helpless..." Jennie asked.

"I think stay here with cook to tend the fire and heat the water. Make sure everyone has the chance to wash up any injuries, and before eating. I'm sure there is soap in the cellar. I'll have the kitchen maid bring up necessaries and be your assistant. She knows where things were in the cellar and you know what to do with what she finds. This will be a big help Jennie." Isabella found the kitchen maid and explained her job to her. The girl nodded and began rounding up soap, towels, linens...anything she could find within the immediate area or the cellar. Isabella found a trunk wedged among some trees containing trousers and shirts.

Grabbing a pair of trousers and a shirt Isabella changed clothes in the thicket, emerging in full blown matriarch on duty, 'just watch me', mode. Isabella was on duty, the devil best hide. No one questioned her ownership of authority at that moment. The men were quite willing to let her orchestrate the groups of workers and prioritize the cleanup and initial set up of emergency shelters and food. Giles and Joshua had inventoried most of the livestock, humanely destroying a few sheep and left Weezie to see to the horses and mules with minor injuries. The field hands had scavenged up the critical tools and materials to begin setting up for the day and into the night.

Giles was truly dumbstruck at the immediate response from the people of Emerald Oaks. They pulled together seamlessly as the rains dwindled into drizzles, and the drizzles gave way to clearing skies. Jennie pitched in fearlessly although still in agony and traumatized. Giles realized Jennie was as amazing as Isabella, a younger version yet to reach her full potential. The stable boy was trying to get Giles' attention.

"Mister Giles? Mister Giles…Miss Isabella needs you, please." Walking around to face Giles again who apparently didn't see or hear him.

"MISTER GILES? MISS ISABELLA NEEDS YOU, Please?" Giles finally heard the boy and turned to respond.

"What? Who? Oh, Miss Isabella needs me. Of course. Where is she?" Giles watched the boy point toward the steps of the house. "There. Thank you, I'll see what she needs." Giles made his way over to Isabella who was standing on the top step with Andrew's spyglass looking toward the sea. Ashen faced, she handed the spy glass to Giles and pointed where she meant for him to look. Giles took the spy glass and raised it to his eye following the direction of Isabella's gesture.

The hurricane had flattened the cane fields and most of the trees between Emerald Oaks and the sea. Bridgetown was obliterated almost entirely. The garrison still stood. The magnitude of the destruction was surreal. The truly terrifying reality of the harbor was what Giles was meant to see. The ships were destroyed. Every single merchant vessel was sunk or scuttled on the shoreline. There would be no escape from the island until more ships might arrive. Given the time of year that could be months. Barbados was completely cut off from the world until ships could be rebuilt or came into harbor. Giles lowered the glass and collapsed it before handing it back to Isabella.

**SHIPWRECK IN CARLISLE BAY**

"Keep that to yourself, Isabella. I'll see to it we have sentries posted and secure our provisions. Bridgetown survivors will be looking for supplies and looting opportunities. This is going to get worse before it gets better, I'm afraid. God help us." Giles was grief stricken at what he saw and what he knew was to follow. He turned to Isabella and said

"We will manage, Isabella. I do want to see about Father Michael when there is a safe opportunity. I expect he is fine. The church has a well-built cellar and plenty of sacramental wine to keep him away from bad water. I must get back to the required tasks and organize security. I doubt we'll have any issues before tomorrow, but I want to be prepared." Giles sighed, turned and headed back to where the men were building temporary shelters. Jennie watched him walk from Isabella across what used to be the stable yard. She saw Isabella looking toward the sea and the expression on their faces. She knew what that meant. The devastation covered the entire island. Looters and bands of desperate hungry homeless would soon be moving about the island looking for shelter and food. A shiver ran up her spine at the thought of being overtaken by them. Jennie's hands were shaking, and she was having trouble breathing.

Jennie regained consciousness with Isabella holding her head on her lap and her hand with her own. A cool rag was gently patting her neck and face.

"Jennie? What happened girl? You scared the life out of us. Sit up slowly. Are you injured?" Isabella was genuinely distressed at watching Jennie collapse by the fire. Jennie was shaking violently from the anxiety and trauma. Tears rolled down her face as she sobbed in screaming terror and clutched Isabella tightly. Isabella held Jennie until she quit shaking and the color began to return to her face.

"Jennie? What happened girl?" Isabella wanted some idea of what to do.

"I…I'm not sure…exactly. I was helping organize the foods for the pot and saw you and Giles looking…at…the

...sea. There's nothing left is there, Isabella? The desperate and homeless will be here soon, starving and probably sick." Jennie was beginning to hyperventilate again.

"Jennie. Look at me, Jennie. Breathe slowly and focus on me. Yes, that's it. Slowly and deliberately. We are all OK Jennie. We are going to stay OK. Giles is here and helping build temporary structures. The maids and boys are scurrying up everything they can find to salvage. We are finding more than I expected we would. We are fine, Jennie. Temporarily displaced but we are fine." She held Jennie closely until she was breathing normally again.

Jennie sat up and brushed her hair back with one hand. "Thank you, Isabella. I don't understand what's happening to me. I didn't used to be afraid and now everything scares me. I think I'll be fine with a bit of time. Thank you, Isabella. I'll do better if I focus on helping cook for a while. Don't worry, really." Jennie smiled at Isabella as she stood to go help organize the recovery and teams of workers. Isabella patted Jennies hand as she left and smiled with genuine love for Jennie. Jennie stood watching Isabella walk toward the men working on clearing the debris from the barn. As she started to turn back toward the fireplace that now had a fire burning in it, she noticed a figure coming up the driveway from the road.

"Giles! Andrew! We have company coming up the drive!" Jennie called to the men with more fear in her voice than she intended. Cook looked up from where she was cutting up onions with a large sharp knife. Without thinking about her actions Cook gripped the blade firmly and stood between Jennie and the person coming toward them. Giles was between the women and the figure with Joshua immediately behind and to the right with a pitchfork in his hand. Andrew appeared between them with an ax. Jennie had found a board with nails in one end. Jennie recognized Father Michael by his walk, dropped her board and even though she couldn't walk normally pushed past Giles and Andrew to help the injured priest up the hill.

The men got to Michael first. Giles and Joshua each took one of Michael's arms over their shoulders despite his screams of pain and effectively carried him up to the remains of the house. Michael had a gash on his head with blood covering his face. Jennie guessed he had some broken ribs as his breathing was difficult and he was clearly in pain. Isabella and Cook set up a palette by the fire and the men gently lay Michael down.

Michael whispered "Thank you. All." One hand reaching for Giles he managed to say, "the church...rectory...the orphanage...the children...screaming..." and passed out as his hand dropped to the floor. Jennie was on her feet in an instant.

"Giles. The children in the orphanage. They must be trapped for Father Michael to walk to Emerald Oaks with broken ribs and bleeding. We must go quickly. Please, Giles...we must go now!" Jennie was frantic but could barely walk herself. Giles put a hand on each of Jennie's shoulders and urged her to sit next to the Priest.

"Jennie, you must stay here with Michael. I will take Joshua and a few workers with tools and see about the orphans." Turning to Isabella he saw she was already organizing supplies to tend the injured and had sent the cook's maid with Joshua to fetch horses that could make the journey to the orphanage. "One of us will be back with news as soon as possible. Prepare to home the children if we must, Jennie. We need you and Cook to be prepared for the worst." Jennie and Cook nodded in unison. Cook turned and sent a maid to find Toby. They needed to organize quickly to shelter the children.

Joshua was leading three horses. Satan was bridled but the saddles were not yet uncovered. Devlin and the other had halters and lead ropes. The stable boy was leading a draft mule harnessed in an ill-fitting yet useable working harness he dragged out of the rubble. Giles helped Isabella up on Satan and Joshua on the other. Swinging up on Devlin he saw Toby coming with two slave men and two slave women.

237

All were carrying blankets or bags of some supply or another. Toby set the smaller older woman on the mule and swung bags tied together in front and behind her. The group of 4 men and 3 women set off for the parish orphanage as Jennie and Cook tended the kitchen and the priest. Toby watched them move down the drive and out on the road to the parish. Andrew had already gone back to recovery efforts knowing they might soon have many more mouths to feed and bodies to tend. He knew from experience the most difficult days lay ahead. God help them.

§

One of the henchmen tentatively opened the door of the cellar. He saw the priest staggering out of the rectory rubble with his head bleeding and holding his side. He waited until Father Michael was out of sight before climbing up and out of the cellar. The stone walls of the buildings had weathered the storm relatively unscathed. The roofs were gone or caved in on the rooms. The cellar had saved the lives of the children and the Fuller's.

The henchmen and Michael went and saddled the horses in the stables under the rectory. Ethan and Samuel met them in the churchyard, mounted their horses and rode off toward their plantation. Ethan was not confident the house would be standing but had hopes the stone barn would be functional. They left without thanks for shelter and left the orphans alone with the stable manager and two aides. One of whom would not be able to walk properly for days.

The Fullers were long gone by the time the teams arrived from Emerald Oaks and the Tallywhoa. The stable manager was organizing shelter and a meal as best he could when they began to arrive. Giles dismounted Devlin in one motion. Joshua helped the women carry the bundles of supplies into the underground stable where the children were. They inspected them closely and found no injuries. The children were traumatized and hungry, but they were ok. The men quickly set up a fire pit and set a kettle on to boil. Soup would be ready for them soon enough and everyone was starving. The stable manager was trying to get Giles' attention. Eventually he had to step in front of him to be noticed.

Giles stopped short before he plowed the willowy little man. "What do you need, man? I've lots to do. Tell me what's on your mind." Giles was trying to be patient, and finally focused when the words 'raped her' hit his ears.

"What did you say? I'm not sure I heard you proper. 'They raped her'. Who raped who? What are you talking about, man?" His blood was beginning to rise listening to the stable manager's story. Ethan Fuller. Again. Oh, how he wished he had arrived sooner and caught them there.

"Who, what girl did they rape?" Giles had a sick feeling this wasn't going to end well. He was right. God, he hated being right sometimes.

The stable manager whispered to Giles "Mary McKenzie. Colonel McKenzie's daughter, Mary." He was crying as he spoke having witnessed the entire assault. "Ethan Fuller is evil. He…they…all had their turn with her…while the breeding buck covered her as he would a slave girl. Then Ethan…he…he sewed her down…" Sobbing the man couldn't look at Giles as he tried to compose himself. "Mary will never be the same, Mister Giles. And she is likely to carry that buck's child, too. He's good at what he does." Giles was furious Ethan was getting away with this horrendous behavior. Now he had a clue how and why. Colonel McKenzie was somehow involved. And that didn't bode well for anyone.

Giles calmly spoke to the stable manager "you did what you could. You never could have stopped them no matter how hard you tried. Now that I know who is behind Ethan's brazen criminal behavior, I may be able to stop them. Meanwhile, I'll see to Mary's care at once. Thank you for sharing the information with me. You have been more help than you might imagine." He patted the little man on the back and sent him over to help with the damage assessments.

239

Giles was headed to find Isabella to tell her about Mary when the Tallywhoa crew arrived.

Giles immediately took Weezie by the arm and led her to Isabella. He explained the situation with Mary McKenzie and left them to find her and care for her. Isabella was furious with deadly thoughts filling her entire soul while Weezie was stunned. She had no idea this was happening to the ladies as a means of political leverage. They found Mary still lying on the sacks in the cellar, unable to move. Isabella sent Weezie to find Giles to carry Mary up out of the cellar where they could see to care for her.

Giles came down into the cellar to find Mary in the same traumatized state as Jennie had been. Mary had not been drugged and was awake, shaking with fear and pain. She recoiled when Giles tried to touch her, screaming and batting his hands away.

"Mary, we must get you out of this wet, dark cellar. Miss Isabella and Weezie will care for you upstairs but I must carry you. I promise I won't hurt you, Mary. I understand what has happened to you girl. It isn't your fault. I swear to you I will find them. They will be punished for what they've done to you. Please, let me carry you out of the cellar and into the sunlight." Giles waited for her to respond. When Mary's tears began to flow silently down her face, she nodded. Giles gently picked her up with one arm under her shoulders and the other under her knees. He could see the blood stains on her skirts and the sacks where she had laid. She had lost a fair amount of blood but would survive with care.

Giles carried her up the stairs and into the priest's quarters that were still partially standing. A timber from the roof rested against the top of one wall and on the floor at the bottom of the opposite wall. There was blood on the timber. Giles assumed it had hit Michael in the head and knocked him down breaking his ribs. Isabella motioned for him to bring Mary into the bedroom. The window was blown out but the bed was sound. Weezie shook the debris off the bed cover and stepped back for Giles to lay Mary on the bed. Giles stepped back and looked as Isabella and said "Let me know how she is and if you need anything to help her pain or to sleep. I'm sure we can assist with any needs you might have." Isabella knew what he was concerned about. She thought a moment before she spoke.

"Yes, Giles, please bring us some of the sacramental wine. I'm sure it will be soothing to Miss Mary. In fact, make sure there is an ample supply sent to the Tallywhoa and Emerald Oaks." Turning to Weezie she asked "Please go with Giles and bring back the wine and any other necessaries such as hot water, soap, and clean linens. Three glasses for the wine should do nicely." She smiled at Weezie, who was a bit confused, but did as she was asked. There was more to this she and was sure she was about to find out.

Giles led her down to the wine cellar under the priest's quarters. Handing several jugs of wine to Weezie, he managed several himself as they went back up to the small kitchen in the rectory. Using his knife in his boot top, he cut the seal on the wine bottle and pulled the cork out with a corkscrew. Silently he wished he could use the corkscrew on Ethan Fuller at some later date. Maybe he would keep one in his saddle bags just for the occasion, should it arise. Weezie found three glasses as Isabella asked. Giles grabbed a fourth. Weezie started to the bedroom when Giles stopped her.

"Put this much into a glass before you give it to Mary." Giles was drugging Mary's wine glass to make her sleep while Isabella cleaned her up and removed her stitches. "No more than two glasses in 8 hours. NO MORE. Do you understand? Tell me what I said Weezie."

Startled by his aggressiveness Weezie stepped back and repeated exactly what he said. "No more than two glasses in 8 hours. NO MORE. I understand Mr. Giles. I do all the medicinals for the Tallywhoa, although I don't think you realize what that means. Drugs. Many different kinds. I know how to use tranquilizing powders. I'm very careful.

No worries, truly." Giles nodded and held the glasses out for her to fill. The first bottle empty, he opened a second one and partially recorked it to make it easy for Weezie to open as needed. They took the glasses into the bedroom and sat Mary up to drink hers.

Mary's hands were shaking so violently Isabella had to help her hold the glass. At first, she didn't want the wine, but Isabella was not to be denied and she drank it quickly, frowning at the taste. Giles realized she had probably never had wine before. She was only 16 years old, still a girl and not fully a woman yet. Her innocence stolen, terrified, and ignorant of what had really been done to her. Isabella was seething with fury at Ethan Fuller and his son Samuel. She was quite convinced he was becoming a willing participant in his father's sick behaviors, no longer a boy dominated by an oppressive father. Holding Mary as she began to warm up and get drowsy, Isabella looked at Giles to signal he could leave. "Please send a maid with warm water and rum to wash the scissors with. We need to take care of Mary quickly while we can." Giles nodded and left to get the maid.

Weezie was staring at Isabella wondering what on earth she was talking about. Isabella spoke quickly "Help me get her undressed. We must examine her entire body, clean her and remover the stitches before she awakens." It took a few minutes to remove Mary's clothes gently so as not to hurt her. Weezie went ashen when she saw the stitching between her legs.

"Dear God, Isabella. What have they done to her! Why would they do this to Mary?" Tears fell from her cheeks as they cleaned her as best they could, and Isabella worked to remove the stitches. Ethan had sewn her down tightly with many knots and loops. He meant for her to stay stitched until she was well healed over and sick with child. Isabella wondered how he meant for the women to get the stitches out after the skin grew together and before they caused infection. The slave women would be told when to do it, of course.

Getting the last bit of thread removed, Isabella sighed with relief. She cleaned Mary with a soft cloth soaked in rum. Mary moaned and clenched a bit but didn't waken. She wouldn't remember the removal at all. They covered her with blankets and let her sleep. Isabella left a maid there to watch Mary until she awoke. There should be hot food ready by then and a plan made to take the children to the plantations. Mary might have to stay a while at the Tallywhoa until things settled down and her father could come for her.

Meanwhile, there was much work to be done by all. Isabella and Weezie went to help with the children and organize food and transportation plans. The teams had everyone a place to sleep that night and a destination in the morning. The men had scavenged up tools and building supplies as they found them. The sacramental wines were divvied up between the plantations with a few bottles opened to share that evening among them. Thomas was glad Richard had suggested they bring two of the dogs. He did feel safer with them there to alert should strangers or loose animals wander into the parish yard.

Everyone was exhausted by the time the evening food was hot and ready to eat. Isabella and Weezie took a plate in to Mary and relieved the maid for a spell. Weezie helped Mary sit up on the edge of the bed. Isabella held the plate while Mary fed herself as best she could. They were patient and kind. They let her achieve a positive baseline to begin to recover her life. Some things a man just cannot do for a woman. Only other women can help another find her way out of the darkness one forkful of lamb at a time.

Once fed, Mary managed to squat over the chamber pot to relieve herself. She cried in agony as the urine burned her torn and bruised crotch. She leaned forward on Isabella's shoulders as Weezie gently rinsed her with cool water and patted her dry with clean linen. They got her back onto the side of the bed and gave her a second glass of wine. This time she didn't hesitate. She drank it thirstily and wanted more. Weezie filled her glass but didn't add any more powder as Giles had instructed. She knew Mary would soon be fast asleep for the night. Tomorrow she would awaken, and the bruises would appear bright and painful. It would be days or weeks before she would be healed.

Drowsy, Mary lay back down on the bed and they covered her with the blankets. In a matter of minutes she was sleeping soundly. Weezie would stay with her during the first watch. She would be relieved by Isabella in a few hours, and Giles would sit with her late in the night. Come morning Weezie would be there when she awoke. Isabella went out to find a plate of food for Weezie and one for herself as the dogs began to bark. Someone was coming down the road on foot. Two figures. One very small, the other taller walked behind her. Isabella though she was hallucinating at first. But there she was, the grandmother had arrived at the parish.

# 15

As the pair approached the yard the dogs whined with joy and jumped up and down wanting to be let loose to greet them. Joshua couldn't contain them, and the dogs ran to meet the old woman. Raising her hand and extending her palm, the dogs immediately settled and sat quietly as she caressed their ears, tails wagging with joy. The dogs fell in behind her as she approached the fire.

Stopping at the edge of the group seated in front of the fire, the younger girl behind the grandmother spoke.

"The grandmother has come to offer her healing and medicines."

The old woman stood motionless as the girl handed the basket she was carrying to Isabella. She untied the pouch from her belt and placed it on top of the basket. The grandmother let her hood fall behind her head and began to speak, gesturing with arthritic hands as she did. The girl translated every word, showing each item as the grandmother described them.

"The papaya can be sliced and wrapped on wounds to prevent infection or eaten to reduce blood pressure and hypertension. Tea made from the Circee bush leaves can reduce fevers and calm flu and asthma symptoms. The aloe stems can be used to treat skin issues, burns, and aids healing when used topically or when eaten. The milk of the coconut will prevent kidney infections and the oil will help break up a cold." The girl waited for the grandmother to think about what she would say next. Isabella opened her mouth to speak when the grandmother started speaking again.

"You must boil all your water and foods for 2 full moons. Do not eat anything raw that has grown in the soil or sea. Cover your skin day and night to prevent mosquito bites. Watch the sea. When the tides return clear and the fish swim strong in the tide pools it will be safe to return to the sea to fish. It is especially important for the women with child to follow these rules and to not drink rum or wine; they must drink herbal teas. There is sickness in the waters you cannot see. Do not swim until you can drink the water. Two full moons." The girl stopped as the grandmother ceased.

The girl said something in the grandmother's language, holding the small pouch in her hand. The grandmother held out her hand and the girl placed the pouch in her palm. She translated as the grandmother spoke again.

"These seeds are for today, tomorrow, and forever. Use them wisely. Used in tea or smoked they relieve pain and heal many agonies. Plant them carefully and tend the plants with care. The leaves are for teas and smoking. The seeds can be harvested for medicinal use or used to seed another generation of plants. This is the *medicine plant* given to us by the old ones many generations ago. It is for all people. Grow, share, and save." The grandmother closed her eyes, raised her hands palms facing up and began to sing for the ancestors. The girl sang with her. When they stopped singing Isabella and Giles could see the grandmother weeping silently. The girl stepped back with a look of shock on her face. She had never seen the grandmother cry before. She never would again.

The grandmother silently pulled her hood back over her head, reached down to love both the dogs with hugs and kisses, turned around and walked away with the girl following behind her. The girl seemed a bit confused, looking from the grandmother to the group and back again. She pulled her hood up and followed the grandmother back the way they came and up into the hills. The dogs sat and whined as they watched them walk away.

Joshua was perplexed at the dogs' behavior. They clearly knew the old woman, but he had no idea how. Isabella realized the grandmother came around more and knew far more than Isabella had realized. Isabella would give the basket to Weezie. She expected the horse woman already knew what to do with the contents. Isabella returned to the pot to get a hot plate for herself and one for Weezie. The night would be long, and they all needed rest and food. Giles was putting water on to boil again. They both knew the old woman was sharing how to stay well in catastrophic conditions. They would follow her words to the letter. Isabella spoke briefly to Giles.

"Once the water has boiled for 15 minutes and tea steeped strong. Please bring a hot mug to Weezie. She shouldn't drink any more wine or rum again until we are sure…Mary, too." Giles simply nodded he understood and prepared the mugs as Isabella instructed. Watching the water boil, he pulled the pot away from the heat and tossed in tea and herbs. He put the lid on to steep the brew for a few minutes before ladling into the mugs. Giles looked up and scanned the immediate area as he waited. He noticed the rectory stable manager slip into the back of the church alone. Something seemed off.

Giles quietly followed the little man entering via the same back door. After letting his eyes adjust to the dim light, he could see lantern light moving down the corridor toward the parish offices. The lantern went into the vestibule, and then into the private office. Giles followed carefully, listening and looking through the small opening of the semi closed door. He watched as the lantern simply vanished in thin air.

Giles gently opened the door and made his way over to where he last saw the lantern. Stunned, he saw an open doorway behind the bookshelves pulled away from the wall. He could see the lantern light bob as the stable manager descended a staircase. The lantern light stopped moving and Giles could hear keys jingling as the man inserted a key in a lock and turned the bolt. The door creaked open and the lantern light went through. Giles followed down the steps, pausing at the door before following the lantern light down a short hall and into a private office.

The stable manager was looking over the room's contents. He tested a book here, a journal over there. Giles assumed he was checking for water damage from the storm. The man opened a trunk almost hidden in the shadows. Giles could hear coins shifting as the man picked up boxes and bags. He was making sure everything was as it should be. Finally satisfied the private room and its contents were safe he took out a newer ledger from between two old and worn volumes. Opening the book, he sat at the desk and took the quill and began to write at the top of two pages.

The man spoke softly to himself as he wrote 'Jennie Harris', at the top of a page. 'Covered by EF's Michael the night of the fall watcher's conclave. Taken from Emerald Oaks. Returned to Emerald Oaks.' Turning the page, he wrote at the top 'Mary McKenzie', followed by 'Covered by EF's Michael, during the fall hurricane of 1667 at the orphanage.'

The man flipped back a few pages until he found Esmerelda Conn's name and page. He sighed clearly saddened by the entry he must make 'Esmerelda murdered and buried at Emerald Oaks. Two days prior to the fall hurricane of 1667. Both child and mother lost and buried together. Killer unknown. Father Michael investigating.' Blotting the ink to dry it quickly, the stable man closed the book and slid it back between the others where he had found it. He lifted the lantern and gave a last look about the room before he turned to leave.

As the stable man looked up to leave, he discovered Giles standing in the doorway. Silent, his eyes were pitch black in fury as he glared at the little man holding the lantern. He watched as the little man wet himself, shaking with fear. Unable to speak, Giles stepped forward and took the lantern from his hand. Giles pointed to the chair and the little man sat, trembling.

Giles leaned down close to the little man's face and said "what is this? Why are you keeping records of the women assaulted by Ethan Fuller and his men? Speak fast man, I'm not in the mood for falsehoods or misplaced loyalties this night." Squinting he waited for the little man to speak.

"I...I...Father Michael...he...we keep records of incidents that we are aware of. He says there is an evil on the island and means to cut off the head of the snake once he is sure who it is. Or they...it could be more than one person...he says...so..." The little man's voice trailed off as Giles stood straight again. He took the journal from the shelf and thumbed it open.

"Dear God...there are...how long have you and Father Michael been keeping this record?" Giles had gone pale, but the little man couldn't see it in the dark of the lantern light.

"I'm not positive, but at least 17 years. Most entries have been in the last 3 years. Father Michael is certain there is a sadistic psychopath at work directing Ethan Fuller and possibly others." Still shaking the little man paused while Giles looked more closely at the more recent pages. "I...I think you can see the pattern..."

Giles responded "yes. There is a pattern to the incidents. Does Father Michael have any idea why these attacks are happening? I mean why impregnate women and leave a signature? What is all this about? Do you have any idea?" Giles was looking at the little man truly bewildered.

"Father Michael thinks it has to do with the loans and titles to the plantations and cane mills. Prices for products do seem to fluctuate with the cycles. He thinks all of this is about manipulating the sugar markets. Whoever controls the production can command the sales and distribution to America and Europe. The money involved is staggering.

Millions of pounds each year. Someone is making a fortune..."

Giles looked at the little man and said "the head of the snake. Dear God..." He returned the ledger to its place on the shelf. He turned to the little man and said "I must speak with Father Michael privately about all of this tomorrow when we get back to Emerald Oaks. Come, let's go back to the fire before they miss us both." Giles gestured toward the door, hesitating outside while the little man turned the key in the lock and led the way back up to the church offices and out the back of the church.

Returning to the fire Giles poured the well steeped tea into the mugs for Isabella and Weezie. Watching with his peripheral vision he saw the little man return from his room wearing clean clothes and take a plate of food and a mug of wine, sitting by himself. Giles realized he didn't even know the little man's name or where he was from. He would ask Father Michael about him tomorrow. Picking up the mugs he made his way over to the personal quarters where Mary McKenzie slept with Weezie and Isabella watching over her.

Entering the quarters, he found Isabella asleep on a pew in the vestibule with Weezie holding her finger to her lips to shush Giles from speaking. She took both mugs from him and mouthed a 'thank you'. Giles could see Mary was sleeping soundly, drugged into a slumber with a gentle powder and wine. Silently he nodded at Weezie and went back to the fire. The little man was gone. Patrick saw Giles looking about for him and said

"Mister Giles, he went to check on the children. He be back soon he say. Is there something I can do for you?"

"No. No I don't think so, Patrick. I'm going to bed down for a bit. If there are any problems, you or Joshua wake me immediately. I'll take the late watch with Mary. Make sure to wake me to relieve Isabella. Joshua can relieve you out here by the fire later as well." Giles waited for Patrick to nod he understood and lay down in the back of the cart with a blanket over him and mosquito net over the cart. Exhausted he fell asleep almost instantly. Patrick watched over the fire as the activity fell quiet in the night. The dogs stayed with him snoozing next to his feet.

About midnight the dogs picked up their heads and began the deep low growl reserved for alerting without drawing attention. Patrick quickly stood to survey the surroundings. A figure was coming from the priest's quarters toward the fire. Weezie had been relieved by Isabella and was returning the plates and mugs. The dogs relaxed and lay back down again. Patrick laid a bedroll down for Weezie under the table near the fire. Weezie gladly took advantage of the warmth from the fire and the mosquito netting hung over the table. She was asleep in short order, both hounds curled up close to keep her safe and warm.

Patrick smiled to himself at the image of the sleeping woman and the dogs. He sipped his tea and waited for the moon to come into view to the west when he would wake Giles to sit with Mary. The moonlight lit up the fields flattened by the storm. He could see movement far in the distance, probably wild pigs searching for food in the night. The fire would keep them away for the most part and the dogs would alert if they came too close. He made a mental note of where the pigs could be found again. They could well need the food in the future if as much was destroyed as he feared. A movement near the fire caught his eye. He froze. The little man from the orphanage had returned from checking on the children.

The little man nodded at Patrick, filled a mug of tea and sat near the fire. The mosquitos were beginning to become a problem, so he went into the church and crawled into the pallet he had made for himself on a pew, netting cast over the pew for insect protection. Patrick rubbed more citronella salve on his exposed skin and his clothes. Weezie always had tubs full of the stuff for man and beast. The parish quieted and slept.

§

About 3 a.m. Patrick awoke Giles to stay with Mary. They switched places in the back of the cart. Giles made a short detour around the side of the church to relieve himself. The moonlight cast long shadows in the quiet of the night. It seemed the island had found a truce with Mother Nature for just a spell. Morning would return with reality facing them squarely. Giles sighed, rolled his head around to loosen the muscles in his neck and went inside to relieve Isabella.

Isabella looked up from where she was sitting next to Mary as the girl slept. Standing she stepped into the priest's private office off the bedroom to chat briefly with Giles.

"Mary has slept peacefully most of the night. She turned a time or two and settled again. I'm afraid for her, Giles. She is too young for...this..." Isabella was emotionally distraught as well as physically exhausted. "Come wake me if you need me. I'll send a rider to find her mother at first light." She took her hand off Giles' arm where she had steadied herself and went to lay down on the pew under the netting again. Giles went in and sat in the chair near Mary. He picked up the little pot of citronella salve off the side table and smoothed it over his face, neck and arms. In silence he watched as the moonlight shifted across the room until the sunlight began to stream in from the opposite direction. Morning was breaking. Mary began to stir, calling for her mother in her drugged haze.

Isabella woke immediately to Mary's cries and went to her. She held the girl close as she sobbed realizing her ordeal had been real and not a nightmare. Mary was terrified of what would become of her, unsure her parents would take her back defiled and damaged. Enraged at what was being done to the women on the island, Giles slipped out to fetch food and tea for the ladies before his anger scared Mary further. Isabella held Mary until she regained some semblance of composure.

Wiping Mary's tears from her face, Isabella helped her with the chamber pot and managed to get Mary dressed in one of Father Michaels old sleep shifts. Roomy and soft, it was perfect for the trip to the Tallywhoa. Giles returned with mugs of hot tea and plates of hot food. He left Isabella and Mary eating their breakfast and went to find the stable manager and get the children prepared to move temporarily.

Giles found the stable manager, Weezie, and Thomas searching through the debris for the children's clothing and bags to put them in. They wouldn't need much initially as they were fully clothed, fed, and dry. The older children would be able to walk or take turns riding with the smaller children double on the horses. The adults would walk and lead them along. Giles already had a plan to return with a large detail from the garrison to rebuild the orphanage first before any other building in the area. The church had the funds to pay for the supplies and the children needed secure housing as soon as possible. The activity would also give him access to the ledgers without raising suspicions.

The stable manager knew exactly what Giles was about when he suggested sending someone to the garrison to fetch a detail to rebuild the parish buildings immediately. He volunteered to go to the Garrison, noting it was unlikely that anyone would bother him. Everyone knew he was the parish stable manager and had nothing to his name. He passed unnoticed by society all the time. Giles noted that comment, realized it was true. So, he asked

"What is your name? I realized last night I do not know your name. That is shameful on my part to not have asked you your name. I apologize for not doing so sooner." Giles waited or the little stable manager to respond.

Tentatively he told them all "I am Peter. When the Dutch were expelled from Brazil in 1654, I was left as an orphaned boy with Father Michael who brought me to Barbados with him. He has been my family ever since." Peter looked at them nervously. Giles spoke again

"Well, Peter, if you feel you can get to the garrison safely let me write a message to the Colonel for you to deliver. Let's find materials in Michael's office?" Giles gestured toward the rectory and Peter led the way. Giles considered how much to tell the Colonel. Somehow, he felt less was better. Yes, much less, until he could get a better understanding of what and who they were dealing with.

Entering Michael's study Peter found paper in a writing box on the floor under the desk. The box also had a single quill and small bottle of ink. Sealing wax and a candle rounded up the supplies nicely. Giles set to write a brief note to Colonel McKenzie asking him to send a detail to recover the orphanage and secure the safety of the children. He briefly mentioned the children were being taken to the Tallywhoa and Emerald Oaks for temporary shelter and security. Giles folded the letter sides in and top over bottom. He dripped the wax over the edge and used his clan ring to signify the message was genuinely from him. Once cooled he handed it to Peter.

"Take this directly to Colonel McKenzie's office. You may hand it to Lieutenant Evans or Colonel McKenzie himself. No one else. Wait for a response. Return with the detail. Do not come back alone. You won't be safe coming back by yourself. Stay in my quarters if you must. Evan's can show you where they are. Leave now. Take one of the spare horses. You won't be safe on foot from the animals that have gone loose from the storm. Take care, Peter. We are depending on you arriving safely at the garrison." Giles looked at Peter with care and expectation.

Peter responded "Yes, Giles, I will leave at once. I am sure I'll be fine and will be at the Garrison in a couple of hours at the most. It isn't that far and a fairly quick ride for one person." Peter smiled and went out to consult Joshua about a mount. Giles watched him go wondering why he had never noticed Peter before, truly ashamed he had not. Especially since he noticed the green ribbon Peter had tied around his hair. Peter was liaised with the Colonel. 'Note to self' Giles thought. The realization hit Giles like a ton of bricks. Peter was not just a stable manager, an orphan, and in the service of God. Giles would have a conversation with Father Michael when they arrived back at Emerald Oaks.

Giles and Thomas organized the cart and horses while Isabella and Weezie organized the children for departure. Frightened and anxious, the ladies did a wonderful job turning the exodus into an adventure. Things would come right again for them. Today they were off to see new places and meet new people as they worked together to rebuild after the hurricane.

The horses were laden with two or three children each. The cart was full with Mary in the back holding the youngest and most frightened little ones. Caring for someone else was the best medicine for her at that moment. The adults walked alongside the horses or the cart as they departed for their respective plantations. Thomas and Isabella made plans to assess the reconstruction and compare resources daily. The children would be cared for first as they worked to rebuild their homes. Today they headed home.

# 16

Peter rode to Bridgetown with urgency but did not hurry. He and his horse had to navigate debris in the road and gullies cut into the road by the hurricane. The devastation was absolute. Livestock was running loose, crops flattened, and the small streams were roaring over their banks along the way. The sails on the cane mill were ripped to shreds or missing entirely. Peter wondered if the mill would still be operable with minor repairs. He turned in to the mill and dismounted at the mill door.

Peter looped the reins through the ring anchored in the side of the mill's stone façade. Quickly he stepped inside the mill and made his way to the control area for the grinding mechanisms. Opening the housing to the millstone mechanics he found a leather wrapped packet. Inside was a letter bearing the Colonel's stag's head clan seal. Breaking open the seal he read the message intended for his eyes only.

> 'The plan moves forward today. Do as Giles Freeman asks. Chaos will occur and we will be in control of the markets within a fortnight. The *Angeline* will return within 60 days.
>
> *E.M.'*

Peter took a drawing lead from the case he carried and replied

'Understood. However, MM is at the Tallywhoa. EF has defiled and marked her. Fear EF has gone rogue. Please advise.

P''

Peter refolded the letter and replaced it where he found it. Casually he left the mill to appear unconcerned and mounted his horse. He looked about casually, turned his face to the sun until he felt he was not at any risk and headed on to Bridgetown. The watchers would find his response and act as they must. Nudging his horse with his heels the pair broke into a canter to cover the last clear stretch into Bridgetown. The carnage in the fields was absolute. The watchers would move to take over the lands quickly thanks to the hurricane's total destruction across the island. Peter smiled to himself as the outskirts of town came into view.

The horse was happy to slow to a walk as they entered what was left of the city. The ships were in ruin in the port. Sunk or washed ashore in broken heaps the scavengers were already set upon the wreckage strewn across the harbor and beaches. The soldiers from the garrison were trying to maintain some order but were failing rapidly. The market was destroyed or so badly damaged the buildings would be torn down to rebuild. Palmetto trees were broken off or laid over. Dead sea creatures littered the battery along the Careenage. This was the worst and most comprehensive damage Peter had ever witnessed from a hurricane. He was suddenly grateful he had been in the rectory cellar for the worst of the storm.

Nearing the garrison, he rode past carts filled with the bodies of men, women, and children. Scores had drowned or been crushed. The stench was already repulsive. Peter covered his nose with his sleeve as he headed past the piles of death toward the garrison. He could see the walls of the garrison still stood. The canons facing the port silent reminders they could protect from man's invasions but not Mother Nature.

Arriving at the Colonel's private entrance he dismounted and tied his horse to the ring anchored by the door. He knocked on the door and the door slowly swung open. The outer office was empty. Lieutenant Evans was nowhere to be found. Peter called out as he stepped inside

"Colonel McKenzie? Are you here, sir?'

Pausing for a reply, he heard none and moved toward the inner office door and knocked gently as he announced himself again.

"Colonel? Are you here, sir? It's Peter with a message from Mister Freeman. Colonel?"

Still no reply he tried the knob and found the door locked. The Colonel wasn't there either. Not sure what to do, Peter walked back outside into the street. He untied his horse and led him up to the stable entrance standing open. He called inside the stable.

"Hello? Is anyone here?"

"Who's there, and what do you want?" A gruff voice responded from deep inside the stable.

"I'm Peter from the orphanage with a message for Colonel McKenzie from Giles Freeman. Do you know where I can find the Colonel, please?" Peter said what he thought was enough to gain him entre into the stable or at least directions to the Colonel or Evans. He stepped back as footsteps came to the stable entry. Coming into the light Peter was face to face with the Colonel himself.

"Peter. What on earth are you doing here? Come inside quickly man. Bring your horse. It isn't safe outside the garrison right now." The colonel motioned for Peter to follow him into the stable.

He took the reins from Peter and led the horse into a nearby stall. Turning back to Peter he put his hand out for the letter from Giles.

"The letter, Peter. I haven't got all day."

"Oh, yes, right". Peter retrieved the letter out of his inside pocket and handed it to the Colonel. Quietly he waited and the Colonel scrutinized the seal, broke open the letter and read the message. The colonel casually refolded the letter and put it in his back pocket before responding to Peter.

"I'm not sure who I can send just now. You've seen the state of Bridgetown. Every man is working without sleep to stem the emergency situation. I fear we may have extreme looting, fires, and maybe an epidemic or two to deal with shortly. You know where Giles' quarters are? I assume he suggested you use them."

"Yes, he did suggest I use his quarters. No sir, I do not know exactly where to find them, but I think I can with some simple directions."

"Yes, well, across the breezeway and down on the right. Here is a key to the door. It only opens the correct door so that helps. Use his room and bath for now. Clean up and I'll have fresh clothes sent to you. By the time you are refreshed I should have a detail selected to assist you at the orphanage. It may be later this afternoon before you can head back. I'll keep you apprised. Meanwhile, make use of your time while here. Stay out of sight. Bridgetown is not safe right now." The Colonel started to leave and then stopped, turning back to Peter he asked

"Was my Mary at the orphanage when the hurricane hit? I can't remember if she was gone to the plantation yesterday or was yesterday her day to read to the children. Do you happen to know, Peter?" The Colonel had a distressed and grievous look on his face. Peter knew he could not lie to the Colonel about his daughter. Not about Mary.

"Yes, Colonel. Mary was at the orphanage when the hurricane struck. She was safe in the cellar with me and the children." Quickly Peter looked away from the Colonel. He didn't want to be the bearer of the news about the assault on his daughter. The Colonel looked at Peter suspiciously.

"What are you not saying, Peter? I can tell there is more you don't want to say. I suggest you tell me now." The

260

Colonel was not a man to trifle with. A finely trained warrior and tactician he was formidable in battle. Undefeatable when he was defending his family. Peter stepped back a space before continuing.

"Colonel, it is exactly as I said. However, you must be told that Ethan Fuller, his son Samuel, and two of his henchmen appeared as we were descending into the cellar. They…took…Mary and me back to my quarters. I tried to stop them, but I couldn't do anything." The Colonel was catching on quickly, his fury rising rapidly. Peter stepped back again. "They violated Mary repeatedly, each of them. Ethan set his breeder Michael to cover her as he would a slave wench. Ethan sewed her down himself." Peter was weeping having to relive the horror for the Colonel.

The Colonel had gone silent. Rage consumed every fiber of his being. Peter was sure he watched the Colonel's eyes change color from hazel green to black and back to green. The Colonel found his voice and spoke concisely to Peter.

"We will leave with a detail in one hour. Be ready, Peter. Where is Mary now?"

"She has gone to the Tallywhoa with Thomas Dewe and Weezie. They have some of the children. The rest went to Emerald Oaks with Miss Isabella. They came on their own, Colonel, just for the children. She is safe and well cared for. Isabella…took care…of what they did to Mary. Physically she will be fine in a few days." The look on the Colonel's face said the unspoken, 'and likely pregnant with a child sired by a mixed native slave'. His daughter had been ruined by Ethan Fuller. Deliberately. Peter knew the wrath of the Colonel would be swift and severe. He almost pitied Ethan Fuller. Almost.

The Colonel abruptly left the stable to organize a detail. A posse to avenge his daughter would soon be on Ethan Fuller's track. Peter made his way to Giles' quarter to bathe and change into clean clothing. He had to try several doors before the key found home and turned the lock open. Stepping inside he discovered there were clothes already laid out for him and hot water in the bath. He wondered how the Colonel managed to do that. Obviously, they had been overheard and his needs were accommodated immediately.

Peter stripped off the filthy clothes he had been wearing for two days through the hurricane and initial dig out. Slipping into the hot bath was a slice of heaven. The water was scented with eucalyptus. He scrubbed himself with the lavender soap and soaked for a short time before rinsing, and toweling himself dry. Stepping out of the tub he dried his legs and feet. Peter quickly dressed in the clothing left for him by the attendant. Amazingly they fit. They had been seen as well as heard. Note taken.

Stepping out into the hallway and heading back toward the stable Peter noticed Lieutenant Evans in a heated conversation with another soldier near the interior stable entrance. The subordinate scurried off to do whatever it was Evans was scolding him about. Peter looked away discreetly when Evan's looked about for prying eyes. Evans walked over toward Peter, somber faced and serious.

"Peter. I understand you have come to alert the Colonel to the status of the orphanage and the…whereabouts…of his daughter Mary. The Colonel has asked you wait in the stable with your horse. The detail will be ready to leave within a quarter hour at the most. Be ready to ride when so directed. The Colonel dislikes being kept waiting. I take it you've had a chance to bathe and change?" Evans stated the obvious looking at Peter.

"Yes, Lieutenant. Thank you for the bath and fresh clothes. I feel like a new man. I will be ready when the Colonel wants to leave. No worries." Peter smiled tentatively, trying to be polite and handed Evans the key to Giles' quarters. Evans nodded and left to return to his office. Peter stepped relieved into the stable to saddle his horse if needed to be ready to go with the Colonel and his detail.

Entering the aisle, he discovered a bevy of activity as the Colonel's selected detail saddled their horses and a pair of pack animals to head to the orphanage. Peter stepped in the stall to saddle his horse and discovered the animal gone. Panicked, Peter ran out of the stall looking for his mount in one stall to the next. An officer finally called out to him

"Peter. Stop. Your horse is exhausted. The Colonel put him out to rest for the night. You are to ride the grey in the second stall. She's a good mare. She is smart and sensitive to a light leg and hands. The stable manager has your saddle on her already. I believe he added some saddle bags full of supplies as well. The horse you came in on will be sent out to switch in a day or two. No worries mate."

Peter was greatly relieved since it wasn't his horse in the first place. Stepping in the designated stall he found a delightful cob size grey mare. Perfect size for Peter she stood a mere 14'2" hands tall. Easy on and easy off, she was well legged and would cover the ground easier than the taller shorter-coupled war horses. She nuzzled him and he liked her instantly. She made him smile. That hadn't happened for a very long time. Peter asked

"What's her name? I like her already."

"Jodi. She was a gift to the Colonel's daughter, Mary as a foal. Take care with her. The Colonel is partial to the horse and his daughter's attachment to her."

Peter understood at once why the Colonel chose this mare for him. She would be a comfort to his daughter when they found her. Smart man the Colonel. Peter smiled at the notion of 'horses and their women'. Proven true, yet again. He scratched her poll and checked to be sure the girth was snug, but not too tight. He noticed the groom had put citronella salve on her ear tips, around her eyes and nostrils. No doubt there was salve worked into her tail and under her midline as well. Yes, the Colonel would have this precious little mare well cared for as his daughter loved her.

Speaking out loud to the little mare Peter said "well, Jodi, it's you and me girl. Let's go find your lady, shall we?" Smiling unabashedly, he led the mare out of the stall and into the street. He mounted her easily and was ready to ride when the Colonel and his detail emerged from the stable. Witcher led the way fully stoked and ready to go to war. The Colonels mood always transmitted to the big mare and she acted accordingly. Collected and on alert, she carried the Colonel out onto the road out of Bridgetown at a jog fully on the bit. She was ready. He was protected. Peter followed behind them all, happy they were between him and who ever might lay in wait. Jodi jogged along enjoying the sunshine. Warhorse she was not.

## JODI

The group moved past the carts of corpses, rows of flattened buildings, and the harbor full of wreckage. As they left the edge of the city the Colonel let Witcher out a bit into a strong trot. The war horse went boldly to meet the enemy seen or unseen, ears up, eyes bright, nostrils wide to scent any change in the wind. Relaxed down her topline she was a single fluid motion and her tail snapped gracefully at the end side to side with each step. Peter was truly awed by the big mare as she was a force of nature under the Colonel's command.

In short order they were approaching the cane mill. The Colonel didn't bother to even look about or slow down. As they passed the mill the Colonel kicked the war horse into a canter and moved as a single unit jumping over fallen trees, gullies, and debris effortlessly. Peter had no idea the big mare could fly as well as run. The Colonel pulled the group down to a walk as they approached the Parish. Peter noticed movement in the trees. The watchers were there as always. The Colonel had to have seen them and was merely ignoring them. As the group came into the churchyard the Colonel waited for a footman to hold the mare and help him dismount. The drawback to riding the big mare was the distance down to the ground. The Colonel could mount and dismount without assistance, but he preferred to not pull on the mare's withers to do so.

Once on the ground he called for his sergeant to organize a search party and canvas the parish. He wanted an assessment immediately. Peter dismounted and led the little mare down to the stable under the rectory. The footmen led the war horse and his own mount behind Peter. As they came up to the stable doorway Peter stopped dead in his tracks. Hanging dead in the doorway was Ethan Fuller. Ethan's horse grazed loose outside the stable still tacked up and sweating. They had surprised the killer(s) before they could finish their work.

Moving closer Peter realized there was a brand burned on Ethan's chest. It was clearly the stag head crest of the clan McKenzie. He recoiled when he looked down to find Ethan's genitals had been cut off and had been stuffed in his mouth that was sewn shut. Peter gasped in horror at the scene. The footman had dropped the reins of his horse and Witcher and was vomiting into the bushes near the walkway. Peter reclaimed his composure long enough to scream loudly for the Colonel.

The Colonel and his personal guards came running and slid to a stop as they rounded the big mare and came into view of Ethan's corpse. The Colonel stepped slowly toward the body swaying gently with the breeze.

"Ethan Fuller. I knew ye'd come to a bad end one day. Ye deserved to, indeed. But not like this. Dear God. Who has done this? Someone was very angry with ye Ethan. Who, man, has done such a thing to ye?"

Peter pointed to the brand on Ethan's chest. The Colonel blanched white and stepped back as if he had been struck.

"Who...what...SERGEANT! I need you down her NOW, man!" The Colonel shifted into warrior mode with fury and action. Peter stepped back out of the way as the sergeant appeared before the Colonel. He followed the Colonel's glare and gasped at the scene.

"Sergeant. Someone is using the McKenzie clan seal to implicate me in this heinous event. Obviously, I had nothing to do with this. We must find out who did this to Ethan Fuller. I wanted to find him alive and mete out my own punishment. Damn the hide of who ever took that pleasure from me. Cut him down. Bury him out in the unconsecrated ground. Check his pockets for anything important. Maybe the killer left a clue for us to follow. Other than the obvious...message...left for us in his mouth."

Furious the Colonel made his way back up the hill to the churchyard to survey the assessment of the damages. He sent a runner down to the parish cellar to fetch a bottle of sacramental wine. The Colonel sat on the bench and shared the wine with Peter who had come back up after stabling Jodi and Witcher. Neither man could unsee Ethan Fuller hanging in the doorway, emasculated and tortured for his crimes. Who could have done such a thing and so quickly the Colonel wondered out loud. Peter shrugged silently, knowing the watchers had found his note and acted accordingly as he knew they would. They always did. He sat with the Colonel and watched as the men scurried about gathering useful materials inside the remains of the rectory and piling the unusable remains in stacks to the side. Within a few hours the men had established an assessment and proposal for action. The sergeant approached the Colonel with the men to apprise him of their findings.

"Colonel, we have established there is significant damage to all the parish buildings as we expected. There are unexpected areas that are still remarkably sound although they need roofing and windows and such. It will take a few days to patch up the rectory to use as a reconstruction office for the parish and local area. The orphanage and church will require weeks or months depending on the available masons and carpenters. Materials should be relatively attainable with the exception of the stained glass rose window at the front of the church. We have established sanitary facilities downhill from the parish and water supply. The men are finishing up an outdoor kitchen area to keep water boiled for drinking and washing until the wells are deemed safe again."

Peter piped in "two months. We must boil and cook all our food and water for a full two months."

The Colonel and the sergeant glared at Peter as if he were an impertinent child.

"The grandmother came down from the hills and gave us medicines and told us how to keep well. To boil and cook everything for two months and not to fish again until the tide cleared and the fish swim in the tide pools again." The Colonel raised his brows and asked Peter to recant that again.

"Did you say the grandmother came down from the hills with medicines? Dear Lord, you're serious." The Colonel was in awe and was suddenly giving Peter his full attention.

"Well, yes, Colonel. I wouldn't make up a story about the grandmother. Oh heavens no. I think Weezie already knew about most of the things she gave us. There was an odd bag of little seeds I had never seen before. I'm not sure what that was about. Anyway, she said the same thing. Boil and cook. Let the sea come right before venturing out on it again." The Colonel nodded and was still wondering why the grandmother came down from the hills to the rectory of all places. Peter continued

"Joshua's hounds loved her, too. Seemed like they knew her somehow."

The Colonel was soaking up every word Peter uttered at that point. Peter knew what not to say and left them to wonder about the visit. The sergeant continued

"Colonel we are at a collected stopping point. Shall we continue on with cleanup and begin reconstruction immediately or shall we divide up and go to the Tallywhoa and Emerald Oaks to see about the children?"

The Colonel considered for a moment.

"Sergeant, I must go to the Tallywhoa and see about my daughter and the children there. I'll take Peter and two men with me. I want you to take two men and go to Emerald Oaks and see about the children there. We will split up the supplies and share them equally. Leave the rest of the men here to continue the cleanup and begin organizing repairs on the rectory. We can make the excursions to the plantations and be back here by nightfall. At least send a messenger if you must stay behind for any reason."

"Yes Colonel. Immediately, sir." The sergeant set off to organize the parties as ordered. Peter realized it was going to be a very long day as he stood to follow the Colonel back down to the stable and retrieve the mares for the ride to the Tallywhoa.

§

They made their way through the now empty doorway to the stable to find the mares quietly waiting to be tacked up to travel. Peter was contemplating how to get the saddle up on Witcher when a pair of hands took the saddle from him and lifted it up on her back with ease. Peter turned and looked up to see the Colonel had found a stool to stand on. Peter went round the other side to help align things as the Colonel tightened the girth just the way he wanted it.

The big war horse wore a breast plate to keep the saddle from slipping down her powerful back and a crupper to keep the saddle from riding up on her mammoth neck. The Colonel stood on the stool to bridle the mare as well. Her head was longer than the Colonel's torso. The bit was custom made just for her. Regular bits were much too narrow for her mouth. Peter was thinking what fun it would be to ride her but was too terrified to ask to do so. No, he'd stick with Jodi today. He was already attached to the little grey. Witcher was ready to ride. The Colonel led her out of her stall and waited while Peter saddled Jodi to follow.

"Peter, ride Jodi to the Tallywhoa. Bring Ethan's horse along as well. We may need an extra and that bay is a decent ride. Ethan won't mind I shouldn't think...." Peter smirked and led the grey out to the Colonel before getting the bay out of the next stall. Peter tied a longer lead to the bit so he would have some room next to the grey as they rode. They walked out the stable and up to the church yard. The men were ready and grouped to go to the plantations.

The sergeant came over and helped the Colonel mount up on Witcher. Peter mounted Jodi on his own. She stood quietly as he settled in the saddle and organized the lead rope for the bay he led along behind her. The men going to the Tallywhoa fell in behind the Colonel and Peter. The men going to Emerald Oaks fell in behind the sergeant. Neither group had a long way to go but were anxious to get back to the parish for the night if possible. Peter was grateful Thomas had brought his cart when they came to the parish. The slaves had cleared the road of the largest debris and the going was much easier than the road from Bridgetown.

The Colonel was taking in the damages as they rode through the countryside. As he expected the crops were virtually wiped out entirely. Trees were down or broken off, the road was washed out in several places, and livestock was running loose looking for food and decent water. In a day or two most of the animals would wander back home on their own. The wild animals were still out of place as well, their homes destroyed or displaced as were the people.

Peter noticed the water birds were standing on the shoreline. They were avoiding the water. He remembered what the grandmother had said about not going in the water until it cleared to fish or swim. Clearly the old girl knew what she was talking about. He pointed the moment out to the Colonel.

"Colonel, do you see the water birds are on shore, there? Not going in the water like they normally do. I think the grandmother knew what she was saying. To not fish or swim until the waters cleared and the tide pools had fish swimming in them again. Maybe there should be some sort of warning in Bridgeport to stay out of the water and away from the wrecks for a spell. What do you think, sir?"

The Colonel looked over and took notice of what Peter was saying. He pulled Witcher to a stop to watch the birds for a minute or two. He was remembering times past when the storms ravaged the islands. Yes. He did remember the aftermath. The grandmother was right. There was something about the waters when disturbed that was bad. He hadn't put it together until just then, but he lost many men who had been out to salvage the wrecks after storms. Days later they would fall ill and die. He didn't know why exactly or if he truly believed the grandmother's warning. But he would heed the advice, keeping a close count on casualties.

"Peter you may have saved many lives today. I will definitely heed the warnings…from you, the grandmother, and the wading birds. Mother nature tells us all we need to know if we will but listen." He set his heels in Witcher's ribs and hit a strong trot to the Tallywhoa. Peter cantered along on Jody just to barely keep up. She was a jewel of a sweet ride. Smooth, calm, predictable…a perfect fit for Peter. Sadly, he would have to relinquish her for Mary McKenzie to ride home. He had a good idea Ethan Fuller's bay was about to get a new owner named Peter.

They had arrived at the gateway to the Tallywhoa. Looking up the drive they could see the house was flattened and the roof was missing from the barn with the walls collapsed in on it. The Colonel took the lead up the hill to the remains of the Tallywhoa buildings. The detail followed on his heels arriving at the front steps in a group. Peter brought up the rear a bit more casually. Jodi didn't rush. Just not her gig. John stood up from beside the fire and walked out to meet the group. Drying his hands on a towel he welcomed the Colonel and his men to the Tallywhoa. George and the boy Tom hustled out to take Witcher's reins from the Colonel and led her and the sergeant's horse to the stabling area. The horses went inside the temporary lot and were tied temporarily to rings anchored in the fence posts.

George had sent Jane to fetch mugs with hot tea for the Colonel and his men. Only boiled waters could be consumed for at least 2 months. Sarah had already explained the rules to everyone. There would be no sickness on her watch if they listened and acted accordingly. Jane came out of the makeshift cook shack carrying four mugs. Following behind her with 6 more was Richard. Richard had a way with children and always let them learn with positive support. They wondered if he would ever have his own…that he claimed…or just enjoy other peoples' children when he had the chance. Jane was trying to distribute the mugs clumsily.

Peter stepped in and took two from Jane and let her hand out the mugs she held first, giving the second pair of mugs to her to distribute next. Richard stood patiently waiting to hand her two more to hand out as her little hands could manage. Carnage surrounded them literally and figuratively yet there stood two plantation owners, a Colonel, a contingent of officers and enlisted, and a parish stable manager all waiting patiently as the 9-year-old slave girl handed out tea to each one with a curtsy and a 'sir'. When she had handed out all the mugs of tea, she looked to Richard for instructions.

"Thank you, Jane. You may go back to help your mother in the kitchen now. Go on, I think she is making some cookies for later. She will need you to help her stir the dough." Jane grinned and ran off to the cook shack, completely oblivious to the men laughing at Richard with gusto. So much for his bravado in the company of very short females. Epic failure. They laughed until they cried, and they needed to do both.

Richard feigned ignorance and played mortally hurt by their giggles. They all knew Richard was making a hardship a bit easier for the children by letting them help when they actually could. The adults simply had to have a smidgeon of patience and let them. Their respect for Richard grew exponentially in that moment. Richard held his hand out to welcome the Colonel and offer him something stronger for his tea.

"Aye, Richard, ye know I love me scotch. That I do. But I must decline just now. I've come to see about the Tallywhoa, the children form the orphanage, and my daughter Mary. Peter tells me she is here?" The Colonel looked from John to Richard waiting for a reply.

"Mary is resting comfortably just now. Sleeping actually, I think." Thomas had walked up behind the Colonel from the far side of the house. "Did Peter explain her...injuries...to you Colonel?" Thomas had pulled his flask out of his hip pocket and was about to take a swig when the Colonel had a change of heart and held his mug out. Thomas poured in a good two fingers while he waited for the Colonel to respond.

"Aye, Thomas, he did. I understand that Isabella has cared well for my Mary? She will heal up just fine then I think." He left the obvious unknown hanging unsaid. Would Mary be with child or not, time would tell.

Thomas paused a moment before continuing. "Yes, Colonel, I think your Mary will heal just fine with Isabella's immediate care and Sarah's continuing pampering. Mary has already begun to recover both physically and emotionally. Give her some time, Colonel, she will be fine." Thomas looked directly at the Colonel. His not so subtle message fell squarely on the Colonel's ears and he took it heart. Nodding he said

272

"Yes, Thomas, I am sure you are correct. Time to heal. After the last few days we all need some time to heal." Nodding as he sipped his rum with a bit of tea in it, letting the alcohol slowly seep into his bloodstream. The rum was helping settle his anxiety about his massive responsibilities due to the storm. Peter stood silently listening to the men chat casually as he watched the workers busily turning the rubble into livable space again. He was truly amazed at the progress they had made in just two days.

The cook shack was the center of activity. Sarah was directing the crews of slaves and seeing to their needs at the same time. She was truly an amazing woman. He realized watching her she was pregnant. Sarah was just beginning to show an identifiable swelling in her belly. Peter smiled to himself knowing John would be a wonderful father to the baby. He doubted he would ever have children. Meanwhile, he cared for the orphans as if they were his own. They needed him and he loved them dearly. He came back to the present when Ian came hustling down to the group asking Richard to come help with the boys. They were fighting again.

The men all went as a herd of lemmings to deal with the adolescent uprising. Richard wasn't the only sucker for children in the bunch after all. Who knew? Sarah stood exasperated outside the cook shack, her hands on her hips, scolding them in her native language. She may have been saying they had pretty blue eyes for all the boys knew, but it sounded really wicked and she intimidated the little urchins into respecting her…and her wooden spoon…with ease. The tussle having demised before the men reached them, they dejectedly went to check in about the rest of the children and the damages at the Tallywhoa.

The Colonel lagged behind to chat with Sarah about Mary. Once certain no one could overhear their conversation he turned to Sarah. Not quite sure how to ask such questions about his own daughter, Sarah gently explained what had happened to Mary and how Isabella and Weezie had tended to her. Sarah emphasized that Mary would be fine physically very soon. She also explained it could take a very long time for her to recover emotionally and mentally. Sarah might never be the same again after being so brutalized by a group of men. Sarah also suggested she could provide Mary with medicine to prevent an unwanted pregnancy. The Colonel was stunned by her comment and choked on his rum and tea.

The Colonel had never considered there was such a thing that could be done and was highly embarrassed to think such a thought.

"Sarah, I'm not sure what you mean or how you would do what I think you mean…"

Sarah explained "Colonel, I can give Mary the right medicines and she will not conceive a baby from Michael at this time. This early it is easy to prevent. There is no danger to Mary. If she decides later to end the pregnancy she would be highly at risk of death or become unable to have children later. My people have known these medicines for thousands of years. It is how we control our populations. We must or we would starve. For Mary, it might give her a better chance to have a real marriage with a good man. Who will want her with a half breed slave child? Will you raise that child and love it as your grandchild?"

The Colonel glared fiercely at Sarah, and then looked ashamed realizing what he was, yet he knew Sarah was right. Mary's life would be very limited and difficult. The tears rolled down his cheeks as he turned away from Sarah.

"Take care of my Mary, Sarah. You do know what to do. She deserves a better life. I will leave her here with you until she is ready to come home. Send word to me when I should come get her. I assume that will be at least a month?" The Colonel was heartbroken for his daughter and eternally grateful to Sarah. Mary would have the opportunity to heal and thrive as well.

"Do not worry Colonel. Mary will be fine. She will simply get better and never know about the medicine. She doesn't need to know. That secret will die with you and me."

"Thank you, Sarah. I will be in touch." Not looking back at Sarah, he wiped the tears from his face and went to organize his men with the Dewes. Together they made lists of required supplies and existing materials. The first step in reconstruction with limited resources was to inventory what was available across the island. Feeling successful in his trip to the Tallywhoa, his contingent began their return to the parish. The Colonel was eager to hear what the sergeant discovered at Emerald Oaks

§

The sergeant and his contingent arrived at Emerald Oaks at about the same time the Colonel arrived at the Tallywhoa. The devastation was equally comprehensive and overwhelming. The men and women were all working with urgency to construct temporary shelters for man and beast alike. Isabella had a fire going in the fireplace while Jennie tended the kettle hung over the fire. Arriving at the front steps they were greeted by Toby and the stable boy. Toby sent the boy to find Mister Andrew and Miss Isabella, or Mister Giles if he found him first.

The sergeant was mentally cataloging everything he could see while they waited. The men were taking notes. Giles came to meet them first. Shaking hands with his colleagues and pointing to the makeshift stabling area for their horses. The men took the horses and Giles and the sergeant followed the group up the hill, stopping about halfway as they talked.

"Giles, the Colonel has asked for an inventory of any excess useable materials Andrew may have, and a list of materials Andrew needs. You know how this works after a natural disaster. What do you suggest as the best way to inventory? Perhaps this has already been done? We do not want to be a burden or in the way, either."

Giles considered what to share.

"Sergeant, I think the best thing would be to pair up your men with our crews and then combine their lists into one. I seriously doubt there will be an excess of anything, but I could be mistaken. Joshua will know exactly who to pair up. It won't take long. First, there is an important matter to deal with. Has the Colonel been told about the assault on his daughter Mary?"

"Yes." The sergeant was instantly enraged at the thought. "Oh, yes. Peter informed us of the incident. The Colonel has gone to the Tallywhoa to see about Mary and the other children there as well. Ethan Fuller will never have his way with a woman again. He was found hanging and mutilated in the stable doorway. Someone murdered him shortly before we arrived. His genitals had been removed and stuffed in his mouth, which was sewn shut."

Giles was genuinely stunned. "Who? Who could have known and got to Ethan that quickly?" Giles waited for some sort of explanation. The sergeant shrugged and said

"We do not know. Seriously. No idea. The Colonel would give him a medal if he knew. Ethan was a piece of work and deserved to be punished. But this was an act of rage, not just punishment. Someone took him out in a fit of rage and left him hanging as a message to others. I almost believe it was a woman, but no woman could overpower him alone or hang him up like that. He is buried in the unconsecrated section of the parish cemetery. Gruesome, yet fitting for that man."

Giles shook his head in wonder. He wasn't sure he wanted to know what happened to Ethan. He was glad it was done, but there were others involved who also needed to be punished. "And the rest of his men? What about them? Will the Colonel go after them?"

"I expect so. You know the Colonel; he is patient and will get them all eventually. This time it's personal. I expect the retribution will be swift and lethal."

"Yes, I agree. I think we can work together to facilitate that happening. The parish reconstruction may be very useful. I still need to visit with Father Michael about some details. I'll share with the Colonel when I have something concrete. I'm staying to help here at Emerald Oaks a few days. The priest is here, and Jennie Harris needs a few more days to heal herself. We will be along directly. I know being here will be the most useful place for me to be right now. There is much to learn..."

The sergeant raised a brow and knew not to ask more. The other men were divided up and moving off to work with the various teams. He followed Giles' gaze to find Isabella coming toward them.

"Miss Isabella, I am delighted to see you unharmed by the storm. I am here to see about what materials you may have to share and what you need to help reconstruction of Emerald Oaks. Mr. Freeman has graciously organized my men into your teams to expedite the process. We will return to the parish shortly to coordinate with the Colonel and his detail that is currently at the Tallywhoa. Thank you for taking such good care of his daughter, Mary. He, we, are eternally grateful for your kindness towards her and the children from the orphanage."

Isabella came to a stop between the two men. "Sergeant you are most welcome. Of course, we will do whatever we can to be of service in this time of disaster. Fair weather is what we need most for a few days as we get some temporary shelters secured for everyone. I assume the Colonel intends to help with rebuilding the orphanage as soon as possible. Do you have any idea what time frame we should be considering?"

"Actually no, not yet. We will meet at the parish later this evening and determine the plan and timetable. Realistically I think we all know it will be a few weeks to properly prepare for the children to return. We will be bringing materials and food to help care for them here in the meantime. We will keep in close contact to make sure you have everything you need." The sergeant was genuinely gracious and grateful as well. He was once an orphan and knew how valuable the care was to these children. On his watch, they would receive what they needed. Looking at him more closely, Giles realized there was a definite resemblance to Jennie. Another island secret he didn't want to know. Isabella replied equally gracious

"Thank you, sergeant. I appreciate the Colonel's commitment to care for our children. We are most happy to contribute to help others in any way we can. By all means, inventory and assess with our teams. Only good can come of our mutual efforts." Isabella gestured for the sergeant to continue with his appointed duty. As he walked away Giles shared the news about Ethan Fuller.

"Isabella, you will be pleased to know Ethan Fuller is dead."

Stunned Isabella replied "WHAT? HOW? WHEN?"

"Apparently someone caught up with him and hung him after removing his more disgusting appendage, shoving it in his mouth, and sewing his mouth shut. The Colonel's men found him hanging in the stable at the parish this morning. Someone was very angry with Ethan to mutilate him and leave him as a message like that. Someone very dangerous has made a very loud statement. Any ideas who that might be, Isabella?"

"I can think of a number of people who would gladly take credit for doing in Ethan Fuller. But, no, I don't have a clue who. I'd give him a medal if I did. At least he can no longer hurt others. Giles, do you think Samuel will pick up where his father left off?"

"I wondered that myself. Time will tell. He and his father's henchmen are not off the hook in any way. I'm sure the Colonel will bring them in for justice. The question is will they live long enough to do so." Giles and Isabella were silent as they realized Samuel and the others could well suffer the same fate as Ethan.

"Perhaps, Mr. Freeman, the hurricane damages will make it difficult for the Colonel to bring the others to justice in a timely manner. Unfortunately, the hurricane damages will take some time to bring under control. Priorities after all."

"Indeed, Mrs. Conn, we must prioritize our efforts in the best interests of the public. I agree." Simultaneously they smirked, both wondering how long before Samuel and the henchmen would be found hanged and mutilated. Giles headed toward the teams and Isabella headed toward the fireplace. Not another word would be said. They both knew it was too late for Samuel and the henchmen. The Colonel would make a public show of a chase only to find them demised upon arrival. The sergeant would make sure to orchestrate the public records accordingly. In truth, no one wanted to know who killed Ethan and no one would ever be arrested for the crime.

The sergeant and his men finished up their work and headed back to the parish to meet up with the Colonel and plan the reconstruction of the orphanage and parish. Giles would become part of the reconstruction and research the parish records as they worked. Peter would be his eyes and ears at the parish. Isabella and Jennie would be his eyes and ears with the watchers. Giles knew there was much more to learn to determine who killed Esmerelda and determine who 'the head of the snake' was.

§

Sifting through the rubble Giles found the crate where he had left the journal for the watchers. The journal had been returned after the hurricane. Perplexed Giles picked it up and a letter fell out. He picked it up and turned it over revealing the Colonel's seal. Giles slipped out into the thicket where he would not be seen before he opened the letter.

'The Fullers are no longer. Ethan was not Esmerelda's killer. She waits for the *Angeline*. The journal holds the key."

Giles went cold and ashen. He knew what this meant. Samuel and the henchmen were already dead. He was being led to find Esmerelda's killer. The chill ran up his spine at the realization he was being led, not the Colonel. He was baffled. He quickly flipped the journal open to discover it was not Esmerelda's journal, nor Jennies. The handwriting was familiar, but he couldn't place the owner. Giles refolded the letter, tucked it back inside the journal and slid it inside his shirt. Time would reveal all. He prayed the *Angeline* would not return too quickly. He would have to check the manifests and harbor master's calendars to get an idea. If the harbor master was still alive and if the records survived the hurricane. Giles turned and resumed working with the teams to inventory and plan reconstruction. Late afternoon the detail left to return to the parish.

Evening was settling quietly with everyone exhausted yet grateful for food to eat and a place to rest. Giles held Jennie close as they slept near the fire. The moon rose silently and provided light for the watchers. Had he been awake Giles would have noticed the cloaked figures slipping through the shadows near the gate, their horses hooves covered in cloth sacks to quiet their movements and hide their identity. The morning would shine new light on the island. The watchers were changing their world.

# Part 3
# THE WATCHERS

## IXCHEL THE CRONE
*The Grandmother*

# 17

The death of Ethan Fuller, his son Samuel, and his associates had complicated the reconstruction efforts of the Governor and plantation owners. The creditors were at the doors, all of them profiteering off the crop failure for 1667. Debts were being called, lands were being foreclosed, and there was little Henri Izzard could do to stem the bloodletting. Titles and deeds were being filed as fast as he and his scribe could write them. Almost every plantation had been subject to having their debts called in. Most owners were finding refinancing options at exorbitant prices or selling partial ownership to a silent partner, The Conrad Holdings Group (CHG). The 'Avenging Ghosts' Bajan name gave Izzard the creeps.

Izzard had been retained by CHG to make offers to any owner threatened with foreclosure or bankruptcy. So far, every offer had been received favorably with minor negotiations. The group already held a majority interest in sixty percent of the island's sugar production. If the rest of the offers were agreed upon that would become ninety percent ownership of the Barbados sugar industry. The Tallywhoa, Emerald Oaks, and the Highlands were the three remaining properties to receive the CHG offers. Izzard had meetings scheduled with the Dewe brothers, Andrew and Isabella Conn, and Colonel and Elizabeth McKenzie in the next two days.

Henri Izzard had hoped to meet Thomas and Richard Dewe in a pleasant situation. The aftermath of a catastrophic hurricane negotiating for the ownership of their land wasn't what he had in mind. Clearing his desk of all unnecessary paperwork and distractions Henri considered the potential outcomes. The CHG had become incredibly powerful in just a matter of weeks. He had no idea who they were. He had never actually met with the group, just with their representative and courier Jennie Harris.

Izzard knew Ms. Harris was well known in the area as an excellent scribe and record keeper who worked for the Colonel at crime scenes and anyone who needed documents written or negotiated. He had used her services himself many times. Jennie could get the right information and explain the information to others easily. Her services were particularly valuable to new widows, orphans, and natives. Barbados was lucky to have her. A knock on his door and his assistant was announcing the arrival of Thomas, Richard, and John Dewe.

"Counsellor Izzard, the Dewe brothers have arrived. Shall I show them in?"

"Yes. Bring them through immediately." Izzard stood to greet the brothers, shaking their hands as John introduced them.

"Henri meet my brothers Thomas and Richard. I regret we are not here for a social visit as I had originally planned. Thank you for seeing us, we appreciate the invitation to consider the offer you mentioned in your communique. What exactly is the offer and from whom?" The men sat in unison across the desk from Izzard. Henri's assistant was handing out dock glasses of scotch to each of them before taking his seat at the smaller desk off to one side of the Barrister's desk. Dipping his quill, he began to take notes as they spoke.

Henri began "gentlemen, I have been asked to make an offer to you for the Tallywhoa. The buyer is willing to buy the plantation outright and rent it back to you or buy out your debts only and become a silent majority partner. The approaches are distinctly different that yield similar financial outcomes for you."

Stunned, the brothers looked at each other and then back to Izzard. Thomas spoke first.

"In essence you are offering us the frying pan or the fire. Either way we lose control of the Tallywhoa. Who is the buyer? We should consider who makes such an offer as well as the offer itself." John and Richard nodded in agreement.

"The Conrad Holdings Group. The CHG. They have the capital to back their offers. I recommend you consider their offers seriously."

Richard inquired "who are they? What are their names, Henri?'

"I can't say."

John was incensed at the cloak and dagger context "Oh for…really Henri, you don't expect us to negotiate with people you won't disclose? That's absurd. Who are they?"

"I'm serious. I cannot say because I honestly do not know who they are. I deal with them via a courier only. I've never actually met them. I do know their offers are genuine and their money is substantial." Henri didn't like the cloak and dagger either, but the group was powerful and had deep pockets. He knew they could just as easily destroy every owner on the island. He had taken their offer to represent them to prevent just that.

The brothers were speechless. Thomas eyed the councilor and considered their options. Richard looked at Thomas and John was staring at the floor. Henri waited while his assistant held his quill freshly dipped in ink.

Thomas finally spoke.

"What is the actual value of each offer? What is the value in pounds and any other form of commitment? And, what does our father have to say about this? The Tallywhoa actually belongs to him; at least it is his investment as well. Have you considered how to deal with his input or lack thereof?" All three were looking at Izzard.

"The actual value is equal to your debts plus 10 percent for outright purchase of the land. The value to buy a majority share is equal to your debts plus 51 percent of gross income for the next 20 years. The 51 percent is actually payments to buy your share back plus interest for their investment. The minimum annual payments must equal 20 percent of the debt value at time of signing. Based your acreage and past income over the first 20 years of the Tallywhoa operation, the CHG is willing to negotiate the details prior to signing."

John stood abruptly and turned to look out the window. He could see the continuing recovery efforts among the wreckages of the ships destroyed during the hurricane. Thomas looked straight at Izzard while Richard stared into oblivion. Thomas finished his scotch and stood with his hand out to Izzard.

"Henri, thank you for forwarding this opportunity to my brothers and me. Please schedule a time to negotiate details for us to consider further. We cannot ignore any legitimate offers, nor can I guarantee we will accept the CHG offer, but we will seriously consider both contexts of a financial agreement. Please ascertain the legal standing required, and what we hold with or without Colonel Dewe present, to conduct such negotiations. We will return at a mutually agreeable date and time to determine what we can and cannot do, and what the minimum financial requirements might be. We will be staying in town for a couple of days at the garrison. Please leave word with Lieutenant Evans regarding the next meeting details."

Izzard nodded and replied "absolutely, Thomas. I will inform the CHG of your tentative interest and schedule the next meeting."

Richard and John shook hands with Izzard and followed Thomas out the door to the street. Silent, they made their way to the Roaring Boar for a pint and a cheese board.

## THE ROARING BOAR

Izzard and his scribe composed a response to the CHG. Henri signed and sealed the letter and slipped it into the courier bag with the others. After a second glass of scotch, he prepared the next set of documents to meet with Andrew and Isabella Conn later in the afternoon. Meeting with the Colonel and Elizabeth McKenzie would have to be rescheduled. He did not want the Dewe brothers seeing him at the garrison with the Colonel and his wife. He wrote a note to the Colonel, sealed it and had his scribe courier the note to the colonel. Discretion was always a critical piece of negotiating business transactions. A gentle knock on the door startled Henri back to the present.

Henri walked to the door and opened it to find Andrew and Isabella Conn waiting to see him. A quick glance around the vestibule revealed his scribe had not returned from the garrison. He invited the Conns into his office.

289

"Andrew, Isabella, thank you for coming. My scribe will be back shortly but no matter. Do come in and be seated. Isabella may I offer you some tea? Andrew something stronger perhaps?" Henri looked from one to the other waiting for a reply.

Isabella replied "Why thank you Henri. I'd love some of your good scotch."

Henri raised his brows in surprise as Andrew rolled his eyes. Isabella cut to the chase.

"Oh really, gentlemen. Don't look shocked for my benefit. Two fingers, please. I'm not driving the cart on the way home after all."

Henri burst out laughing and fondly poured two full fingers of scotch in a dock glass for Isabella and another for Andrew. Actually, three fingers for Andrew. He was going home with Isabella after all. Henri smiled to himself and poured a glass for himself.

Andrew graciously took the glasses from Henri and tried to hand Isabella the smaller pour. Not having it, Isabella took the other glass and glared at her husband as she did. What could he do? She wasn't driving the cart home that was true…

Henri began with chit chat until his scribe returned.

"Andrew how are things coming along at Emerald Oaks?"

Andrew replied "actually much better than I had first anticipated. The Colonel has been most generous with materials for the orphans staying with us, and for the parish buildings as well. We have been able to share our surplus materials with him and others. The Sergeant has done a remarkable job pulling things together across the island. The children should be able to return to the parish orphanage within a fortnight I should think. The Tallywhoa has been most helpful with the children as well. What we don't have they do it seems. Things could be so much worse."

Henri listened quietly, letting Andrew and Isabella share freely about their situation.

"Andrew is being modest, Henri. We are blessed in many ways. We have good neighbors, a dutiful parish, the garrison detail has been splendid to everyone. Replanting has commenced in the gardens and the fields. Our losses were negligible compared to the low country areas." Isabella knew how to spin her standing before negotiating for anything. Andrew just wasn't on to why they were there. Isabella sipped her scotch as the scribe returned and hurried in, removing his hat and coat as he did. He nodded to Henri as he dipped his quill and waited.

Henri began "I've asked you both here today to present an offer to you. The CHG is interested in purchasing your land or purchasing a majority share in your land. The amount would either buy out your debts entirely or facilitate the retirement of the debts over time. They are aware of the island wide devastation and hope to keep the lands in the hands of the owners, at least partially."

Andrew sat speechless, glass halfway to his mouth. Isabella calmly sipped her scotch and looked straight at Henri. Henri looked back and forth waiting for a response. Andrew stuttered

"Someone wants to BUY Emerald Oaks? BUY out a majority share? You've got to be kidding! Absolutely not! There is no.."

"Tell us more Henri. Who exactly is making this offer, and what is the amount of the offer? We will be gracious enough to hear what an investment group has to offer. I don't guarantee they will be pleased with our decision, but we will hear them out." She sipped and waited while Andrew stuttered and swigged. Henri refilled Andrew's glass.

"Conrad Holdings Group is the 'who'. The individuals I have no idea. I deal with them through a courier. So far, their money has been good, and they follow through on their contracts. To the letter. They have provided a lifeline to others. It is entirely your decision to negotiate or not. I am just making the offer as requested." Henri sipped, the scribe scribed, Isabella watched intently, and Andrew slunk in his chair.

"What do you need from Andrew and I to further the conversation? Isabella's eyes narrowed. The nitty gritty was coming into view.

"They will make an offer based on the value of your debts and the gross receipts of Emerald Oaks for the last 20 years. That information will be required. The actual value is equal to your debts plus 10 percent for outright purchase of the land. The value to buy a majority share is equal to your debts plus 51 percent of gross income for the next 20 years. The 51 percent is actually payments to buy your share back plus interest for their investment. The minimum annual payments must equal 20 percent of the debt value at time of signing. Based your acreage and past income over the first 20 years of the Emerald Oaks operation, the CHG is willing to negotiate the details prior to signing." Henri repeated the offer he had already made to dozens of landowners verbatim.

Andrew sat aghast at the prospects. He knew the offer was more than fair compared to losing the land all together. But they weren't going to lose their land. He had seen to the figures himself. "Henri we aren't in a position to need their offer. We will have losses this year from the crops wiped out by the hurricane, but we are on sound financial footing otherwise. Why are you, your clients, thinking we need their financing?"

"Andrew, Isabella, the CHG now owns far more than a majority share of the sugar production on Barbados. They can ruin you in one season. They do not have to offer you anything, they could wait. Starve you out and take the land for a small percentage of the debt value when your creditors are desperate to sell your uncollectable debts. I will say I do not like this method of acquisition. I am working for them to know exactly what they are doing and to protect local interests as best I can. They can do what I'm describing. They have the finance behind them to do so. I suggest you take their offer seriously, Andrew. Go home and think about it. I will arrange another meeting if you want to do so. I recommend you do so."

Isabella raised a brow and finished her scotch. "Well Henri. Thank you for your honesty. As refreshing as your scotch, truly. Yes. I suggest we set up a meeting to hear their actual terms before we make a final decision. Andrew, do you concur?" Henri looked at Andrew waiting for a reply, Isabella looked at Henri.

Andrew replied "yes. I think we must inquire further. Isabella, I agree. I am far from convinced we must, but I will review the ledgers prior to our meeting. Thank you, Henri. I appreciate your commitment to the local producers. Indeed." Andrew stood and offered his hand to Isabella as she rose. Henri shook Andrew's hand and kissed the back of Isabella's. The French did know how to treat a lady. Isabella smiled as she turned to leave the room ahead of her husband. She would smile all the way back to Emerald Oaks.

Henri collected the notes from his scribe, penned a message to the CHG for the courier bag and waited for the courier to arrive. He was not entirely sure who the CHG was, but he was quite sure they were about to hold complete control over the island's economy and finance. The group had money and lots of it. Here, on the island. There had been no ships arriving in port since the hurricane. This was no fly by night group. This was years in the making, carefully crafted, patiently waiting for the right opportunity. That opportunity blew in with the hurricane. Clever. Smart. Positioned. God, he wanted to know who they were. The scribe knocked gently to announce the courier had arrived.

Henri stood and held the courier bag out for Jennie to deliver to the CHG. No one noticed a woman traveling between plantations or homes, especially a scribe often seen going about writing down wills, directives, and day to day letters. Jennie didn't know who the CHG was either. She had never met them in person. She would leave the messages at a different designated location each time. As much as Izzard wanted to know, he hadn't been able to trip them up. He had tried but could not. It was as if they had eyes everywhere. Jennie took the courier's bag and turned to leave. She had to make haste to deliver the bag on time to the new location discreetly.

# 18

Jennie's horse was nondescript and looked like a hundred other horses on the island. She blended in wherever she went. She was preparing to mount up when a rush of weakness hit her. She held on to the mane tightly and closed her eyes until the episode passed. These incapacitations were coming more frequently now. She wouldn't be able to hide her swelling belly much longer. Only Giles knew about her pregnancy. He had wanted to marry immediately once she was sure. She knew she wanted to be Giles' wife, but not like this. They needed to talk to the Colonel and Father Michael first. She wasn't sure they could marry. Giles would need approval from his superior and she needed the priest's blessing since she was unwed and pregnant. It was time to make the decision. She would bring it up to Giles that night. Jennie mounted up and headed down the road out of Bridgetown.

The ride to the mill was just long enough to make sure she wasn't followed, and not too far to make in an afternoon. Jennie nudged her mount into a slow jog. Watching her surroundings with her peripheral vision she felt she wasn't being followed. Just to be sure she made an unplanned change in direction up the road to the Highlands. There was a thicket not far up the drive where she could slip in on her horse and watch the road for followers. She waited a good 15 minutes and was about to head back toward the mill when Giles came along on Devlin. He stopped at the Highlands drive and waited for Jennie to show herself. He knew she was there. He had shown it to her and taught her how to use the tactic. Jennie rode down to the road to meet up with Giles. Whatever he wanted it must be important for him to follow her out to the mill.

Jennie rode up next to Giles with her hand up shading her eyes. Giles looked down at her and said

"Jennie. After you drop off your bag…yes, I know what you're up to…we need to ride on to the parish. It's time we talked to Father Michael. You almost collapsed at Izzard's office. I saw you." Jennie started to protest, and Giles cut her off.

"Jennie. Don't even start with me today. I've waited long enough. WE have waited long enough. Please. Let's move forward with our lives together. Today."

Jennie was in tears as he spoke. She nodded in acceptance. Giles reached over and wiped her tears with the cuff of his shirt.

"Come on then. Let's go find the hidey hole for your pouch and then we go to see Father Michael. If he agrees, the Colonel will not object." Together they rode on to the mill.

Once at the mill they both dismounted. Jennie held the horses as Giles checked inside for any lurking intruders. Satisfied Jennie would be safe inside the mill, he let her go inside to stash the bag inside the mechanism housing. Opening the cover, she gasped and stepped back.

"Giles. I think I need you to s…" Jennie fainted into Giles' arms. He laid her down softly on the floor.

"Jennie? Jennie can you hear me? Dear lord now what…Jennie!" Giles was gently shaking Jennie, stroking her hair. Slowly she began to come around. "Jennie? What on earth…are you ok?" Giles was frantic. Jennie came to her senses, more or less, and began to point in horror at the housing. Giles helped her sit up against the wall before he went to investigate what scared her.

Looking down into the housing even Giles gasped and stepped back. Covering his nose and mouth he looked back again to be positive of what he saw. There in the bottom of the housing was what appeared to be a mummified newborn infant. There was a note pinned to the ratty old bit of linen wrapping the child. Giles carefully removed the note. It was new, clearly left for Jennie to find. The note read

'This is Esmerelda Conn, daughter of Isabella Conn. Her father is Moses. Her mother mercifully let her die. Father Michael must tell you the rest himself."

Giles gave the note to Jennie who sat upright to read it twice. She looked up at Giles quizzically.

"Giles? What is this about? Why would someone do this…leave a mummified baby for me to find? Is this a sick game of some kind?" Jennie's hands were shaking as she held the note.

"I think I'm beginning to understand some things. Father Michael has the answers."

"What answers? I don't understand." Jennie was still woozy. She held her hand out and Giles helped her stand. He led her outside for the fresh air.

"Who was the Esmerelda that was killed on the road?" Giles asked the obvious. "Does her parentage have something to do with her death? Someone clearly thinks so." Jennie sat down in the shade on a rock. "Wait here while I collect the…remains…Father Michael has some explaining to do and a child to bury properly." Giles went back into the mill. He emptied the courier's pouch and gently put the wee corpse inside. He placed the letters in the housing as arranged and closed the cover. Giles carried the pouch carefully, as the wee baby was still someone's child and deserved the respect due any child.

Giles helped Jennie mount up and handed her the pouch to hold while he mounted up on Devlin. He reached over and took the bag from Jennie and gently hung the bag across his chest with the shoulder strap, the bag behind his arm. Without comment, they headed to the parish. Father Michael had some explaining to do. And a blessing to give. Giles would have both that day, which was decided.

Jennie was unnerved and feeling dreadful by the time they arrived at the parish. Giles helped her down and steadied her as her knees tried to give way under her again. Peter took the horses without asking any questions. He merely stated Father Michael was in the rectory, to go straight in. Giles nodded and half carried Jennie into the vestibule.

"Father Michael? Are you here?" Giles called out for the priest upon opening the door. He led Jennie into the private dining area and let her sit in a chair at the table. Father Michael tottered into the room wiping furniture wax off his hands.

"Pews wait for no man, Giles. What can I do for you and Miss Jennie today?"

Giles said nothing, he just handed the bag to the priest. Father Michael looked quizzical and asked, "and what's this?" Looking at Giles and Jennie his joviality waned. "What is this? Giles, Jennie…what is this and why are you here?"

"Open it. You tell us." Giles had gone quite cold and Jennie was silent. The priest set the bottom of the pouch on the table and opened the flap. Peering in he quickly dropped the flap back over the top.

"Dear God." Eyes closed, his face downward, he asked again. "What is this about? Why have you brought such a thing into the rectory?" He opened his eyes as he raised his face and looked from Giles to Jennie and back. "WHAT is this about?"

Giles handed him the note that was attached to the infant. The priest sunk into a chair, realization finding a home in his gut.

"Where did you find this note and this long dead child? She was interred respectfully and with the blessings of the church. WHO HAS DONE THIS! I WILL KNOW WHO HAS DONE SUCH A THING!!!" Furious, the priest stood up, shaking with rage.

"Michael. Someone wants us to know about the real Esmerelda and how she was not the girl that was killed on the road. Tell US what this is about. The child was left for us to find and the note was left for us to find YOU."

Ashen faced, Michael nodded. "Yes. I can see you are correct. But first we must…"

"No, Michael. Tell us now." Giles wasn't letting Michael leave the room until he shared the truth about Esmerelda.

"Isabella was pregnant with another man's child. Andrew wanted nothing to do with the birth or the child. He arranged for Isabella to birth here and she would leave the child with us. In return he would allow her to remain his wife. When Isabella went into labor, he dropped her off and went to Bridgetown. Her labor was long and horrible. Esmerelda was born after a full two days of excruciating labor. Isabella came close to bleeding to death. I truly thought she would not survive. The child was, as you can see, deformed. Anencephalic. She had no brain. She didn't live to take her first breath. Isabella, by the grace of God, cried for her daughter. We gave her last rights and I interred her into a crypt at the back of the church. A blessing, a kindness the child never knew pain or suffering. Esmerelda's father was Moses. Andrew's breeding buck.

"Are you saying Isabella was having an affair with Moses?" Giles was unbelieving in what he was hearing.

"No. I'm not." Michael looked from Giles to Jennie. "Dear Lord. You don't know. You truly don't know. Andrew can be quite an abusive man. He set Moses to cover Isabella in a drunken rage when Isabella found out about John Dewe's wife carrying Andrew's child. This happened on a regular basis until Isabella's belly began to swell. Oh yes, Andrew is quite a nasty character behind closed doors."

Giles and Jennie were dumbstruck. "So, who was the Esmerelda raised as their daughter?" Jennie asked the obvious question.

"The same night Esmerelda was born, Penelope Fuller...Ethan Fuller's wife...gave birth to twins. A girl and a boy. Penelope died before she could hold them both. Ethan brought the girl to us. Isabella needed a baby to nurse, and the wee girl needed a mother. God's hand put them together. When Andrew returned, he was truly perplexed. We all let him believe the baby was his, that he had fathered the girl. It was possible so we just didn't tell him otherwise. He never knew. Until the Rosebud Cotillion.

Jennie put the puzzle together stood and covered her mouth with her hands in horror. "Samuel. Samuel Fuller was her brother. Her twin brother. Andrew must have seen them together as young adults and saw the family resemblance." Jennie had her hands twined in her hair, pacing in fury. "Isabella had to tell her the truth and she went to Andrew to confirm her mother's story...but she TOLD her mother's story...oh. My. God." Jennie sat down heavily in the chair, eyes closed, head in her hands.

Giles was piecing more together as the priest nodded. "Ethan and Samuel were furious at being spurned, but Andrew wouldn't say why. Ethan puts his buck Michael on to cover his own daughter, unbeknownst to him." The priest nodded again.

"Samuel was distraught because he believes he will be blamed for Esmerelda's death. That was why he was here waiting for you after her funeral. But you couldn't tell him the truth. He would've killed his father himself." Michael nodded again and paused.

"How did you know he was here after the funeral?"

"I came to watch who might come by...but Samuel was already here. I just saw him rail at you and leave. You were kind not to tell him. No good would have come from that." Giles gave the priest credit for trying not to destroy Samuels's family all together.

300

"Thank you, Giles. I appreciate the understanding. There is no excuse. Life just gets messy sometimes. But we still don't know who killed Esmerelda. Do we?" Michael puzzled the question to them.

Giles answered, "No. No we do not." He stood quiet for a bit, considering what they did know. The assaults on the women over the years..." Michael, I want to see your records of the assaults on the island women. I've seen it briefly once. Now I need to study the dates and names. Let's put this wee girl back to rest and then fetch the journal. We have a killer to catch."

Father Michael stood and nodded with purpose. He gently picked up the baby Esmerelda's corpse and led them to the back of the church to the consecrated crypt where she was originally interred. The lid was barely out of place. He wouldn't have noticed at all unless he knew the baby had been removed. Giles helped him slide the marble lid aside. The priest laid her back into the arms of a priest long dead. This time she would rest undisturbed for eternity. A prayer, a blessing, and they slid the lid shut.

§

Father Michael was now a man on a mission and led them directly to the underground hidden office and records. He lit three lanterns and hung them strategically around the room for full lighting. Giles and Jennie watched as he pulled the precise journal Peter had written in out of its place and opened it on the table. Jennie turned it around and started reading the names in reverse order, most recent to oldest. The records went back 20 years. The magnitude of the deviant behaviors perpetrated on the island women was sickening.

"Father Michael. Why did you keep these records? What purpose is there to know these things?" Jennie kept turning the pages, growing nauseous as she did.

"To have evidence for the future. Look closely at the patterns and names. The same man is responsible for the assaults for the first 16, almost 17 years. The women would never testify it was assault. They all came here to give birth and leave the babies with us. Within a day or two the children would be taken to a wet nurse at a plantation. This was about breeding new blood into the slave population. They used their own daughters to do it. They controlled the women by keeping them pregnant and increased their slave holdings at the same time. Look closely. Some of these poor girls have had five or six slave babies born to them and sold away. Look at this…this girl was 13 when she gave birth! She was 12 years old when her own father let Andrew put Moses on her! I can't prove it was him, but I know it wasn't anyone else. The girl went on to birth 7 more babies before she finally hung herself. I buried her myself in hallowed ground. She earned it."

Michael was pacing fury and rage at this point. Giles and Jennie were beginning to understand the magnitude of the sickness.

"Now…look…let's see…HERE. LOOK HERE. The events become far more sadistic starting here. This is a new perpetrator. A partner, I think. With a new buck. I think at this point Ethan and Andrew were working together. Ethan would use his new breeder for top dollar, and Andrew still used Moses for repeat clients and to get full breed black babies. Not everyone wanted a half breed native buck." Michael was spitting mad at this point. "I am so angry with them. But I have no real proof. This is just an anecdotal record. Ethan and Samuel are both dead. Someone knew and did unto them, clearly. Giles do you have any idea who is behind Esmerelda's death? Ethan's?"

Giles was considering the information dates and notes. "Michael, I think we have two killers. I don't yet know who killed Esmerelda, but I have a gut feeling it had nothing to do with Ethan or the slave baby she carried. I think she knew or discovered something she shouldn't have and was on her way to share that information with…someone…and was intercepted. I have a theory Ethan and Samuel were killed because of the assault on Mary McKenzie. Ethan was careless. I expect the entire Island knew what they had done before he got back to his plantation that morning. I just missed them at the orphanage."

"You are insinuating the Colonel took revenge…"

"No, Michael, I am not. I think it was closer to home. I think it was Elizabeth McKenzie that killed Ethan and Samuel or had them killed." The priest stood straight in disbelief.

"Elizabeth McKenzie? You must be joking. Seriously Michael…"

Giles looked at him and didn't speak as he let the reality sink in Michael's thinking.

Jennie spoke quietly "if Mary were my daughter, I'd have ripped Ethan apart with my bare hands. I can easily see Elizabeth avenging her daughter. Oh, yes. Yes, I can."

Michael was speechless. "So, what do we do? The Colonel is not likely to arrest his wife for avenging their daughter."

"What would you have us do, Father?" Jennie was staring at the priest with hard, lethal eyes. "Tell me, what would you have us do?"

Michael simply shrugged and said "I guess there is nothing to do. We don't actually know, there is no evidence…just our conjecture and an anecdotal set of notes."

Giles continued "but we still have Esmerelda's killer at large. That person must be discovered. I think we can." Giles pulled the journal out of his shirt and showed Jennie and the priest. They both looked up at Giles and said

"SHE?"

"That was my first reaction. The message clearly intends for us to be looking for a woman. But which woman? What is in the journal that makes any sense? Both of you look at it closely. I can't make heads or tails out of it with regards to Esmerelda."

Jennie and Michael poured over the journal for some minutes while Giles fingered the spines of the volumes next

303

to where Michael found the first one. Something was tickling his brain…he slowly pulled one of the journals out and opened the cover revealing neat rows of numbers, sums, and subtractions. The handwriting. This matched the journal left for him to study. "Michael. Whose handwriting is this? The penmanship is perfect. A perfect match to the journal…"

Michael looked from the journal to the ledger. It was indeed the same hand that wrote in both volumes. Jennie took them and compared them under one of the lanterns.

"Giles is correct. These were written by the same hand." Jennie looked at the priest. "Who wrote these figures? And what is this ledger for? Father Michael?"

"These are the real records for the Parish. The books I keep for the Bishop are upstairs for his use. Don't look at me like that. You can compare them if you want to. The real books are what I use to keep the money local. The Bishop's books reflect a meager, yet worthwhile parish. If I let him see the real books, I would have nothing left to feed and clothe the children at the orphanage. Nothing to give to parishioners when their homes burn, or their crops die. I am indeed a man of God, but I am a man first. The glory of Rome isn't always so, well, glorious when it counts. Where do you think I'm getting the money to buy the materials to rebuild the parish and half a dozen plantation homes? Every parish on the island keeps these sets of books. The bishop knows. He likes good rum. He gets deliveries with every ship."

Giles couldn't help but laugh. Jennie had to giggle, too.

Giles spoke first "speaking of rum…let's get to the details here. Jennie, go through the journal closely. Look for a something that might give us an idea what we are looking for. Michael…how long has it been since you accounted for your balances…the real balances?"

Michael was pouring rum in small cups he kept in the office. "I balance them every week. At least once. So far everything has been perfect. Peter double checks everything

I do." Michael and Giles looked at each other and looked to Jennie. Michael spoke first

"Jennie, look for common threads of thought or speech. What is that journal about, really. The handwriting is Peter's, as are the ledgers. He is my scribe and thus he knows every detail of the finances of the parish. There is a lot of money I have set aside for the parish and he knows exactly what and where it is. I'm not suggesting Peter is our killer, but he may have accidentally said something to whoever it is. The note did say "she" waits for the *Angeline* as well. I am perplexed who 'she' might be. No idea. Look closely Jennie…"

Giles and Michael sat and sipped their rum while Jennie combed the journal. Michael noticed she hadn't touched her cup. He looked at Jennie's pallor in the lantern light and immediately knew the girl was pregnant. Giles caught Michael looking Jennie over and realized he knew. He quietly put his hand on the priest's arm to get his attention. Michael looked at Giles and realized Giles knew. Giles was the father. Giles was pleading with his eyes for Michael to not say anything to Jennie. Let her bring it up. Michael nodded in agreement and they waited for Jennie to finish. Michael was smiling over his rum. His Jennie was with child. He couldn't help the thrill of seeing her become a mother. Giles squeezed his arm softly to keep his joy under control. The truth might not be quite so happy for him.

Giles finally interrupted Jennie knowing Michael couldn't contain himself much longer.

"Jennie, can you pause for a moment. I think we need to tell Father Michael why we are here today. This needs to come from you, Jennie. And me. I'm here with you and always will be."

Ashamed, Jennie looked away as the tears cascaded down her cheeks. "Forgive me, Father. I am so ashamed." Weeping into her hands the priest went around to her and held her as he did when she was a wee girl.

"Jennie, my sweet Jennie. Do not be ashamed. You bring joy to this old man no matter your trouble. Tell me what

305

hurts you so? No one here will abandon you. Not ever. Tell me, Jennie. I think I know from your pale skin and tired eyes, you haven't touched your rum. Am I right Jennie? Will you bring new life into this world soon?"

Jennie turned away from the priest sobbing. "You don't understand, Father. This...this...child within me...it is the product of...oh, God... I can't even say it..." Giles took her hands in his and said it for her.

"Father, Jennie is pregnant with a child sired by Ethan Fuller's buck, Michael. She was abducted, raped, abused, and returned to my hands as a message." Giles was crying as he spoke in gasps. "I...I couldn't...stop them. I did try...Truly...I couldn't stop them." Sobbing into her hands he finally gave into his own guilt. This was done to both of them. He finally admitted that to himself. "Jennie is my life, Father, we planned to marry before the assault, but now Jennie...I don't know what to say...she has refused me repeatedly. I don't understand. She is my life, and I can't watch her hurt anymore. Her child can be my child, it is hers and thus it will be mine, too."

Michael was crying with them. He stood and put his hands on top of their heads. "Oh, my children. Do not weep. Do NOT weep. Take joy in each other. Heal each other. There is not guilt for either of you. Not this day, not ever. Jennie, do you want to wed Giles? Do you want him for your husband?" Jennie nodded without any hesitation. She did love Giles with her soul and body. "Do you love Giles? Will you let Giles love you and all your children...ALL your children, Jennie?"

"Yes, Father, but I am afraid he will grow to hate me and this child. This child will not look like our children we may have together. I could not bear to watch him learn to hate us." Jennie looked down ashamed of herself and her pregnancy. Tears flowed silently as she wept, agonizing in her solitary reality of having been assaulted.

"Jennie. Look at me." The priest was gently bringing her back to them. "Look at me, Jennie." Slowly she raised her eyes to look at Michael. "You are not to blame. You are to be a mother, Jennie. I expect Giles would have fathered this child had you let him, yes?" Jennie nodded; Giles blushed. "Then this is Giles' child, Jennie. Accept that in God's eyes and heart, this is Giles's child and he will love this child as you do. As I have loved you, Jennie. You are my daughter in all ways but one. Accept Giles as the father of your child and he will be."

Michael turned to Giles "Giles, you have my blessing to wed Jennie, and she has mine to wed you. I get a grandchild!" Michael was ecstatic and his joy took Jennie's doubts away for good. She would wed Giles and she knew he would indeed be the child's father. He would be the father of all her children. If he didn't suffocate her hugging her so tightly, she couldn't breathe. "Giles. I can't breathe, Giles. You can put me down now, Giles. GILES I CAN'T BREATHE!" Giles set her down and kissed her as a woman should be kissed.

Michael mused, "Well she's already pregnant..." and laughed louder. Giles blushed like a schoolgirl and couldn't help but laugh, too. Jennie just rolled her eyes and went back to the journal. They had a killer to catch. Michael poured rum for the men and went to fetch a water for Jennie. A grandchild. Glory be, a grand day it was indeed!

Giles sat with Jennie on his lap as they combed over the journal. As they settled into normalcy, Jennie began to see a pattern. "Giles look here. The dates. Peter was keeping track of ships traffic as well as the church records. And here, he refers to a...I think this says Maria, yes...Maria meeting with...Giles...this says Lieutenant Evans. Who is Maria?"

Giles slid the journal nearer the lantern. "It does say Maria...meeting Lieutenant Evans. And here...meeting with a...Charles. What on earth? What are these sums about? Regular recurring sums..." Giles went cold silent. He wasn't sure what this was about, but he knew it wasn't good. "Jennie. Put this away in your bag." Giles ripped out several complete pages and handed them to Jennie. He slid the journal in his shirt. "Do not show that to anyone. No one. I don't think Michael realizes what this is or might be. I'm sure he thinks Peter is skimming the church accounts. I'm not so sure." He slid Jennie off his lap and stood up with her. "Come on, we have a wedding to plan and a killer to catch."

Jennie realized Giles had an idea he had to prove. She had chills realizing he was afraid for their safety, dividing up the evidence. The answer was in the journal. The answer WAS the journal.

# 19

The bow of the *Angeline* rose and fell with the waves. Spray blew up alongside the Sakakawea figurehead pointing the way. She had led the Captain safely and steered him to skirt the hurricane that plowed over Barbados and ravaged the eastern seaboard of the American continent. The *Angeline* had lay low in various harbors for weeks making her way back to Barbados filled with desperately needed goods. The hurricane had delayed their arrival by several months and her passengers were anxious to arrive in Bridgetown. Finally, the lookout cried 'land ho!' as Barbados was sighted in the eyeglass. They had arrived at last.

Captain William Douglass of the *Angeline* felt a great weight lift from his shoulders as they dropped anchor in Carlisle Bay once again. The journey had been treacherous and unusually difficult, but they had arrived safely. Scanning the harbor, the Captain quickly realized they would be further out in the harbor than normal. There were ships wrecked from the hurricane in the shallows and on the beaches. Getting to the dock was going to be an adventure in freight transportation. The lighters were beginning to row from shore as the anchor took hold in the seabed and held fast.

The Captain had no way of knowing they were directly over the *Turmalina*. She was a Brazilian beauty laden with emeralds, gold, and fine silks trying to escape the hurricane and failed. Much of the cargo had washed up on the shore, looters enjoying the bounty cast upon them by the winds and surf. Many years would pass and several more hurricanes would roar through before the wreck was fully buried, added upon, and buried yet again. Such was the way of the sea and all who dared to sail upon her. The lighters were nearing the *Angeline,* the dock workers holding up bottles of rum for the thirsty crew.

"Permission to come aboard, Captain!" The oarsman in the first lighter called.

"Aye, mate, welcome aboard the *Angeline!* Tis our pleasure to welcome you on deck. Crew, welcome the dockhands from Bridgetown!" The Captain called and the crew roared with greetings for the dock workers with bottles of rum to greet them. The Captain noticed there were…ladies…in the lighters as well. Wasted no time, the enterprising girls that they were. "Gentlemen make sure everyone is accommodated as our guests. Just make sure the passengers and freight are unloaded before you unload your cocks!" The crew roared in laughter but knew the Captain meant business. They would get the ship's passengers and freight safely to land before they indulged in any debauchery. The Captain was a good and fair man, but he would not allow anything less than professional behaviors while on board the *Angeline.* The crew was thirsty and horny, and thus they worked fast yet with skill and accuracy. The Captain smirked and went to his cabin to pack his critical items for shore.

Captain Douglass was sorting through his manifests and contracts he would need on shore. He glanced out the window at the back of his cabin with a view of the port wondering where he would find the people he needed to see.

310

The market and business districts were essentially gone with a few temporary structures functioning as reconstruction offices. He would go to the garrison first and find Colonel McKenzie. The Captain was confident either the Colonel or his lieutenant would have a suggestion of where to start. The Colonel was usually a good bet for excellent accommodations as well. A case of good scotch usually opened those doors for as long as he wanted the bed.

Looking at his bunk in the tiny ships cabin he pulled out the duffle from underneath and began packing his clothes for shore. He would take almost everything to be freshly laundered and repaired as necessary. It was unlikely he would be able to find a tailor to make anything new this soon after the hurricane. Trousers, shirts, sleep shirts, socks, and undergarments all went into the shore bag with his small leather kit for shaving and another for writing. The leather officer's case over one shoulder and the duffle over the other the Captain headed out of his cabin and toward the ladder down to the lighters. He set his gear down on the deck near the gateway in the railing. He looked about until he found the First Mate, Charles Michaelson and motioned to him to come.

"Charles, I'm headed to the garrison to try and find Colonel McKenzie and arrange accommodations there as you and I usually do. Given the hurricane damages to Bridgetown that may or may not happen. I will leave word with Lieutenant Evans either way. When you and the men are finished unloading the freight that comes off here in Bridgetown make sure there is a watch on board and the men take turns so everyone gets shore time. As you can see there isn't much to do right now except help with the reconstruction. I will be offering hands to the Colonel while we are here. He does us well in security and docking every time we drop anchor. Helping out is the least we can do. Any questions before I head to shore?"

"No sir, Captain. We know the routine. She'll be done right as always. The men take pride in their standards and ethics. I know where to look for ye if I need ye."

"Excellent, Charles. There is coin for the crew in the usual place. Make sure every man gets to enjoy time on shore. Well done, Charles, and thank you. Oh yes, I almost forgot…please bring the case of the scotch for the Colonel. You know he is expecting an addition to his cabinet." He and Charles rolled their eyes as the Captain tipped his hand to his hat in an informal salute and Charles responded likewise. A routine of respect and familiarity that made the long sea voyages tolerable.

Charles turned back to the crew and the enormous job of unloading the ship. The dock workers had arrived, and the *Angeline* was a beehive of activity with several rows of lighters at her side to move people and freight to shore. The Captain had boarded a fully loaded lighter heading in and was helping row the heavily laden boat. They dodged several wrecks as the surf took them into the Careenage docks. Tying off at the shallower end he climbed out and up onto the dock. The oarsman tossed up his duffle and officer's case with ease and he set them aside to help the men set up to unload the freight. At that point he was in the way. They could unload the boat faster than show him how.

The Captain slung the officer's case strap across his shoulder and chest and tossed the duffle over his shoulder. He set out for the garrison thoroughly enjoying the sensation of terra firma under his feet again. Crossing the bridge over the inlet to the Careenage docks he could see the true extent of the storm damage. Temporary huts dotted the way to the outer walls of the garrison. Enterprise was returning one hut at a time.

§

The Captain made his way to the Colonel's office entrance without incident. Tapping gently on the door he waited a short time and Lieutenant Evans opened the door as gracious as ever.

"Why Captain! What a pleasure to see you again. I saw the *Angeline* drop anchor earlier. I know the Colonel is expecting you and asked me to make sure you have your accommodations prepared as usual. Please come in and I will let the Colonel know you are here." Evans stepped back to let the Captain enter unobstructed and walked over to the Colonel's private office door. He tapped softly and said to the Colonel through the now partially opened door

"Colonel, the Captain of the *Angeline* has arrived. Shall I send him in immediately or settle him in his room first?" Evans waited for the Colonel to respond.

"By all means send him in, Evans. Please take his duffle to the laundry and provide him with fresh clothes if he needs them immediately. Make sure he has a key to his room."

"Yes, sir." Evans nodded, pushed the door fully open and stepped back to let the Captain enter. He held his hand out as the duffle was handed to him.

"Thank you, Evans. I appreciate the services tremendously. Yes, fresh set of clothes for this evening while my own are laundered would be splendid."

"Of course, Captain. It is my pleasure." Evans smiled, handed the Captain the key to his room, and nodded to the Colonel as he gently shut the door behind him as he left to deliver the duffle and arrange the amenities. The Captain sank into a chair as the Colonel handed him a dock glass of fine scotch.

Raising his glass, the Colonel said "A toast, old friend! Another safe arrival is always a blessing. Well done!" They men raised their glasses but were too far apart to clink them. "How was your voyage? Other than way off schedule due to weather..." The Colonel sat back to hear what the Captain had to say.

"Actually, the voyage was remarkably uneventful with excellent sailing. The difficulty was in port. Every port was as broken and tossed as Bridgetown. It will be a long time before they recover. Some may not, I fear. At least everyone is working under the same hardships and somehow that seems to make things just a tad less harsh. The hurricane's destruction was merciless, obliterated much of the eastern seaboard. Bridgetown can step up her game. The world is at her fingertips." The Captain sipped his scotch, eyes closed and simply not thinking of anything for a few moments. "How badly broken is Barbados…the port appears totaled. I know you will rebuild better than it was. What is the outlook for crops, and the holdings across the island?" His eyes stayed closed as he listed to the Colonel reply.

"The island is for all intents and purposes destroyed, in terms of crops, structures, and trade. If a person has something to sell, there is nowhere to sell it…no ships until your arrival, seriously…and the roads are so washed out there is almost no way to move anything. The repairs are happening. They are just going to take some time. People-wise we lost many here in the port and some in the low country areas. The hill ground plantations lost their crops and buildings…save a few…the garrison is the least damaged structure on the island and we still don't have the entire roof put back on." The Colonel sipped bigger.

The two old friends sipped scotch and just sat enjoying the other man's company. Neither had many real friends, other leaders of men with which to collaborate or consult. They cherished the brief interludes of camaraderie and collegiality.

"How is Miss Elizabeth? And your girls? I hope everyone is well."

The Colonel considered and chose not to say anything about the assault on Mary just yet. There were so enjoying just being in the company of each other. "They are fine, Captain. They will be delighted to see you again I'm sure. Especially if you have brought new silks from Paris?"

"Absolutely. Would I deprive your wife from emptying your wallet for her and your daughters? Perish the thought!" The Captain giggled. They had this same banter every time he landed.

"You're a conniving accessory to larceny, Captain. Feminine larceny enabled by a salty old seadog extortionist." The Colonel's took his turn to giggle.

"And curmudgeonly old kilt laden highlander that you are wouldn't have it any other way." The Captain was pleased with his quick and snarky come back. They broke up laughing in unison.

"More scotch, Captain? "

"If I must, Colonel. If I must."

"I insist, therefore you must." The Colonel, poured, the men drank their scotch telling stories and laughing loudly. In tears the Captain finally called a stop to the refills.

"Colonel, I must get up and bathe before dinner. Perhaps even a nap. We can chat real business later. I must find the merchants that go with my manifests and invoices. My men and the dock hands will have the *Angeline* unloaded by nightfall. Maybe a bit left for morning since they are further out than normal. Thank you for your wonderful welcome, as always. My First Mate, Charles, will be showing up when he can. I assume Evans will have a key ready for him?"

"Yes, yes of course. I expect he already does. Evans is thorough and does his job very well. Anything you need just let him know." Standing, the Captain stood in unison, swallowing his last bit of scotch before he left for his room. The Colonel stepped to the door to let him out. "Dinner is planned for 8:00 as usual. I'll see you then unless you sleep through. Good to have you here again, Captain."

"Thank you, Colonel, I plan to be there at 8:00." The Captain nodded, tucked his officer's case under his arm and headed to his room. Walking across the breezeway he could smell the hibiscus blooms in the hedges, the earth under his feet, and clean fresh scent of laundry drying in the breeze. The simple things he missed at sea. Stepping briskly up the steps and turning down the hall he passed through the first set of double doors and used the key Evans gave him to open the door to his usual room.

Entering the room, he found fresh clothes on the bed and he could smell the lavender petals steeping in the bath. Heaven couldn't be this good. It simply wasn't possible he thought as he undressed and headed for the bath. He set his documents case where he could see it from the tub, stepped lightly across the cold floor and stepped into the hot water with pure pleasure as he settled in. He closed his eyes and was instantly asleep. The scotch and hot water did him in, bliss took over. But not for long.

A loud knock on the door to his room woke the Captain. He stepped out of the tub and wrapped himself in a warm towel and went to see who was in need of his attention. Whoever it was had better have a good reason for interrupting. Downright snarly when he opened the door, he found a courier's pouch on the floor just outside the door. Opening the door wider to see who had left the pouch he saw the outer double doors shutting and the courier gone. Perplexed he picked up the pouch, shut the door, and made his way over to the small desk across from the bath door.

Opening the pouch, he found a stack of letters addressed to CHG, the seal unknown to the Captain. The letters had been erroneously delivered to his door. He put the letters back in the pouch, all 17 of them, and decided he would take them to the Colonel at dinner. Seeing his freshly laundered and dried clothing on his bed he realized dinner would be happening sooner than he expected and set to shave and dress in fresh attire. He had stayed as the Colonel's guest many times and thought nothing of the attendant coming in his room as he slept in the tub. It was their job to be discreet and comprehensive in their services. His personal attendant knew his tastes and proclivities. The chosen partner would be waiting for him when he returned that evening to entertain and provide for his every need. The Captain smiled to himself at the thought of what the evening might provide.

Finally, dressed and ready, the Captain was hungry and thirsty. The Colonel's table would be a welcome change to *Angeline's* galley. Courier's pouch in hand he locked the door and made his way to the Colonel's private dining room. A real dining room with china, silver, hot foods that required a knife and fork…oh yes, he was ready for dinner.

## 20

Entering the dining room the Captain found old faces and a few new faces, too. He always enjoyed meeting new people and typically the Colonel put people together that could and would help each other, and thus him. The Colonel made the Captain's life easier when he was in Bridgetown. The Captain went out of his way to make it worth the Colonel's efforts to do so. The sideboard was sporting several decanters of different varieties of scotch, boards with cheeses and meats, and chocolates. Dinner would be served in about an hour. No telling what wonderful and succulent entrée the chef would present to them this evening. God the Captain loved Bridgetown. The Highland warrior knew how to take care of his own, and thus those that enabled his charity.

Sipping on a particularly smoky old scotch and nibbling on a beautiful aged cheese and tongue tidbit, the Captain was fully engaged in culinary delights. He chit chatted with the people he knew and was most gracious introduced to those he was meeting for the first time. The Colonel always gave his guests a few minutes to interact before his arrival. The Captain held the courier's pouch under his left arm waiting for the Colonel to arrive.

The Colonel came in the room at 7:30 to greet his guests. Lieutenant Evans was two steps behind him when they entered the dining room. Ever the excellent host, the Colonel greeted each guest by first name, shook hand, asked about their service, and let Evans refer any adjustments required to the subordinate staff. The Captain was most gracious about his accommodation, the scotch and his anticipation of a delightful meal. The Colonel smiled, pleased that his guests were well taken care of and enjoying their evening.

The Captain almost forgot about the pouch and stopped the Colonel as he began to turn away. "Colonel, hang on just a moment." The Captain set his glass of scotch on the sideboard and took the pouch out from under the other arm, extending the pouch out toward the Colonel. "This was left at my door earlier. The letters are addressed to someone other than me. Do you think Evans could make sure it is delivered to the correct recipient?"

Frowning slightly, the Colonel took the pouch and opened it far enough to look inside at the address on the letters. His face went ashen when he realized who they were intended for. Recovering as quickly as he had been surprised, he said

"Thank you, Captain. I'm sure Evans can deliver to the proper person. I'm sure they will be most grateful for your honesty in returning the pouch to them in a timely manner." He turned to Evans with a dead cold stare, handed him the pouch, and continued. "Evans, please see to it these get to the intended party. Let me know when you have done so."

Evans took the pouch with a quizzical look on his face and replied "of course Colonel. Right away sir." He turned and left the room to find a proper courier for the pouch. Opening the pouch as he walked, he looked inside to ascertain to whom it was to be delivered. Evans stopped dead in his tracks at the CHG initials. He pulled out one letter and turned it over. The seal was unmistakably Henri Izzard's. Quickly he returned the letter to the pouch and closed the pouch tightly. He looked around to be sure he wasn't being observed. Satisfied, he went straight to the Colonel's private quarters. He knocked softly on the door and waited. When the door opened, Elizabeth McKenzie looked Evans straight in the eye and said

"Yes, Lieutenant? What can I do for you? I'm sure you are aware the Colonel is already gone to his dining room."

Evans replied "Yes, Lady Elizabeth. The Colonel asked that I deliver this pouch to the appropriate recipient. It was errantly left at the door of the Captain of the *Angeline* earlier. I'm truly not sure to whom I should give the pouch. Please look at the address and suggest..." Elizabeth took the pouch and opened it to see the address as Evans had done just moments prior. Without any reaction at all she said

"Who is the representative for the CIIG? I have heard of them as everyone has since the hurricane, but I don't know who they are. I'm truly baffled. Why would you bring this to me in the first place? Did the Colonel suggest you do so? If he did, then I will take it and keep it for him until he returns later. Otherwise, I'm afraid I'm of absolutely no help to you." She waited for Evans to reply. He raised one brow before he spoke.

"Lady Elizabeth, I am aware of the couriers that frequent your door. No one gets in the garrison and near your door I don't know about. I have seen many a pouch identical to this one taken by your hands. If you say this is not for you, then I have no idea what to do with it." He looked coldly at the woman trifling with his professional competence. She had a difficult time not breaking into loud and raucous laughter at his offense. She calmly replied

"Lieutenant, I'll hold it for the Colonel until he returns. He can decide what to do with the letters then. If that suits you?" Elizabeth waited until Evans made his decision.

"Very well then. Keep them for the Colonel to review later. If you need me to deliver them elsewhere by all means let me know. Good evening Lady Elizabeth" He nodded and turned to leave.

"Thank you, Evans." Elizabeth closed the door and took the pouch directly to her private desk. Opening the lid with the key she wore on a ribbon around her neck she laid the front down into the writing position. She set the pouch down, opened it and began to look at the letters one by one over a candle to read the bits she could decipher through the paper. Izzard just had to use premium heavy stock to ensure his correspondence was private. Yes, he did. Frustrated at what she couldn't quite read, she knew she would have to let her husband return the pouch to Izzard to resend. It would take another day or two to get her hands on them through the correct channels and read them. So close and yet so far.

Elizabeth sighed and returned the letters to the pouch. The next to the last item caught on the last letter and the letter popped open without breaking the seal. Curious, she carefully unfolded the letter to read it.

'CHG, just to confirm Andrew and Isabella Conn have agreed to the majority of your terms. There are a few minor points they wish to discuss. We are to meet again in a fortnight to conclude the negotiations and create the contracts. I will forward a sample to you at that time for your approval and signature. *HI, QC Barbados'*

Elizabeth smiled. Assuming the rest of the letters contained similar information, the CHG was about to control 90% of the sugar industry on Barbados. Once they did, they would have the leverage to control the production and price for sugar in the entire West Indies. She smiled smugly to herself. She refolded the letter and slipped in between the others as it originally was, closed the pouch and waited for her husband to return. Pouring herself three fingers of his very best scotch, she twirled with delight at the thought of CHG holding complete control. Her share alone would be worth a small fortune every year. Laughing she went into her dressing room to change for dinner. Tonight, she would hostess in her finest silk and pearls. Why yes, yes, she would.

§

Elizabeth had chosen a glorious purple gown with white purls sewn in decorative motif along the low-cut bodice. Her husband was particularly fond of this gown as it showcased her assets perfectly. She knew what he would want later, and she lusted for the dinner to be over sooner rather than later. She pulled the attendants bell cord. When he arrived, she requested the tray of fine deserts and wine be ready when she and the Colonel returned. He nodded and stepped back for her to exit the room. He closed and locked the door and put out his arm to escort Lady Elizabeth to the dining hall.

Arriving at the hall the attendant opened the door and let Lady Elizabeth enter ahead of him. The dining room attendant immediately put out his arm for her to escort her to her husband. Every dining guest either bowed or curtsied to her as she made her way over to the Colonel. She graciously thanked each person or couple for being their guest that evening. The Colonel smiled devilishly at his wife and the effect she had on every man in the room. His libido stirred slightly. He knew the night would end splendidly. He mused at how skilled Elizabeth was at setting him up to lust for her. How easily she could harden his cock from across the room. Realizing almost every man in the room was resisting an erection made his all the more lustful. But he would wait, he could wait. She would be going to bed with him. The Colonel greeted his wife warmly.

"Elizabeth. What a wonderful surprise. Thank you for joining us this evening." He kissed her cheek and pinched her ass where no one could see as she came up next to him. She began to moisten as he did. "Captain, you remember my wife Elizabeth I'm sure."

The Captain nodded as a gentleman acknowledges another man's wife. "Yes of course, Colonel. Good evening Lady Elizabeth. How delightful to see you again. I hope you and your daughters are well?" Safe conversation only with the Colonel's wife. Anything less a man could disappear forever. The Captain sipped his scotch and munched a bit of cheese. The Colonel was handing his wife a glass of white wine as they spoke.

"As always a pleasure to see you Captain. I hope your presence means we have new and glorious fabrics again? It has been positively dreadful not having real materials for gowns since the hurricane." Elizabeth could be the ditzy wife on command at any given moment. Her husband knew better, but fully understood why. The Captain most graciously replied

"Why of course Lady Elizabeth. I have brought a lovely selection of fabrics, laces, and buttons for the ladies of Barbados. I will let the proprietors in question know of your interest in the best products. They should be available for your review within a day or two." The Captain nodded and said, "excuse me while I refill my glass...and yours as well Lady Elizabeth?" He held his hand out for her wine glass.

"Why thank you Captain. Yes of course. A bit more of the white please." She handed her glass to the Captain as her husband inched his hand lower down her backside and felt her cheeks. Her breasts were pressing hard against her bodice. Her lust was blossoming rapidly as the Captain returned with her wine.

"Thank you, Captain. You are most kind." Elizabeth was trying hard not to show her heightened desires, but her flushed face gave her away. The Captain smirked slightly knowing her husband would be pounding her hard shortly after dinner. Lucky bastard. But no matter, he had dessert waiting for him in his room as well.

"You are most welcome, my lady. Excuse me while I chat boring business with the proprietors of Bridgetown for a bit. Colonel." The Captain nodded to the Colonel and kissed the back of Elizabeth's hand, turned on his heel and began to mingle with the other guests. Elizabeth smiled as she watched the Captain walk away. Fine figure of a man, some lady somewhere was going to catch his eye one day. Turning to her husband she said

"Colonel, your wife is starving. Let's eat."

The Colonel replied "Why of course Lady Elizabeth. Dinner first. Dessert later." He casually set his glass at the head of the table and gestured for the guests to be seated. He held the chair for his wife as a gentleman does for a lady. He was contemplating the curve of her shoulder as he gently scooted her chair underneath her as she sat. She sat straight in her chair, her back never touching the back of the chair. Well trained in the arts of being a Lady, Elizabeth was an excellent hostess and a welcome addition to any gathering. The Colonel knew the value of his Lady and treated her well. Later she would treat him well, too. Oh my, but a lady of a different flame behind closed doors.

Elizabeth watched and listened as the guests chatted about the continuing reconstruction, the costs of recovery, and the salvation offered to them through the CHG. Soon the group would have control of the sugar industry. Quietly, yet completely, they would own the lands, mills, and men who worked them. She smiled to her guests pleased with the progress the watchers had made. Yes, they were about to have absolute control. They would also use their position to change and imbed culture more amenable to workers and distribute income more equitably. Indenture would be phased out as would slavery. The markets would adjust with even handed adjustments. Everyone would become better off and live more secure lives in every phase of the sugar production and sales. Elizabeth sipped her wine as the waiter served her plate first. She graciously waited until everyone had been served before she took up her fork and the guests followed suit.

The Captain was always impressed with the civility the Colonel and his wife could maintain even in the most difficult circumstances. The hurricane had decimated the island, yet the Colonel managed to maintain and share kind words, clear actions, and support both financial and practical. The accommodations he enjoyed were a particularly nice gesture. He enjoyed knowing he wouldn't be alone later. The Lieutenant knew the amenities to provide with discretion. The Captain did have a wife back in England. He kept her pregnant most of the time. They had sex almost constantly when he was home. He left her pregnant and nursing virtually nonstop. She was nursing her 5th child when he last saw her, and her belly was swelling with another. She would drop the new baby any time now. He would impregnate her again when he returned home in a few months. She was a good wife and mother to his children. As long as he kept her pregnant, he could be sure she wouldn't stray from his bed while he was gone. Just the thought of her made him long for a wench. Shifting in his chair, he focused his attention on the merchant across the table from him.

"Seriously Colonel, I don't know what the missus and I would have done if your men hadn't come to help us when they did. We are nearing completion of the initial reconstruction of the Roaring Boar and hope to be open for normal business in a fortnight at the latest." His wife nodded in agreement. The Colonel replied

"Splendid! I know I'm looking forward to your ale and cheese boards again. A good game of cards or darts. Excellent indeed! A toast to your successful rebuilding! I look forward to your success!" The Colonel raised his glass as the group all cheered the good news for the Roaring Boar proprietor. These stories of successful turnaround were indeed welcome news and were happening more daily. The Colonel was truly pleased. The rest of the evening passed with laughter, good food, and the men growing horny as they grew rested and fed. Elizabeth initiated the end of the evening as she rose to retire for the evening. The guests thanked the Colonel and his Lady for a fine evening. The tottered out to the street and made their way home in whichever direction home lay. The Colonel and his Lady retired to their quarters and the Captain ambled back to his guest room.

# 21

As the Captain expected there was company when he arrived.

"Good evening, Captain. Tis good to see you have arrived safely in Bridgetown once again." The apothecary shopkeeper's daughter smiled warmly, set the book she had been reading open and face down on the table, and reached up to hold the Captain's face in her hands as she kissed him tenderly. The Captain wrapped his arms around her and pulled her close. She could feel his erection through his clothes and reached down with one hand to loosen his trousers.

The Captain unlaced her bodice and dropped it as she stepped out of her skirts. She unbuttoned his shirt and helped him lift it over his head. Breathing rapidly, they kissed. He nibbled her neck as he picked her up and took her to the bed. The Captain sat on the side of the bed and removed his boots and trousers. He stood and went to the sideboard and poured them each a glass of red wine. He handed the girl a glass of wine and offered her a choice of chocolates the attendant had left for them. She picked two and enjoyed them as he sipped his wine and relaxed.

327

"Captain, will you be in Bridgetown long? I so enjoy my time with you..."

"I'm not sure actually. Probably a few weeks depending on who arrives in port and what I find to load the *Angeline* for the trip to Virginia, and then England again. I enjoy my time with you as well." She was nuzzling his neck and feeling her way south again.

"I've missed you. You know how to please me, sir." She nipped at his ear teasingly. He ran a finger down her neck over one breast and down her belly to her crotch. She yielded to his touch, moaning softly to encourage him. Gently he nibbled and kissed and teased his way down her ear and neck. Finally, he whispered

"And when were you going to tell me about the wee one you carry? Is it mine?" He waited patiently for her to answer.

"I wasn't going to tell you at all. I know you'll be gone soon, and I may never see you again. You're a sea Captain married to his ship...and a wife in England with...how many children has she born you? But yes, the child I carry is yours. You needn't worry yourself about either of us. I'm well cared for and will raise him or her well. Right now, I want to concentrate on enjoying you while you are here." She went back to nuzzling and cooing softly as he stopped her.

"My lady, I am not the sort to ignore or abandon any child of mine. I only have your word what you carry is from my seed. Once the child is old enough to see family resemblance or not, we can have this conversation again. My wife's children are stamped with my image. I expect your child will be as well, if it is indeed my issue. I have no worry about you or your child. Motherhood is not the service I pay you for."

She enjoyed her work and kept the Captain entertained well into the wee hours of the night. Fully exhausted they slept soundly until the first rays of sun pried open the dawn through the window. The Captain silently arose and went to the bath to wash and dress for the morning. He slid several pound notes inside her book as a bookmark, pulled the bell cord to alert the attendant and left silently for breakfast. The attendant would bring a tray of hot foods for the lady in the bed chamber and discreetly assist her with her bath before leading her out through the bath access stairway. The Captain had ladies in a number of places and always made sure they were well cared for. A man of his times, it was just how life was.

§

The Captain was enjoying a hot breakfast in the officers dining hall, watching the activity in the breezeway through the same window as had Thomas Dewe. The First Mate, Charles, from the *Angeline* wandered in about half an hour after the Captain.

"Morning Captain." He sat across from his boss and waited for the ever present attendant to produce a pot of tea, a round of warm bread and a pot of fresh butter. He had taken advantage of the bath and company barber early and was famished for real food again. "The Colonel has provided for us in fine style, sir. I am most grateful for his generosity and kindness. If I don't get to tell him myself, please tell him for me. The hot baths are a wonder after weeks at sea." He closed his eyes remembering the bliss of hot water washing over him as he sank into the tub the night before.

"Indeed. The Colonel is a good man to know. A gentleman of the first order." The Captain sipped his tea as Charles was served a hot plate brimming with long missed foods. "Were than any issues unloading the *Angeline*?"

The mate swallowed, shaking his head. "No, sir. Went smooth as silk. The dock crews here are good workers. Good men. Know how to work together." He forked another sausage and bit half off. "We had to bring it all to the garrison warehouse for storage. Everything else is either blown away or completely filled with salvaged goods.

"Excellent. When you are rested and have had time to get things organized get the signed delivery manifests to me. I need to compare them to the loading documents…weights, numbers…you know the routine." He sipped his tea between hunks of bread with butter and jam, planning to inventory the freight later that morning. How convenient the freight was just underneath his feet.

"Aye, Captain. I know the routine. The case of scotch for the Colonel is in his private office, as we always do. I hope that was the correct of me. I didn't want to…wake you last night." The mate was looking at his plate, eating and talking. The Captain knew that meant Evans let him in to leave the scotch for the Colonel and gone straight to his room in preparation for his liaison with his lover, Maria. The man was in love with Maria even though they could never marry. The Captain understood what it meant to truly love someone and allowed him his privacy. He was the best First Mate he had ever employed and meant to keep him.

"Thank you. I'm sure the Colonel will be delighted to find his favorite scotch when arrives this morning. What are your plans for the day?" The Captain only wanted general information. He let his sailors have their lives when on shore leave. Charles thought for a minute and replied

"I think I'll hire a horse…or maybe the Colonel will loan me one for our stay…and ride out to the country. See something other than the sea for a while. I miss the livestock…and the gardens. There's a parish not far from here. I think the priest will let me stay if I help out around the church for a while. Help them rebuild." He chewed on bread and gazed out the window as he spoke.

"Sounds like a wonderful retreat. I wish I'd thought of it myself." The Captain sipped and considered the allure of the countryside, the aromas of the earth and foliage. "Enjoy your excursion. You've earned it." He pulled several pounds in coins out of his pocket and slid them over to the mate. "Here…no take it…you truly have earned extra. Enjoy your time on the island. Get some new clothes…boots…whatever you need. Take care of you for a change." The Captain genuinely cared for his men. Charles worked harder than five men.

Charles nodded and took the coins, grateful to his Captain for his kindness and generosity. The Captain was the first man to employ him that didn't shun him or abuse him for his proclivities. "Captain, thank you. You're easy to work for. Ye respect a man for his skills and work. I will find a tailor and cobbler. They will need extra work right now so I may get a good price. A few days in the country and my things will be made and ready when I return." He smiled and put the coins in his poke and slid it back into the inside pocket of his trousers and went back to consuming his platter of food. The Captain smiled watching the man enjoy the simplest of God's pleasures in peace, a welcome change.

Finished with his tea the Captain stood to stretch his legs around the dock area. He wanted to see the damages and reconstruction efforts firsthand. Charles said

"I'll check in with you…and Evans, too…before I leave the city…in case anything comes up you need me for."

"Excellent. I doubt you'll be needed but thank you. It's a very different Bridgetown than the one we left a few months ago." Enjoy your breakfast. I'll be in touch as needed. The Captain nodded and left the dining hall, descended to the breezeway and made his way out to the street past the Colonel's inner office door. Out on the street, he turned his face to the sun for just a moment to savor the warmth on his skin. Looking toward the old market area, he chose to head for the battery and walk the docks casually. Carriages were making their way along the streets with patches of new cobblestone where the storm had torn out sections of odd sizes. He came to a milliner selling straw hats out of a box. He found one that fit reasonably well and was pleased to shade his eyes and face as he strolled.

The Captain hadn't gone far when he began to overhear the conversations about reconstruction and a company called the CHG that was buying up all the debts and lands across the island. Curious, he realized whoever they were they were quickly gaining control over the sugar market in Barbados, and as result would control the entire industry in the West

331

Indies. Very interesting. He was sure he would learn more if he just paid attention. Such an economic shift could mean vast wealth opportunities for him, or complete ruin depending on how he managed his contracts. He would indeed learn more. He sensed a sugar war was brewing.

Walking along the battery further he enjoyed fresh fruits and spent some time listening to the local music. Bridgetown may have blown away with the hurricane, but her culture certainly survived. He was smiling as they played when he saw the First Mate ride out of town headed for the parish just out past the cane mill. He said a mental prayer for his friend and hoped the priest would indeed welcome him as he always had. The Captain stood and began his return stroll to the garrison. He had work to do and wanted it done before noon. Then he would enjoy browsing the shops further and a pint at the Roaring Boar.

# 22

Charles took his time as he rode out of Bridgetown. He had the green ribbon tied around his hair as Evans instructed him to do whenever he left the city. The horse Evans provided was more than decent, calm, gentle…an easy ride with a smooth gait. He had forgotten how much he enjoyed riding and took the time to enjoy this nondescript yet truly fine ride. Evans had sent bags of food and a few supplies he knew the priest was waiting for with Charles and thus could justify the use of the horse by non-military personnel. The Colonel would never know and wouldn't care if he did find out. Charles was nearing the cane mill and slowed his horse down from a jog to a casual walk. He was watchful for movement in the trees and thicket. He heard a hog grunt as the horse put his ears forward and sniffed the breeze to locate the source.

He kept the horse on the far side of the road keeping a tight seat in case the hog moved suddenly and spooked the horse. The horse snorted as he gingerly walked past the source, unseen by the rider the sow felt secure. Her piglets scurried through the undergrowth back to their mother and the horse snorted and arched his neck and side-stepped quickly past them. Charles heard the sow grunt at her babies as they swarmed around behind her. He could just make out her shape in the shadows. She was huge and dangerous. He would let the priest know she was lurking about the cane mill. She needed to be caught or killed. He set the horse into a trot and moved out of the sow's threat zone quickly. He mused there were sharks on land as well as in the sea. Once safely away he let the horse relax into a walk again as they headed for the parish which he could see in the distance over the treetops.

Father Michael was out feeding the chickens when Charles rode into the churchyard. He shielded his eyes from the sun with his hand and grinned widely when he realized who had arrived. "Charles! How wonderful to see you again. I heard the *Angeline* had dropped anchor yesterday. Do you how long she'll be in port?" The priest hugged Charles as he stepped down off the borrowed horse. Charles hugged him back, truly glad to be home again. Charles was but a baby when the priest took him in oh so very many years ago.

"No, I don't know how long we'll be in port. The Captain said probably a few weeks depending on the load and weather. He gave me leave to come help rebuild the parish if you need me. It's good to be home, Father. I've missed everyone terribly." They hugged again and the priest called for Peter.

"Peter! Come see who's arrived!" The priest was walking with Charles toward the stable. "Peter! Where are you man? We've a special guest!" Peter stepped out of the door to the orphanage where he had been working to see what the priest was on about now. Peter stared in disbelief and dropped the linen towel as he hurried over to greet Charles. The men hugged and patted each other on the back so glad to find each other well and safe.

"When did you arrive in Bridgetown?" Peter knew but wouldn't let on to Father Michael. "Will you be staying for a while?"

Charles responded "We dropped anchor yesterday morning about noon. Took way into the night to unload her.

Thanks to the dock hands in port we were done at least a day sooner that we would have been on our own. Staying at the garrison with the Captain as always. Should be in port at least a few weeks." Charles handed the reins to Peter and they walked into the stable as they talked. Father Michael followed to the doorway and said

"I must get back to the chucks and then see about a meal for later. You two enjoy catching up and perhaps Charles can help you with some of the more difficult tasks we've set aside. You know where to find me if you need me." The men nodded and turned back to unsaddling the borrowed horse. Charles removed the bags of supplies and ran after the priest. "Father Michael, hang on just a moment." Charles handed the bags to the priest. "Evans sent these with me for you. Said you were expecting them."

Father Michael took the bags and replied "thank you Charles. Yes, I know what this is, and we definitely have been waiting for them. Medicines and some necessaries." They nodded to each other and Charles returned to the stable where Peter was rubbing the horse down and letting the horse drink a bucket of water. Charles tossed a couple forks full of hay into the manger as Peter closed the stall door.

"I've missed you terribly, Charles." Peter quietly spoke eyes cast down. "I was afraid I'd never see you again." Tears were running down his face at the thought he might lose Charles forever one day. Charles stepped over and dried Peters tear with the rag he had used to rub down the horse.

"Peter that's enough. You know that God willing I will always come back to you." They held each other tightly, neither speaking as they simply held the man they loved. "Let's see about some of those chores Father Michael mentioned. I am here to help any way I can, Peter. We've time for us later. You know Father Michael gives us our space and time and why. But right now, we need to get the orphanage back to functionality. What do you say?" Peter didn't want to let go, but he did. "Yes, let's see to those chores. We will have time for us later. We are lucky you and

I. We do have Father Michael who watches over us." Peter smiled and the men went to the orphanage to plan.

The priest watched Charles and Peter as they began to work together. He so wanted good things for them. Both had suffered horribly physically and mentally at the hands of the priest in Brazil. They found solace and a measure of safety in each other when the world abused them. When he had the opportunity to take the position at this parish he immediately left and brought Peter and Charles with him from Brazil. Michael was sure the pedophile priest in Brazil would have eventually killed them, if Michael didn't kill the abuser first. With hope in his heart the priest left them to their own company, went into the rectory to plan the menu, and poured himself a substantial glass of sacramental wine. One Hail Mary, a genuflect to the crucifix by the door and he was good with life.

# 23

Elizabeth McKenzie slipped silently out of the garrison stable and made her way to the cane mill unnoticed. Years of planning and patience had paid off at last. The Watchers owned 90% of the sugar plantations and crop on Barbados, and thus controlled the sugar industry in the West Indies. Smiling smugly to herself she carried the last letters of ownership to share with the group, each letter going to the proper new owner, the wives and daughters of the men who lost their worldly goods to a hurricane of smart women.

She tossed her hood backward off her head, shook her hair loose, put her heels in the side of her horse and rode flat out ensconced in the full moonlight through the fields. The grandmother watched from the hilltop. She could see in her mind how Elizabeth glowed with an aura normally reserved for native healers and holy women. Elizabeth and Jennie had the glow. Together they created a formidable presence among men and women alike. The old woman continued to make her way down the hill toward the mill. Tonight would be the telling.

Elizabeth pulled her horse down to a walk as they arrived at the mill. Barely winded, she handed the reins to Maria who kept watch on the horses as they met. She carried the pouch over her shoulder as she entered the mill. Almost everyone had arrived. The meeting would begin soon. The women were chatting animatedly, sharing the news of their good fortune and plans they were making for the future. The remaining ladies arrived a few at a time, Jennie Harris being almost the last. Elizabeth welcomed her personally and left her to make her way to the front and begin the meeting. No one noticed as Maria slipped in the back as the grandmother entered the mill.

The group fell silent as she stood waiting for the group to quiet, her staff in her hand and her hood fallen away, her white hair glowed in the moonlight through the window above the millworks. Looking to her left and then to her right, she smiled and walked straight to Jennie. She placed her hand on Jennies belly beginning to swell with child and nodded in approval. Speaking in her native language the girl ever behind her translated

"The ancestors are pleased. Conceived in the devastation of a great hurricane, your child, and her children after her will continue our line of strong women who do good things for their people. All your children carry the blood of our people. This child..." the old woman firmly grabbed Jennie's belly "this child will return the blood of the ancestors in the south to the blood of the children in the north. It is as it should be." The old woman smiled, raised her hands as she closed her eyes looking toward the moon and sang a prayer in an ancient tongue. Not even the girl with her knew what she said. Yet Jennie and Elizabeth understood every word. She sang of the love of a mother for her children and a grandmother for her people, praising the wisdom of the old ones for their mercy and wisdom.

The grandmother turned toward Elizabeth and walked to the center of the room, the women parting the way as the sea parted for Moses. Upon reaching Elizabeth she turned to face the group and said

"You have done as the old ones asked. You have accomplished a great task for all people everywhere. You have begun the most difficult part of your journey. Take the blessings the hurricane has given you and make more, make them a hundred times more for all people. Feed the hungry, clothe and house the poor, be kind to each other in all things. The old ones will be with you if you always keep reverence for the power of the storms be they hurricanes, earthquakes, or men. Know that as the matriarchs of your peoples you have the power to move mountains, ease suffering, and teach those who come after you."

The grandmother raised her staff and struck the ground with it five times. The first time she called to the power of the winds and the winds howled through the mill. The second time she called on the power of the light and a blinding flash of moonlight lit the night across the island. The third time she called for the power of the waters and the tides rose in a great swell to wash the beaches clean of the wrecks. The fourth time she called on the power of fire and the volcanos on the neighboring island shot flames high into the night sky. Last she called on the power of the sacred mother earth and stuck her staff sharply in the floor of the mill. The earth beneath them began to shake and undulate as she spoke again, calling on the all the elements of the universe to seal the pact of the watchers with the ancestors. The women were tossed about, some falling on the floor, others holding on to each other. Elizabeth and Jennie hovered inches off the floor, unmoving, aglow with the presence of the old ones in them.

The grandmother let her arms fall back to her side and grasped her staff with her right hand. She pulled the stick from the earth and the earth settled, the moonlight shone clear on her back, the winds calmed, the seas settled, and the fires ceased to roar. Jennie and Elizabeth were once again standing on firm ground, unsure if they had moved at all.

The grandmother calmed the group by lifting her hand. Smiling she spoke softly and blessed them all as only a grandmother can bless her children. The girl translating was in tears as she spoke. She had never seen the grandmother cry before, much less invoke the elements to bless and carry the people into the future. The grandmother walked through the group as they parted before, pausing to touch both Elizabeth and Jenny on their hearts as she left. The women had the breath sucked out of them as she did, Clasping the old woman's hand as she touched them. They knew pure joy for a moment. Jennies felt her baby stir and knew the grandmother had blessed her and all her children with a wonderful life to come. They would be leaders, healers, teachers, mothers, and grandmothers.

The grandmother left the mill silently. Hood fallen back she walked back toward the hills with her great, great, granddaughter walking behind her. Joy in her heart she went back up the hill knowing she would see great things come to her people and all the people of the island. The tears on her face were for the one who could not be saved from her past, from the burdens and horrors visited upon him as a child. With great sorrow she prayed to the ancestors to take him home gently, to love him as all the others before him. The girl saw the grandmother's tears and asked

"Why do you cry grandmother? What makes you weep in a time of such joy?"

The grandmother replied

"I cry for the one who does not know how to love himself, the one the vilest of oppressors have wounded and left to cry unheard." The grandmother stopped and was looking up at the girl, the moonlight on the girl's face. "I cry for the haunted one who in fear for those he loves destroys his earthly body. I cry for those who love him and may lose him and cry from their broken hearts at their loss. Be careful my granddaughter. Tread softly on the souls of others who are easily wounded. You will know them when they find you. Be kind. You may always be kind." The grandmother turned and sang a prayer through her tears for Maria as she made her way across the ridge of the hill with the full moon lighting their way home.

Maria helped the women mount up and make their way out of the cane mill yard in groups of 3 to five riders. They were safer traveling in small groups, separating as they dropped off at their home plantation. She tidied up the mill house, closed and locked the door before leaving on the horse Charles had borrowed from the garrison. The horse was skittish around the mill yard. He could still smell the sow that had been there earlier in the day. She had moved her piglets further down the hill when the ladies began arriving in groups. Maria knew the horse smelled something and guessed it was the sow. she mounted up and left quickly. She did not want to challenge the sow alone and unarmed in the dark. She and Charles would see about the sow in a few days when they had more men and some dogs to help hunt her down safely.

§

The ride to the parish wasn't far and Maria arrived quietly, leading the bay into the stable unnoticed. Once the horse was properly stabled Maria made her way to the orphanage. She entered her quarters where Charles was waiting for her, reading a book by the window. Charles smiled as she entered, standing to kiss Maria passionately as a man does after a long absence from his love.

Maria put her arms around Charles' neck and held him in a long embrace. Charles' erection was obvious through his trousers, his shirt hanging loosely untucked from his waist. Maria slid one hand down as Charles whispered in Maria's ear.

"Oh God how I've missed you. You are the light of my life. Do not ever be afraid…I will never leave you…God willing I will always return for you. Only you, Maria." He kissed her passionately on her mouth, nibbled her ears and down her neck to her shoulders. Standing between Charles' arms, they kissed deeply and embraced each other, holding each other tightly. Completely in love, they were life partners dedicated to the other always.

Maria tucked her head against Charles' chest and began to cry softly. She knew Charles would leave again soon and it broke her heart every time he left. Charles lifted her head and kissed her tear away. Caressing her hair, her neck, her shoulders, and grasping her buttocks he held her close to him, her shirt shifting upwards as he held her tightly. Charles spoke softly to his love

"Do not weep my sweet. I am here and will always be with you. You know this. Please, do not weep. We are safe here. We can love here unconditionally as we are loved unconditionally. Take heart in our faith in each other here, in this room, where we have loved and laughed, and cherished each other always. Do not weep."

Maria nodded her head and let Charles begin to undress her. He untied her shirt and pulled it over her head and let it fall to the floor. Maria undid her riding trousers and let them slip to her ankles. She kicked off her riding shoes and her trousers fell to the floor on top of them. Naked, they held each other in the moonlight. They were joined as one again in the shadows of the parish and they both slept well for the first time in many weeks together in each other's arms.

# Part 4
# REVELATIONS

# 24

The sun began to stream through the windows as Father Michael was tending to the chucks and collecting the eggs. He talked to them loudly enough to announce his presence but not disturb people either. The hens were hungrily scratching the crumbs as he tossed them into their coop. The priest had his eye on a young rooster that needed a new purpose in life. That one would fit nicely in a pot in a day or two. The rooster eyed the priest watching him suspiciously and stayed out of reach. Chattering with his girls, the priest collected up a couple dozen eggs into his egg basket. Far more than he needed, he would distribute the extras to the families in need of food first and leave a cache under a hen to raise chicks to replace those killed by the storm. It would take time, but eventually the island would replenish itself with chucks from the priest's nests.

Stepping out of the coop Michael turned to find Charles out by the pump shirtless washing out his clothes from the ride. Michael was always surprised to see his boys had grown into powerful adult men. They were truly beautiful in their physique and strength of youth. He was so proud of them. He smiled and waved at Charles as he tottered back to the rectory to start breakfast. Eggs, sausages, tomatoes and fresh local fruits would grace their table this beautiful sunny morning.

God did work in mysterious ways. Michael joined the priesthood after his own beloved Mary had been taken from him in childbirth. Unable to move out of his grief-stricken life, he had left everything behind and taken passage on a ship to Brazil. The Captain had allowed him to come along free of fare if he could pass himself off as the recently deceased ship's priest. No one ever knew he was not the real Michael and was not ordained by the church. He merely took over the real priest's identity. Time passed and he became Father Michael more effectively and more genuinely than the man who died at sea so many years ago.

Some day he would tell Peter and Charles his story. He didn't want them to die believing his lie. He wanted them to know he truly loved them as a man would his own children. As he had loved his twin sons, holding them as they both perished within hours after their mother died birthing them prematurely. God had given him Peter and Charles as a second chance to be a father to two wonderful sons. Michael practically floated above the floor as he hummed and cooked for his boys. They would always be his boys.

Charles and Peter stood in the doorway thoroughly enjoying watching the aging priest dancing about the kitchen cooking and singing as he cooked. Perplexed they managed not to laugh for quite some time. Charles eventually couldn't contain himself and broke up into hysterics at the priest's antics. Startled, Michael missed and dropped the eggs he had been juggling on the floor. The cats came running to clean up the mess as the men laughed until they cried at the humor in the kitchen. Michael feigned distress just to entertain them as he had when they were little, loving every minute of his comedy on the spot. They were indeed home.

They all worked together and soon had a marvelous breakfast on the table. As they said grace, they held hands as they had always, only tighter these days. Life was fragile and they had learned to treasure each other deeply. As they began serving their plates there was a knock at the door. Charles stood up to answer the door wiping his mouth with his linen napkin as he walked across the room. Opening the door, he was face to face with John Dewe.

"Charles? Charles! I had no idea you were here. Welcome home!

"John Dewe. What a joy to see you again. Come in and share breakfast with us!" Charles stepped back and held the door open as John stepped inside the priest's private quarters. He and Charles hugged briefly and walked to the table where Peter and Michael were seated. Father Michael swallowed and gestured for Charles to bring another plate for John to join them. Charles already had a plate and fork in his hand, a linen napkin held underneath the plate as he handed them to John.

Taking his seat John asked "when did you arrive? You must meet my brothers Thomas and Richard. They will be delighted to meet you. It seems you have always missed each other be it here, England or the colonies." John filled his plate as Charles smiled at John's warm welcome.

"Actually, I do know Thomas and Richard. They made the journey on the *Angeline* when they came to Barbados not long ago. I expect they simply haven't had time to mention our conversations. They are both delightful gentlemen." Charles was enjoying his breakfast and deftly managing not to ruin John's. The sea journey with Thomas and Richard had been trying at best and they rarely had time to even speak, much less spend time together. He was honest about their integrity as gentlemen. Not so forthright about the harrowing journey John's brothers survived to get to Barbados. Charles would let them explain the crossing themselves. Charles prayed they would never have such a voyage again. "Do try the tomatoes. Father Michael has taken great pains to resuscitate the vines from the storm ravaged garden. God works through his hands."

John snagged two pear shaped tomato halves along with several sausages, scrambled eggs, a hunk of bread with fresh butter and jam. The men caught up on the news both near and far and told stories about each other with abandon and more than a little embellishment. Fully stuffed they all sat back in their chairs and sipped their tea, simply enjoying a rare moment of peace among dear friends. Michael finally brought them back to the present asking

"John, what brings you to the parish this lovely morning? Is something amiss at the Tallywhoa? Is Sarah doing well? She is getting near to dropping her baby I should think…" Michael sipped and let John ponder how to respond. Charles and Peter started to get up and leave when John stopped them.

"No. Stay, please. Charles is the person who may be the most help this morning." John sipped his tea pensively. Charles and Peter sat back down and sipped, too. Charles focused on John while Peter respectfully looked out the window. Charles asked

"John, I don't know what a First Mate can do for you, but I will help ye if I can. You know I will. What's your trouble, mate?"

"I'm sure you're aware of the buy up of lands and debts since the hurricane." They all nodded in unison. "Thomas and Richard were able to pay the entire debt load on the Tallywhoa. We have sold only a small share to the CHG." The men sat quietly as John went on. "I've been on Barbados for some years now. It's been quite a struggle. I lost my wife and child, had crops destroyed by storms and pests. I'm tired. Tired of the struggle and the politics that come with the struggle. I guess you could say I'm done in. I am leaving my share of the Tallywhoa with my brothers and plan to return to Carolina to help father with his lands there. But I need assistance getting off Barbados with Sarah and a load of freight…goods…for father." Charles raised his brows completely surprised by John's comments.

"What can I do to help you, John? I'm at a loss here…what are you needing from me…from us?" Charles gestured at Peter and Michael as he spoke.

"Sarah will never pass as my wife to get on board the *Angeline*. She will have to go as a servant since she is native. I won't leave her behind. Michael is correct. She is likely to give birth in about 6 weeks at the most. I'm hoping to get her and father's...freight...to the Carolina's first."

Michael was perplexed. "I don't understand the problem, John. Can you explain more clearly to this old man?"

John replied "Sarah cannot spend the voyage traveling as a slave. She must be with me in my cabin. I think she will be fine to make the voyage if she can be with me the entire trip. Father's freight is a bigger worry. With the CHG taking ownership of the plantations...the vast majority...on Barbados, I expect getting goods in and out of the port will suddenly become difficult. Nothing has been said yet but I expect excessive tariffs or taxes...harbor fees...you name it, are just around the corner. I want to get off the island and father's freight to him as soon as possible. What do you think Charles? You're privy to the Captain's contracts..."

Charles sat back in his chair to consider John's dilemma. He truly didn't know what to say. Peter spoke quietly and broke the silence.

"I have an idea..." Charles looked at him cold faced and a bit panicked. "Oh, stop Charles and hear me out." Charles relaxed a bit and sipped his tea. "I want to go to Carolina myself." Father Michael almost choked on his tea.

"WHAT? This is the first I've heard of this...Peter...NO!" Peter put up both hands to shush the priest.

"I'm tired, too, of the smallness of this island. I'm a grown man now Michael. Just as Charles is a grown man and out in the world. I want to go to Carolina and see what that new world has to offer." Charles reached over and put his hand on Peters.

"Father Michael, maybe it is time for Peter to have a chance at a life outside the parish. Surely, you're willing to help him make such a step, as you did me?" Charles was staring at Michael willing him to let go of Peter just a bit. It was time.

Michael stood up and turned his back to the others, trying to hide the tears that cascaded down his cheeks at the thought of losing both his sons to the sea and distant lands. He couldn't speak but he did nod his approval. Peter stood and hugged him, and they cried together. Michael at impending loss, Peter at impending life. John spoke first.

"Michael, you do realize you could come with us. Take a year's relief and make the journey with us. There is the novice in the western district who could manage for you in your absence. You've been a long time gone from those you left behind all those years ago. Many of them are in Virginia or Charles Town now."

John spoke wisdom at his breakfast table. Michael had been a long time gone and he could not let Peter and Charles leave without him. He just could NOT lose two sons at one time again.

"Yes. Yes, I will take a year's leave and make the crossing with you. If Peter and Charles have no objections." Turning to his sons he held his heart in his throat. What if they didn't want him? He couldn't bear that.

Peter was beaming with relief and Charles smiled and said

"Do you think we could leave you behind? Truly? Of course, you must come with us! The ship needs a priest and I think we can solve the problem for Sarah." Charles and Peter shared a knowing smile and said no more.

John looked quizzical at Michael who merely shrugged and said, "don't look at me, I've no clue!" Charles sipped his tea and conspired mentally with his dearest friend in life and simply said

"John, no worries mate. Leave the details to me. I'll give you plenty of lead time of our departure. If I can of course. The Captain must know but he will be supportive of my plan. Please just trust me. The less you know now the better."

350

"Well...I guess we've no choice, really. What do you need from me, Charles?"

"I will need precise information on your freight...size, weight, contents. We can discuss how to frame those parameters later, but size and weight matter most. The Captain will be honest and fair, but not free. The voyage into port this trip cost him dearly with the extended delays. I'll be here at the parish for a while. Let's chat more when you have solid information I can work with. Meanwhile, enjoy your tea. It is truly wonderful to see you again." Charles toasted John's mug as his mental wheels began to spin a web that would catch them all safely aboard and off to Carolina. Peter sat quietly, worried about how they would manage to get away, the freight on the ship, and to Carolina without mishap. He looked hopefully at Charles, and at Father Michael who was smiling and ready to make life happen for them all.

Michael commented "I'll make the inquiry with the western parish about the novice taking over here for a year. He is very close to being fully ordained and everyone knows him already. He is going to be an excellent priest. I think Charles will remember him. William Edwards. He was a year or two older than you and Peter. His parents died of fever and he stayed with us for a few years until he went off to England for school. Yes, he will be perfect. He is ready. Ideal solution. I'll speak with the priest there tomorrow."

Charles spoke softly "Our Willie? A priest? I had no idea! Well good on him...yes, yes Michael I agree. What good news. He is perfect to be here in your absence. May I go with you to talk to the priest? I haven't seen Willie...I can't remember actually but it has been years." Suddenly saddened by the reality of how many people he had lost touch with or lost entirely Charles looked downcast over his tea mug. Michael said

"Charles, William has grown into a fine man. A man of God, truly. More so than I will ever be. I can credit you and Peter for much of his character. No, truly, I can. William is kind, gentle, tolerant, and loving. Truly loving toward everyone as the church would have us all be. You must come with me. Both of you. What a fine way to spend a day together." Truly happy, Michael was overcome with joy, relief, and anticipation of good things to come.

Peter smiled and sipped his tea. He was a bit more cynical and would feel secure when they were safely aboard and far out to sea. Charles had reached over to hold Peter's hand under the table to comfort him. He knew how much Peter feared change and new situations. Peter had been treated so badly as a child. Horrible conditions. Just remembering made Charles angry and tearful to think of what he watched Peter suffer through for others. He believed Michael never knew. Peter took the punishment for everyone. He saved many children suffering on a daily basis. Peter would never be whole again. Too much had been stolen from him as a child.

But Michael did know. He had tried to protect Peter but could not be everywhere all the time. He had spent his life working to help Peter heal and grow into a man. Peter made remarkable progress and had indeed grown into a fine man. But not whole and they all knew he never would be. But that was OK. Charles loved him dearly. Michael had accepted their love for each other long ago. Who was he, a man masquerading as a priest to judge who another might love? No, Michael would protect them with his life. They were the most honest men he had ever known. He was proud of his sons, never more than he was that morning at breakfast.

John sipped his tea, relieved at having begun the next in his life. His life with Sarah and their child. She would be accepted in Carolina, an asset to him in his trading endeavors with the Cherokee and Creek Indians in the area. He knew about Charles and Peter and envied their devotion to each other, and he too, was proud of the good men they had grown up to be. Already he was considering how the two might fit into his plans trading along the seaboard. Time would tell. Pleased with his morning and his decision to come see

Michael, John made his thank you and headed home to the Tallywhoa. Thomas and Richard would be saddened to see him leave so soon after their arrival, but they would understand and wish him well. They would no doubt meet up again in Carolina or Virginia again soon. There would be many voyages back and forth to manage the plantation and market their crops. His leaving wouldn't be goodbye forever. Meanwhile there was much to be done.

§

John nudged his horse into a trot and sat a bit taller in the saddle. It was indeed a good day and would enjoy every moment. As John came into the main gate at the Tallywhoa he could see the temporary structures taking shape on top of the hill. Smoke came out of the kitchen chimney and he could see Ian and Richard were teaching the older boys how to use the hand tools required in building framing for houses, sheds, and even ships. These were good men teaching these orphaned boys how to be men through example. John smiled as he walked his horse over to the temporary stabling paddock.

Sarah saw John ride up and could see he was in a much better mood than when he left. She wondered what might have happened to change his day so profoundly. She would ask him later. It would keep. She went back to organizing the vegetables for the afternoon soup kettle. So far, her cooking had kept everyone healthy. Sarah was a skilled healer as well as a chef. Her knives were sharp, her medicines powerful. She smiled and went back to planning the meals. John was headed to see her. She could feel him thinking about her without looking at him. She put the knife down and wiped her hands on her apron. John put his arms around her from behind and drank in the aroma of her hair, and her neck. He was happy for a change. That hadn't been the case for some time. She waited, knowing he would tell her in his own time.

"John. I'm trying to cook here..." He nuzzled, she closed her eyes and let him.

"Yes. I can see that. We will chat later. Good news my love." He nipped her ear gently and left as quickly as he had come in. Puzzled, Sarah watched him head toward the warehouse where Thomas and Richard were busy rebuilding the primary framing for a new structure. They put down their tools and walked out toward the cane fields together. Whatever it was, John was not going to be overheard. Sarah went from puzzled to worried as the three brothers disappeared around the hillside.

Once they were clear of being seen or heard John stopped and began to explain his decision to leave Barbados.

"Brothers. I have decided to leave Barbados and go to Carolina. I've had all I can take of storms, pests, and the isolation of this island. You two have come at the right time to take over the Tallywhoa. I will be taking Sarah with me of course. I want my child born in America." John waited patiently for his brothers to digest what he said. Thomas and Richard were disappointed but not surprised. John had born the weight of the Tallywhoa operation on his own for years. He was tired and burnt out. John wanted to go to Carolina and work with their father at the other end of their business. John continued

"I plan to manage the sugar products from the Tallywhoa at the distribution end along the Eastern seaboard. There is a lot of money to be made trading with the natives as well as the colonists. Sarah will be a significant asset to us. She will give us entre to those transactions with the native women who control the trade." Thomas replied

"Managing the sugar product at the distribution points up and down the eastern seaboard is the logical next step. John, you are the most qualified to do so. I think you're on to something. Excellent idea. What can Richard and I do to help?" Richard nodded and smiled in agreement.

"We must organize what needs to be shipped on the *Angeline* with me when I leave. Enough product to be legitimate in our offers and provide samples to liaisons. Not so much that we attract too much attention before we establish our trade routes and sites. I've made arrangements for discretion aboard ship leaving Barbados so as not to show our hand to any other distribution managers or the CHG. Looking further into the future, I can see our planation business model being adopted and implemented in the Virginia colonies and Carolina as well. The political environment is perfect to establish dynastic land holdings producing an array of crops. Father may be critical to fostering such a governance scheme in the south. That is a legitimate potential outcome if we are successful in utilizing the sugar distribution and trade routes."

John looked to his brothers and concluded

"I must have your support to make this work. Please do not be hurt I must leave the Tallywhoa behind and in your hands. I trust you will make her prosper as never before. Life is messy sometimes. I must go while I have the opportunity and the health to do so." Nodding their acceptance and support the brothers hugged and headed back to the rebuilding sites. The future looked bright for them in every way.

Sarah saw them coming back smiling and jovial. Something was definitely in the wind. She could feel the shift in the atmosphere. A chill ran up her spine, she knew her world was about to change forever. She returned to stirring the soup as the bread rose in the sunshine. She made a mental note to take a starter of her yeast with her as she began to make her list of what to pack for the new world. Somehow, she just knew, and she was happy. Smiling and humming when John returned to tell her his plans, they embraced without speaking for an extended moment. Sarah calmly said

"I can be packed and ready to leave with short notice. Just tell me what you need me to do." John kissed her and replied

"Sarah, you are my life and my love. Prepare what you might need to live and bring a new life into a new world. We leave with the *Angeline*. We have a week or two at the most. Do not share our plans with anyone. We must be discreet.

The future of the Tallywhoa and our future in Caroline depend on our confidentiality." Sarah smiled warmly at the man who loved her so. She was terrified but she would not let him see it, she would go with honor and confidence into her new world. John kissed her again, hugged her tightly and went back to work at the warehouse. His plan was taking shape and moving forward. He and Sarah would indeed sail with the *Angeline*.

# 25

Father Michael, Charles, and Peter had a wonderful day visiting with William Edwards. William and his supervising priest had both agreed to Michael's request for the novice to provide relief care at the parish while he went to the colonies for a year. William was indeed ready for his collar and this opportunity would provide him the capstone he needed to be full ordained. The young men went fishing, swimming, and played like children for the afternoon. They had a blast just being young men again. Their elders had more fun watching them be the fine men they had raised them to be. At the end of the afternoon they all hugged and vowed to see each other again soon. They would not let years come between them again. Michael and his sons rode toward home laughing and full of happiness.

As they reached the parish Michael mentioned he needed to go to Emerald Oaks and explain his impending absence to Andrew and Isabella Conn. They were housing most of the orphans until the reconstruction of the orphanage was complete. They deserved to have advance warning of the impending change in parish governance. Charles and Peter agreed. Michael rode on to Emerald Oaks alone as Charles and Peter went to the rectory to see about evening chores and get supper cooking. They were happy and content, looking forward to their future. Michael was considering what to say and what not to say to the Conn's as he rode through the gate and headed up to the steps of Emerald Oaks.

Toby came to great Michael and led his horse away to the stabling area as Isabella came out of the kitchen to greet her dear friend and confidant.

"Father Michael, what a pleasure to see you here this afternoon. I do hope you'll stay for supper later?"

"Isabella, I need to speak with both you and Andrew. Is he about nearby by chance?" Michael needed to conduct his business and get back to the parish to begin his preparations for leaving the island for a year.

Isabella replied "I think Andrew is up by the old slave cabins. Toby? Toby would you please go find Mister Andrew and ask him to come to the house? Father Michael is here with news about the orphanage." Isabella correctly surmised the orphanage was the basis for the priest's visit. "Do come up to the table and at least have some tea while we wait for Andrew." Isabella turned and headed toward the house as Michael stepped in beside her.

"Thank you, Isabella. I am parched and would much appreciate some tea." Looking about he commented "I see the reconstruction is progressing well. The stable looks nearly complete. Nicely done, too." Michael was genuinely impressed at the craftsmanship he could see from across the yard. Isabella handed Michael a mug of tea and they sat at the kitchen table to wait for Andrew.

Isabella said "Michael, we have the twins born during the hurricane that need to be baptized. Their mother is still healing. Time will tell if she can bear more children or not. She has been able to nurse her babies about half the time. Fortunately, we have a couple of wet nurses available who have helped her. You know it does not matter to me if they are slaves or not. I want every child born at Emerald Oaks baptized properly. Can we arrange that soon?"

"Why yes of course Isabella. I believe I baptized their mother as a baby did I not? Her children will be as well. Let's aim to do that later this week. I look forward to doing so." Michael truly loved the baptism of infants. Ordained or not, he was sure God blessed the child and judged not the man holding the child. Michael was a more genuine priest than those that studied and made their place through the Holy church. The parish congregation was testament to his effective and caring talent as God's will.

Andrew entered the kitchen and Isabella handed him the mug of tea she had waiting for him. "Father Michael what a delightful surprise. To what do we owe the honor of your presence here today?" Andrew took a seat across from the priest out of the sunlight.

"Andrew, Isabella I have come here today to inform you of my impending departure for a year."

Isabella cried out "WHAT? You can't be serious! Leave us now with the parish in near ruin, the orphanage partially habitable?" Clearly panicked Michael calmed her with his hand on her arm.

"Isabella. I must take leave to go to the colonies for a year. The novice priest from the western parish is going to take over in my absence. You remember him, William Edwards? He is familiar with the entire parish community and is a fine priest. Young and strong he will have the parish rebuilt in short order. Better than it was! I wanted you to know in order to make the transition smooth for everyone, especially for you and the children. I am hoping you will personally be able to help William reestablish the orphanage seamlessly. The children deserve some continuity and familiarity. Jennie Harris will be a tremendous help to you. Many of the children remember when she lived there with them. Giles Freeman comes with her. You know they are to be married very soon?"

Isabella gasped "Really? That's wonderful news! When? We must prepare a fine welcome for them as a married couple. OH yes, Michael, I am thrilled to help with these projects. Indeed I am." Beaming with joy, Isabella hugged the priest and continued. "I am so saddened you won't be here to see the children return, or Jennie's baby come into this world. But rest assured we will care for them all as our own. You know we will."

Andrew added "Let us know what we need to do to help. Of course, you have our support. Thank you for coming to tell us all your wonderful news. This is indeed worthy of a celebration." Andrew stood and went immediately to find Giles Freeman. There was work to be done, and a wedding to plan. Sneaky bastard hadn't let on a peep. Giles was a fine man and Jennie was literally his daughter. Isabella had accepted her and they both would see her happily wed with the man she loved.

Andrew found Ian first. "Joshua, do you know if Giles is back from Bridgetown? I have some things to discuss with him immediately."

"Yes, Mister Andrew. He got back way late last night. He's out in the north cane fields measuring for replanting, I think. I'll go find him. I was headed out there anyway."

"Excellent. Tell him to find me inside the new stable."

"Yes sir, Mister Andrew." Joshua took the nearest horse and rode bareback with a halter and lead rope to find Giles. It was a short ride to the north fields but a long walk home. He found Giles stepping off rows of cane plantings calculating how much would be needed for replanting. Joshua slid off the horse and Giles jumped up and headed back to the house. Joshua began the long walk back, enjoying the afternoon amble in the beautiful late of the day.

Giles rode up to the stable and tied the horse where Joshua had found him. Andrew had seen him coming and was there to meet him as he got to the stable doorway.

"Giles. Yes, we need to talk. Come into the stable if you would, please." Giles followed Andrew into the stable curious to find out what was on his mind.

"Father Michael was here earlier with interesting news. He is taking a year's leave from the parish to go to the colonies."

Stunned Giles simply said "REALLY?"

"Yes. The young priest over in western parish will take over for him in his absence. Michael asked that Jennie Harris be available to help the children transition to the orphanage when it is ready for them."

Giles nodded and said "that is an excellent idea, Andrew. Most of them remember when she lived there. Jennie will love the assignment I'm sure. I'll have her go see Michael as soon as possible. Splendid idea." Smiling, he turned to go back to the fields until Andrew stopped him.

"Not so fast, Freeman." Giles stopped dead in his tracks completely taken aback by Andrews immediate change in demeanor.

"Father Michael also mentioned Jennie Harris would not be available, but that a Jennie FREEMAN would be." Andrew was beaming with joy, but it took Giles a moment to catch on. He hadn't thought of Jennie as becoming Mrs. Freeman, just his wife. Giles blushed, embarrassed at his own male density.

"Yes, Andrew, Jennie and I have Michael's blessing and he will wed us. Soon. Jennie is beginning to swell noticeably. Only the few of us know by whom. As far as Jennie, myself, and Father Michael are concerned Jennie carries my child. For I feel that it will be. I know I would have been the child's father had she not been abducted at that precise time. So yes, we are to marry and have our family."

"Giles. You do not have to explain to Isabella or me. We know you will be a wonderful husband to Jennie and father to all your children. We must have your wedding before Father Michael and Sarah sail with the *Angeline*." Andrew slapped Giles on the back as they walked out of the stable. "What say this Saturday? I think Isabella can organize a lovely wedding and reception on short notice. Force of nature that she can be. Go find Jennie and share this news with her. Make sure she knows it is her choice of course. But also make sure she knows how badly Michael wants to be the priest to wed you."

Giles' mind was racing. Marry in short order. Michael was leaving on the *Angeline*. He most certainly needed to find Jennie and fast. He now had a lead on discovering who Esmerelda's killer might be. The passenger and crew manifests of the *Angeline*. Turning to Andrew Giles said

"Andrew. I must find Jennie immediately. Please explain to Joshua and Isabella. I should be back with her by tomorrow afternoon. Thank you for everything Andrew. I cannot express my thanks enough." He hugged Andrew and went to saddle Devlin for the ride to Bridgetown to find Jennie. Izzard would know where she was and he intended to find her by morning, if not sooner.

§

Devlin was antsy as his master was nervously adjusting his tack. Giles mounted quickly and was out the gate of Emerald Oaks in short order. Isabella and Andrew giggled thinking he was off excited about his impending nuptials. That was true, but Giles' was on the track of a killer. A killer he had to catch before the *Angeline* set sail for Carolina. Giles and Devlin raced through the setting sunlight to Bridgetown. Giles sent the agile dun along the little-known shortcuts he had discovered following the watchers home from their meetings. Devlin flew over the built-in cross-country hunter fences just to facilitate the watchers' movements in the dark. Giles and Devlin arrived at Bridgetown in record time. He let the little dun walk to the office of Henri Izzard.

Devlin was breathing almost normal by the time he tied him at the councilor's door. Giles stepped off, patted his partner gently and went to knock on the door. A candle burning cast just enough light to make him believe the councilor was in. Footsteps coming to the door confirmed his ascertain. Much to Giles surprise, the face that greeted him wasn't the councilor, it was Jennie.

"Giles, what on earth are you doing here at this hour?" Jennie looked to see if Giles was alone or had someone in tow. She opened the door fully to let Giles enter. Perplexed at his presence and demeanor.

"Jennie, are you here alone?" Giles was looking about the vestibule and in Izzard's office. Jennie just stood and watched him dash about a bit.

"Yes, Giles. I'm the only one here. I'm quite safe I think. What on earth has got in to you?" Jennie inquired as Giles looked out the windows and behind the doors.

Giles let the curtains drop over the windows and returned to Jennie standing bewildered in the center of the room. He took her in his arms and kissed her. Jennie's arms flailed about until she caught her balance, wrapped them around her man and kissed him right back. Jennie whispered to Giles "you can come visit me at work anytime, handsome…" and kissed him again.

Giles was clearly kissing her back and reaching lower when he recovered himself and why he was there. Well, the other reason he was there. He would come back to the present reason soon enough.

"Jennie, Michael is leaving the parish for a year and will sail with the *Angeline* in two weeks or less. Andrew found out and insists we marry before Michael this weekend."

"WHAT? OH, you did NOT agree to that without asking me…tell me you did NOT…"

"Jennie, please listen to me. Father Michael is leaving Barbados for a year. I do want him to marry us. I know it is short notice, but please Jennie. I really want this to happen now. Your belly swells as we speak and I want my child…MY child, Jennie…to be born to wedded parents with the blessings of the father that raised you. Please, Jennie." Giles hadn't intended to be so emotional, but he couldn't help himself. Valiant warrior that he was, he was

363

wet noodles in Jennie's hands. Jennie couldn't stifle a wee giggle.

"Oh my, my sweet Giles. Yes. Yes of course we will have Michael wed us before he leaves with the...did you say the *Angeline*?" Jennie finally grasped Michael's panicked behavior fully. "Giles, we haven't much time to catch Esmerelda's killer. We must use our wedding to flush her out...if it is a her...I mean we..."

"Yes, Jennie, that's important. But that we wed matters more." Jennie was standing arms crossed, toe tapping, fingers rhythmically drumming her arm...she wasn't fully buying his disclaimer. "Jennie, please!"

"You're a sneaky one, Giles Freeman. But not sneaky enough. I am on to you, don't think I'm not." At which point she broke into hysterical laughter at the comedy of the moment. "Oh...Giles...the...look...your face...kiss me again ya big brute, and then we'll plan our wedding and lay a trap for a killer...*seriously*...kiss......me..." And he did. Mostly to keep himself from cracking up and proving her right. The woman did know how to push his buttons. She sure did. A lifetime with Jennie? Oh yes, he was going full in...and he did. Repeatedly...in the vestibule, the office...Izzard's desk...the other desk. He had no idea what pregnancy did to a woman's desires, but wow!

They left after midnight and went to his quarters at the garrison to sleep. He mused at the humor in that fact. They would enlighten the Colonel about their impending wedding in the morning. Meanwhile they needed a hot bath and sleep. He handed Jennie the key to his room as he took Devlin into the stable to bed him down. Poor horse had been left standing outside listening for hours. Thank god he couldn't repeat what he'd heard. Giles laughed until he had tears in his eyes. Patted his dear mount, who obviously thought his master was looney, went through the breezeway and into his quarters. Jennie had bathed and was fast asleep in his bed. The sight overwhelmed him, and he wept at the joy of having her with him, and that he always would. Giles bathed quietly and slipped in behind Jennie. She softly stirred and rolled over to snuggle up next to him and fell hard asleep before he could cover her with the blanket again. Bliss. He finally knew bliss. Giles slept at peace, but with one ear awake as a soldier always does. Jennie knew she was safe in his arms and in his bed. Morning would come too soon, and life would begin anew.

# 26

Giles and Jennie were waiting for the Colonel in his office when he arrived the next morning. Jennie sat in one of the leather covered chairs as Giles watched out the window overlooking the inner garrison courtyard. The Colonel came in as Evans was briefing him on his visitors.

"Colonel, Giles Freeman and Jennie Harris are waiting...for...you..." Evans' voice trailed off as the Colonel made his way in to greet Giles and Jennie.

"Well you two are here early. What brings you to this old man's office before I've had my third cup of tea? Hmm? Must be important..." The Colonel sat on the front of his desk looking from one to the other waiting on a reply. Giles noticed the door was still open and moved to close it. The Colonel beat him to it.

"The door Evans, if you please. Privacy is a courtesy to my guests." Evans dejectedly closed the door softly but totally pissed off. The Colonel looked back at Giles.

"One of you please tell me what this is about. This isn't a social call. I'm not daft."

Giles put his hand up to stop Jennie as she started to speak.

"You are correct, Colonel. This isn't a social call. Jennie and I are here for two reasons. First, we are on a strong lead to the killer of Esmerelda Conn. Please give us the leeway to not say more at this time. We are not entirely sure of everyone involved and we want them to incriminate themselves. At our wedding. This weekend." Giles just said it the way it was. Jennie just sat with her mouth open thinking the day they taught tact at school Giles was out playing hooky. She rolled her eyes and looked out the window until she was less pissed. The Colonel brought her attention back to the important.

"Really? Wedding? AND a murderer revealed?" the Colonel looked from one to the other and stopped smiling when he realized "Dear LORD…you're serious." He stood and faced Giles straight on. "You need to explain yourself soldier. What are you talking about?"

Giles stood straight as he addressed his commanding officer.

"Colonel, Jennie and I have a very strong lead on Esmerelda's killer. We…I…believe we can flush the killer out of hiding at our wedding this weekend. Please don't ask me to explain. I don't want to show our hand inadvertently, sir. Please trust me about this, sir." Giles was practically pleading with the Colonel. The Colonel's eyes narrowed without looking away from Giles. Giles didn't budge or flinch. He could stare down the devil if needed. Almost as if he were the Colonel's son, which unbeknownst to him, he was. Go figure.

"I do trust you Giles. Completely. I will leave the conversation about the suspects for now. I expect you to keep me informed as I can be. I won't be left surprised. But you know that. I know you do. You have demonstrated excellent judgment always. Alright. You have my permission to maintain discretion until I must be told." Giles was greatly relieved and relaxed substantially.

"HOWEVER! I will not be kept in the dark about your…WEDDING? Oh, now I'm offended. I'm the last one to know, aren't I? But you must have my permission to wed as an active duty soldier. HAH! Seriously? You come here last and just expect...me..." by now he was laughing so hard he couldn't speak. Giles was deflated...he didn't find his impending bliss at all funny. Quite the contrary.

"Oh, please, Giles...Jennie do not be offended. I'm thrilled! What on earth took you so long? I've been expecting this conversation for some months now. Everyone in Barbados that knows you has been watching and wondering when you would make it official. Seriously. You two are the perfect couple and we are all overjoyed for you both. Oh I wish you both the best life has to offer. And please, Jennie, move into Giles' quarters with him. It is spacious enough for you both for some time yet. Even your wee one...yes Jennie we are aware and thrilled for you both...will have space here if needed."

Jennie blushed at the thought the world knew...everything. Or did they? The sudden doubts took her smile away and the Colonel noticed...and read her thoughts exactly.

"Jennie. My sweet girl Jennie. You have been another daughter to Elizabeth and me. We are well aware of your situation. We are over the moon for a grandchild! And this IS Giles' child in our eyes...and obviously in his heart." Jennie was in tears as her fears were set aside. The Colonel was sincere. She had to have known Elizabeth knew what happened and the Colonel was watching out for her all along. Jennie finally understood what family meant. She'd had a good one all along in unusual places.

"So, my sweet Jennie...you will allow Lady Elizabeth and Lady Isabella the pleasure of creating your wedding and reception? If they don't kill each other in the process it will be a fine affair." They all three cracked up laughing at the reality of what he suggested. Oh my. But there was much to do and little time so perhaps they wouldn't have time to try and outdo the other. There was always prayer for that.

Serious settling in again the Colonel concluded the meeting with "yes, Giles catch us Esmerelda's killer. Do whatever you must. Evans will be at your disposal without question. I'll see to that. No matter what you might hear or think of Evans, he is my man. He does much behind the scenes that might lead you to a different conclusion if you are unaware of my purposes. Do not mistake me on this Giles. Evans is my man. Trust him. The only man I trust more is you. Go on then. Get that wedding planned! I have champagne to uncover in the stores...somewhere..." The Colonel grinned with delight. Giles knew the Colonel knew exactly where he kept his best Champagne. The wedding would be spectacular indeed.

Jenny stood and hugged the Colonel for a long hug. Giles and the Colonel hugged as a father and son would, and did, though they didn't know it. The Colonel opened the door and followed them out of his office with a smart smile on his face.

"Evans, we've a wedding to attend, and a killer to catch. No matter what Giles or Jennie asks of you. Do it. Without question. Do you understand me, Evans?" The Colonel turned his head slowly to look Evans in the eye, his glance cold and deadly threatening toward the Lieutenant.

Evans replied "Yes, Colonel. I understand completely." Actually, no he didn't understand. Not at all. But he knew he was not to ask. The Colonel had a plan happening and he would play his part exactly as ordered. Tho he did venture to ask, "a wedding, sir?"

"Yes, Evans. A wedding. Giles and Miss Harris are finally getting wed. I will need an inventory of our champagnes and finer chocolates for the reception. I intend this event to be a baseline for all future events on the island. For Saturday, Evans. I know, short notice but you've got this." Grinning, he winked at Evans and went back in his office. He poured himself three fingers of his best scotch and toasted Giles and Jennie and his grandchild to be. A fine day it was after all. Lady Elizabeth would be in her element and vigorously lustful when she returned each night. Oh yes, this would be a fine week. He loved weddings. He giggled. His cock wanted to go back to their quarters and practice. Perhaps he would...he sipped his scotch and his cock beckoned to him again, perhaps he would.

The Colonel left the office with his glass in hand and headed to his private quarters. Elizabeth was seated at her mirror brushing her hair when he came into the bedroom. She could see his erection even in the mirror. Looking up at him in the reflection, the Colonel stepped behind her and nuzzled her neck as he pressed himself against her. He reached around and began fondling her breasts. She moaned with pleasure at his advances. "Why husband, what a pleasant surprise. Please, let me help you with your morning...constitutional..."

Whatever had him excited, she wanted to know what it was. This was by far the best sex they'd had in a long time. The Colonel bathed and dressed before Elizabeth did. He explained he had committed her to help with Giles and Jennies wedding.

"WHAT? A wedding? GILES and JENNIE! What wonderful news, Duncan, truly. Oh yes, a wedding to plan!"

She stood up quickly and immediately regretted it. Damn her husband.

"Now Elizabeth, Isabella will also be working on the festivities. She will be a great help to you in your...limited...capacity."

He bent and kissed her neck as she scowled at him. "Oh stop, Elizabeth. You know very well you love rough sex more than I do. And it pleases me when I can tell I did my job well. You love it." He nipped her neck and kissed lovingly. He truly loved Elizabeth and she him. He was out the door and on his way to get some other island work taken care of. Smirking all the way.

§

The Colonel made his way to the stable and called for the stable manager to saddle up Witcher and fetch the sergeant to ride with him. He had a priest to see about and a First Mate to consult. The stable manager made haste as the Colonel went to his office to inform Evans he was going out for a bit. Keep the lid on things while he was gone. The Colonel locked his office with his private key in the lock only he had a key for. He didn't use it often but today he needed to be sure only he had access to his office. He wanted to protect Evans from any impending accusations. Only he could protect his devoted assistant. And he would.

Smiling and a quip of a salute and he was out the front door where Witcher and the stable manger waited. The sergeant was already mounted as the manager gave the Colonel a leg up on his war horse. Stepping back away from the giant mare, he and Evans watched the two men ride out of Bridgetown. Both perplexed by what on earth was under the Colonels skin this beautiful day. It was a killer, and the Colonel meant to have the killer caught. He would set the stage to flush the quarry and Giles would be there to catch and kill if necessary. The Colonel was a man first, a father second, and a warrior always. The killer was about to learn how lethal that combination could be.

The Colonel and the sergeant rode along at a brisk pace all the way to the parish. Peter and Charles came out to greet them and take care of their horses while they visited with Father Michael. Peter's instincts told him to give the Colonel a wide berth and keep quiet. The man was in full warrior mode noticing every detail that day. He stepped between Charles and the sergeant before Charles could speak and give away his voice. The officers went into the rectory as the priest welcomed them. Charles took the sergeant's horse as Peter led Witcher.

Charles looked up at the monster of a horse in awe. She was truly as powerful and magnificent an animal as he had ever seen. And gentle to Peter as a wee pup. Charles realized the mare absolutely adored Peter. And Peter loved her as she nuzzled him slobbering fresh grass green slime all over his white linen shirt. Charles laughed at the ewwwww moment but somehow Peter didn't care. The mare gave him unconditional love…and green slime…whenever he was near her. Charles realized Peter was the stable manager for a reason.

The horses were therapy for Peter. They did love him unconditionally and he needed that desperately when Charles was at sea. He finally understood why Father Michael had objected…flat refused…to take Peter out of the stable chores and move him into "gainful" employment. Peter was exactly where he needed to be. Charles walked up behind Peter as he rubbed the big war horse down. He wrapped his arms around Peter and whispered "I'm so sorry Peter. I didn't realize. This is truly your love and support when I'm gone from you. I had no idea. Please accept my apology. I am so very sorry. They love you unconditionally in my place, don't they? Good, Peter. Never leave the work of a stable. It suits you perfectly." Peter reached up and held Charles' hand tightly for a moment, kissed him on his forearm, and went back to brushing the biggest and gentlest horse either of them had ever had love them as a single tear traced down Peter's cheek. It was true; the outside of a horse was good for the inside of a man.

Meanwhile, the Colonel and the priest were planning a wedding while the principal parties haggled over details. Little did they know. It was a done deal before 3 p.m. Michael and the Colonel had dealt with enough weddings to know how to make it work…in spite of the organizers and nearly wedded. The Colonel's champagne was the key ingredient to distract and conquer the event. Ever the tacticians and strategists, the Colonel and Priest had them out maneuvered from the get-go. Hah! They all had a bit too much sacramental wine, tho the sergeant drank less to keep order in the rectory. Peter and Charles just sort of watched the show from the fringe and enjoyed the wine.

When it came time for the Colonel to head back to the garrison, Peter and Charles had their horses ready and waiting. It took the three of them to get the Colonel up on his war horse. Witcher was clearly pissed her rider was schnockered. Well lit. Blitzed. Drunk as a skunk. Charles would swear later the horse rolled her eyes at his breath. The sergeant was relatively upright, and they knew he would get the Colonel back safely. They left out of the yard with the sergeant's horse in the lead, the big war horse pinning her ears at the obnoxious behavior of her...rider...and pretty much stomping her hooves with each step to make him miserable for embarrassing her like that.

Once the Colonel and sergeant were well down the road and out of earshot the rectory trio flat broke up into hysterics. Oh. My. God. This was a day that would live in infamy. They would be able to leverage the story for years to come. And the Colonel would be the one telling it on himself. He was honest about his misguided adventures and used them appropriately. What the priest knew but Charles and Peter did not was that once they were out of earshot and sight line, somehow the Colonel sobered up in moments. As did the sergeant. Anyone watching the parish thought exactly what he wanted the Island to believe. A wedding was happening, and he was distracted from all else. He had let himself go during working hours and was vulnerable. Like hell.

§

The second half of the detail that day was watching hidden in the trees above the parish. They would report back late that evening about watchers or visitors before and after his performance. To make it work, Peter and Charles had to believe, and they did. Father Michael was part of the hoax. He knew the stakes were high and wanted to catch Esmerelda's killer as bad as the Colonel. So the soldiers hid and watched and waited.

It wasn't long before the movements began. Isabella Conn rode into the rectory yard on horseback from the direction of the Tallywhoa. Elizabeth McKenzie arrived at the rectory shortly thereafter on horseback cutting across the fields behind them and taking her horse at a dead run through the thickets and over hidden fences. The soldiers were terrified the women were doomed to crash and die or worse, live long enough for their husbands to hang themselves trying to care for the independent women in their houses. Giles Freeman and Jennie made a stop by, as did almost every parishioner in the area. The news was out. A wedding was on.

One of the men had a spy glass while the other took notes. They were thorough yet not the best forged anchors in the harbor. The colonel didn't need them to think, just watch and take notes and not assume anything. Just listening was hilarious.

"Oh, yeh, another FE-MALE at the rectory."

"FE-MALE…at..rect…rect…spell that agin mate…"

"C…H…U…R…C…H. Rectory. Should I spell it agin for ye?"

"Don't sound like ye spelled it, Mason. Are ye sure?"

"Oh, for God's sake man it's CHURCH. C…H…U…R…C…H!"

"Oh. Right. Church. C..H..U..R..C..H. Got it. Thanks, mate. FE-MALE at CHURCH. Anything else I need to write down with church, mate?"

The man with the spy glass rolled his eyes to heaven and prayed 'Dear God. Give me the strength not to kill em too soon. Please. Deliver me…'. Where upon a movement at the 'church' caught his eye. A sign from God. Must be I can't kill em yet...

Looking at the new arrival he was truly surprised and spoke to his…comrade…carefully and seriously. "Zach. We got us a live one, mate. I ain't never seen this girl before nowhere. I wonder who she is. Zach are you getting this down, mate. This one is important. For real the Colonel wants to know about this one."

"Ok, Mason. What do you see. Give me a description." The comedy was gone, and the men were on their game.

Well she's taller than most women…as tall as the priest but not as tall as Charles the First Mate. Dark hair way down her back. Rides in trousers like Lady Isabella and Lady

Elizabeth. Straw hat with a green ribbon around the crown. Ohhh my...she knows Charles...well by the look of it. Hell of kisser she is, too. Well done Charles! Got a pretty one that kisses in front of a priest yet!"

"Kissing Charles? In front of the priest? Give me that spy glass fool...that can't be right." Zach snagged the spy glass from Mason and whistled. "I wouldn't have believed if I didn't see it with my own eyes. She's kissing Charles like she realllly knows him in front of the Priest! And now Father Michael is hugging her and Charles both!" Zach handed the spyglass back to Mason and sat down in complete disbelief. "I don't get it. How does a sailor like Charles, you know what I mean, all serious like all the time, find a woman like that? It's not fair is what it is."

Mason was still watching as the priest went back into the rectory and the woman went into the stable with Charles. "Write this down Zach. Michael went in the...church...and the woman went into the stable with Charles. Holding hands all lovey like as they went into the stable. Something is really off with this Zach. Seriously. Stop yer self-pity and listen to what I'm telling you to note. That horse she was riding was Ethan Fuller's old horse. Wasn't he in the stables just the other day? How did it get here?"

"That I can answer. Evans let Charles have him to use while he's in port for a week or two. So, no issue with that. But who's the woman? That is a good question that I cannot answer."

"May I have a piece of your paper, please. And a charcoal. I want to sketch her basic look while I remember it." Zach handed him the materials and swapped for the spy glass. The men were silent as Mason sketched and Zach watched. Neither noticed the old woman standing on the hill behind them watching them watch the parish. The girl behind her didn't like the situation and suggested to the old woman they move on. In time she did. Satisfied the men were merely watching as she was. Though for very different reasons.

Zach was taking in much he didn't say. The priest came outside and tended the chucks. He never ventured near the stable or orphanage while the woman was in there with Charles. After a while Peter came out to the pump to wash up for supper. Apparently, he had been in there all day working. Something about Peter made Zach uneasy. He focused in as close as he could with the rudimentary spy glass. Looked closely at Peter as he washed up at the pump. His hair was tussled, his trousers loose around his hips as he washed with a linen cloth. Something…what was it that was bugging him about Peter? Zach started to say something when he stopped himself. There. No. His eyes were playing tricks on him. But he could swear the woman wore the same boots as Peter. They must use the same cobbler to make their footwear. That was all. Still it unsettled him. He made a mental note but didn't share it with Mason. Not yet.

Mason finished his drawing and asked Zach to look it over. "What do you think? Did I remember her correctly? Did I miss anything important?" He handed the drawing to Zach who froze when looked at the sketch. Right there in front of him were the same boots Peter was wearing at the pump. One boot was missing a high-top buckle, as was the same boot that Peter was wearing."

"Zach? Is it that bad? I thought I got a good look at her…maybe I.."

"Mason you captured her perfectly. We need to get to the colonel. Fast."

"Zach? What did I do, mate? Are ye mad at me?" Mason was terrified of the Colonel's wrath and petrified he had done something to draw that wrath upon himself.

"No Mason. Oh no. You did a perfect job. We just need to get this to the Colonel as fast as we can without raising attention. He will definitely want to know about her. Oh yes, yes he will." Greatly relieved Mason gathered up his charcoal, quill and ink, packed them carefully in his scribe's case and slid them in his saddle bags. The men tacked up their horses tied in the shadows and headed back to the garrison briskly but not fast enough to alarm anyone who might see them.

As they made their way along the road their horses stopped and shied away from the mill side of the road just ahead of the mill. They side-stepped past the shadowy thicket where the sow was bedded with her piglets for the night. Even the men could smell them and were rightfully wary of getting past her without raising her alarms. The dusk was settling into night by the time they arrived back at the garrison. Mason took the horses into the stable as Zach made a bee line for the Colonel's office. The outer door was locked and the rooms dark. Neither the Colonel nor Evans was about. He would have to wait until morning to report in. Zach went back to the stable to help Mason with the horses. He set the scribe's case with the notes and sketches on the table in the tack room while he and Mason fed, watered, and rubbed down the horses. When he returned to get the case and retire for the night it was gone. Panicked he ran back to Mason and asked

"Mason. Did you take the scribes pack? I left it on the table in the tack room to keep it safe and clean. Did you move it?"

"No mate. I haven't been in the tack room tonight. Let's have a good look tho." They both searched the tack room, feed room, hallway…saddle bags. The pack was gone. Zach had a bad feeling about this. Someone knew where it was. Saw him put it on the table and somehow managed to take it without Mason or himself seeing them do so. Terror crept up Zach's spine. Someone had been watching them. Someone was watching them now.

"Mason. Let it go. We need to get to the dining hall and back to the barracks before we miss roll call."

Mason started to protest "Zach we can…"

"Mason. We need to go. Now." He turned and gave Zach a look that chilled Zach where he stood.

"Ok, Zach. Let's go get some grub fast like and turn in on time." Mason knew something was dreadfully wrong but no idea what. He followed Zach's lead and kept both alive that night. She slid her knife silently back into its sheath tied to her waist.

The watcher waited until they were truly away before she left carrying the scribe's case. In her haste she dropped the green ribbon that had been tied on the shoulder strap of the case in the back stall nearest the outer wall. She closed the hidden panel behind her silently, made her way down the narrow passageway and exited in the attendants' vestibule under the guest room baths. She hung her cloak on a hook and put her dressing robe on over her sleeping gown. Elizabeth slipped up the stairs and into their bath without being seen or heard. She closed the door to the bath and bolted them both. She needed absolute privacy to review the scribes notes and sketches.

The notes were informative but nothing incriminating. Except her husband would figure out she and Isabella could move unseen and unheard between locations all over the island rather quickly if he read the notes as a narrative and not just bullet points. Then she got to the sketch of the woman with Charles. Stunned, she gasped. That was Maria. What was she doing with Charles? She and Charles were obviously lovers. The notes supported the sketch perfectly. But what was in the sketch that had Zach terrified. She couldn't place that reaction just yet. Something had spooked the soldier. Really scared him. She had to know what. She had an idea…in the morning she would take the pouch to Evans and claim she found it in the stall with her horse. He must have pulled it off the hook during the night or something. Stir the pot Elizabeth. See what rises. She slid everything back in the way she found it and tucked in the bottom of her wardrobe in the bedroom with her knife underneath. She unbolted the access door and waited patiently for her husband to return. The day had been exhilarating. She and Isabella had the wedding plans organized. Tomorrow she would have her tailor measure Jennie for a dress.

There were several already made Jennie could choose from that had been abandoned after the hurricane. The girls were killed or financially ruined. The tailor could alter one quickly if there was one she liked. In truth, so many girls were wed well into a pregnancy the concept didn't matter to anyone. It's just the way life was. The fifty percent of girls that lived through childbirth were more important than who was wed with child. Life was a crap shoot with barely even odds for women. Once the dress was chosen all Jennie had to do was let herself be pampered and primped by the Barbados queens of pampering and primping. Both of whom claimed her as a daughter and were trying to outdo each other before sunset.

Jennie and Giles were gracious in their reception of attention. As much as they might prefer a simple ceremony with just Charles and Peter to witness Michael marry them, they knew it would never happen. Jennie endured the fluff and puff with grace, a smile, and a few well-timed giggles to suppress the screaming she would have preferred. Giles endured the man-uppery from the fringe pouring much scotch into flasks he hid in his shirt or the nearest plant to avoid complete inebriation and the associated Tom Foolery that would inevitably follow. Giles and Jennie would have an ample supply of good scotch for their honeymoon, and Jennie received many lovely pieces of lingerie for…later. Lingerie and lust, scotch and sex. It worked.

# 27

By the time Saturday rolled around the couple was ready to row a lighter to a nearby island and find a native holy man to wed them and never return to Barbados. Sadly, all the lighters were closely guarded. It wasn't going to happen. Saturday morning arrived glorious and sunny, the night rains freshened the air and washed away the trials of the preparations. Giles watched the dawn break gently through their window as he held Jennie while she slept. He wanted the moment to never end.

Giles smelled Jennie's hair, closed his eyes to imprint the scent in his brain forever. He mentally sketched the outline of her body warm against his skin to never forget her touch, her shape, and her desire for him. He held her tighter than he realized, and she began to wake. Jennie cuddled closer and softly, oh so softly, kissed his chest and nuzzled him with her cheek still half asleep.

The sunlight broke through the window and cast light on Jennie's face waking her from her bliss. She groaned and rolled over to avoid the light in her eyes. Giles patted her gently on her backside and slid out of the bed to bathe and dress. He was learning that pregnant women sleep more and eat for more than two. The thought of her bringing a new life in the world for them made him smile. He was so excited and could hardly wait to hold the wee babe. Would she look like her mother? Or, would he grow to be like his father? The thought the child could be a boy and grow to be a serious piece of male made him smile bigger. While he didn't sire the child, he knew who had and the man was indeed very much like Giles. Michael, the native half black slave was a very impressive man physically and smart, too. He cherished the idea of raising this child and had a hunch Michael would be very pleased, supportive even, that the child would be loved and raised well be it a daughter or a son.

"Giles, what are you smiling about so gleefully? Do you know something I do not?" Jennie startled him out of his thoughts of their future. He replied

"Jennie. You're awake. No, my love, I do not know anything you do not. I was smiling at the thought of waking with you every day. It is time we wed. He bent down and kissed her, one hand holding chin and cheek, the other hand on her swelling belly feeling the baby kick. Jennie was caught and surprised at the strength of the baby's kicks and giggled. Giles just kissed her again. Jennie had to shove him back just to breathe a bit.

"Ok, Giles. Time to get serious about the day. We do have a wedding to get to this afternoon…our own. Let's get some breakfast first. I'm famished!"

Giles smirked. Hungry. She was always hungry these days. For food.

"Me, too, my dearest. Starving." He smiled, pecked her on the cheek, and went to the bath to dress. He could hear Jennie dressing in the next room in her casual scribe's trousers and loose-fitting shirt. She needed a few things from the tailor to fit her better in the few months remaining in her pregnancy. He would see to that next week. Assuming he would survive the wedding, the reception, and the flood of champagne and scotch. He would need more flasks in which to hide what they thought he was drinking. Mental note. Get more flasks in the market on the way to the parish.

As Jennie was tying her shoes there was a knock at the door. Jennie looked up as Giles went to see who it was. Opening the door, he found Evans with an entourage of men.

"What's this? What has happened?" Giles was genuinely alarmed something catastrophic had occurred.

"Giles Freeman. By order of Colonel Duncan McKenzie, you are hereby under arrest. You are to be taken, by force if necessary, directly to the Colonel's private dining room for trial and summary judgement." Evan's somehow managed to maintain a straight face. The men behind him did not. Giles knew something was afoot. He also knew he had no choice. They would forcibly take him if they had to. Crap. So much for breakfast with his bride to be.

"Jennie. I'm afraid I'm being forcibly detained by the Colonel and his...men...breakfast is off. Sorry sweets." Giles turned to kiss her goodbye, but they grabbed him before he could. "Oh no you don't soldier. Not before the wedding!" Giles was abducted and disappeared before Jennie's eyes. The irony of abducting a man away from his pregnant fiancé in his own quarters was ignored. They would have their fun with him. Giles was taken to the Colonel's dining room and properly fed a fantastic breakfast before they loaded him in a cart full of crates of champagne and scotch and a host of other decadences headed for Emerald Oaks where the reception would be held. The Colonel was no man's fool. He knew Giles could row her to any of the nearby islands all by himself. Not on his watch. Not happening. All the oars for the lighters had been removed and carefully stowed under lock and key in the garrison storehouse. Jennie had laughed so hard she had tears in her eyes and could hardly breathe.

When she turned to close the door, it wouldn't shut.

A feminine hand wearing a gold ring with an oval center diamond surrounded by emeralds caught the door and pushed it open. Isabella and Elizabeth stood before her with an entourage of ladies. "Miss Harris. It has come to our attention that your fiancé has improper thoughts about having his way with you before you are properly wed." No one could keep a straight face. Elizabeth continued

"By order of Colonel Duncan McKenzie, my husband, you are to be remanded to our care until such time as your fiancé can be trusted in your company. That would be at 2:00 p.m. this afternoon at the parish for your wedding. If you try to resist, we will forcibly remove you to a location unknown to you or your fiancé until such time as the Colonel himself may discover your whereabouts and deliver you to the church. And, it's time for your pre wedding breakfast and we are famished." At which point they all cracked up and Jennie left with the ladies to enjoy her wedding day in spectacular fashion. As if she had a choice.

Jennie was taken with the ladies to the Roaring Boar. The one place the men would never look for a gaggle of women on a wedding day. The proprietor had been well paid to cook a magnificent breakfast for Jennie's wedding party and had engaged the apothecary's daughter and his indentured girl to do the place up proper for a bride to be. When they entered Jennie was stunned to find the entire pub decorated in fine linens, fresh flowers on the long table running across the room, and Elizabeth McKenzie's fine china and silverware set with cut crystal filled with juices and champagne. Jennie couldn't speak through her tears.

Elizabeth held her close, noticing Jennie held her belly as the child kicked and squirmed inside her. Elizabeth simply said

"Jennie, you are our daughter and you deserve a fine wedding day. We could never not give you these things as you wed a wonderful man. Come girl. Let's eat!" Jennie nodded as she cried and was seated at the head of the table. The rest of the ladies found their seats as the breakfast was served by the bar maid, the apothecary's daughter, Elizabeth, and Isabella. This was their finest moment, and everyone was going to know it. Jennie was to be respected and honored as their daughter as she prepared to wed Giles Freeman. Hunger took over and Jennie ate for more than two. The wonderful food exactly what she needed that particular morning.

The breakfast finished, Elizabeth and Isabella nodded it was time to head for the parish. Leaving the pub Jennie stepped out to find a row of carriages to take them all to the church. Jennie rode with Isabella and Elizabeth and her wedding dress in the box next to Elizabeth. The sun shone brightly on the bride to be and her family. The trip to the parish was uneventful. The old sow had moved off begrudgingly when the cart load of joviality and debauchery came along loud and obnoxious as they ambled the groom to the plantation. The ladies were telling stories, giggling and laughing as ladies do when they arrived at the parish.

Father Michael was there to greet them. Jennie was first out of the carriage and the priest hugged her as if she was his daughter. Having raised her, she was. Peter took the wedding dress box from Elizabeth and took it into the rectory. Isabella and the others stepped down from their carriages and they ushered Jennie inside to continue their revelry and primping of the bride. Charles and Peter helped the drivers move the carriages that would stay out of the way and unhitched the horses to stable them still harnessed to facilitate hitching quickly after the wedding. Most of the carriages returned to their home plantations to fetch the husbands and families of the women who had escorted Jennie to the church.

Jennie was walked through the church to see the decorations. The local tropical flowers were in vases and tied into garlands wrapping candelabra in sight and scent. It was a glorious sight. The women had spent hours putting it all together. Jennie was truly overwhelmed.

"Oh…it is just beautiful. However did you manage all this? Perfect…just perfect. Thank you. I never expected any of this. I'm overwhelmed…it is truly perfect…and the aroma…" Jennie closed her eyes and breathed in the fresh aroma. She smiled as they began to drag her away. "I was enjoying the aroma…" The ladies giggled and herded her into the completed and renovated section of the orphanage.

## The Parrish

Jennie hadn't seen what the workers had been doing in the reconstruction. The orphanage would be a true home for the children with beautiful woodwork, functioning windows with fine silk screens, and Venetian floors tiles scavenged off the beach after the hurricane. The bath and private quarters for the house mother were nothing short of a palace with wall coverings from Milan, copper bathtub and fixtures, and hot water piped in from the roof. The Colonel had been good to his word. These children would have a home and comforts. Jennie had been his inspiration.

Jennie's dress was displayed on a dress form near the bed. On the dressing table was a silver brush and comb. A scattering of ribbons and pearled hair ornaments cluttered the table waiting for her maids to dress her. Jennie beamed with joy. This was truly her wedding day. What a wonder and deliverance of love and support.

The ladies began to undress her as Elizabeth and Isabella prepared her bath. Lavender oil was dripped in the hot water as it poured into the tub from the spigot. The aroma filled the entire suite. They wrapped Jennie in a large bath wrap and ushered her into the tub. Pure heaven she let herself sink into the hot water, ensconced in lavender as they bathed her with sponges and finely milled soap from France. Her baby kicked hard enough to cause Jennie to wince.

"Jennie? Are you all right girl?" Isabella asked in a concerned but not alarmed voice.

"Yes, Isabella I'm fine. I think this is a boy the way the baby kicks. Moves around a lot...kicks me all over!" Elizabeth and Isabella exchanged a glance but kept quiet. They would take care to watch Jennie closely.

"Oh, good. Let's get you out before you turn into a lavender prune." The ladies helped her stand, her swollen belly making her unbalanced at times. Jennie stepped out on the rug and let them dry her off and anoint her with scented lotions and perfumes. The girl smelled like a field of flowers that didn't even grow on Barbados. Jennie had never smelled most of them before. She loved every minute and every new experience that day.

The duly appointed hair dressing ladies wrapped Jennie in a robe and sat her in front of the dressing table on the rotating stool. She closed her eyes and let them entertain themselves fixing her hair in a style to compliment her face and her gown. They added ribbons and pearls, flowers and perfumes. When they were finished, they handed Jennie the silver mirror and turned around so she could see the reflection of the back of her head in the big mirror on the dressing table behind her.

Jennie didn't recognize herself. She was a stunningly beautiful woman. Her mixed blood heritage gave her perfect skin, a lovely complexion, and almond shaped eyes over high cheekbones. Her dark hair was arranged to frame her face and allowed her neckline to be seen easily. Speechless, she looked at herself as if she was seeing a stranger in the mirror. She had never had her hair done for her before by women. Peter was talented with her hair and often had done it for her as children. Father Michael had let him until a comment was made by a prudish parishioner about Peter combing out her hair after she washed it one day out by the pump. "Isabella, would you go find Peter for me? He was the one who did my hair all the time I lived in the orphanage. He will be heartbroken if he doesn't get the last word." Jennie glanced up to see Isabella begin to object, the ladies perplexed. "Please, Isabella. This is for Peter and his gentleness and kindness to me all my life." Isabella thought for a moment and had a compromise.

"Jennie you know men are not allowed to view the bride before the wedding." Jennie started to protest but Isabella cut her off. "What say I go fetch Maria? She could tell him all about your hair and help dress you in your gown even? I think THAT is a splendid idea!" Jennie's smile grew smugly as Isabella ever so kindly meant to include Peter in the best way possible. The ladies were totally confused. Only Elizabeth, Jennie and Isabella understood.

"Well, if you think that's best, I can live with it. I suppose it is the best we can do." Jennie patted her hair as she looked in her hand-held mirror. Isabella slipped out the door and headed for the stable. The ladies had no clue.

Almost running to the stable Isabella found Peter and quickly explained she must find Maria quickly. Jennie must have her to help dress her and prepare her for the wedding with her dearest friend from the orphanage. Charles stepped in as Peter suddenly didn't know what to do or say.

"Isabella, no worries. I'll find Maria for you and bring her to Jennie. I agree, she must have Maria to assist her on this, her wedding day."

"Oh, thank you Charles. You have no idea what this means to me…to Jennie and Elizabeth as well. Find her promptly, please?" Isabella nodded to Peter and was gone back to Jennie. Peter was afraid.

"Charles…I …I …"

Charles took Peter by the arm to their quarters. He simply said 'strip, now' as he took the pitcher to fetch clean water from the pump. He returned with a fresh linen for washing and one for drying. "Wash and dry yourself. You shaved earlier so you're good there already. Go on, get cleaned up and smell good!" Charles busied himself getting Maria out of the trunk as Peter bathed from the basin. Once bathed Peter dressed as Maria just for Jennie. He would risk being found out only for Jennie.

Charles smiled at Maria and just had to kiss her. A handsome man, Peter was more beautiful as Maria. A ruse begun to hide their relationship years ago, the disguise had become quite useful over the years. "You are gorgeous as always. The ladies will be quite jealous...and curious. You know what to say or not. And don't worry if you are found out. I think you'll be surprised how accepting women are, Peter. Consider who came to fetch Maria. You are safe with these ladies or she wouldn't have come for her.

Maria smiled and kissed Charles warmly before she left to find Jennie, her dearest and oldest friend in the world. They were brother and sister in every sense but one. He would protect Jennie with his life if he had to. Arriving at the new door with the hardware from Milan, Maria knocked gently. Isabella let her in with a hug and a smile. "I am so glad you are here, Maria. Please join us in our ladies' celebration with the bride." Maria hugged back with genuine love for the opportunity.

Jennie looked up at Maria and beamed. "LOOK! Look what they've done with my hair Maria! It isn't quite what you used to do, but it is lovely. What do you think? Is it missing anything?" The ladies immediately knew Maria was not as she appeared. They guessed who was under the wig and dress. They didn't care. In fact, they were miffed they hadn't known sooner. Maria would soon have an entire clientele to consult with about hair, gowns, and shoes. Maria loved shoes. They glared at Isabella as one simply asked "and where have you been hiding Maria? And not share her with us? Really Isabella? And you call us your friends? Well, consider yourself on temporary standing until you are willing to share Maria more often. Oh no, girl, you do not get to hoard her for yourself. Oh no."

Maria blushed and cried as they mass hugged her with Jennie.

"Ok, Maria, show us your best work. You Go girl!" The ladies stepped back and let Jennie and Maria be brother and sister the best way they knew how. Maria loved what they had done with her hair. She added only a few touches, moved a pin or two. The outcome was stunning.

"Ok, girlfriend, you are SO doing my hair from now on. Oh yes, you are."

"What? NO, I get her first. I have a niece getting married in a fortnight and must have Maria for the bride and the attendants!" And so it went. Jennie, Isabella, and Elizabeth were in hysterics at the antics. Maria was happier than she had been in years. Accepted and loved just as Charles had said she would be.

It was time to dress the bride. Jennie didn't hesitate to drop her wrap in front of Maria. They had no secrets from each other, and no one would shame her or Maria, ever.

"Maria, please help me with my gown. I can't put it on without ruining my hair."

Maria gently took the gown off the form as the ladies helped slide it off and over. Together they turned and lifted it up over Jennies head, arms raised and lowered it down, one sleeve and then the other, dropping the skirting softly over her swollen belly and down to the floor. Maria stepped behind Jennie and carefully pulled the lacing snug enough to show off the bride and her gown without constricting her belly or tender breasts.

Elizabeth stepped up and draped a diamond encrusted necklace around her neck. One of the ladies on her right added a matching earring and a lady on her left added the other. Maria held her ankles softly as she slid her foot into each shoe. Fully dressed they all stood back to admire the bride. The baby kicked hard. Jennie winced and bent over to ease the pain. She quickly said "ladies I'm fine. The little

Dickens is just feisty and active. No Worries. I really am fine." Smiling she stood and blushed with joy. Maria hugged her long and tight, and kissed Jennie on her cheek before she left to find Peter to help with the guests' horses as they arrived. Jennie squeezed Maria's hand in gratitude as she left. They sat and enjoyed a glass of light wine as they waited for the service to begin.

Maria hustled back to her quarters. Charles was out helping the guests and needed Peter to assist him. Maria opened the trunk and tossed Maria back in as Peter emerged from underneath the wig and dress with false breasts stuffed into it. Peter dressed quickly, checked himself over to be sure he hadn't missed anything and went out to help Charles in the stables. He walked on air as he reached the churchyard. Charles smiled to himself knowing things had gone very well for Maria. The guests were arriving, and the groom was getting dressed in the priest's quarters in the rectory. The grandmother watched from the hilltop unnoticed in the bevy of excitement.

Finally, the hour had arrived, and Jennie was escorted to the church. Music played from inside the church. Elizabeth had commandeered the garrison's musicians to play for Jennie's wedding. They were finely trained musicians and did a lovely job for Jennie and Giles. As she entered the church, Jennie could see the pews were filled and people stood at the back. One of the orphan girls was the flower girl and walked ahead of Jennie dropping rose petals for her to walk on up to the altar. Giles was waiting for her at the altar in his full-dress kilt attire. The highland Scot was a magnificent sight dressed in his formal clan tartan, something she had never seen before. She felt faint realizing she had underestimated the man she would marry. He was far more than she had known and suddenly realized the remarkable resemblance to the man on whose arm she walked to the altar. She knew in that instant that Giles was the son of Colonel Duncan McKenzie. Now two people on the island knew. Giles' stepmother and his bride.

Elizabeth was watching Jennie look at Giles and then Duncan. She and Jennie caught a knowing glance. Jennie would keep their secret. She knew it would destroy the Colonel's marriage if he ever found out he had been deceived about a son stolen from him all those years ago. No. She wouldn't destroy their illusion. But she wouldn't forget it either. Someone good had raised Giles as their own. No wonder the man would love her child as his own. Jennie's tears came knowing why Elizabeth had gone all out for her wedding. It was also her stepson's wedding. She did it for Duncan, for her husband's son, and her as well.

Jennie smiled at Elizabeth as Duncan gave her away to Giles and went to sit with his wife, hands entwined, smiling with Joy. Elizabeth's tears came with the relief Jennie would indeed bring grandchildren to her husband. He didn't get to raise his son, but he might a grandson. Duncan patted Elizabeth's hand as he beamed, bursting with pride for his assumed son and the girl he wed that day. That was his grandbaby she carried, and he could hardly contain himself.

Elizabeth ached to tell Duncan that life had come full circle for him, that Jennie's children would be truly his grandchildren. That the love he lost in a weak moment as a young and foolish man had come back to him and to the island in a beautiful and positive way. Giles' mother was one hell of a woman. Unbeknownst to Duncan, she was in the back of the church beaming with joy for her son and new daughter in law.

Elizabeth had sent for her when Thomas and Richard arrived talking about the unrest and upheavals in England and Scotland. She wasn't safe there with her husband dead, his clan under siege. Elizabeth had been a conspirator with his mother to see him raised free of the bitter battle that would have raged over his birth. She deserved to be kept safe and see him wed to a fine woman. And she did. No one had noticed when Charles escorted her off the *Angeline* amid the milling confusion that exists when a ship comes into port.

No one cared that Elizabeth greeted her sister with joy after so many years unseen. She would bring Giles and Jennie to see her in the stable at Emerald Oaks later. She smiled thinking of Giles' joy learning of his mother's presence at his wedding. He hadn't seen her in almost 15 years. She had kept away so Duncan would not discover the man he chose to be his closest officer in the field was his illegitimate son, all knowledge hidden from him by his wife and her sister, his mistress for one night.

The wedding service was closing as Father Michael presented Mr. and Mrs. Giles Freeman to the congregation. Raucous cheers and clapping ensued as the couple walked out the aisle toward the carriage that waited to take them to Emerald Oaks. The horses and carriages were all waiting to take everyone to the reception. Peter reached up from the far side of her carriage and pulled Jennie down to kiss the new Mrs. Freeman. She cried and kissed his cheek and said, thank you Maria, I love you dearly. Do not ever change, dear brother. She squeezed his hand as the carriage pulled them apart.

Peter would be at the reception later. But first he and Charles had to help Father Michael clear the church. Normally that waited until the next day, but the priest had insisted. As the last carriage left and the churchyard emptied of guests. Peter and Charles went in to help Michael with the decorations. Michael was still standing in front of the altar. Colonel McKenzie on his right, and the Sea Captain on his left.

Charles stopped and asked suspiciously "what is this? What is going on here?" Instinctively he had his arm out to protect Peter from the men looking at them expressionless. Michael began to explain.

"Charles, it has been brought to our attention that Maria was here today and assisted Mrs. Freeman in preparation for her wedding. Is this true?" The men stared at Charles and Peter with no hint of their intentions.

Peter answered from behind Charles "yes. Maria was here today, Father Michael."

Charles was getting very angry very quickly. He could hear the tears in Peter's voice and said "What is this about, gentlemen? I think you need to explain yourselves."

The Captain spoke quietly "we cannot allow a relationship such as yours and Maria to go on as it is. You have been seen in romantically involved actions, at this parish, by others. A complaint has been filed with the Colonel." The color drained fully out of Charles' and Peter's faces. Father Michael was smiling however.

The Colonel spoke next. "Therefore, Charles and Peter must be banished to live in sin on an island somewhere not far from here. Where we could all visit discreetly. But that would be difficult."

Father Michael finished the offer. "I offered a compromise. Charles and Maria must wed, here in the presence of family, paternity, and me. Then no one can say a thing about anything because all of us that love you both as our sons do love you both as our sons. You get three fathers for the price of one bride. Peter, I think you'll find Maria waiting for you in the confessional." Peter was dumbstruck until he realized what the patriarchs of the island had cooked up for them. Jumping up and down squealing with joy he ran to confessional opened the door and found Maria waiting for him. He stepped in, closed the door and in mere minutes Maria stepped out in a beautiful gown with silk threads and pearls. The men forgot the fake boobs, but they didn't care. Maria was glowing. Her wig was crooked, and Charles adjusted it as best he could.

When they were finally satisfied they were ready Michael began the wedding service again but stopped as Jennie came running down the aisle with Giles close behind. She hugged Maria and exclaimed "I couldn't miss this. Never could I miss this! Continue please Father Michael". And so, they did. Colonel McKenzie gave the bride away and the Captain was indeed the groom's best man and handed him a gold ring with an oval diamond in the center surrounded by emeralds. Isabella would see her daughter's ring on the hand of a bride her daughter respected and loved. The bride's sister was his maid of honor whose husband was completely confused but had a flask full of the Colonel's best scotch. Which they all shared with gusto as they left the church and loaded into a carriage for Emerald Oaks. The real church record's show an entry for two marriages that day. Both with the blessings of the church, and in the presence of those who loved them. Freeman family legend says the first marriage of two men in a catholic parish occurred in 1667, in a small parish church not far outside Bridgetown, Barbados. Father Michael hoarded the flask. God help him if the world ever found out.

# 28

The journey to Emerald Oaks was far too short. Maria had stepped out not far from the gate, kissed her husband and disappeared into the thicket. Charles took the reins as the others stepped out of the carriage. When the carriage arrived at the Emerald Oak stables Peter took hold of the near horse's bridle as Charles pulled the team to a stop. While Jennie and Giles were busy enjoying their reception Charles and Peter took care of the stable and guest's horses. Later in the evening Isabella appeared out of nowhere and scared the bejesus out of them.

"Well, if it isn't the newlyweds. Is the happy couple ready for their reception?" Elizabeth, Jennie, and her ladies appeared behind Isabella as if by magic. Charles leaned over to see the panel open at the back of the stall. So that's how they did it. Tunnels. Looking back at Isabella and the ladies, he realized they came fully loaded. With champagne, food, deserts and flowers. They all crowded around and shared their joy for a short time. Jennie would be missed at her reception and promised to come spend time with them soon. One by one the ladies left to avoid being missed. Isabella left last. Tears in her eyes she held them both close.

"Hold your love close, my sons. And remember, we love you both dearly and will always be here for you. Always." She kissed them both and went back through the tunnel to the parlor. Charles and Peter sat at the makeshift table of hay bales and celebrated their union as a couple. They didn't have to hide who they were anymore. Father Michael had set them up to be safe and secure for all their days.

The blissful evening lasted until the Captain came to the stable. "Charles, I'm afraid I have unfortunate news I must share with you tonight. The *Angeline* will sail much sooner than I had anticipated. We must set sail in two days. We have landed a major contract with the CHG transporting a full cargo of sugar and tobacco to Carolina and Virginia. I am truly sorry you will have to leave…Maria…behind so soon. Breaks my heart it's not fair. I am sorry." The Captain was genuinely heartbroken to hand his First Mate his dream of life with the man he loved and take it away in the same day. It wasn't fair. He hated himself for doing this to Charles and Peter, but it couldn't be helped. This contract would get them back into some profit after the huge losses incurred evading the hurricane and her aftermath. "I need you at the docks first light tomorrow to begin loading the freight."

The Captain hung his head and turned to leave when Charles stopped him.

"Nay Captain. It's not a bad thing. It's a good thing." The Captain looked at Charles completely confused.

"You did hear me say first light…?"

"Aye Captain. Let's chat just a bit more before you go back to the party if we might. I think you'll be pleased with my news, too." Charles gestured for the Captain to join them at their makeshift table with candles, wine, and roses. Charles poured a glass of a beautiful full bodied red and handed the Captain a plate to share in their bounty. The Captain was actually hungry and did so. Charles let him get settled before he continued.

"Captain, John Dewe has asked to buy fare for himself and his wife on the *Angeline*. He intends to sail out with us if you can accommodate him and a small shipment of materials to his father, Colonel Thomas Dewe in the Virginia colonies."

The Captain replied "I think we can accommodate John Dewe with no problem. I'm not sure about his freight tho. Depends on how much...size and weight as you well know. If not this trip we could bring freight next go, or part of it. Do you know what he carries?"

Charles shook his head. "No, I'm not sure yet. My hunch is it is samples of their crops and maybe some root stock and the like. I don't think it's anything of terrible value except to John and his father. Nothing commercial in other words. That was what he described to me the other day."

The Captain nodded affirmatively. 'I expect we can accommodate his limited cargo one way or another. Does he know our fares?"

"No, I didn't give him a quote. There is a small glitch the port authority won't care for I'm afraid."

The Captain stopped chewing and waited for Charles to tell the rest.

"John's wife isn't really his wife, Captain. Sarah is a native girl and can only travel as a slave or indentured servant as ye well know. She is far along with child and he wants to get her to Carolina before the baby is born."

The Captain said sadly 'Well, there's not anything I can do about any of that. She will have to come through the port authority as his slave girl. Traveling in steerage won't be good for her or the baby. Not good at all. I don't know what to say, Charles."

Peter finally chimed in. "I do, Captain. Maria can come aboard as John Dewe's wife to make the port authorities happy, and to get me on board as well. Once at sea Sarah can be brought to travel with John and I can cabin with my...husband...as well. When we reach Charles Town we can easily switch before we drop anchor. Maria leaves the ship with her husband John, and Sarah comes ashore with them as their slave. No one will notice either of us that way."

The Captain smiled and sat back, leaning against the stall wall behind him. "You two have cooked this up, haven't you?" Charles nodded, Peter didn't deny it. Laughing the Captain said, "a bit more of that red might help smooth things over with your Captain, First Mate Charles." He popped a chocolate and some fruit in his mouth and toasted the conspiracy fully afoot. Pleased with the outcome and simple solution no one would care about even if found out, the Captain hugged them both and went back in to help organize the chivaree for the newlyweds. The catch was finding out where they would spend their wedding night. Charles and Peter already had that covered.

§

The new loft above them was set up splendidly for the couple. When they went to change to leave they would simply vanish down into the tunnel hidden in the floor behind the temporary walls under reconstruction. The guests would think them sneaked away by conspiring hands. True, but not the hands they thought. Giles, Elizabeth and Isabella had arranged this for Jennie complete with moonlight, a feather mattress, fine wine, chocolates, massaging oils, and absolute privacy. The evening was winding down and the guests were making their way home as Charles and Peter saddled and harnessed several dozen horses and teams with the help of the Colonel and Captain. A perfect ending to a perfect day. The warrior and the sea salt made their way back to the main house area laughing, enjoying fine cigars and sharing a flask of good scotch.

Charles and Peter let the last of the Emerald Oaks horses out into the paddock for the evening and returned inside the stables just as Giles and Jennie were disappearing up the ladder to the loft. They took their lantern and slid into the tack room, turning the light down low, but not completely out. Exhausted, they curled up together on the pallet by the far wall and fell asleep in each other arms barely hearing a giggle or two from Jennie and Giles above them.

Jennie and Giles were too tired to do anything but cuddle and fall asleep with the moonlight shining on them as they slept. Not long before dawn Jennie awoke with a horrible pain in her belly. She shifted and the pain seemed to subside for a while. A few minutes later she was racked with excruciating pain and cried out, waking Giles abruptly. Terrified Giles called panicked "Jennie? Jennie what's wrong?" Jennie was gasping for breath as the pain wracked her body. Clearly, she was going into premature labor. "Oh, God. Jennie, no it's too early...Jennie..." Jennie couldn't respond she just gasped for breath. Giles pulled on his shirt and trousers and was headed down the ladder. Peter was at the bottom asking what was wrong.

"Giles why is Jennie screaming? What have you done to her?" Terrified and angry, but mostly confused, Charles grabbed Peter before he could take a swing at the Scot that outweighed him by 50 stone.

"Peter, I don't know. I must get one of the women...or a midwife...is there one nearby? Oh God, she's losing the baby I'm afraid...Peter? Who? Who can help her...think man?" Peter's mind went blank and Charles was about to speak when the grandmother appeared in the stable entry. She silently walked to the ladder and went up to Jennie, the girl followed her. Giles followed but the girl stopped him with one glance. The grandmother went to Jennie and knelt beside her.

Delirious with pain Jennie reached out and grabbed the old woman's hand. The old woman placed her hand on Jennies belly and felt the contractions begin again as Jennie screamed. She spoke to the girl in her native language who turned to the men and said

"The grandmother needs hot water in flasks or skins. Something that will stay warm against her skin. Quickly." The men ran to the kitchen and began filling flasks and jars, anything with a lid with hot water. Isabella heard the ruckus and went to see who was in her kitchen. She knew immediately when she saw who it was that something was dreadfully wrong with Jennie. She grabbed her medicinals bag and ran barefoot with no wrap to the stable. The men closely on her heels.

"Why didn't you come get me first? Good Lord none of you know anything about pregnant women. Giles, what are you doing with hot water bottles? Seriously...Good Lord..." Climbing up the ladder Isabella came face to face with the grandmother's girl who stopped her dead in her tracks.

"Move girl, I must get to Jennie!" But the girl didn't move. The grandmother spoke to Isabella and the girl translated.

"Do you have the hot water for Jennie? Calm yourself woman or you will make Jennie worse. Calm yourself if you want to see her carry to term."

Isabella was flummoxed and more than a little perturbed. "What? What is she doing to Jennie! Get out of my way girl!" The girl did not move. Giles finally stepped in.

"Isabella. Stop. Calm down. Let's see what she is doing. Jennie has stopped screaming at least." He was handing the hot water bottles to the girl who ferried to the old woman. The old woman finally said something softly and the girl gestured for Giles to come up.

She motioned for Giles to sit across from her where Jennie could see him, and he could hold both of her hands. The grandmother was massaging Jennies back and belly in slow rhythmic circles using oil that smelled like chamomile. She was softly chanting to Jennie as she rubbed her belly. Jennie was going limp in front of Giles who began to panic. The grandmother simply placed her hand on his arm to calm him, and thus Jennie.

Once relieved of the pain, Jennie fell into a deep sleep like trance. The grandmother then began to examine Jennie feeling her belly, the size of her belly and even the feel of her breasts. Giles was perplexed and fascinated at the same time. Isabella had come up into the loft as was watching from a distance in complete amazement. The old woman spoke quietly, and the girl translated.

"Jennie has almost lost her babies. She carries two. The boy is stronger and kicks hard. The girl is small and weaker. The excitement today was too much for Jennie's body to hold both babies without objecting. Jennie must rest and stay quiet until the babies are big enough to survive being born and take their first breath. Jennie may bleed a little off and on if she does too much." Looking at Giles through blind eyes she continued. "You are her man and must see to her needs before your own. Jennie carries the blood of my daughter, her mother and the blood of my father's clan in her babies. They are the future of our people in the new world. I will return to check on her regularly and will be here when she gives birth. It will be a difficult time and a risky birth but there is no choice. The babies will come when they are ready if you care for her as you must."

The old woman and the girl placed the jars of hot water around Jennie and covered her with a blanket to keep the warmth in. "Rub her softly with this oil if the false labor returns again this night. Soup and no alcohol. She needs rest and quiet now. She put her hand on Jennies head and Giles shoulder. He felt fire flow through his body from her touch that took his breath away. It was a warning from the grandmother. He was on notice to care for her Jennie.

The old woman left and Jennie slept peacefully the rest of the night. Giles and Isabella, Charles and Peter all kept watch over her until the dawn broke, the sun on Jennies face waking her to find them all sleeping in the loft, Giles head hanging down as he sat leaning on the wall holding her hands as he slept. She smiled and held one hand to his face.

"Giles. Are you awake my love?" Giles was instantly attentive to his bride. "I had the strangest dream…the grandmother was here, and she told me I was going to have a boy and a girl." Jennie giggled and the others all begin to awaked with her. "Can you imagine me with twins? What a silly dream." Giles kissed her hands and softly whispered to her.

"It wasn't a dream Jennie. We almost lost you and your babies. It was the grandmother who brought you back to us. You must rest Jennie. She says you carry a son and a daughter, but your body is not ready to carry them to term. You must rest a lot Jennie, or you will lose your babies. Our babies, Jennie. You do carry the blood of your people as do I, as do we all. But you must rest to carry these two wee ones until they are big enough to survive outside your womb. Do you understand me Jennie?"

Jennie nodded as she looked around to see Isabella, Charles and Peter looking afraid and worried. "Yes, Giles, I do understand you. I'm sore this morning from the…contractions…oh dear God…" Jennie began to panic when she realized she had bled in the night. Giles calmed her quickly.

"Jennie. Look at me Jennie. The grandmother said you might bleed off and on if you do too much. You just must rest and eat well. The babies will still probably come early, Jennie. We just have to help you hold them as long as you can." Jennie was beginning to cry when she realized she very likely would lose her babies anyway. Giles held her and soothed her for some time. The others had left the loft to turn to their chores. Isabella returned with hot soup and clean clothes.

"Jennie you're a very lucky girl. Giles knew to trust the grandmother and she did know how to help you. Sit up if you can and sip on this broth. When you are feeling a bit more stable, we will clean you and change your clothes. Giles will stay with you today and tonight and as long as you need him. Elizabeth and I will care for you as well. You will be fine girl. Come on now, sip." Jennie sat up against Giles and took the mug of broth. It tasted wonderful. "I'll be back in an hour or so." Giles set the mug down as she drifted off to sleep again in his arms. He had her head against one shoulder and his hands crossed around her, both hands holding her belly he could feel the babies moving as she slept. He felt he would die with them if they came too soon.

He dozed off and they slept until Isabella returned to clean and dress Jennie in fresh clothes.

Giles let the ladies alone for a few minutes and went outside to the pump and the latrine. The sun rose beautifully across the island again. The plantation was bustling with activity rebuilding and replanting. He and Jennie would stay here at least a day or two and he knew Andrew would take Jennie to their apartment at the garrison in his carriage when she was able to travel safely. He overheard Andrew telling Joshua they needed to get what sugar was still saleable out of the stores to ship out on the *Angeline* in two days. Giles walked over to hear the details.

"What did you say about the *Angeline* sailing in two days?" Giles was aghast. He still had a killer to catch and only two days to do it and Jennie's health precarious.

"Oh, yes, you and Jennie left before the Captain shared his good fortune with us. The CHG has contracted the entire space on her to move a full load of sugar and tobacco to Carolina and Virginia and then on to England later I suppose. Charles left earlier to head for the docks to begin loading the freight. Carts and assinigoes will be arriving all day and night from all over the island. Everyone is being paid at the dock scales as they load the freight."

Giles was stunned. The CHG was moving fast. Way faster than he ever imagined they could. "Thank you, Andrew. You've been most helpful. I'm impressed!" He was terrified. Giles was so distracted he barely noticed when Isabella and Elizabeth went into the stables to see about Jennie. Mentally Giles was babbling. The night too short, the wine too much, Jennie's screams way too loud. He went to the kitchen to get a mug of tea. Elizabeth handed it to him as Giles looked at her oddly.

# 29

"What is it Giles? You look like you've seen a ghost."
She smiled until he continued to stare at her unmoved by her
humor. "Giles. What's wrong, you're scaring me."

"Didn't I just see you walk into the stables with Isabella?"
Giles stepped back truly afraid his mind was playing sick
tricks on him. He set the mug down turned and ran back to
Jennie with Elizabeth close behind him. Who knew a man as
big as an ox could run like a gazelle, barefoot and feeling no
pain. Elizabeth just saw him disappear up the loft ladder.

She followed him up to the loft and found Isabella on the
far side of Jennie looking worried as Elizabeth walked softly
up behind Giles. Giles was staring down at the back of the
hand of the woman sitting with Jennie, stroking her hair and
feeling the babies kick under her other hand.

Giles froze staring at the woman's hand. There on her
right-hand ring finger was a ring with the seal of the
McKenzie clan. The ring she had been given by her mother
with a stag's head and the motto Lucceo Non Uro, I shine
not burn inscribed inside the band. He knew it was there, but
who dared to wear his mother's clan ring. On Barbados. Fury
rose throughout his body and replaced his fear in less than a
heartbeat. His eyes changed from green to black.

"Woman I don't know who you are or why you are here. But you will take your hands off my wife and explain how you come to wear my mother's ring." None of the women there had ever seen Giles in full McKenzie patriarch mode before and they were rightly terrified by the fury and rage standing before them ready to kill the woman who wore his mother's clan ring. Elizabeth saw his father in him immediately. Isabella was confused. Jennie reached up to her husband and spoke

"Husband. I am in no danger. Please, welcome the grandmother of our babies as we have." She held her hand up until Giles knelt down and took it in his, his anger ebbing as he did. He closed his eyes and held her hand against his cheek. The woman let her hood fall down her back and turned to speak to Giles.

"Giles, you have wed a wonderful woman who will give you many children I am sure. I see you are already a wonderful husband to her. And I will wear my clan ring until my death, my son."

The sound of a mother's voice is never forgotten. Giles looked up, dropped Jennie's hand and lifted his mother off the ground in one highland scot sweeping hug.

"MOTHER! What…how…oh it is wonderful to see you. Is father, here too? Oh I can't wait for him to meet Jennie…why did you not tell me you were planning to voyage to Barbados?"

Elizabeth stepped in to explain the short notice to bring his mother to Barbados. The conditions in England and Scotland were truly wretched. She feared for her sister's life. And she wanted her to see her son wed.

Giles wasn't hearing anything about his father, he realized quickly. "Mother, where is father? Did he not come with you?" Giles watched as his mother's face fell with a sadness he had not seen in many years. "Mother what has happened?"

Giles' mother calmly explained "Your father was killed in the insurrections some three years ago. I wouldn't let them tell you. You'd have tried to come home to me, and it was not, still is not, safe for you in England or Scotland. Elizabeth's invitation was a godsend to me, Giles. I was able to leave the country safely, but I came alone I am afraid."

"Why didn't you come to the wedding yesterday? Or the reception? You were here and couldn't come to my wedding mother? Why? My father is dead, and you could not come to my wedding and tell me?" Giles stepped back from his mother hurt beyond words.

Elizabeth spoke "Isabella, could you give us a few minutes alone, please?" Isabella stood and quickly left the loft, waiting outside the stable. She had a bad feeling this was going to get worse. Little did she know.

"Mother explain yourself." Giles was in tears as was his mother, but he would not let her touch him. Elizabeth stood next to Jennie and spoke calmly and rationally.

"Giles. Giles look at me please." It took him a bit, but he finally looked at Elizabeth still weeping. "Your mother did attend your wedding. She was there at the back of the church." Giles looked at his mother puzzled.

"You were there? You wouldn't stand with me? You let another represent you at my wedding? What sort of sickness is this?" He stepped back again.

Elizabeth continued. "Giles. Please. Let me explain. Please look at me and let me explain. It is time you knew the truth." Giles looked at the women totally afraid and beginning to panic. "Giles. Your father, Freeman is dead. But he was your stepfather Giles. Not your father."

Incredulous Giles tried to object; Elizabeth cut him off.

"Giles. You are the spitting image of your father at your age. Do you not see it when you look in a mirror?"

"Elizabeth what are you talking about? Mother? What is she talking about?"

Softly his mother spoke to him as he wept. "Giles. Elizabeth is my sister and your aunt. She is also your stepmother. Duncan McKenzie is your father."

Giles lost all the color in his face and sat down hard on a bale of hay. He looked up at his mother and Aunt who had not moved. They were identical twins. He could see that now they were next to each other. Dear God. They were twins.

"Mother. What have you done? How…when…Oh dear God. Does Duncan know? He doesn't know anything about me does he?" Giles was calculating the fallout quickly. Looking hard at Elizabeth he said "Elizabeth, you cannot tell Duncan this by yourself. We both know how dangerous and lethal he can be if truly warranted. You're sitting on a powder keg. Dear God, Elizabeth. The two of you hid this from both of us. Why?"

"Giles, Duncan and I…it wasn't even an affair. One night, one moment. He was very drunk, and he thought I was Elizabeth. There's really nothing else to say. But I ended up unwed and pregnant with a child sired by my sister's husband, a patriarch in a rival clan. You know full well where that would have led if Duncan knew about you. He already had Elizabeth's seal, he could have and would have taken my son and killed me. The bloodletting would still be going on. We hid you to protect you from both of your clans. Freeman couldn't have children and stepped up to hide you as his own. And he did Giles. He was your father in every way but one. He loved you more than life itself. He kept our secret and watched you grow into an adult that fate would put in the hands of the man who sired you. Do you have any idea how hard that was for him? But he kept his silence to protect you still. You owe my life and Elizabeth's to the man that raised you Giles. Do not ever forget that."

Jennie finally spoke weakly "Giles? Come to me my husband." Giles immediately went to Jennie. "You must forgive your mother, her sister, and your stepfather. Their unconditional love for you raised a fine man who will be a wonderful father to all our children. They chose the right path for you Giles. Think about what your mother tells you. You know she speaks the truth. Duncan would have taken you and killed her and had Elizabeth raise you as hers. The

410

feud would be never ending. They choose the best path and you, my wonderful husband, are living proof."

Giles smiled through his tears and kissed Jennie's hand again before standing. He turned to his mother and her twin and calmly said. "This ends today. WE will find Duncan and tell him the truth. He will not hurt either of you. I will not let him. He loves Jennie and wants to hold his grandchildren…and they truly will be his grandchildren. Do you think he would turn on you and lose everything, now? How do you know he doesn't already wonder? He has given me more than is acceptable to a subordinate for years. Now I wonder why. Give him the grace to hear the truth mother. He deserves that much."

"Very well, Giles. Let's go find your father."

§

They didn't have to go far. As they made their way down the ladder Colonel Duncan McKenzie was waiting for an update on Jennie and then take Elizabeth to take her back to the garrison. When he saw the two sisters standing side by side, fear, and utter terror flashed through his body.

Elizabeth spoke first "Duncan, husband? Do you not remember my sister, Eleanor?" Eleanor stepped forward to take Duncan's hand.

"Hello Duncan. It is truly a pleasure to see you again."

Duncan couldn't speak. Petrified Elizabeth would discover his secret he though long buried he took his hand away as he stepped backwards hitting the front of the stall. He could back up no further.

Elizabeth spoke coldly from a distance. "Duncan, how rude of you. Can you not respond to Eleanor? The mother of your son?"

Duncan looked at Eleanor and Elizabeth as if they'd lost their minds completely. Giles was standing with his hands on his mother's shoulders. At last the obvious came to Duncan. He went from terrified to enraged at the deception the sisters had pulled off. They had taken and hid his only son from him. They kept his birth from him. They let another

411

man raise him and gave him Freeman's name. Duncan was completely out of control and lunged at Eleanor. Giles pulled her out of the way and quickly subdued his father, pinning him against the wall of the barn.

"I see now they were right to keep me from you…father. You would have killed my mother and taken me from my mother's clan. You will not lay a finger on either of these ladies. Not tonight, not ever. I am of the Clan McKenzie by birth and by wise women who still live. If you want to live to see and hold your grandchildren, you will never speak of this again. I will never speak of this again. My mother shall walk freely among us and I will keep the name of the man who raised me. Freeman. But my children will have their clan name and carry it proudly. My name was denied to me because of your selfishness and rage, but your grandchildren will be McKenzie. Giles reached up and took the clan ring off of Duncan's finger that was rightfully his upon the death of his grandmother. Challenge me father and I will kill you."

Giles let Duncan loose and he shrank away from the massive highlander towering over him, far more lethal in that one moment than Duncan had been in his entire life. He looked up at his son weeping. You are my flesh and blood. They never told me. Not one word. That was not right either, Giles. Your grandmother would have protected your mother and your Aunt. Yes, Elizabeth and I would have raised you. Your mother was unwed and that was the way of the clans. But I would not have harmed her physically. That I could never do, no matter what you see here today. They hid your very existence from me. My only son. They kept you from me…always…" Duncan was sobbing as he realized how close he came to never knowing at all. "Please forgive me my one…ONE…indiscretion of adultery. I truly did not know the woman I lay with that night was Eleanor until the next morning. I was so drunk. Way too drunk. I believed I was bedding my wife. I have never deliberately cheated on my wife. Never."

Duncan continued to sob as Elizabeth looked oddly at her sister. Giles caught on real fast and got between them. "He thought he was bedding me? Why did he think that Eleanor? Eleanor was quietly stepping away until Giles grabbed her by the arm. "Oh, no mother. This ends here. This ends today. You will face your sister and clear this air for good." Eleanor was shamefully staring at the floor. Elizabeth was crying in realization.

"You let my husband believe he was with me? You deliberately lay with your sister's husband and let him believe? Why Eleanor? How could you do such a vile thing?"

Giles stayed between them. The only place on earth that terrified him was between two angry women. And these were twins. And one was his mother. He suddenly feared for his life. "Mother? Answer your sister."

"I was a foolish, jealous girl, Elizabeth. I didn't plan on any of it. I didn't. Duncan can tell you it was just coincidence we ran into each other. He was so drunk and thought I was you. I…just…didn't tell him…otherwise. I was stupid. Never considered the consequences. We shared everything once and it really, foolishly, didn't occur to me a night with Duncan was so bad…I never dreamed he would settle a child in me. Never crossed my mind until I started heaving up my socks. I was so ashamed Elizabeth. I let you believe ill of your husband I was so afraid you would hate me and abandon me and take my child as your own. Which clearly Duncan had the right to do and would have done just that. I can't change the past Elizabeth. But you can steer our futures."

Giles thought…'well said mother'…a little late but still well said. They were having a staring and choking tear filled standoff when a weak voice came from the bottom of the ladder.

"Giles, you must heal their wounds. Only you can do that. They are divided over who you will honor and love. I know this feeling Giles. I was raised divorced from parents as you

413

have been. Mine are long dead, yours are here before you. Choose wisely husband. I cannot carry these babies to term if I must forever referee your family quarrels. With that Jennie collapsed on the floor writhing in agony and bleeding again. Mortified, they all worked together and had her carefully resting on a palette by the fireplace in short order. Her contractions stopped as Giles rubbed her back and belly with the oil. The bleeding ceased slowly but it did stop. They hadn't realized how fragile Jennie really was.

Duncan and Andrew were gathering men and materials. They would build a weather safe room around Jennie where she lay. She clearly wouldn't be traveling anytime soon. Giles was heartsick she would lose her babies. He wanted them so badly it brought him to tears. The sisters quickly overcame their past and took on the health of the future. They never spoke about Eleanor's night with Duncan again. Somehow it truly no longer mattered.

Giles would take some time to bring this to a comfortable place in his mind and heart. He loved the man that raised him. Freeman was truly his father in every way but one. His mother made the right decision. He was well raised by wonderful people. He claimed clan rights from two clans and four grandmothers. He spun the stag's head ring on his little finger. The ring was far too small for his ring finger as Duncan had worn it. The truth revealed and the mantle of patriarch passed. Duncan was surprisingly at peace. Giles decided he would allow Duncan the son he never knew. He was cheated out of that. He did not abandon Giles. He knew nothing about his conception or birth. That wasn't fair to him, he was right about that. Giles had taken unmistakable ownership of the power of the clans from both his mother and father that day. A new era had begun and would be carried forward with the twins Jennie held in her womb.

# 30

Giles returned to his quarters to gather up what he would need to split his time between the garrison and Emerald Oaks. With luck Jennie would carry the twins full term, but that was a full three months from now. Most likely they wouldn't hold that long, but hopefully long enough. He was stuffing things in his duffle when the journal dropped on the floor. In the rush of the wedding he had forgotten about the journal being in the drawer with his shirts. He opened the journal and sat by the window to see the entries clearly.

Alone and in the quiet he was able to concentrate on the names, amounts and calculations. First, he realized that these were transactions between several men and Maria, Peter's alias persona. At first Giles thought Peter was being paid for sex with men around the island. But Peter was faithful to Charles. He was sure of it. If Peter had been a promiscuous homosexual the Colonel would have intervened somehow. The Colonel knew about Peter and Charles and even protected them as Father Michael protected them. Even the sea Captain knew and protected them. No, Peter wasn't prostituting himself as Maria. He was collecting money the men were skimming off the barons they worked for or with and giving it to Maria. On account. Savings of some sort.

The next obvious question was where's the money? The chest in the parish's hidden office. That's what Peter was doing down there that night. He was adding to the chest. It wasn't church money at all. Those records were a banking system. An independent banking system.

Giles stood up abruptly as the scheme became clear. The CHG banking system ran from inside the parish's hidden offices. Michael was in on the whole thing. Peter was a natural cross dresser and he was the go between with the watchers and the account holders. It was genius. He smiled and began to laugh. He laughed so hard he cried until he couldn't breathe. The women of Barbados had stolen from their husbands and employers for years and accumulated immense wealth just waiting for a disaster to make their debts unpayable. And now they owned the island. They owned the land their husbands were leasing from them. The simplicity and ease of implementation taught Giles a lesson few men ever learn. Good women keep good men alive and well fed. He would never doubt Jennie's value. Never. These women were a force of nature, as nature intended.

The odd piece that didn't fit was what did any of this have to do with Esmerelda's murderer? Who was she? Maria? Maria was Peter. Giles was sure it was Elizabeth who left him the journal to find the killer. What did she see in the entries that could tell her who killed Esmerelda? Giles sat down and went through the pages again. He realized he didn't have the pages he had given to Jennie. He went and began searching her drawers but came up empty. Frustrated he kicked the side of the wardrobe and the bottom drawer fell out on the floor, breaking the sides loose from the bottom. Irked at damaging the drawer he picked up the pieces and meant to set them on the bed when an envelope fell from underneath the bottom piece.

Giles picked up the envelope and went back to the table. Inside were the pages he had given to Jenny. He thumbed through them seeing the same pattern as the other accounts. All additions but no withdrawals. Except one. Esmerelda

Conn had withdrawn her entire savings. A huge amount of money, almost ten thousand pounds. Giles sat back in his chair and whistled. What could Esmerelda need with ten thousand pounds? He looked at the dates and sat up straight. She had withdrawn the money two days before the *Angeline* arrived and dropped anchor with Thomas and Richard Dewe on board. Esmerelda was leaving Barbados behind her parent's back. No, behind her father's back.

Giles remembered Isabella's composure at the sight of her daughter's corpse. Truly grief stricken, but not surprised. That was what was missing that day that had bothered Giles at the time. Isabella knew her daughter was not going to return to her, believing she would escape Barbados with the sailing of the *Angeline* two days later. Something had gone wrong. *Someone* had gone wrong. Who was waiting for the *Angeline*?

Giles went pale and prayed he was wrong. Flipping through the journal he didn't find her, but there in the pages he had given Jennie was the answer. Jennie had circled her name and left a question mark. Giles was suddenly nauseous and lost his breakfast. It was all clear to him now. The CHG was exactly who he thought they were. But much, much more. This was an international banking ring. It was designed and operated by the matriarchs from the highlands. He knew who had killed Esmerelda and why. He was sick again and cried in anguish at the truth. Another horrible secret he did not want to know. He slid with his back down the wall of his room, sobbing, holding his guts as they twisted in his agony. Evil finds a way, it always does. Freeman had taught him that and cautioned Giles as a lad not to fear evil but hold great respect for what evil can do to you.

Screaming in anguish Giles beat the back of his head on the wall until he bled profusely down his shirt. "No. Dear Lord, please, do not let this be so. God. No..." He put the heels of his hands against his eyes to try and block the image of Esmerelda's mutilated corpse from his mind. The tiny child that would never take a breath. The killer that took them both from her mother and the child's grandparents. He had no choice. He had to tell the Colonel who killed Esmerelda Conn. The repercussions would be lethal. The killer would hang. He, Giles Freeman, would be the executioner. He was ill again and screamed in silence as he wept. "God. I pray to thee…make this not true…I…no…"

Elizabeth was pushing past the attendant as he unlocked Giles' private bath access. She found Giles curled up and incoherent on the floor, laying in his own vomit sobbing.

"Giles? Giles! GILES!" He looked at Elizabeth from the corner of his eye. "Giles what on earth…are you ill Giles? Has something happened to Jennie? You're scaring me." Elizabeth was crying in terror she was watching her stepson die before her eyes. She turned to the attendant. Quickly, run find Lieutenant Evans. The Colonel is down at the docks. Get Evans NOW! The attendant ran to the office and found Evans at his desk. Evans immediately went to help Elizabeth with Giles while the attendant fetched fresh water and some linens.

When he arrived at Giles quarters Elizabeth had managed to get him sitting up against the wall. The massive scot was still weeping into his hands. They were all sure something had happened to Jennie. But he shook his head 'no'. They finally got him calmed enough to sip some water, but it came back up quickly. Elizabeth was asking Evans to fetch the physician when Giles finally spoke coherently.

"No. I'm not ill. Jennie is fine. But I have a duty I must fulfill. A horrible duty that I alone must do. Evan's when does the *Angeline* sail out for Carolina?"

Evans though a moment and replied "I believe they are loading her now and plan to set sail first light in the morning. Why?"

"Elizabeth. I need you to leave Evans and me to speak privately please."

"What? Giles you're not..."

"Now, Elizabeth. Please." Elizabeth was completely perplexed but did as she was asked. The attendant left with her and he escorted her back to her quarters. He knew Giles did not want her to overhear anything.

Giles looked up at Evans. The Colonel did say Evans was his man, to trust him to catch the killer. Evans spoke cautiously "Giles, what is this about? You are scaring even me. What is this about?"

Giles put his hand up and Evan's helped him stand.

"Evans, I need you to help me catch a killer. A very dangerous, cunning, lethal killer who will slip away with the *Angeline* if we are not more clever."

Evans eyes narrowed and he said "Now you have me terrified. Judging by your appearance and behavior you have me absolutely terrified. Dear God Giles. WHO are we after?"

Giles choked up and could barely speak. He whispered through his tears, "Esmerelda Conn's killer. We are after my mother, Eleanor Freeman, sister of Elizabeth McKenzie. We must catch her Evans. And I am the one who must hang her."

Evans stepped back and said "Giles you've lost your mind. Eleanor Freeman? Seriously, this isn't amusing Giles. Do you have sort of separation hatred for your mother or something? Stop this at once. I'll not hear any…"

Giles had the journal open to Esmerelda's accounts. Evans looked at it no idea what he was looking at. "What is this Giles? These look like bank ledgers. Are these some sort of …?"

"These are just some of the individual accounts of the CHG. The women and a few men were pooling assets to take over the sugar industry on Barbados. They've been at this for decades. When the hurricane took out the island's crops and the debts couldn't be met, they were ready. They had huge reserves just for this purpose. Esmerelda withdrew ten thousand pounds to leave Barbados and start a new life for herself and her child sired by Ethan's buck Michael. She knew her baby would be taken from her and sold or killed at birth. Her father would never have let her keep the baby. Isabella wanted her to raise her grandchild and agreed to let

Esmerelda leave the island. But someone found out she had taken her money out and was leaving Barbados that did not want her to go. That person was Eleanor Freeman. She had arrived just days before Esmerelda's body was found, but not on the *Angeline*, she lied about that. She came in on one of the other ships. Eleanor was probably secreted out by one of the sea Captains fighting against the crown since the King of England imprisoned or killed her people. Eleanor managed to escape to Barbados. I'm not sure what happened exactly, but she followed Esmerelda and meant to rob her of the money. I know it is Eleanor Freeman. The timing fits, the records prove she is a primary share holder." Giles flipped to the back where Eleanor's account was listed on one of the pages he'd torn out for Jennie.

Evan's took one look and his mouth dropped open. "I've never seen that many zeros in one number before in my life, Giles. There are two comas…dear Lord…15 MILLION pounds? Is this real?" Evans was staring with his mouth open at Giles.

"Aye, Evans, tis real all right. I know where she came by most of it. The man that raised me was a banker from a wealthy family in the highlands. They made their money using the same methods. Only more painfully and with sharp cutting instruments if you failed to contribute on time. Eleanor learned how to skim and manipulate finances from the very best, tightest, stingiest people that ever lived. My grandparents. It's Eleanor, Evans. I know that it is. We must catch her before the ship leaves Barbados, or we will never catch her."

"You know she's on the island? How"

"She came to my wedding and hid at the back. Elizabeth brought her to meet Jennie early this morning. I hadn't seen her in almost 15 years. I had forgotten she and Elizabeth are identical twins. There's ill blood among them Evans. I don't care to share all that right now. We must find Eleanor before she can board the ship. She'll have Esmerelda's money on her or in her luggage if I'm right. And I am quite sure I am correct."

Evans got real quiet as he realized what Giles was saying to him. The evidence fit. The motive fit. And she had the opportunity. "Giles, how could Eleanor Freeman...a tiny woman...overpower a young strong Esmerelda? That makes no sense to me at all."

"Eleanor comes from a long line of healers and mystics. She probably poisoned Esmerelda with kindness and tea. She knows how. I've seen her put sick and injured animals down. I know she's taken more than one life to end a person's suffering that begged her to help them die. She's lethal Evans. Do not forget that. She can and will kill you if she feels she must. Elizabeth can as well. But Elizabeth isn't lethal like Eleanor is. Elizabeth gets what she wants with her wiles, not her blade."

Evans was floored "Elizabeth carries a knife? You're joking..."

"Oh no, I'm not joking. You've never spoken to Elizabeth she didn't have at least one very sharp blade on her person. The highland men learn as babes not to push a highland lady too far. She will cut you at one end or the other and has every right to do so. Elizabeth is not a killer unless she's cornered. No, that is Eleanor. I didn't know that until just before you found me. I can't talk about that yet...not yet...I..." Giles looked out the window still emotionally destroyed. Evans nodded and said

"Get a hot bath and some clean clothes. You and I are going to the Roaring Boar and then we will catch a killer. WE, Giles. Not YOU, but WE will catch her. And if WE are correct, you will not hang your own mother. Hell no. If she has done what we believe she has, I expect Isabella will gladly trip the door. You will not hang your mother. You will not watch her hang. You will only visit her grave long after her headstone is placed. Do you HEAR ME, Giles?" Giles nodded and whispered "Thank you Evans. I'm not handling this well, am I. That is the kindest thing anyone has ever offered to do for me."

Evans simply replied "No more than you would do for me, Giles. And yes, I do know you are Duncan McKenzie's son. I am sure many people wonder when they see you together. The resemblance is striking. Especially in uniform. Why do you think he keeps you in plain clothes all the time? He's always had suspicions. I have never confirmed them simply because of Elizabeth. She begged me not to reveal her secret and why. I've known for years. Get cleaned up and meet me downstairs." Giles nodded and Evans left to change into civilian clothes. He left instructions with the stable manager to have Devlin and Elizabeth's horse ready to ride. Puzzled, the stable hand simply did what Evans ordered.

Giles was waiting for him at the office door. Ashen faced, Giles was still wobbly but managed to keep himself upright to the pub. As they entered Evans picked the table at the back where they could watch the door. Giles decided it was in the blood of officers to sit facing the door. Evans ordered water for Giles first, and some light bread and cheese to settle his stomach. If he kept that down they would order real food and some ale.

The bar keep was keeping an eye on the customers as the bar maid served the pints and boards. Many pinched her ass or groped a breast and she playfully slapped them away. She would earn plenty that night. The *Angeline* was set to sail early, and the crew was eager to find some comfort before they shipped out. She would pleasure many that night. It didn't matter to her. She was already a good 5 months pregnant by someone. She had no idea who. Meanwhile she made her money, did her job, and would be able to buy her way out of indenture soon. Evans was watching and listening to the sailors for hints of passengers or freight irregularities. Tonight, just the usual chatter until the senior sailor reminded them they had to be back and ready to load passengers extra early. Especially the Lady that was kin to Miss Elizabeth.

Giles and Evans were tuned in and kept eating like they weren't listening at all. The men were arguing who would be there to help her Ladyship get to the ship while it was still dark. She did not want to be seen on the docks with the regular passengers. Snobby bitch, they called her. Arrogant cunt, they laughed about her. Giles was beginning to feel sick again. He couldn't handle hearing these greasy men talk about his mother in such ugly ways. He looked at Evans, took a handful of cheese and the loaf of bread and left. Evans stayed and listened long enough to know which dock and what time. He left more than enough coin on the table and went to find Giles. Giles hadn't gone far and was nibbling the bread with his eyes closed trying to keep food down. He was managing just barely.

Evans clapped his hand on Giles shoulder and said come on, we have work to do. Giles followed Evans into the stables to find Devlin and Elizabeth's horse saddled and waiting. "Where are we going?"

Evans replied "Us? Nowhere" But someone is going to believe that you and Elizabeth have ridden to Emerald Oaks. Giles looked up to see the two soldiers that had been sent to watch the parish walk in the stable. They were in ridiculous disguises but in the dark a watcher would believe it was Giles and Elizabeth streaking through the night. Devlin would be a dead giveaway, and no one would look closely at the riders. Brilliant. The Colonel was correct, Evans was brilliant and efficient. They thought so much alike he could be the Colonel's...no he wouldn't even finish the sarcastic thought. Not tonight.

The men disguised as Elizabeth and Giles led the horses outside, mounted and left out of Bridgetown fast enough to draw attention. The city now believed they were gone. Evans closed the garrison stable doors and put the lanterns down very low. From the outside it appeared dark and empty. He led Giles to the back stall and opened the panel to the walkway to the bath attendant's room. Giles had never been through it but knew it was there. Evans stopped at the door and gently looked through the peep hole before he opened the door. He froze. Elizabeth McKenzie was changing into her riding clothes. Apparently, she didn't know she had already ridden out of town. As Evans was considering the best plan, the door opened and there stood Elizabeth.

"What on earth is going on here, Evans? Giles?" Evans looked about to be sure Elizabeth was alone and quickly pulled her into the passageway with them. Elizabeth opened her mouth to scream and Evans reflexively put his hand over her mouth while Giles grabbed her arms.

"I am sorry Lady Elizabeth but screaming isn't an option right at the moment. And we mustn't be seen either." Elizabeth finally realized that 1. She could never get away from them if they chose to stop her, and 2. They were up to something serious and she wanted to know what. Evans did not play games nor mince words. If either of them had intent to harm her she'd be dead already. And they had no way to know she was headed to the passageway door.

"Evans, Giles…what is going on here? I need to ride out to…Emerald Oaks and check on Jennie." They didn't seem to believe her.

Giles said "Try again Elizabeth. Where were you riding to this evening? My guess was a meeting of the watchers at the cane mill. Or at the parish to check the accounts?"

Elizabeth was suddenly very quiet. They knew too much. But how? Things had gone like clockwork. The contracts were all signed, the plan was in motion. Why now?

Giles shifted his weight and loomed over Elizabeth a bit closer. "Elizabeth. We. Know. Everything. Accounts and their owners and their balances. We know Elizabeth. WHERE were you going tonight and why?" He knew she would probably lie to him. He wondered if she really knew who killed Esmerelda. He played a hunch.

"Elizabeth. Did you see Maria kill Esmerelda? Is that why you left the journal for me to find? To catch Maria or to expose Peter and Charles? You don't like what they are do you?"

Evans raised one brow and let Giles lean in closer.

"I will find out Elizabeth and when I do I will not be kind to anyone who is hurtful to Peter, Charles or his wife Maria."

Elizabeth was furious. "What do you mean hurtful to Charles and Maria or Peter? I would never hurt them! I remember when they came to the island with Father Michael. What had been done to those boys...dear GOD Giles. No. They finally have some peace and support in this life. Your father is one of their protectors. YES, he is and always has been. They will always be surrogate children to us. Duncan...Duncan didn't have his own son, only two daughters that he loves with his very being...but not his son. You have no idea what those two mean to him. It was the best I could do to help fill the void you never could."

Giles was genuinely taken aback. He had struck a very raw nerve. Her reply had been genuine. Elizabeth did not try to set Maria up. He took another stab.

"Elizabeth, why did you leave the journal for me to find? Who do you think killed Esmerelda?" She looked truly puzzled.

"What journal? I left you no journal?" Giles and Evans looked at each other and at Elizabeth. "One of you might want to explain...?" Giles nodded. "Come on. My quarters. Evans is coming with us. But you and I can't be seen since we are riding to Emerald Oaks."

"We're WHAT?"

"Riding to Emerald Oaks. Just hush and come on. Or I tie you up and gag you. Your choice." She knew he'd do it. He was his father's son tho he hadn't known it for long. She willingly went with them up the access stairs to Giles' apartment completely intrigued. Once in the room Giles and Evans showed her the journal and the note. If she was lying it was a damn fine job.

"I didn't write this note Giles. This is Peter's handwriting." Giles was confused. The journal he held and the ledgers at the church were Peter's work. Father Michael had said so and Giles had seen him writing in them himself. This writing was similar but not quite the same as the journal. He finally understood.

Giles said "this journal is not Peter's handwriting. This is Maria's handwriting. It is different enough to the casual eye to not notice the same hand writes for Peter and Maria. Clever. And very difficult to do. Wow."

Evans gently took the journal and the note to compare them. "I agree. They are the same hand, yet deliberately different. I wouldn't have noticed if I hadn't really seen them side by side."

"Elizabeth was beginning to catch on. Peter knew who killed Esmerelda. He wants you to find...her. HER? A woman killed Esmerelda? Let me see that again..." She reread the note repeatedly. Flipped through the accounts. She dropped the journal on the table when she put the dates and transactions together. She looked up at Giles horrified. Elizabeth was a good actress but not this good. She covered her mouth with the back of her hand and stepped back from the table.

"Dear. God. She plans to sail out with the *Angeline* at first light. Oh, Giles...please tell me I'm wrong. How could she..." The tears fell in genuine heartbreak for her nephew. "She could though couldn't she. After her other behaviors and her lies...we both know she is capable, has the skills. The banking she learned from Freeman. Giles...what if he is still alive...we don't know if anything she said is true! Except that she deliberately deceived my husband and me for decades. She could do this. She could do all of it. Dear Lord, Giles. She did."

The mortified expression told Giles everything he and Evans needed to know. He held Elizabeth as she wept in agony and he cried with her.

Evans was the sole dry eye in the room. "Giles, we must catch her before she boards the ship, or we may lose her. I need both of you to make this work. Elizabeth, you have ridden out to Emerald Oaks tonight with Giles. We have all the elements to spring a neat trap." Evans was smiling wickedly. Giles was afraid of him at that moment. Evans had a plan. Boy howdy did he have a plan.

# 31

Elizabeth dressed her part. Rather Eleanor's part. Giles waited out of sight while Evans processed the dock papers and stamped her ticket and sent 'Eleanor' out to the ship to receive Eleanor's luggage. Evans stayed at the passenger loading dock waiting for 'Elizabeth' to appear, too late to see her sister off. As 'Eleanor' was climbing onto the deck of the *Angeline*, Evans greeted 'Elizabeth' as she came to the dock master's table.

"Good Morning Lady Elizabeth. I am so sorry, but you just missed your sister Lady Eleanor. She waited for some time to tell you goodbye, but the Captain is anxious to get under way. She did ask me to relay her regrets she couldn't wait."

Stunned, 'Eleanor' watched as her twin clambered aboard the ship. She didn't know what to say at first. But recovered quickly.

"Well, could I go to the ship and tell her goodbye? I won't see her again for a very long time. Oh, Please Lieutenant...let me go to her and tell her goodbye." 'Eleanor' was beginning to cry real tears. Her sister was about to make off with...millions...of her pounds and ten thousand pounds that she stole from Esmerelda Conn. She began to panic. She noticed Evans look past her at someone and turned to find her stepson standing before her. "What is this? If you're looking for you mother you just missed her, Giles."

'Eleanor' was genuinely frustrated and had both hands on top of her head. Evans and Giles looked at each other and 'Eleanor' oddly.

"What? Have I suddenly grown a second head or something? Damn!" Giles was looking at her hands...she had no clan ring on her right hand. And her nails were longer than Eleanor's. This was Elizabeth. They had been duped by a very clever con artist. A cold calculating killer.

"Evans...how fast can your men row to the *Angeline*? We've got the wrong sister."

"WHAT? No, this is Eleanor...we sent Elizabeth out to the ship...didn't we?"

"I'm afraid not Evans! Just to prove my point, I know you have a pair of moles next to a scattering of buckshot scars in a very unusual location. No one but Elizabeth could know that. She picked the buckshot out of your ass when you were too embarrassed to see the physician. Remember me picking the buckshot out of your ass, Evans? All 27 pieces of BUCKSHOT OUT OF YOUR..."

"Giles, this is not Eleanor. How did you know?"

Giles held up his clan ring he had taken from the Colonel. Too small for his finger and barely able to get on his pinky, he knew it had been Elizabeth's which rightly went to her husband when they wed. He took it off his finger and it slid perfectly onto the ring finger of her right hand. Evans' jaw dropped.

Elizabeth put it in his palm and closed his fist. "No, Giles. That is rightfully yours now. You are the patriarch of the Clan McKenzie from two direct lines, cousins a ways back got frisky. You've earned the right to wear it. Do so with wisdom, kindness, and loyalty. Giles put the ring back on his finger. Now, go get that scum sister of mine so I can hang the bitch! I'm sorry Giles, she is your mother and I shouldn't speak about her like that to you. Forgive me." Elizabeth turned to Evans and pointed to the ship. "Bring the fucking cunt back to me alive. I will hang her sorry ass from the gallows myself. ALIVE Evans. I want that cock sucking wanton adulterous bitch sister of mine alive!" Stunned by Lady Elizabeth's unusual verbiage, Evans nodded and headed for a lighter. He was about to push off from the dock when the Colonel himself jumped down into the boat.

He grabbed a set of oars and simply said ROW. And they did. Evans could see Giles standing on the dock holding his stepmother close. He wasn't sure who was comforting who, but it was Duncan who took charge of the race to the *Angeline*. Evans had no idea the old man was a seaman in a former life. The lighter was a child's toy in his hands. They made it ship side just as the Captain was ordering Charles to pull up the ladder. The Colonel called up to the Captain for permission to come aboard.

Normally the Captain wouldn't' grant permission once the ladder was up and he was ready to be under way. But something was wrong here for the Colonel to row himself out to his ship. He knew he would seriously regret not bringing him on board.

"Of course, Colonel! You are always welcome aboard any ship under my command. Mate drop the ladder down for the Colonel and his men. Quick like. We don't have all day." He gave a subtle reminder to the Colonel he needed to weigh anchor and catch the breeze as she rose. The Colonel and his men were up the ladder and on board in short order, one man remaining in the lighter to steady her with the ship.

The Colonel walked toward the Captain and headed for the bow. Talking quietly as they went, not to be overheard.

"Captain I am afraid you have a criminal on board. I must arrest her and take her back to port." The Captain was stunned.

"Her? A woman on board my ship is a criminal? Oh, really Colonel...what could she have done...I only have two, well three with Maria...well you know. Sarah or

431

Eleanor? The pregnant wife of John Dewe or Eleanor, your sister in law?" The Captain was being highly sarcastic until he realized the Colonel was dead serious.

"Eleanor Freeman. Eleanor McKenzie Freeman actually. I must take her back to port Captain. Would you bring her up on deck? I think you can find her faster than I can. And we must retriever her luggage. She has some…things…that do not belong to her."

"Oh, so she is a thief. Very well if you think it's worth the effort. But I'm not refunding her fare or waiting for her to clear this up."

Sadness had overcome the Colonel's face. "Captain. Eleanor is an international theft ring organizer and a murderer. She killed Esmerelda Conn. You need not worry about her fare or waiting for her. She will not be going back to anywhere. She will hang within a fortnight…for her crimes of which there are many."

The Captain was stricken with horror.

"Dear God. Your serious. My apologies Colonel. I thought perhaps her sister was trying to delay…I am so sorry. Let me get her found and her luggage brought up on deck." The Captain turned and called "CHARLES! I need you here NOW man!" Charles was there in mere seconds. He was all business on ship and knew his job well.

"Charles…we have an issue."

"Aye Captain, I seen the Colonel come on board…What can I do?"

"Find Eleanor Freeman and bring her to the Colonel. Alive, Charles. And be careful. She will have a blade on her. All highland women carry a blade…or two. Once we have her to the Colonel, he needs all her luggage unloaded as well. Charles. I'm serious. She is very dangerous and knows how to use a blade faster than you can see her take it out. I know the clan McKenzie women. My mother was a McKenzie. What Colonel, you didn't know? Small world isn't it…Go now Charles, find her."

"Aye Captain. We will be careful." Charles left them standing at the bow, took a handful of deck hands with him and set out to find Eleanor McKenzie Freeman. They searched her cabin and she wasn't there. One of the hands quietly said "Charles…"and pointed toward the door to the lower deck ajar. The men lit a lantern to take down with them. It was pitch black down below. She could hide almost anywhere in the dark.

Charles said quietly "get the cook's dogs. They will rat her out." They waited while the sailor went to fetch the dogs and returned with the little yappers in his arms. "She can't hide from both of them…" Charles nodded, and they opened the door and went down the stairs with the lantern and the two terriers. And the bottom of the stairs, the sailor set the dogs down and said "FIND". The dogs immediately began hunting for rats and any other vermin. They were on board just for this reason. The Cook always took them with him into the hold. He hated rats. Scared the bejesus out of him. Thanks to him and his dogs, there were very few rats on board the ship.

Today they were after one big rat. If she was in the hold, they would find her. The men worked their way through the stacks of freight. Eleanor was slipping unnoticed back behind them, a knife in each hand. When she thought she was clear she sprinted to the stairs and had one foot on the first step when one of the dock hands called out "there she is…FIND!" And the dogs were at her ankles in an instant. Eleanor was swinging wildly at the dogs when a pair of very strong hands grabbed her wrists in midair.

Startled she turned to find Duncan McKenzie, eyes black as coal gripping her wrists so tightly her hands sprung open and her knives clattered to the floor. The terriers had been snagged by the dock hands that stood back as the Colonel managed to hold his rage and not break her neck right there. Not a man would say a word if he did. Duncan knew he could kill her right there and walk away. But no. Duncan wanted her to officially pay for every crime. Every lie. Every year of hell they had endured because of her. Maybe he wouldn't hang her. Maybe he would sell her to the slavers. First, he had to get her to shore with her luggage and find the trove of coins she had taken from the rectory.

The CHG was smart. The priest was pragmatic. He knew the women would need the Colonel's protection. Today was that day. Duncan seethed as he pulled her hands down behind her back and tied them tightly. Looking to the burly freight man he stepped aside as the man tossed Eleanor over his shoulder with one hand. Kicking and screaming he carried her up the stairs to the top deck where the Captain and the others were waiting. He climbed down and put Eleanor in the lighter and stayed there until one of the officers came down to hold her until the Colonel returned. He tied her ankles as well. Eleanor was caught.

The men found her luggage and hauled everything upstairs and to the lighter with Eleanor. The Captain thanked the Colonel for taking her off his ship. The men hugged and patted backs knowing they would throw back good scotch again soon as the Colonel set off to shore with his catch of the day. Eleanor was furious and snarling like a cornered dog. Fitting thought the Colonel. Bitch can snarl all she wants. I have a cage for that.

The Colonel looked up and waved to John and Sarah, Charles and Peter...Maria...and smiled. Truly happy for his adopted sons. He hoped he would see them again someday. His heart ached at the thought he might not. Sarah would bring new life in the new world. That pleased him and hoped he would one day meet their child. And there beside them was Father Michael. Beaming with pride and joy for them all. Somehow the Colonel knew this was not the end of their story. There would be more to tell.

He settled in as the men rowed them to shore. Evans quietly staring at Eleanor. He noticed the stags head ring on her right hand. How did he miss that? At least they had Esmerelda's killer which was a great achievement. He looked toward shore to see Giles and Elizabeth waiting right where they left them. The Colonel followed Evans gaze and then looked back at Evans. Sick at heart at what he must now do he couldn't look at them.

Once at the dock the Colonel got out first and went to Giles and Elizabeth. He gently took them by their elbows and led them away. He would NOT let them see Eleanor taken through town to the garrison and put in a cell like the animal she was. Giles pulled away from Duncan's grip weeping and angry. Duncan gave him a moment and then essentially ordered him to take Elizabeth home. Ever the soldier, Giles complied. He took Elizabeth to her quarters and returned to his own. He sat with his head in his hands and wept for his mother. How could a man gain a father and lose his mother in the same day? What kind of God would do that to a man? Giles was still inconsolable when Duncan came to his quarters.

Giles simply said 'come in' to whoever was knocking. The Colonel was at a total loss on how to console this young man he treated as his son all his life and now that he knew the truth, he didn't know what to say. He just stood there beside him, put his hand on his shoulder and wept silently for his son. Giles hugged his father around his waist and sobbed. He knew the Colonel would hang her. He had no choice. They just stayed there trying not to die from their broken hearts.

§

About noon Evans came to find the Colonel. He let himself in the open doorway and gently announced himself.

"Colonel. We have a problem. We can't find the bulk of the money. We found ten thousand pounds in one small bag. There is nothing more in the luggage we took off of the ship. Either it was never aboard the ship, or someone else on the ship has it." Stunned the Colonel had a good idea where it was and just smiled. Time would tell but if he was right, the orphanage would soon begin receiving remarkable materials. The church would have the finest stained-glass windows and his sons…all of them…and daughters…all of them, would never know hardship. Nothing could have pleased him more.

Evans was confused. "Colonel?"

"Not to worry Evans. The Conns will get Esmerelda's money back. They need it to rebuild and replant. Giles let's get some lunch and chat. I think I may have news to help cheer you just a bit."

Walking down the balcony to Colonel's private dining hall Giles glanced out over the harbor to see the *Angeline* had raised her sails and fully caught the rising wind. The Colonel followed his gaze and smiled as she rose and fell with the waves taking her passengers and cargo to Carolina. They would see them again, many times in the years to come. They watched as she slowly disappeared, the sun glistening off her fresh white sails as she slipped gracefully through the surface of the sea. The *Angeline* was a uniquely beautiful ship built by the master shipwrights of Virginia. Sakakawea pointed the way for her Captain for many voyages. Little did they know she led the way for the women who would create a modern vibrant country in the world from whence she came. But that is another story…

*THE END*

**Sakakawea Figurehead**

# ACKNOWLEDGMENTS

The Kill Devill series could never have been written without the dedicated research on our family genealogy by my cousin Katherine Allen Fazio. I found her and my biological father's family thru DNA analysis that matched us as first cousins. Katherine's meticulous research and vast family knowledge provided the foundations for this series. She knows the truths and fictions within. I am forever grateful to her for introducing me to the family, chauffeuring me around the historical locations, and her friendship. The adventure continues.

I also thank the North Carolina Division of Family Services for placing me with my adoptive parents, C. Brice and Betty Brown Ratchford. Wonderful people who gave me a life that enabled me to become a scholarly researcher, world traveler, artist, and author. The Kill Devill series is a material outcome I leave to my children and grandson.

My draft reader, Ariel Robinson, PhD, was instrumental in providing professional critique. Thank you for being the professional I knew you would become.

My PhD advisor, Jerry Valentine, Professor Emeritus, taught me how to be an author. Without his guidance, this book and those that follow would not exist. Lighting the way is an art. I accept the torch and will hold it high for others. Thank you, Professor, always.

*Next* ::::::::::::

**ULISI**

TEWTZ E VONN, aka Mary Ratchford Douglass, PhD, has worked as a strawberry picker, teacher, school bus driver, research assistant, B&B owner, artist, florist winemaker, mother and grandmother. She is a policy analyst, world traveler, chef, gardener, photographer, quilter, and equestrienne. Mary lives in Columbia, Missouri with her dogs Sally and Stripper, her cat Gremlin, and her Goldfish Guido 1 and Guido 2. She has three sons, Joseph, Jonathan, and William, and one grandson Colton.